ONE STEP TO DANGER

JOHN GUBERT

ONE STEP TO DANGER

Matador
9 De Montfort Mews
Leicester LE1 7FW, UK
Tel: (+44) 116 255 9311 / 9312
Email: books@troubador.co.uk
Web: www.troubador.co.uk/matador

ISBN 978 1906221 355

This is a work of fiction. Characters, companies and locations are either the product
of the author's imagination or, in the case of locations, if real, used fictitiously
without any intent to describe their actual environment.

Typeset in 11pt Bembo by Troubador Publishing Ltd, Leicester, UK
Printed in the UK by The Cromwell Press Ltd, Trowbridge, Wilts, UK

Matador is an imprint of Troubador Publishing Ltd

To Anne and Charles

JUST A BILLION DOLLARS

Friday September 15. It was late afternoon. And the scam was about to begin.

John Ryder held his breath, looking intently at the screen. This was going to change their lives. The screen read a billion dollars. The cursor blinked on the "confirm" box. He swallowed nervously. His heart was pounding. He hesitated. This was the point of no return. Then it was done.

The PC was already powering down. He was moving out of the office – his box with a view of a wall. Gone forever! Not that he would miss it. As he moved down to ground level, the glass-backed lift gave him a full view of the bank lobby. Buzzing as the business day came to a close. Outside, he walked to a waiting car, and said curtly, "Let's go."

The timing had been intentional. They needed to miss the worst of the weekend traffic. Time was of the essence. Nothing must go wrong.

An hour later, they were at the airport. But the hour felt like an age. Each time they heard a siren, they froze. Each time they saw a police car they held their breath. Every policeman appeared to look at them with suspicion. The traffic slowed down and they looked at each other in near panic. A car hooting, someone shouting or people pointing all made them start. They were new to this fear. They did not know yet that it was just a passing phase. Tomorrow it would be gone, if they were still free.

As planned they had cut it fine. Each waiting minute added to the danger. And the stakes were high. They walked quickly through the airport. They passed the rows of shops without a flicker of interest. Each announcement made them start. The official at passport control waved them through, but in their nervous state they thought he had stopped them. They almost panicked and ran. At the desk, the stewardess asked them to wait a moment and fear struck them again. "I hope you have a nice flight to Paris," she said a moment later as she let them through to the plane.

On board, they waited as the moments ticked by. They wondered why they had not left on time. Then the motors purred as the plane taxied away. A quarter of an hour later, the plane was on its way to France.

She turned to him. "Will it work? Will it really work?"

He sounded more confident than he was. But he had to re-assure her. "Of course it will work. We have planned every possible move."

It was simple. Simple because he was not concerned that they would know he had done it.

"They will know who it was. They will seek us out. But they cannot follow the trail. And they will try to play it down as it will be a huge embarrassment. That will help us disappear."

Once he had pressed the return key, the billion dollars had left the bank's account. He had toyed with the idea of making it more than a billion, but that would have raised too many queries. A billion was a good round sum. It was material enough, but not that noteworthy in the world of high finance. And that was his world.

The money had moved through a series of fictitious company accounts. It had been changed into Euros, into the Japanese Yen, into Euros again and finally back to dollars. Eventually, the money had ended up in a dollar account in the Cayman Islands. The introduction of real time settlement systems by the banks meant that the dollars were all on the account during the same day in the Caymans. And time zones meant that it was just after lunch there although it was the end of the working day in London.

He laughed to himself. They would only discover something was wrong after the weekend. After the weekend he would not be there and his trail would be cold. His phone number would ring but there would be no answer. They would initially be concerned about him but not suspicious. His house would be unoccupied but it would be there. All the contents would be there. His bank accounts and other assets would be there. He had had no scruples about leaving them behind. A couple of million jettisoned to ensure they gained a billion. That was the sort of return people dreamt of. This would puzzle them. In time, when they discovered the loss, it might make them wonder if he was the perpetrator or a victim.

It was only when they could not balance their books that they would start to worry. But that would be Tuesday at the earliest. The banks had built systems that allowed one to move money globally in a few seconds. They had introduced services that allowed you to swap any major currency into dollars on the same day. But they still used lowly paid clerks to see that it all went well. And in reality, the clerks only looked for errors. Not for fraud.

The system had to be built on trust. But trust depended on fear. Fear of being caught. If you overcame that fear, as long as you weren't too greedy, you could get away with murder. And unfortunately, he thought ruefully, we'll have to get away with that as well.

At that moment, Charles was at the First International Bank in Cayman. He wished to withdraw a hundred million dollars in cash from his account. Ample cover should have come that day from London. The bank was willing to comply for a commission of a million dollars and the pleasure of earning another few million or so a year on the remainder of the money. They treated Charles respectfully, pleased that he was so casual with his funds and feeling no scruples that this must mean this was illegal money. Charles had explained that Global Financial Enterprises Inc, the account holder, wanted the money to be available at all times and would therefore prefer it to be on a cashing account.

Thus motivated by greed, First International Bank willingly complied. It suspected that Charles, the grandly named President and Chief Executive Officer of Global, was involved in the drugs trade or money laundering. It realised that he was operating under a false name. It most likely even saw through the heavy disguise he was wearing. But they did not even give it a thought.

Drugs and money laundering were both illegal, but then First International Bank was known for its flexibility rather than its integrity. And, as Charles had appreciated when selecting it, intentional stupidity and greed rather than high principles drove its officers to success.

Charles soon left the bank with the cash – he would move most of the rest of the money electronically through another myriad of accounts the next day. The last hundred million would remain with First International, if only to ensure their continued silence, however suspicious they might become.

He drove to the airport and within the hour was heading by an ageing charter prop jet to Panama, although the flight plan stated otherwise and he was not on any passenger manifest. Once the plane had landed and Charles was on a scheduled Air France service to Paris, the pilot took off again in accordance with his instructions. As he sent out his Mayday message, he parachuted out at the agreed location. If his parachute had opened and had not been switched by Charles, he would have been in a bar as planned some half hour later, waiting for a bus to take him to Mexico City.

So he never collected his five million dollars fee although he did have the half million advance in an account somewhere. He never realised that the plan was strange. That he should have been wary about the need for total silence. That he should have questioned the need to get rid of the plane. And that the promise of a regular role in Global with another passport, another location and another name was just too good to be true when you are on the most wanted list of a series of drug agencies across the world. But then, the pilot had been willing to believe anything for he needed to get away from an ex-wife, from a pregnant mistress and most of all an angry loan shark.

Coast guards never worked out why he was so far off course. They could not understand where he was during the missing hours. Customs never knew Charles was a passenger. In fact nobody even knew who Charles really was. And they did not even know if the man in the bank had actually left the Islands.

For Charles was no longer Charles Ryder according to the Air France passenger list. He had used a false name and appeared to be a French student on the return leg from an exchange visit to South America. Indeed, on our flight from London to France, Anne-Marie and I had also used false names.

Anne-Marie had dyed her hair. She had cut it short. She wore oversized glasses and carried a novel by an unknown avant garde writer nobody had ever understood. Her clothes were baggy and she looked a good stone heavier than she really was. Nobody would have thought she looked like the photo they circulated when the search started. Long dark hair, a great figure and always elegantly dressed in one or another designer label.

I had put on a straggly wig, coloured contact lenses and a long brown tweed coat of the type that went out of fashion in the early sixties. I was the personification of an ageing hippy. Not the conservative banker whose only concession to personal taste was slightly long hair, nestling just over his ears.

It had all been so easy.

The bank trusted me. I was authorised to make large payments but had needed a second person to approve the one for a billion dollars. That had been simple for I often needed to make large value payments on a rushed basis. Jim was heading out to a meeting. He did not realise that the agreement he gave was for a series of dubious transfers to unusual locations. He would be fired for negligence. He would be unemployable for a long time. Serve the bastard right! I had picked him intentionally. He had already been the end of many good peoples' careers. Their only crime was that they had stood in his way. Now he would know how it felt to be on the receiving end. It was tough luck, Jim. You never got to taste life at the top despite your ambition!

First International Bank never got to earn much interest on the dollars they retained. They were traced and had to be returned. Unfortunately the other nine hundred million dollars brought more trouble than they had bargained for. Regulators thought they were implicated in the transfers. Nobody believed that they could be so stupid even in a business where clean fingernails rate higher than IQ points. The major banks shunned them. Clients started to move to other banks. Most of the clients and their new chosen banks were as bad as First International, but they had the advantage of not having been caught. Hot money does not like high profiles. It attracts the wrong sort of attention. So it's Adios First International. You did not deserve to survive.

Do I regret my actions for my old employers lost close to a billion dollars? Not really for they could afford it. Better to lose it, if they had to lose it, to us than in lending to property sharks or corrupt regimes. They were dumb to trust me. They were dumb to give me the authority. They were dumb to leave me in a role where I was bored. But then that gave me the time to work out the plans, even while they paid me.

They will not trace the De Roches, as we were then known, or the other alibis we had to adopt on our road back to legitimacy. We look different from the old days when we were the Ryder family. In France we changed identities again. And since then, we have changed further. Plastic surgery, a healthier lifestyle, a good tan and hair dye has seen to that. And once again that was achieved by way of a trail through many countries. We spent time in Latin America, Switzerland and the USA. They all validated our forged papers with their visas and entry stamps, and helped change our appearances and our identity pictures with the rare abandon that is normal with a million dollar spend.

Once Charles had arrived from Latin America, we got down to business. Laundering the money would be easy. We needed to allow time for the trail to get cold. So we drove from Paris to the South of France and rented a place in the holiday resort of La Croix Valmer. It was smart but not ostentatious. It was discreet.

We headed along the coast to Cannes and walked into the imposing branch of one of the large French banks, putting the rest of the cash into a safe deposit box and keeping back only a sum for our expenses.

Our plan was simple. We would lay low for a year or so. We now had two things to do. Change our appearances and let the trail go cold. That would take three to six months and take us through to spring

The first challenge was to move the cash into a legal bank account and establish a track record. And then we had to do the same with the rest of the money we had moved from Cayman. Once we were legal, we could move out of the shadows. Charles would be fine as the front man, but I had got to keep low for the rest of my life. You don't suddenly burst onto the scene at my age. And Ryder would always be taboo as a name. And, in any event, we liked La Croix Valmer and that region of France. This would be our long term base.

My story would be both simple and credible. I would have taken early retirement to the South of France after a fairly successful business career. I would be well off but not flash. We would be unmemorable. I could take that for a year or so before we set off anew. I would tell my new friends that I got bored in retirement. I would want to join in the rough and tumble of the financial markets again. And indeed I would, not full time and not as the front man, but definitely in the swing of the money game.

We would say that Charles had got bored with working for others and was setting up a hedge fund with some of his and my former major clients. We would say that he was drawing up his plans and would often be visiting us. In reality his and my prime role was to launder the money we had stashed away in cash in Cannes and round the world in a myriad of bank accounts.

"Dad, you never explained why you chose that bank in Cannes" commented Charles. "After all it's hardly a top rate bank, even by French standards"

He was right. It was a prime example of a bank with ambitions to be a leading player on the world stage. And it had fallen on hard times. I smiled as I thought through the falls so many big names had taken.

Midland Bank had been ruined by paying through the nose for Crocker National in California; and then being forced to sell that out for a song to the hard men of Wells Fargo. Wells' background pitted them against armed robbery. In the deal with Midland they showed they could make more money than the robbers without even getting their pens dirty!

A trader with unlimited authority had destroyed Barings. He had taken them for nearly a billion. Did they know about it? Perhaps they did, perhaps not. Typically they did not feel the need to ask questions when the going was good. Typically they cried foul when the chips were down. Typically, they were horrified when they learnt that all their friends elsewhere in the City of London, who would have bailed them out in the old days, had been sent into early retirement to their country estates. And poor Barings, they ended up in the arms of a Dutch savings bank that still yearned for global fame.

The ups and downs of the banking world had caused many to go down or go near the brink. Continental Illinois of Chicago, Bank of Credit and Commerce International of Luxembourg, Herstatt of Germany and Ambrosiana of Italy were just a few of the famous names that over-stretched themselves and were allowed to fall. Many others did the same but were deemed too big to fail. However, many people never knew how close they came to opening a paper and seeing their bank was bust.

My chosen French bank was one of the banks that had been near the brink. It was dependent on state handouts. It was forced to sell off assets. I felt its staff had to be demoralised as they read, day after day, of its problems. I doubted that they would question too much. They would surely be only too pleased to get the rental of their vault. They would not see any of the money for I had no interest in their type of banking.

I had established a series of accounts at discrete banks and most of our cash would end up there. They were Banque Fucquet in Geneva; Bankhaus Hochzeit in Zurich; the Monte Carlo branch of United Bank of Europe. Finally, I had a further but small account at the Jersey offices of my former employer. The last was from a sense of duty, or perhaps a well developed taste for irony.

I mused about the set up, and I looked out over the sea as we drove along the coast.

The road from Cannes to St Tropez skirts the sea almost all the way. It passes through one resort after another. On a bleak day the whole area looks very similar to an out of season English seaside town. The warts of the seaside are hidden in the sunshine. A grey sky and rain make them more pronounced than they really are. The sea fronts become uglier than the different towns inland.

They are stripped of their ornaments, the tables and chairs, the bright tablecloths, the gaudy shops full of swimwear and other seaside baubles. Their ambient population deserts them. Men dressed in T-shirt and shorts, sometimes suitable but often laughable. Their stomachs hiding their knees, their breasts wobbling like frightened jellies. The women dressed in sarongs and skimpy bikinis. Sometimes they were breathtaking, often attracting a second glance. And then sometimes they were caricatures of corpulence with their bulging thighs, bouncing flesh and mammoth

7

breasts, hoping to hide behind strips of cloth more suited to something more seductive.

In the winter, the sleek are lost in their layers of clothing. The absurd is hidden behind their layers of cloth. People blend into a covert world and only become attractive or ugly again as they unpack themselves from the anonymity of their own wrapping paper.

Today, though, the day was not like that. The weather was cool but clear. The streets were littered with locals enjoying the freshness of the breeze from the sea. It gently played with girls' skirts. I noticed Charles glancing hungrily from time to time at a tanned thigh winking at us mischievously.

"Keep your eyes on the road," I laughed. "That's jail bait of about fourteen. I think you better give them a chance to put away their school books first."

"It's all right. I am hardly likely to get attracted to something that young. Mind you, if she has an older sister that would be rather agreeable. I think I'll wander over to St Tropez and look in at a couple of the clubs tonight. I know that it's Sunday but they should be quite busy. And I need to relax."

"Do as you wish but remember that you have to keep your cover. Otherwise there will be no girls. All you'll get is a cell for a few years."

"Don't worry," he said, "I can handle that. I am looking for a fun night, not a relationship. At least not until we have done the laundry – cash wise."

I rather liked that turn of phrase and laughed appreciatively.

"OK smart arse. Let's get moving. We are only at Agay and I don't want to get caught up in the evening traffic. Anyway we plan to go up into the mountains this evening for dinner. Don't wake us up when you come home. And if you do bring a girl, drop a note so that we don't get a shock. The last time we were all together, I walked naked to the kitchen and did not like the idea of some blond telling me that she could see the family resemblance."

"She was nice kid," said Charles. "But that was a couple of years ago. I wonder if I still have her number? We had a great time that night. I was surprised you knew nothing about it. She was really noisy."

I knew a lot of that was bravado. Something had not been right for months. Charles had always been sociable. Girlfriend followed girlfriend. Some would last a bit longer. He never had been in love. His aim was always to enjoy himself. Yet since the summer he had been quieter. He went out but without the joy of before. He talked of women as if remembering things in the past rather than looking to the future. I hoped we would find out what it was that was bothering him.

We had asked but he had always laughed and denied anything had happened. We knew that was not the case. We knew one day the sadness would go away. Perhaps one day he would tell us what it was. Maybe he had been in love. Maybe it hadn't worked out. I wondered if we would ever know.

That night, Anne-Marie and I went up into the mountains at Gassin, where there is a group of very French restaurants. In the tourist season they maintain their veneer of French originality but often regress in the turmoil to the charm of a fast food joint staffed by Parisian street café waiters. In the off season, it is different. The patron will have time to talk. They will have spent time on the menu. They made their money in the season and now they can relish in their art.

Our meal was delicious. We looked across the forest of pines and vineyards, dotted with the occasional house, over to the coastline of the St Tropez peninsula. The sea was calm in the distance, the clouds low and soft, and the stars smiling conspiratorially with only the quarter moon looking grim. I lifted my glass of house red from the region, "Let's drink to a new beginning. We are going to have fun again; real fun."

Anne-Marie sighed. "Sometimes I thought we shouldn't do it," she said, "but you were right. We needed to get away. We were getting bored. It will be great to start up again and have fun. But if it doesn't work what do we do?"

"Don't worry, it will work. We will use the funds as seed money. I'll find a way out. I'll do something like ending up with a big stake in a bank and that will give us access to more funds. Perhaps one day we'll even buy my old firm. Who knows? Even the best run banks can get it wrong and then their shares fall and predators like us, without scruples about the past, can turn them around."

My plan was simple. It was a vague plan. I did not want to constrain my actions by making too detailed plans. I knew what we would do in general. I also knew that the plans could change if we were to really make money. Otherwise we would not take advantage of the unexpected.

We were going to go for bust on the financial markets. We would give speculation a new meaning. We would play for broke on up to five hundred million dollars of our stolen capital. If it worked we would then move to greenmail. Greenmail is basically financial blackmail. You force

9

companies to do things they would never do by their own free will. But they have to do as you dictate as you have taken a major stake in them. And, if that worked, we would then buy respectability. It all would work because we were not afraid of losing. After all, even if we lost we had several millions in the kitty as a reserve for the rainy days!

I saw it as three steps. If the first step – speculation – failed, we reverted to a reserve strategy. That was quite simply living a quiet, but wealthy life, on the St Tropez peninsula at Croix Valmer. If the second step – greenmail – failed we were just super rich and as for the third stage, it could not fail if we got past step two!

We looked at the other guests in the restaurant. There were shopkeepers. They were celebrating a good season. An elderly man was leering at his companion and getting excited whenever she called him papa in a very un-daughterly way. There was an older woman and perhaps her daughter or niece, both of whom seemed somewhat out of place. I looked at them carefully. It was late for tourists and yet they were not local. They had still the pale skins of the city. They seemed nervous about their surroundings. With that second sense that comes from being a fugitive, I knew that they too were running away. From what I may never know.

I smiled over at my wife, "You know, Anne-Marie, Charles will be sorry that he did not join us. He would have tried to get to know the girl. She is definitely his type."

Don't be silly," she said. I was surprised by the unusually tart response. "Let Charles do his own hunting. I sometimes wish it would be like the old days when he would appear in the morning with some girl. I used to get annoyed or embarrassed if I knew the parents. Now I think I would be pleased."

She looked at me again, raising her eyebrows and flashing her eyes. "And don't use it as an excuse to eye up every bit of talent you see," she joked, dropping purposely into the jargon of the male chauvinist pig as she called it.

We chatted casually as we finished our food, and then decided it was time to move. "Tomorrow evening we head off for Brazil via Madrid," I reminded her. "So let's get some sleep now. Just think, soon the dentist gives you perfect teeth and the surgeon reduces my rather prominent chin. In the meantime, let's make love for one of the last times in our old shapes. If the design is as you have drawn up, it could be even more fun in the new ones."

We were not going in for major changes. It is amazing how small changes can alter one. And that is all the more the case if you drop out of circulation for a bit. Our plan was actually quite modest and quite simple.

Anne-Marie would have her teeth capped and a couple of her older crowns would be replaced. An expert who would make it all appear as if she had never had dental work at all would do the dentistry. Even her dentist in London would find it difficult to reconcile the old with the new.

I would have my chin remodelled. That would both reduce it and reshape it.

We would then go to the US and reshape our bodies. That needed two things. First of all there would be a series of medical routines. I disliked the sound of them but had been persuaded that they were necessary. Then there was a plan for some liposuction. All that would though be accompanied by a three month concentrated stint of physical exercise and controlled diet. This would tone up our bodies to perfection.

I was keen to do that for health reasons alone. From my perspective, getting rid of the flab would streamline my appearance. Gone would be the symbols of a lifetime of office routine and business lunches. This part of the process would have less impact on Anne-Marie, but the driver for her was the thought of getting super fit.

The final part of the process was to take place in Italy. We were going to have our hairstyles reshaped. My hair would be toned and become a pale, distinguished grey. At the moment it was a light brown, speckled with grey around the ears. I would also have some treatment to thicken out the balding patch that had started to appear a couple of years ago.

Anne-Marie was going to stick to remodelling her style. She also planned an intensive henna treatment to bring out the true, lustrous colour.

Both of us would stop wearing glasses. I wore them all the time although Anne-Marie only used them for driving and reading. We would be fitted with contact lenses. Charles had already done that from the time that he had left England. He had, though, been wearing spectacles with plain glass during that period to further his disguise during the Cayman scam. He was not changing much else. He was going to focus on dental treatment and exercise. He was quite slight and wanted to put on another stone. Not through over-indulging but rather through determined bodybuilding.

We actually were all quite pleased with the plans. They should make us all look as well as feel better. And they would make it more difficult for people; especially those who did not know us well, to relate us to the past. For Anne-Marie and my details could be with the police forces of the world for some years to come. But those would be the details of our former selves.

Charles had also insisted that we restyled our wardrobes. We had agreed and would be using wonderfully named "style consultants" for this. Anne-Marie was overjoyed with the idea of a quarter of a million-dollar budget to replace all her clothes. We would also change our jewellery. That could identify us. We had put that into the bank and left it behind. We had done the same with our old clothes. Together, this helped sow doubt in people's minds as to our role. And we never knew how that could play for us.

I had built up the bank accounts in my new identity over a period of a year. We used a series of companies and our new names. Currently the accounts also held the eight hundred millions we had moved electronically from the Cayman Islands. We had carefully spread it over several banks and ensured it arrived to each of them at a million or so at a time. We had explained that that was seed money for our fund management company from wealthy backers. I had also made it clear to them that further substantial funds had already been committed. Banks are always worried about large unplanned inflows. Advising them in advance makes it easy to get over those fears. And I had made certain that the money came to them directly from well regulated banks in the right countries to avoid them asking too many questions about their origins.

As we left the restaurant, I noticed the older woman and the girl were walking ahead of us. They were already standing by their car and were having an animated discussion. They still looked nervous. They glanced at us, then looked away as if fearful that we would approach them or worse. They stopped talking and the older woman went to open the door.

I opened our car and we climbed in. The older woman was talking to the girl again. We heard her say in a loud and irritated voice, "Get in. We are safe. Nobody is going to hurt me while you are with me."

I shrugged my shoulders. Sounded as if there had been a family quarrel I thought. As I pulled out of the car park, I saw that the old lady was just getting into the car. And then suddenly, with a screech of tyres, a large black sedan pulled across my path.

"What the hell is he doing?" I gasped as I skidded to avoid him. The next moment the noise of gunfire cut through the night. Bullets ricocheted off parked cars and hit us.

"Duck," I shouted to Anne-Marie. "Duck, they've found us and sent an assassination squad. I don't believe it. It can't be true. How did they know where we were? Why kill us?"

The gunfire stopped as suddenly as it had begun and we heard sobs and screams from outside the car. There was a further screech of tyres and shouts of concern in the distance.

Shaken and white faced, we sat up in our seats. The car was against a lamppost. The front wing staved in but otherwise sound. The car belonging to the older woman and her daughter or niece was peppered with holes. The girl, her clothes spattered with blood, was crying over the motionless body of the older woman.

"They killed her. They killed her," she sobbed to nobody in particular. "And now they will come after me."

"We better get moving," I said "we can't afford to be caught up in this. Move."

"No," said Anne-Marie. "People will have seen us and the car. If we move we will be reported to the police. If they haven't got the number, they will describe the car and us. Better they have our names and not our pictures."

"You're right," I said. "Well done. I wasn't thinking straight. Let's help the girl. She's hysterical."

We ran over to the girl who was sobbing violently. She was sprawled against the car. Her face was averted from the staring eyes of the dead woman. We reached her ahead of the crowd that was now running from the restaurant. We drew her away from the victim, wrapped her in my jacket and Anne-Marie tried to soothe her. I kept the others away, reminding them that the police would come soon and would want to ensure that no clues were disturbed.

Anne-Marie was talking with the girl. She looked concerned and called me across. "I don't know what to believe. She has just spun me the most amazing story."

She went on. "Her name is Jacqueline, they call her Jacqui. Her mother is French and her father is American. They are separated. She hasn't seen her mother in years. She lives with her father. She says it's the Mafia.

"The older woman has a place here. She is a distant relative. The old woman told the girl in the restaurant that she had been to the police about a murder committed by one of the Mafia families. The girl did not want to stay when she heard that. She was scared. She does not trust the police to keep a secret. And now she knows she was right for the men must have been hired killers. Somehow, the girl knows them. And they told the girl she would be next if she helped the police."

I turned to the girl. "Why did your aunt or whoever she was get no police protection?"

The girl was so distraught that she started talking fast. I think she realised she needed help and decided instantly to enlist our sympathy. The only way she knew was by telling us why she was now so afraid. She looked me over and then replied to the question.

"The police told her that they would not reveal their source and that she was safe. She had come here on holiday, there was nothing secret. I was passing through and stopped over for a couple of nights. There was no reason that the evidence she gave the police should be traced back to her unless someone in the police gave away her name."

She continued her story about her aunt. "She told me that she had promised them she could back up her accusations. She says she has a video of a brutal killing that showed the killers. The video had been put together by one of the Mafia dons to show others as an example of what happened if they breached the code. The police must have leaked her name. Or perhaps the Mafia has an insider in the police. They have quite a few. Somehow, the family got to know. She was sure they would not learn but that was stupid. I knew she was wrong. Once they learn that someone has grassed, then there's a contract out, and they execute it quickly and ruthlessly. The quicker the grass is dead the less danger they will be. I know the laws of that jungle even if I am not part of it. I am a spectator really. Father got rich on crime but he wants the next generation to be legitimate."

I noted that she knew more about the Mafia than I would have expected. My senses told me not to get involved. I suspected that she and her family were very central to the Mafia. I sensed trouble. This was more than a run of the mill criminal family.

She then seemed to calm down from her initial shock. All the pallor left. Colour returned to her face. The eyes were soft. The face was determined. It was a face that attracted, then fascinated and finally entranced one by its character and beauty. My first impression had been correct. This girl would attract most men.

I quickly told her, "Tell the police you saw no faces. Say you knew nobody. Tell them you don't know why they attacked you."

Anne-Marie said, "I will say my window was open and that I think one shouted to the other 'we got the wrong one' in French or similar words. Don't worry, we'll help you."

"Why do you say that?" I gasped. "We have to leave tomorrow. We don't have a choice."

"We must help her. She's all on her own. We can't walk away. We would not have done so before yesterday. We can sort it out."

I shrugged in despair. I hated complications. But there was no choice. The sirens were finally whooping in the distance as the police arrived alongside an ambulance.

As usual in the off season, the local policeman was going to be more at home directing traffic than solving murder cases. That would make the idiots more likely to accept our story. We needed a quick explanation. I needed anything to stop this becoming a long running saga. If we played our cards right, we could pull it off.

I quickly turned to the shivering girl, "Where are you staying?"

"At the Rue de Provence, in St Tropez. I was going to move on to Nice tomorrow."

"Did anyone know about Nice?"

"No. I had not booked even. At this time of the year there is always room."

"Come back with us and we can help you. But get away from the police. We can't spend time at the police station."

"What about my aunt? She's dead," sobbed the girl.

"You can't help her then. But tomorrow we must leave. It's safer for you and we need to as well. Trust us."

The policeman came to us and asked what had happened. It was fairly evident but we gave our side of the story.

"We were just driving out when a car drove in at speed. It all happened so quickly. I tried to avoid it and hit the lamppost. Then I ducked and so did my wife as guns were fired. Then they left. There was shouting. We heard their car leave. When we looked up the older woman was lying against the car and the girl was screaming and sobbing in terror. My wife went over to comfort her."

"Are you acquainted with the girl and the older lady?" asked the policeman with strange formality.

"No. They were in the restaurant and so were we. We all left roughly at the same time. Our car was closer and we must have reached it before them. We were about to drive away."

My wife added, "It was strange. When they drove away one man was yelling that they got the wrong one."

"I didn't hear that. I heard shouts and shouted conversation. I must have been too shocked."

The girl had recovered well. "Why me?" she cried. "I was on a tour. I wanted a break. I was visiting my aunt. I had not seen her in years. She is only a distant relative. Her sons live in Paris. She is a widow. Who could have done this? Why did they do this? My father will be..." She did not finish. Undoubtedly her father would react, but as I discovered later, hardly in sorrow, as he appeared to have been the cause of the shooting. The policemen were not to know.

Others in the growing crowd embellished the story. People who had been miles away appeared to think that they were on hand. One added to Anne-Marie's story and asserted that the tall dark assassin had shouted out "Shit we screwed up. It was the wrong one. It was the wrong fucking bitch."

The police appeared to be pleased with this line. I supposed that murder in error was better than a gangland killing. By now they were loading the old lady's body into the ambulance and surrounding the car and its immediate area with a fence of police tape. They called for forensics on the radio and asked what they should do with the girl.

I intervened and said, "Look, the poor kid has just seen her aunt killed. She saw little. She is in a state of shock. We are willing to take her home. I assume she has family there. Why don't you just get her details and talk to her tomorrow?"

The police seemed to buy the idea. I saw no reason to give the police an inkling of our earlier conversation. "Can we take you home? Do you have friends or relatives here?"

The girl was sharp. She was really in shock but she knew she had to continue playing along. "We were on our own. I had come down for a break. Tomorrow I was supposed to leave. I don't know anyone here."

Anne-Marie looked sympathetically on. "Would you like to come back with us? We have room. Perhaps we should pick up your things and then you can stay with us overnight."

I shuddered at the thought of hitting their apartment alone in the dark. You never knew what those thugs would do. "Perhaps it would be better if you went back tomorrow. I am sure we can fix you up for the night. You are shivering. Officer, Can we take her?"

The girl seemed to agree. She said nothing. The policeman turned to me and asked for my address. I gave it to him and said that we were planning to leave the next day.

"I think it is an open and shut case, Monsieur, obviously one of mistaken identity. It is all so unfortunate; so very tragic. We should meet tomorrow morning to complete the formalities with the young lady," he added.

I was surprised how eagerly he had swallowed the story. I had been concerned that he would latch onto the case. Perhaps he would have dreams of hitting the headlines in a great crime that he alone would resolve. I had though over-estimated the man's ambition. His main concern, as I overheard him later note to another of the policemen, was that he was a bit late for his "cinq a sept". I thought back to my office days in Paris in former years and remembered that was the French jargon for a bit on the side. The guy had a mistress waiting and was getting itchy. No wonder the criminals usually win!

We packed the girl into the car and drove towards our home. She sobbed gently to herself but I could see she was tough. With possibly a Mafia father, and definitely a crooked one, she would have needed to be. I wandered if we would find out what lay behind her story. Somehow it hadn't rung entirely true. But that could wait. It would have to wait.

RE-UNITED

They were actually quite sweet. They could have walked away. But I was concerned about two things.

My aunt had noticed them and had immediately said that they were running from something. The woman had started nervously in the restaurant whenever sirens were heard in the distance. The man looked too carefully at people when they came into the restaurant. And he seemed only to relax again when he realised that he did not recognise them. But then he had acted out of character at the shooting. Why? If they were fleeing the law, they would want nothing to do with the police. Who were they? I would need to find out.

I also did not want them to know that I had been the one who had stolen the recording. I had tried to use it to get some money from my father. I wanted to get out of the house. I didn't want to be surrounded by thugs. I shuddered at the thought of some forced marriage to the scion of one of his circle. I had reckoned that a few million would give me independence. I had stayed with my aunt by chance. I had arrived in St Tropez on a whim, waiting for a response from my father. I had called my aunt who insisted that I stayed with her. She had seemed pleased to see me although we had never been close.

And then she had seen the video. She picked it up accidentally. How could I have been so careless as to leave it lying around in my room? The stupid bitch had planned to take it to the police. She must have called them to arrange a meeting and hinted about the reason. Somehow they had got the message to my father. She may have told the police about me and my role. If so, I was in trouble. More likely though, she did not tell them about me. Otherwise they would have got me. I had recognised Bruno. He wouldn't have missed. I started crying, out of anger, out of frustration.

Anne-Marie looked back and sought to comfort me. She thought that I was mourning my aunt. I was sorry that she had been killed. But why on earth had the stupid cow done what she did? There must have been a reason. It must have been something that had happened in the past. She risked her life to get her revenge. The problem was the tape would always be like dynamite. The police could have the full story. Surely they would look for the tape. How would we get out of it? When would they realise who had been killed? When would they learn who I was?

We drove down the winding hill and across the flat peninsula to St Tropez. Their house was a pleasant villa. It had a good view down to the bay. It was a decent place for a holiday, but little else. I still felt suspicious. Somehow it did not all fit together.

"Would you like a drink?" said Jean Pierre.

"A virgin Mary, please, with lots of spice," I answered. Then I took the plunge. "You're not French. Why have you got French names?"

"What do you mean?" was the sharp response. "Why do you think we are not French?"

"Your English is too good. I hardly heard you speak French although you obviously can. You chatted quite a bit with the police."

"We lived a long time in England. We are French originally. We came from Martinique."

"My father was a plantation owner and my husband's were teachers," Anne-Marie added quickly. She was not convincing. Spoke too quickly, too glibly. I decided that I should accept their explanation. I did not want to upset them. I would snoop around later.

I downed my drink and felt the spices in the smooth juice burn my throat.

"I would like to get some sleep," I said. "Would you mind? Perhaps we could talk tomorrow? I really can't take any more today."

Anne-Marie was immediately sympathetic. "Of course you can, my dear. Let me get you some wash things and a nightdress. You will be sleeping in the spare room that is opposite our bedroom. If you need anything or want to talk or anything, just knock on our door."

She returned with a black slinky nightdress, a bit tight on me but a decent fit I thought. She also had a towel and a new toothbrush. "The bathroom is just here. Don't forget, call if you need anything. Sleep well. Or would you like a tablet?"

I asked for a tablet, thinking that would make them believe I was asleep fairly quickly. I wanted them to go to bed for I was really exhausted and did not want to fall asleep myself before I had gone through the house. I had to find out who they were. There was an outside chance that they were involved with my father. Somehow, though, I felt that that was unlikely. I quickly brushed my teeth and headed to the bedroom. I pulled off my clothes and went to the window. I opened the window and looked out to the sea, relishing in the cool air that gently caressed all the contours of my naked body.

I had always loved going around without clothes. I felt refreshed and invigorated. There was something erotic about the cool air creeping into my body.

I turned away and quickly shut the window as I thought that we could have been followed. My father's thugs could be lurking in the garden. For a moment I almost panicked. Then I calmed myself. I still checked the window again. Then I drew the curtains. I pulled the nightdress over my head and realised it was tighter than I thought.

I had inherited my mother's figure. My last boyfriend had called it voluptuous and I guess that it was. I missed him so much. He had been great. We had been great. Then somehow it had all fallen apart. Not helped by my father who had kicked him out of the house. He had beaten me too and called me a fucking whore in front of everyone. I was twenty. Did he really expect me to be a virgin? Was it so terrible that we were in bed? It wasn't as if I was a serial man eater like some of my friends. That boyfriend had been one of three, and since him, there had been no one.

I shook these thoughts away. That was the past. I switched off the light and went to bed. I listened carefully for signs that everyone was asleep. I noticed it was nearly midnight. I shut my eyes for a few moments and then woke up with a start. I looked at the clock. It was two in the morning. I had dozed off. But never matter. They would now be asleep and I could start searching for clues. I needed to know who they were.

I crept downstairs. It was light from the moon. I had noticed a small study just off the hall. There was a desk. In it were papers, all in the name of De Roche. There were others in the name of Feraud. He had rented the house for a year in the first name; it wasn't his house. He was an authorised resident of Monaco through his wife whose parents had lived there. She had been born there. They had an address there. It was an apartment but I did not recognise the street. Mind you, that meant nothing as Monaco is hardly a fun city and I had done little more than pass through on a visit to its casino.

Then I noticed the briefcase. It had a combination lock and was shut. What would be in it? I looked in his passport. Most people used a combination of the days, months or year of their birth on such locks. He was born 14th July 1955. I tried 1407 on the lock. Nothing happened. I tried 1455. Again nothing happened. Then I realised the case was slim, more a lady's. I picked up her passport. She was born 2nd January 1958. I tried 0201 and heard the pleasing sound of a lock opening.

Inside the case were a series of air tickets. They took them from Madrid to Rio. Then they went from Rio to Miami. And they continued on from Miami to Los Angeles. Finally they took them from Los Angeles to Geneva. There was a list of addresses. Each was a doctor or a hospital. There were three in each location. This was getting stranger and stranger.

I checked the issue dates on the tickets. They were all identical. Three sets. They were for Jean Pierre, Anne-Marie and Charles De Roche. Who was Charles? Anyway he wasn't around. I thought through my find. The dates on the tickets ran through to Christmas although the last two were open ones.

There was a large manila envelope in the case. Inside it were two sheets of paper. From these I learnt that my mystery rescuers had an involvement with an investment management company, but its name did not ring any bells. Perhaps they owned shares in it. They also had accounts at several banks. I recognised three names including the secretive Banque Fucquet in Geneva and Bankhaus Hochzeit in Zurich. Otherwise the banks were major names, United and so on.

I pondered what this could mean. I moved backwards. A hand clamped over my mouth. An arm pressed down on my throat. I knew the voice that said "Who the fuck are you? What are you doing here?"

I couldn't place it, but I knew it. It was so familiar. But it was in the wrong place. I knew it so well. But why was it here? And who was it? I knew and yet I did not know. I screamed to myself in anger and frustration.

"Scream as much as you like," he snarled. "You'll only wake my parents and they won't help you. And answer me truthfully or you'll be pushing up the daisies in the spring."

He talked like Mafia, but he did not sound like them. How though did I know the voice? I struggled to get a glimpse of him. I wondered if he was one of my father's people.

"Don't try to look bitch; you're better off not seeing me, not being able to recognise me." He had pulled me away from the window into the middle of the small study.

He again asked, "What were you doing here?" I was wondering what to say. I thought how I was going to get out of this predicament. I had been caught looking through confidential papers. What could I say? This must be the Charles I had heard mention of.

I said stupidly, "Charles, trust me..." The arm around my throat tightened. I felt myself choking.

"You know who I am," he snarled. I thought I heard real fear in his voice. I recognised though that there was more, a strength that I had heard before at home. He would kill if needed, not perhaps without compunction, as my father would, but out of necessity.

I could hardly breathe. My mind ran over recent events. I stole the tape. I had run away. I had turned up in St Tropez. I had gone to my Aunt's house. Then there had been her betrayal and her death. Nothing was working to plan. No tape, no ransom and now up to my neck in trouble. I struggled to loosen his grip. I heard a tear. The strap of the nightdress fell in two and I felt the flimsy material fall away and the chill air touch my left breast. It no longer felt erotic as it had in front of the window. I thought I felt the chill of death. I could hardly bear my weight. My legs went shaky. Then everything turned black and, for the first time in my life, I fainted.

I don't know how long it was till I came to. I was no longer in the study. I was on a bed. A cool sheet was over me. The window was open and I could see a tall figure gazing out at the early signs of daybreak.

I moved and the noise alerted him. "Jacqui, what were you doing here? Why were you in this house in a nightdress? Why were you trying to rob us?"

I gasped and felt weak again. So much had happened in the last twenty-four hours and now this. It was that Charles. Charles was Charles Ryder.

I looked at Jacqui. Her long dark hair glistened against the white pillow. It was dishevelled, but not untidy. Her face was white. Those big eyes were even more pronounced than usual. They were dark against a pallid backcloth. The colour was slowly coming to her cheeks but I could see strain marks around her eyes. "Well why are you here. Tell me what's wrong."

Jacqui sat up. The flimsy black negligee was still clinging to her body. One glorious breast was uncovered where the strap had torn in the struggle. I looked at her and thought back to the times we had made love. The nipple was sitting calmly on top of its smooth firm mound of flesh. She saw me looking at her, noticed my swallow. She blushed slightly as she felt her nipples harden. Then she looked up at me with a longing on her face. "Come to me first. Make love to me. Last time we had to stop in the middle. Please come to me." Her eyes were pleading. She wetted her lips. I could sense her heart beating. Mine was too and I wondered if she noticed.

I took a pace forward. She stretched out her arms and, as I bent down, had them round my neck. Her lips, red as wine and glistening with moisture, brushed over mine. Her tongue was darting forward; I let mine join hers. We drew back as if shocked, but then came together again. My hand moved up to her bare breast. I cupped her in my trembling hand. My other pulled down the other strap of the negligee, and I gently lowered it to her waist. I pulled her towards me. I gloried in her naked flesh. I sensed, through the thin fabric of my shirt, the longing that had waited for so long to be satisfied inside both of us. It had waited unsatisfied since that fateful day the last summer when her father burst into our love making and had brutally torn us apart.

Her hands were on my chest, gently undoing one button after the other. Soon the shirt was on the floor and her breasts were playing with the hairs on my chest. They seemed to skate through them, sending tremors down my body with all the sensation being channelled through her now proudly firm nipples. I wondered if she too was feeling these sensations. I wanted it to carry on. I never wanted them to end.

I nevertheless took a step back and looked at her reclining body. The bedclothes covered her to her thighs. The nightdress still was clinging to her body below the waist. Her stomach was flat below a slim waist and I could see the swell of her hips and the inviting smoothness of her thighs through the translucent silkiness that still hid them from view. With a groan I pulled off my trousers and pants, stepped out of my shoes, moving to her under the bedclothes as she pulled down the night dress and turned to take me again.

My hand moved down and caressed the inside of her leg. I felt the smooth skin taut and warm. I now could hear her groans. I felt her hand encircling me and she groaned again as she felt my pulsating firmness.

We let go of each other. We then moved closely together again in a tight embrace. It could only lead us to our final lovemaking. Her body crushed eagerly up to me, and mine to hers.

"Darling, I can't wait. It's been so long" I groaned as I felt each part of our touching bodies search out for each other. Slowly she lay on her back, and I went with her. As she drew her legs up, her wetness pulled me into her. It seemed to be over at once and yet it lasted forever. She was soft, warm, moist, tight, pulsating, moister, looser, tighter, and wetter. It would never end. The beginning was mixed with the end as we made love and exploded into each other as if we had never been apart. Then we slowly separated again, only to fall into each other's arms. Her face was moist with tears and I kissed them away. "Don't cry," I said.

"It was just so lovely. It was as if we had never left each other." We lay together, caressing and kissing from time to time. The sun was now rising over the horizon. We could see the sea gleaming in the distance. I knew that the hills around would soon be noisy with life. But in the room, it was quiet, peaceful and I was fearful of breaking the spell. Yet I knew I would have to.

I waited for as long as possible and then turned to her. "What's wrong darling? What can I do to help?"

"Let me tell you all, but then you need to explain things to me as well." She explained how she had stolen the tape. She told me how she had sought to blackmail her father. She told the story of her aunt. And she solved the mystery of how she came into our house. "So my parents know everything except the fact that you were the person who stole the tape and the fact that you blackmailed, or tried to blackmail, your father."

I then considered her problem. "Your father will find you. His thugs will have the details of my parents' car. They were professionals and they would have noted that, even in the rush to get away. The police also may know about you and the tape. The question is how many of them and what will they do? Your aunt will be in the morgue and her funeral is really a matter for her sons. You don't even have to attend; you could be recovering from the shock. The police may want to ask questions about her death, all the more so if they link her to the tape. If they don't, if the police who were told about it were all corrupt, in the pay of your father or whoever and therefore kept it quiet, nobody may make that link. At least not officially."

"Surely then the first thing that I have to do is to find out what's happening at the police station," she said.

I agreed. "We'll wait till my parents get up and get them on side. Then we will tell you about us. We'll also explain why we have changed our identity. From now on, though, you must call me Charles. You must never mention Ryder. Not even as a joke. It's too dangerous. It's a link to the past. Charles is OK. There are a lot of Charles around in France and England."

She laughed deliciously. "I want to stay with you. I am sure my father won't want me back. His men would have grabbed me last night if that were the case. If we could get back the tape, I think he would agree just to disown me. He knows I would keep the vow of silence. That was why he would not respond to the blackmail. He always said that I was too much one of the family to betray them. He told me that the family was in my blood. The problem was that it was not in my heart."

I was not convinced. "It will be hard to get back the tape, although he might be the one who gets it back rather than us."

At that moment, we heard footsteps outside. My mother's voice sounded anxious. "Charles, do you have a friend with you? Can we talk?"

"I'm coming," I called. "We'll see you in the breakfast room."

"I need to talk to you on your own. It is important."

I didn't explain who the other part of the 'we' was. Obviously my mother had found Jacqui's bed empty and was concerned. Jacqui pulled her negligee back on and looked around for something to fix the strap.

"You can't go down stairs like that. Much too revealing. My father will get excited. That flusters mother. And I will want you again half way through the cornflakes."

I went into the spare room and picked up Jacqui's clothes. She was in the shower singing to herself when I came back. She knew how to survive. She would not be a problem. Mind you I only wish I could have said the same about her father and the police.

I followed her into the shower. She made room for me and we kissed each other. I felt myself being aroused again, but we both drew away. There was no sense in rushing things. We would have time to enjoy each other and we wanted each time to be special.

Once dressed, we went downstairs. I held her hand. We walked into the breakfast room. The look on my parents' faces was wonderful. At one level, they were relieved. Perhaps that Jacqui had not left for they must have known that she had been in the study. At another, they could not believe that we would have ended up in bed with each other.

"You both look a bit astonished. Let me explain. Jacqui was suspicious. She did not know who you really were. She suspected you were not whom you said. I caught her in the study. We knew each other in New York. We went out together. Do you remember me talking of a girl called Jacqui Di Maglio? That's Jacqui. She did not tell you all her story. Let me explain it to you for her. Then, I think, we need to give her an explanation."

I ran through Jacqui's story. I told them of my analysis. They agreed. I then turned to my father and asked him to run through our position. When she heard all, Jacqui thought for a moment. "Could you delay Rio for a month, at least for Charles?" she asked.

"With a couple of phone calls," my father replied. "We don't all have to go together. We could meet him there. After all Charles is only going to have his teeth done, his hairstyle revamped. He already has the contact lenses. He is not really being sought as he was disguised in the Cayman's and used a false name. Moreover we planned in advance that we should be estranged from him and that he would move abroad. His trail went cold about a year or so ago."

"Well Charles and I could launder your money. We could even pass a chunk of it through the banking system — especially if you are using the right banks in Switzerland as they will never query a large transfer, up to a point, if it is even vaguely associated with my family name. Also, nobody is going to be surprised to see me in a Casino with a pile of cash. Casinos have a role in our family business. Nobody will question me. They will assume I am there for my father. They can legalise wo rse than stolen money. But your plan is wrong. You may need more than one casino for money of that scale. But I know them all from illegal gaming clubs through to the top casinos. When I was a kid, I used to enjoy watching my father's banke rs at work in the casinos. I know all the tricks. I would love to run the show for you. But first of all we would need to sort out my aunt and my father."

"I like the idea" said my father. "Don't get angry Jacqui. Charles, can we really trust her with the laundering?"

"Yes," I said without hesitation. "The real issue though is how we keep her father off the scene. He'll know what she has laundered."

My father thought for a moment. "She could be acting as our partner to get a fee, I suppose. I suspect, if her father thinks she has enough money, he will be happier. He may disown her but he does not want to drive her to becoming a kept woman or worse."

"You're right" said Jacqui. "One can steal, sell drugs, kill and worse. But the family have to be pure."

"The danger," I said "is that he may blackmail us. We need protection against him, Jacqui. We need that tape. Wait. You said your aunt may have told the police about the tape. She would not have given them it. Yet she took it from you. What did she do with it? Where would she have hidden it? She wouldn't have had time to make a copy would she?

"We need to get to her house. I know what worried me. I could not work out why she had not given the tape to the police after she talked to them. I wonder if she may only have pretended to talk to them. Perhaps she just wanted to use the tape for blackmail. Perhaps she wanted to blackmail your father? That would explain why he killed her.

"I know the police here are not hot. But they are not totally dumb. If the tape is at her house, then we must get it and keep it as insurance. It's our insurance against your father harming my parents or us. I would not use it for anything else. But we need to act quickly. The police may not all be corrupt. We can't be sure that they are unaware of the tape. We can't take the risk in any case that they find it by chance. They could come to your aunt's house and look for it once they make the connection between her and the shooting. If they don't, your father's people will definitely come once the coast is clear."

"What do we do?" said Jacqui.

"You and I should go to your aunt's house. I suggest we go with the police. You said you would call on them in the morning. Let's meet them at your aunt's. You can say that you need to pick up your clothes and you can scan the place. Is there anywhere you think she would hide something like a tape? Somewhere your father would not look."

My mother said, "Hold on. You're running ahead of us. Do we want to launder the money immediately or not? I thought we wanted the trail to go cold first."

"I did," said my father. "But there are many advantages of prompt action. And, if Jacqui is used to money laundering, that reduces the risks. The way the markets are going I would like to put the currencies in play sooner rather than later. But we only do that if we are sure that the police are off the scent and we have insurance. Otherwise we revisit our plans."

Jacqui picked up the phone and called the St Tropez police. I listened carefully on the extension. They were sympathetic and did not appear to have any concerns. The two sons were coming down to take charge of the body. It was unfortunate. It was a scandal. It was a random shooting.

It had evidently been a case of mistaken identity. Among the cars in the car park was one belonging to a Mr. Big in import and export of goods from Marseilles. The police were questioning him. Had he enemies? He had two convictions for the import of a certain white powder.

They did not think he was the culprit. He was though with his favourite mistress and his wife. Had someone tried to frighten him? Had they thought that Mademoiselle's aunt was the mistress? Or even the wife. They would never know. It seemed so far fetched even allowing for the strange threesome they had described. The old lady was gone sixty, hardly mistress material! Still if it got them off the trail, who cared?

27

We had already established from Jacqui that the sons were not too straight. One was an accountant and the other was a lawyer. Their clients were not shopkeepers and people seeking to establish family trusts. Most of them would be friends or enemies of Jacqui's father. They too would have no interest in getting involved with the police. They did not want their names in the papers. If they found out or guessed who might be behind the death of their mother, they would back off. They knew the price for curiosity was terminal.

Jacqui's parents were in fact second-generation Mafia. Their parents had both come from Italy to America. That was at the time of the prohibition. They never made the big time but both sides of the family carved a niche out for themselves at the rough end of the business. They specialised in prostitution, protection rackets and blackmail.

After her parents married, Jacqui's father and an uncle got to run both of the gangs. Then one day there was a big raid. Nobody ever knew how the police got to know where the family was meeting. Her father was there but he managed to escape. He got a bullet in the stomach but still crawled away and hid. He stayed put till the coast was clear. He turned up the next day.

But the police left the house where the meeting was taking place with several members of the family. They were led away in handcuffs. And there were body bags as well for three other members of the family. It seemed a devastating blow.

There had been enough incriminating evidence in the house to charge the survivors with a series of crimes. In the subsequent investigation and trial, two were sent to death row and the others got sentences ranging from ten years to life. Jacqui's father got the best lawyers to argue for them but they got no leniency. And surprisingly he was not arrested. Some time later, I heard hints that he may have engineered the raid to get total control.

Left in total and undisputed charge of his gangs, her father moved into big time. He realised that the future lay in drugs and built up a series of connections in Latin America. He was especially friendly with the Colombian syndicates.

He used the cash flow from his petty crimes to finance the drugs. It was all too simple. He used a variety of ways to bring in the drugs. They usually came in by boat or plane. They were hardly ever detected. The planes landed in small airports and remote airstrips. The boats were not tankers or cargo boats but yachts used by the super rich. All you needed to do was to put a mule on the yacht. The role of the steward was the favourite. No shipment was ever too large.

But the cumulative value of the shipments was huge. From time to time people were used to carry the drugs. They were often girls who had run out of money while travelling around the world. Their choice was smuggling or prostitution. Australians and New Zealanders were the common targets. Sometimes they got through and picked up their five thousand dollars. Sometimes not. It was important that the police made regular hauls or they got upset and tackled the big stuff.

The profit from the drugs funded other activities. Big time gambling was a favourite. They also developed a series of legitimate businesses and her father had said that he wanted her to be straight. That was quite common apparently with the modern Mafia families. They made fortunes through illegal ways and then became pillars of society.

The bulk of his assets were legitimate. The bulk of his income was still illegal. So prostitution and protection rackets financed the drugs. And the drugs financed a chain of holdings in the financial, leisure and pharmaceutical industries.

They were actually even more closely interlinked. The money was laundered through the first two. The pharmaceutical side provided a good cover for some of the drug imports.

In the end her father was a billionaire. I thought that we could be too if our financial plans worked out. Perhaps there was not that much of difference between her family and mine after all!

Jacqui though had wanted out. She did not believe that they could split the two worlds. She knew her father had ensured that nobody could uncover the link between his Mafia activities and the legitimate business world behind which he masqueraded. He was based in Switzerland although he lived all over the world. He kept his US citizenship. Jacqui suspected that he may even have had immunity from prosecution, and that would have been for two reasons. He had definitely helped the CIA on many occasions. Indeed the Mafia is a good source of intelligence for them. He had also generously financed the election of many politicians, and had handled some slightly more delicate work for them at the same time.

Jacqui had been given a convent education. She had been shielded from most of the crime syndicate activities. But she had to know, for the family could not afford any errors. Ignorance was as dangerous as knowledge. Knowledge though incriminated. That was the advantage of ensuring she knew. She had also been involved and taught how to launder money in the casinos that her father owned. And also in many that he did not. That was going to be useful for us. She felt she could launder our funds in a month or so. People were used to seeing her as a big roller. We would have had to be more circumspect.

Jacqui appeared relaxed about helping us. But she did not want to launder drug money. She despised drugs. That had been the main reason for wanting to get away from her father. She therefore developed her plan and stole the video. But she had misjudged the reaction that would cause.

It would be much harder making him let go than she had realised. And indeed it was uncertain that he would let go. There was a rationale in his obstinacy. He had many enemies. He had betrayed many people in the past. He had tricked Colombian drug barons. He had shipped other gangland leaders. He had fought with other crime syndicates. He had ruthlessly destroyed any one who stood in his way. The family would want her in the fold to protect her as much as for any other reason.

But Jacqui was clear. She wanted out. And I knew that I wanted her out too. I wanted to be with her. And that was impossible inside the family.

So we needed to get out of St Tropez. And we needed to do that fast. So we asked the police to accompany us to the house. Jacqui needed her things. And she needed to see if she could find the tape. She doubted it but perhaps once in the house it would be easier for her to identify possible hiding places.

The police were agreeable. They would look around the house with us. They were pleased that we were leaving everything to them. That made it easier to manage. We agreed to meet them there. They understood only too well the fact that we were nervous and that Jacqui wanted to get away from the scene of such anguish as soon as possible. They found nothing strange about my story. I was the son of the De Roches and would accompany Jacqui as moral support.

They had my parent's statement. Of course Mr. and Mrs. De Roche could proceed with their plans. They had given their statement. They were just bystanders. When the culprits were caught they may be needed as witnesses but till then they should go on with their planned trip. I could not see the police being successful in this case; and felt that we were unlikely to be bothered by them again.

We quickly agreed that my parents would head off to Madrid and then on to Rio. I knew where they would stay and would call them once we had laundered the money. Or earlier, if there were problems. We said our good-byes and they went inside to pack and prepare their luggage and new identities.

Jacqui and I drove to the house. Just outside the town, Jacqui said, "My Aunt had a wall safe behind a picture in the hall. She took her jewellery from there. I can guess the code; she used it on everything. She was an amateur. She always used the year of her 21st birthday. It was a big joke in the family. The only people who did not know it were her two sons. And it was better that they didn't for they would have robbed her. As it was they tried to bleed her dry. But she was a bit smarter than they were. Although that's not saying much. The number is 211965, 1965 was the year of her 21st."

As we came to the house, the police were already there. Jacqui had taken a pair of mother's sunglasses to hide her eyes. She had put sun block on her face and it gave her a ghostly pallor. She looked the part.

"I am glad I had that shower," she said, "or they might have realised that I had been in bed with you. I always reckon I can tell. There is a sort of sweet smell on a girl and it clings. It's not erotic, unless it's on you. I always found that strange."

"Stop, this isn't the time for talk about sex. I always get excited if you talk like that. That's not going to do you any good at a time like this. We've got to be serious."

We walked into the house and Jacqui said, "I must get my ring. I left it in the wall safe." She calmly walked over to the picture, as I asked the police if they would like to check the locks with me. "After all the house will be left unattended until Madame's sons arrive. It would be horrific if there was a burglary as well."

The police went with me and we had soon gone round the house. It was in a fashionable area and had a good-sized garden. It had two rooms downstairs, a sitting room with a pleasant terrace and a dining room off a modern kitchen. The bushes and shrubs were void of blossom at this time of the year but I realised that in summer the garden would have been a sea of colour. Upstairs there were three bedrooms, two with bathrooms en suite. Nothing spectacular. But the whole place gave the impression of quiet wealth. A bourgeois in retirement. Or, in reality, the wife of a minor hood living off black money.

When we went downstairs, Jacqui was closing a medium sized suitcase. "I had hardly unpacked," she said, "That's everything. What do I need to do now?"

"We have your statement typed up. As it is the key one, we need you to sign it." They were understanding about her desire to leave the scene of so much sorrow and return to the arms of her loving father. If only they knew!

We went to the police station. As soon as we were alone in the car, I started to ask. "I have it," she said. "It's in the case." We drew up outside the station.

"Let me wait in the car. I don't want the case to be unattended. We could have been seen going into the house." Jacqui nodded and headed into the grey police station. It was a strange building. The only sign of life was the flickering blue sign over the entrance. And that flickering was unintentional. It was just caused by a poor connection. I did not get the impression that there would be a quick reaction if I got attacked.

I sat in the car and kept a watch for any strange activity. When you are looking for something unusual, everything seems suspicious. The car slowing down for no reason. The man loitering at the corner. The car coming towards one and jumping the lights. The man carrying a coat but what was underneath it? Then I heard an irritated hooting of a horn. There was no obvious reason for it. I was nervous. I had seen what Jacqui's people could do.

When her father found us in bed together, he had threatened me. He was careful not to hit me in front of her. He knew how to scare one. He believed I had taken her virginity. He thought it had happened that day. Neither of us had been that innocent but I knew better than to contradict him. He had wanted his daughter to be pure at her wedding. I had despoiled her. I was to leave and leave her alone. If I did not, she would suffer. Acid in her face. A car accident that left her a cripple. It was up to me. And that was why I needed insurance. Jacqui and I hadn't talked about the incident. But she knew the score.

Within minutes she left the police station.

I said, "We need to get to Monte Carlo and to the bank. We have an account at the United. They have a vault. It has twenty four-hour security. It is more reliable than the one in Cannes. We need two copies of the tape. We will have to get to a tape recorder and copy it. That means that we won't get everything finished today. First of all we need to get back to the house for the recorder. I also need to pick up my stuff; and I want a gun. There is a revolver there. I am not the greatest of shots, but I have been trained. And it is best to be prepared."

Jacqui nodded and we headed back out of town. At the exit to St Tropez there was a huge roundabout. I passed the turnoff to Grimaud. We would be taking that later in the day. And it was then that I noticed the black sedan. I needed to get into the right lane for Croix Valmer and a van was in my way. I took advantage of a small gap that opened up and swerved in front of it at the last minute. There was an angry exchange of flashing lights and horns, but not at me. The van driver raised his fist and muttered "conard" or so it seemed through my rear mirror. Now the cars behind reacted noisily as a large black car with shaded windows drew in a couple of cars behind me. A black sedan. Just like the one they had seen the night before at the murder scene.

Jacqui had noticed it, too. "Trouble," she said, "We have to lose them."

"They're faster than me. It's going to be difficult. I need to think."

Jacqui said, "There's only one way. You can't shake them off on a road like this. But they also won't try anything too risky. They will prefer to wait till we stop and get out. The getaway is not easy in a stream of traffic. Even if it is fairly light. It would be all right for them at night but in the daytime they could get caught behind lorries and things. We can only hope that we can get them to crash. The question is how."

"Make sure your seat belt is tight. This is going to be the drive from hell. It's the only way."

The road to Croix Valmer is not a fast road. It is mainly two lanes. There are several intersections. It is winding. And slippery at the bends. Only a fool takes it at more than 80 km an hour in the bad parts and it is difficult to make more than 120 on any section. I pressed down on the accelerator. My C class Mercedes convertible, a good run-around for the region but no more, burst into life and the speedometer climbed quickly. 60 to 80 to 100 and on to 140.

"Oh my God," said Jacqui and I thought she was praying. In the end that convent education always shows itself. Convent girls have two common traits. They are either frigid or they love sex; that's a reaction to the high walls of their convent schools from which all men are barred save their priest and a couple of aged retainers who mow the lawns and tend the boilers. And convent girls will revert to prayer in extreme circumstances, even if they give up mass, holy retreats and all the other rituals of their schooldays the moment they graduate to more liberal environments.

We came to the end of the straight road. We were just below the picturesque village of Gassin. That was the place where my parents had gone the night before. The town looked medieval from the road below. It is an old town with some good hill restaurants. Not too tarnished by the twentieth century. Perched high up a steep hill, it looked like an impregnable fortress set over the plains of the peninsular.

I pulled towards the junction that leads to Gassin. It is a nasty crossing. A staggered four-way junction. A white car pulled across my path and stopped in fright in the middle of the dual carriageway. I wrenched the wheel to the right. My car shrieked across the road. I pulled the wheel the other way and we veered to the left and right before gathering speed again as we drove on to Croix Valmer. I heard the horn of my pursuer and others as they in turn swerved round the unfortunate driver. I wondered when he would have the courage to restart his engine and get to safety. "France," I said. "It's full of blind bloody drivers. That or they're blind drunk."

I knew the sedan had realised they had been spotted. They had now drawn up behind us and were keeping pace with no difficulty.

"Here comes the dangerous bit. You'd better pray. For my driving because it won't be as good as the guy behind. And for luck as we overtake in tight spots. But don't forget he's wider and longer than I am. So the odds are stacked a bit in our favour."

"Holy shit," said Jacqui.

"No, pray to God" I said, "He may be more useful."

I pressed further down on the accelerator. The car screeched round the corner hitting nearly one hundred and sixty. I felt the wheels lift slightly from the ground as I wrenched the steering wheel round. The car had skidded into the centre of the road. A car on the other side screeched to slow down. It slid across the road. The black sedan had taken the corner easily. There was a grind of metal. The small car on the other side seemed to bounce off the side of the sedan and I guessed it crashed back into the bushes at the verge on its side of the road. All I saw was the sedan swerving a bit as it regained full control. "First score to us at least," I shouted.

We hit a straight stretch of road. It was in need of repair and the car bounced dangerously as it gathered speed. I hoped the suspension would hold. At times we seemed to be flying. At others we seemed to try to plough over the bumps.

We were already in the next bend and hitting it at 180. I felt the car sway. I sensed it getting out of control. "Too fast, just too fast. I need to slow down," I muttered. Jacqui's lips just moved. I wondered to whom she was praying.

As we came into the bend I tried to accelerate gently and saw we were holding our speed. I knew I couldn't brake. Once again I felt the car rise on its side and this time it appeared to bounce as I slipped in a skid right across the carriageway. I was straightening up on the wrong side of the road as I came into the second part of the S bend. At that moment I saw the oncoming lorry and pulled further across, still facing the oncoming traffic. I tried to get onto the narrow grass verge and out of its way. I was slowing and bouncing as half the car ran on the grass verge and the other half on the road. The bushes and small trees were scraping the side of the car. Jacqui sat stiff, her mouth open, and her eyes wide in terror.

The lorry appeared to swerve away from me and that pulled him over the centre of the road in a shower of sparks. There was a loud crack as the mirror on the far side of the car shattered as it hit the side of the lorry but then I was clear and already pulling back over to my side. There were frightened shouts and noises from the cars behind the lorry. Luckily the first one, a small Fiat, was going slowly and had held all the others back. The gap was large enough for me, now that I had brought the Mercedes under control again. I veered through the gap between the Fiat and the lorry and cut across again to the right side of the road.

The Fiat went out of control and I saw it hit the verge. It jumped into the air and rolled over, crashing into the bushes and trees at the side of the road.

By now I had slowed down to 120. I was pulling away from the looks of fury and horror from drivers now shunting together in the wake of the crash ahead. For a crash there was. It may have already happened, for it seemed in the past by the time I registered.

I realised it at that moment when I became aware of the noise. A huge explosion and a ball of fire. Had the sedan hit the lorry? If so, it looked as if it had blown up. I thought quickly and said to Jacqui, "It must have been going at our speed and so it would have been well over the road. It must have hit the lorry and it could even have been head on. In that case I don't think we will see them again. But we can't check. We need to drive on and we need to change cars. This one will be wanted."

"Won't they be able trace it back to you?" queried Jacqui.

"I doubt it," I replied. " We bought both our cars with false papers. They were registered in the name of Feraud. That was after my mother's favourite off the peg designer. You know Louis Feraud. They both have insurance in that name and I carry an ID card as Charles Feraud as well as De Roche. We reckoned we needed one additional escape route in case the De Roche name was discovered. We used the Feraud documents for the cars as we thought that we would need the cars and new identities if we were discovered immediately after the scam. Once we had got through a few weeks and were sure the trail had gone cold, our De Roche identities would be established and we would just re-register the cars in our names, having bought them from the Ferauds."

Jacqui said, "They definitely did not make it through or they would be up with us."

"We can't be sure," I said, "By now they would have guessed that we were heading for the house. They could have decided to hang back or to take us out at the house later. We still better be careful. In any event let's listen to the radio."

As we drove back, a warning came over the radio about an accident and the fact that the road would be blocked. No more details. "We will need to monitor what comes out," I said as we turned into Croix Valmer. I drove down towards Gigaro Beach where we had our villa and pulled into a private road that led to a development of tourist cottages. Although it was off-season the place would still be half full. The car park was at the top of the property and only used when the residents could not find a nearer spot. Just next to the rubbish bins, there was space for half a dozen cars and I pulled in next to a little Twingo hire car. We would be unnoticed there, at least by the security people. They would assume we were visiting friends. The side mirror was a mess but that was a good thing. "When did you last see a car without a dent in it in this part of the world?" I joked to Jacqui.

MEETING THE MAFIA

I took Jacqui's hand and we walked through the grounds down to the main road. Our house was five minutes away but we approached it with care. We had good cover, as the area is full of bushes and trees. The house seemed quiet. There was no movement. I turned to Jacqui.

"Hold on to the tape and wait for me. Let me investigate. If I switch the light in the hallway on and off three times within the next five minutes, everything's OK. But, if not, run back to the car and get out. You have the tape and that's our insurance. If I'm caught, I will use that to bargain with you. Take this phone. I can contact you through it."

I walked to the back of the house. I quietly tried the door to the porch adjoining the kitchen. It was locked but I had the keys. I opened the door hesitantly and carefully walked in. I breathed a sigh of relief. There was no sign of life.

I entered the kitchen and peered round the door into the hall. Again no sign of life. I went into the study, squeezing gingerly through the half-opened door. I quietly lifted out the ventilator cover and took out the gun and ammunition. I placed the bullets on the study table and the gun in my trouser belt. I had checked and it was loaded. I looked around the study. It was all too neat. I felt it had been looked over. My parents would have taken all the papers and I had mine in my jacket. Someone had been here. Of that I was certain. The question was whether he or she was still around. I took the gun from the waistband of my trousers and took out the safety latch.

I crept back into the hall. I peered into the lounge. There sitting in a chair was a tall, dark-haired man in a black jacket over a black T-shirt. He did not look legitimate, but I had to be sure. I suspected he would not be alone, and then I saw her.

She could not see my gun. She did not realise that I could see her in the mirror on the wall. And it wasn't a lipstick in her hand. It was a small gun and it was pointing at me. She had made no noise and that meant she wanted me alive. I had no such need. I knew that sort of gun was not effective at any distance and had no plans to let her get close. I turned round and fired. The bullet took her in the stomach and she fell. The gun clattered out of her hand and rattled across the parquet floor.

I turned back. The man was on his feet, gun in hand and diving for cover. I fired. The gun roared again and, out of luck rather than anything else, I realised he was dead. The body had dropped lifeless onto the floor and, as I moved closer, I saw that I had struck him clean between the eyes. I turned back to the injured woman. She was in a bad state. Yet she had managed to crawl over to the gun. A trail of blood smeared the floor behind her. A shot rang out. She was accurate, but weak from her wound. Her hand must have been trembling. Nevertheless the bullet clipped my arm. I felt a sharp pain. But somehow I held onto my gun. I pressed the trigger and saw the trail of the bullets as they spat out and hit her in the chest, the throat and the face. And then into the ceiling as, in fright, my hand continued in its upward path.

I pulled myself together and ran into the kitchen. I had to reload. I did not even know if I had any bullets left. I doubted there was anyone else but I had to check. I reloaded the gun and quickly looked over the house. Empty. I went to the hall and flashed the lights. It was an ashen Jacqui who came running. She saw me, gun in hand and bleeding slightly from my arm. She stopped as she came to the hall.

"Maria Angelica," she gasped. Then she followed my gaze into the lounge. "Claudio Pasquale," she muttered. She threw her arms around me. "They are killers. They are not part of our family. Never allowed to know more than they need. Only half trusted. Simply they were seen as too evil. Nobody wanted them around. They would have been sent to torture us to get the tape and to kill us. They would have been good at that. The car was only a back up then." She turned to me, "What do we do now?"

"We sort out the tape and get out of here. We need to clean the place. We need to get rid of the bodies. And we must leave pretty soon."

She had a quick look at my arm. She went to the kitchen and came back with a plaster and some antiseptic spray. In a minute she had finished. I winced as the spray hit the open wound. "Don't be a baby," she joked. "It won't even leave a scar. Which is more than we can say about your handiwork."

We got down to work quickly. It was lucky that the television in my bedroom had an in-built tape recorder. The lounge television had a separate one. We took it to the bedroom and I told Jacqui to get to work.

I packed one case and then went down, telling her that I would deal with the bodies.

I grabbed some sheets and wrapped the bodies in them. One by one I pulled them over to the front door. Checking that nobody was around, I lifted up the woman first and put her over my shoulder. I dumped her in the garage. I then did the same thing with the man.

I put the two guns on the table. I also went through the woman's bag but there was nothing in it of any interest. I took that to the garage as well. They had no ID papers, no credit cards. They were totally anonymous. An idea came to me. A way to rid ourselves of the car and the bodies. A way to confuse the police.

I got a mop and started cleaning up the floor. I needed to get the blood off the floor and walls. I also needed to tidy up the bullet damage. I had fired six times and she had fired once. The bodies still had four bullets in them. I had checked that out. There were entry wounds but no exit ones. I quickly found one bullet in the wall near the mirror and the other in the ceiling.

I switched on the TV and saw the news was on. The announcer said "And now to the fatal accident in St Tropez." I called Jacqui to watch. We gasped as we saw the picture of the sedan. It had crashed into the lorry. In fact it had crashed underneath the lorry. All four occupants had been decapitated. The lorry had crashed into another car before coming to a stop. The lorry driver had had a miraculous escape. He was suffering from shock and nothing more. The other car involved had two occupants. One had light injuries and the other was suffering from head injuries but was said to be in no immediate danger. A black Mercedes was being sought. The sedan had been chasing it. The sedan had been linked to the murder at Gassin the night before. The killers must have been chasing their true targets. The Mercedes had caused another car to crash and several to shunt into each other but all that chaos caused just a few scratches and bruises.

I breathed a sigh of relief. I had no compunction about the sedan and its occupants. At least there were no innocents hurt. I asked Jacqui how she was getting on. The tape was only 20 minutes long. She had recorded it twice and was just running through the copies. She would be finished in half an hour.

I said, "I will be too and then we need to get the car. There's too much about it on the news to leave it up by the houses."

"Charles, why do we need two copies? You never explained. I didn't think of asking earlier."

"I want to put one in the bank in Monte Carlo and one in Fucquet in Geneva. We will then call your father and arrange to hand over the original. But, I will make arrangements that, if anything happens to me, the tapes will be discovered and handed to the police and the television channels. CBS would love them. In addition, if anything happens to you or any of my family, I will do the same. I can make those arrangements on the phone. But we need a new car and we must drive to Monte Carlo. We can deposit the first tape first thing in the morning and the second before the banks close in Geneva."

She nodded her agreement. "Are we going to stay together?"

"I want to," I said, "but you are free to choose. That does not change the arrangement I need to make with your father. If ever you want to leave, I will see that you do not go empty handed. You are going to help us. You will be free. You won't have to blackmail your father again."

I took her in my arms and kissed her gently, "I love you though. Don't leave me."

She laid her head on my shoulder and clung to me, just for a minute. Then she started. "Come on let's get moving. We need to be careful 'till we've sorted this out."

We did our best to cover our tracks. I suspect forensics would have been able to find traces of blood and bullets. But there was no reason w hy they should look at the house, at least as long as we re not caught.

I handed Jacqui the small gun. I also passed her a couple of rounds of extra ammunition that I had found on the girl. "Keep that in your bag. But only use it if you are desperate. I doubt it would be very accurate at any distance. Shoot low as the gun jerks up when fired."

I put my father's gun in my waistband and the gangster's in my jacket pocket. I picked up the ammunition – both guns took the same – and returned it to its hiding places behind the grill. I removed the tapes and placed the copies in the same place. The original I put in my other pocket.

We walked out carefully. I said, "We'll have to scout around the car in case it has been identified. I doubt it, though, as the news is only 40 minutes old. But we need to be careful. When we come back, is it possible that your father would have ordered more people here? After all, he should already know about the sedan."

"He'll know about the car but not the killings. We would avoid radio contact at times like this. There would be a rendezvous planned for later today or tomorrow with the killers. The meet would take place whatever happened. That's the process. The instructions are always the same. They are simple. Do the job and then get out and away. If the targets have not turned up, stay put only for as long as you have been told. If they don't turn up, get further orders at the meet. In extreme cases call, but only in extreme cases. Use a public phone. Never pick up the house phone, as you don't know who is calling or whether calls can be traced. And avoid mobiles, as they are not secure. That's the way it goes. I think we can stay in the house tonight."

"Let me explain later but I plan to be out in an hour or so. But first of all, how would they have got to the house?"

"You would never use a car on a job like that. They would either have instructions to take you or kill you. They would use your car to get away. They would be left at the house and the delivery car would leave. A parked car causes suspicion. It is of no benefit."

We came to the parking space the same way as we had left it. Nobody was there. The car was parked next to the Twingo. A couple of others had left, but it was as we left it. I could see nobody around.

I turned to Jacqui. "Head down to the main entrance. Here is the tape. Same routine as before if I am caught. Although this time it is more likely to be the police than your father."

She quickly headed off and I strolled over to the car. I got in and quickly immobilised the alarm. I held my breath. I had known it to be temperamental and go off for no apparent reason. But it didn't. I drove down the deserted street and stopped at the junction with the main road. Jacqui came out of the bushes and jumped in beside me. We drove off to the house.

"I am still a bit edgy when I am without you," she said. "Together and I feel safe."

"I'll be with you all the time," I said. "Let's get this car in the garage and then we have a couple of urgent phone calls to make."

Once at the house, we quickly checked it out for visitors and found none. We did it together this time. It was getting dark as night drew in.

"Jacqui, call and hire a car. We need a good four door, and we need to pick it up this evening." She did as asked and was soon giving her credit card details. They offered to deliver it. "Hold on a minute," she said, and covering the mouthpiece asked me what she should do.

"Can we pick it up in an hour? Can they wait?"

After a minute on the phone, she said, "They shut in half an hour and they say they have nobody available."

"OK we will be there. Am I right that they are just off the road to St Tropez. Just after the big bend as we leave Croix Valmer?"

She confirmed the details with them and said goodbye. "Let's move," I said. We went to the kitchen for the bullets and the tapes. I put them in a holdall, picked up my case and we headed out. I locked the house and opened the garage. "Open the boot," I said, and then put the case and the holdall on the back seat of the Mercedes.

She then came to help me place the two sheets with their gory contents into the boot of the car. They actually fitted neatly in together.

"They never laid on top of each other in real life," observed Jacqui with a grin. "He only liked rough stuff, the rougher the better, and she was a dyke of the first order."

"Well it's nice to give them a chance to taste it straight," I joked. "After all, I doubt he has ever been as stiff as he is today."

With that we drove off to the car hire place. Up the side road with the car blending well into the night. We agreed Jacqui should go alone and, as she drew out, I would follow her back to Croix Valmer. We would take the back road to Gassin and on to Remantuelle. I knew those roads well and they would be quite deserted at this time of the year. My plan was quite simple. We would get to the top of the cliffs, wipe my car down and send it into the sea with our two dead friends in the front. Once found, they would be linked to the sedan. The police would assume that they had been the targets and, given that they could not establish the exact time of the murder, they would have assumed that friends of the occupants of the sedan had been the perpetrators of the crime. A case well closed in their mind.

The only other thing we needed to do was to get my parents to dump their car. They would have it in Madrid tomorrow and I knew where to contact them from tonight. That would be easy for we needed to avoid any connection with the mysterious Ferauds. After all, the police would assume that they were the people in the car.

The road to the car hire firm was dark and deserted. I dropped Jacqui off outside, and, as agreed, moved up to the junction and pulled into a side road. From there I could watch the entrance to the car hire firm and the main road.

Everything appeared very quiet. By now Jacqui should be inspecting one of the cars in the parking area in front of the hire firm. Yet there was no movement. I felt nervous and glanced at my watch. Then in the half dark I saw Jacqui emerging from the offices. There were two men with her. They were dressed in suits. They were definitely not in the car hire business.

I quickly moved from the car. I locked the doors and, my heart thumping, moved down to the car hire area. They must be expecting me, I thought. Yet I could see no lookout. I was sure nobody had been watching me. If they were going to take me out or capture me, they had ample opportunity earlier. They would not have waited till I was suspicious.

I got closer to the gate and crouched by the fence. I held my gun ready.

I then heard Jacqui. She was sobbing. "Let go of my arm. You're hurting me. I don't want to go back to my father. I want to get away. That's why I wanted a car. I want to be on my own. Let me go, please let me go."

A rough voice replied, "Get in the car and shut up bitch. You're more trouble than you are worth. If I were your pa, I'd beat the fucking daylights out of you."

"You're not my father," she said. "You're my cousin and he's my uncle. If you touch me, my father will kill you. Whether you are family or not. Let go of my arm."

Somehow I knew she thought I would be close. The message was clear. They did not think I was there. Perhaps the fact that I drove away had led them to believe that my car was a taxi. In the half dark it would have been difficult to identify from a distance. Also I knew that uncle and cousin were not going to harm Jacqui. They would be wary of a shootout. I also suspected that they did not know that she was armed.

I decided to use surprise tactics. I stood up and called out, "Police. Let the girl go or I shoot."

They swirled round to me, pushing Jacqui away behind a van for cover. They hesitated as they looked to see if I was really the police. I was half hidden from their view by a large dark blue estate car. They lost precious moments as they searched for others. I was surprised they did not attempt to make it a fight. I supposed that they saw that I had them covered and so made no attempt to draw guns. Then I saw why. Jacqui had used the diversion to take her gun from her bag, and they had seen it before me. Two guns against two in their holsters are no match for two drawn ones.

"Back off to the wall," I said. "Now."

They complied uneasily.

"Now get into the office." They complied. "Lie on the floor and spread your arms out. One bad move and I shoot."

I turned to Jacqui, "What happened to the car hire?"

"Let me look if anything was done," she said. "Yes, all the paperwork is here. There is the Peugeot. All they needed to do was to swipe my credit card, confirm my licence and get my signature. I can do the paperwork myself. That makes the hire legal, including insurance and things. I don't want to get stopped by the police, although I resent paying after what they did."

"What did you tell the car hire people? How did you know Jacqui was going to be here?" I asked the uncle.

"We know the firm," he said. "We put them on notice. We were in St Tropez co-ordinating operations."

"What operations?" I snapped.

He mentioned the sedan and the accident. He knew we had been involved. He said nothing about the house and the killers. They saw no need to tell me. I felt there was no need for him to know.

"OK Jacqui wants to get away from this all and I agreed to drive her here. I am now going to drive along with her. If you follow her, there will be trouble. I know what her father really wants and if I do not call a friend by tomorrow night, then the goods are handed to the police. And the hand over will be at senior level and a copy will be passed to the US embassy in Paris. We know their organised crime people there. Tell her father that we will call him on Wednesday morning; that's the day after tomorrow. He will be safe as long as nothing happens to either of us, or any of our friends. Have you understood?"

The uncle looked worried. "OK," he said, "but don't go back to your house. There are people waiting for you there."

I hesitated. "Why don't you call them?"

He looked worried. "We always maintain total silence on these operations. They would not answer. They will leave tomorrow night if you don't turn up. It would be dangerous to break the rules."

That relieved me, as I now knew that we had time to spare. I also knew that the uncle was worried by my threat. He couldn't be sure that I was not bluffing but couldn't risk it either. Fortunately, at this moment they thought they had nothing to lose by playing along.

"Once we leave, you stay for five minutes. Then go back to St Tropez. Don't even try to follow us."

I was certain he wouldn't. I thought of cutting off the phone but they most likely had mobiles. And we did not have time to mess around.

Jacqui said, "I'm ready." We backed out of the room.

"Change of plan," I said. "Follow me. We'll take a different route, as they may be able to see the road we take if we go the back way. But we need to drive fast."

She jumped into the car and started it up. "The tank's full," she said. I walked alongside her as we made our way to my car. I then got in, started the engine and pulled ahead of her. I turned right and she followed. I then drove steadily for five to ten minutes till I got to the Gassin turnoff. Then I led her cross-country to Remantuelle and drove up through it to get to the coast road and the cliffs. It was from there that I needed to dispatch the car. I knew a good place that was protected from the road, overlooking the sea at a point that I believed was quite deep. That suited my plan.

As we drove round the old square in the centre of Remantuelle, it was getting dark. And there were menacing clouds approaching. I knew that there could be violent storms soon. I only hoped that they would not hit us until we had finished our jobs.

I watched carefully in the rear view mirror as we drove along the winding back roads. There was hardly any traffic and I was pretty sure we had not been followed. If Jacqui's uncle had watched us go, he would assume we were heading to St Tropez and beyond rather than doubling back to Remantuelle and the coast.

As I pulled off the road I saw that the dark and ever more menacing storm clouds were even closer and that a strong wind had whipped up. Jacqui drew up behind me and shivered as she got out of her car. She was dressed in a white blouse and short blue skirt. She wore light shoes.

"Have you warmer clothes in the car?" I asked. She shook her head.

"Take my jacket then. Most of my stuff is summery things as I was planning to move on and buy as I needed. I have a light sweater in my case and I'll put that on. Take the gun and the tape from the jacket pockets and put them in the glove compartment of your car. Always hold onto your bag with the other tape though. I'll empty out the car."

I grabbed our bags and shoved them into the boot of Jacqui's Peugeot. I then opened my case and pulled out a light cashmere sweater and put it on. I still felt cold and could see that Jacqui did too. The wind tugged petulantly at her clothes and seemed to blow through them. She pulled the jacket around herself for more warmth.

"Let's get moving," I said. "First we need to wipe down the car to remove our fingerprints. I don't know what the sea will do to the car but we should take no risks. Here are some rubber gloves that I took from the kitchen. You take the right hand one and I'll take the left. Spray the car with this, it's an alcohol-based spray, and wipe the front of the car clean. I'll do the same around the doors and in the back. You at least can sit out of the wind."

She nodded and got to work. I did too and we felt we had done all we could although it took longer than I had thought. How do you rub off fingerprints when you cannot see them? I hoped we had done a good job and felt somewhat more confident when I reflected that we had never been in trouble with the police and so they would not have a copy of our fingerprints in any case.

By the time we had finished it was already raining. It started slowly and then got heavier in minutes. The thunder in the distance was already rumbling and then a sharp flash of lightening seemed to shoot out of the sky and disappear into the hills on the other side of the bay.

"Let's hurry," I said. "We are too exposed here and I don't like the idea of pushing a car in this storm. I want to be away from the metal and the trees. Help me get the bodies out of the back."

We pulled the girl out first and unrolled her from the sheet. There was another flash of lightning in the distance and it threw its shadow across our cliff top. The dead girl's face seemed to move eerily. The eyeballs appeared to move. The open mouth seemed to click. I almost screamed and Jacqui looked about to faint.

"Give me your glove," I said. "I'll put her in the car. We need to avoid any fingerprints."

I pulled the body to the passenger seat. I lifted it into the car. I placed a seat belt around it. I wondered if the air bag would inflate in the crash. Not that that would help. We pulled the second body out and I slammed the boot. Again I took off the sheet and lugged him to the driver's side. I called to Jacqui to tear up the sheets as best she could but not to lose any bits of them. He was heavier and I fought his weight, I struggled, too, against the wind and the now teeming rain. I somehow got him into the seat and secured with the seat belt. I saw that my clothes were blood-stained. I would need to change before we hit the next town.

As I looked up there was a roar of thunder and a blast of wind that had me reeling backwards. I turned to Jacqui and felt the lightning soar towards us. There was a crack about thirty yards away. It hit a large tree and, as we looked, it crashed down falling between the road and us. It missed the Peugeot by a few yards.

I went to Jacqui. "I'm going to push the car over now. Give me the sheets and drive your car to the road."

I took the sheets and grabbed a bag that had been in my car. I saw it was from a supermarket. I couldn't recall from when. I was amused that this irritated me. I stuffed the sheets inside, picked up some stones from nearby and shoved them into the bag. I tied the top together, pushed out the air and flung the bag over the cliff into the sea. I watched from the edge and saw it plummet down into the water. At least they'll be washed but they'll always be stained, I thought.

With the gloves still on, I released the hand brake and put the car into neutral. I pushed. It slowly moved. The muddy ground made it difficult. I could hardly see for the rain. It thundered again. Somewhere in the distance I was conscious of another flash of lightning. I took a deep breath and saw that Jacqui was driving to the road. She did not want to get stuck in the mud. By me it was looking like a quagmire. I put my back to the car again. I pushed and felt it give as it inched to the edge of the cliff. I felt a jerk and then it came to a halt. I slid down the back of the car and fell over into the mud. My knees sank into it. I steadied myself with my hands. I tried to get up but slipped again, falling heavily on my shoulder.

By now I was covered in mud, soaked and exhausted. And I was scared by the raging storm. I knew it was dangerous. I hurried round to the car and saw the front wheels were over the edge. The underside of the car was jammed, stopping it moving forward. I pushed again. No movement. I pushed harder. It edged slightly. It either shifted sideways or just a bit forward. I could not tell. I cried out in frustration and ducked as a bolt of lightning seared across the angry sky. Its forked tongue coming straight at me. It pushed the rain in front of it, soaking me again. The mud ran from my hair into my eyes. I tried to wipe my face but only made it worse. I blinked to clear my eyes but that hardly helped. I did not know where the lightning had struck. I knew it had missed me, that was all.

I turned to the car in fury now and heaved at it once again. I felt it give and yelled, "Move, fuck you, move." It did and I could feel it tipping forward and I pulled back. I went onto my knees and watched it, as it disappeared over the cliff in slow motion. It bounced once half way down and seemed to shoot out to sea. It sank below the rough sea, throwing up a high spray and then disappearing into the angry depths.

I turned round to the sound of yet more thunder. But now I was past caring. I stumbled round the fallen tree and blinked, seeing only out of one eye. The other seemed to be full of mud and rain. The car was there. Jacqui had moved over to the passenger seat. She was crying to herself. Her blouse was torn. It was soaked through. Her bra was visible beneath the now transparent material. Her skirt was riding high. Her tights were torn. Her shoes were caked in mud. She drew my coat around her shivering body.

I knew that I was little better. I was muddy, wet, cold, despairing, frightened, exhausted and I just wanted to be warm, dry, comfortable and comforted. I knew, however, that that was not possible at the moment.

"Darling, we must change. We can't clean up. I'll find us things to wear. We will have to say that we got caught out on the way. That we got lost. Got a puncture. We'll get a hotel. The best is to find one well away from this coast. I think it best we head for Frejus and look for one there. I prefer it to Grimaud. That's too close to St Tropez."

I looked in her case and found some trousers and a black T-shirt. Also some fresh tights.

"Change in the car," I said, smearing some mud on the new clothes. We needed them dirty but also dry. With my wet coat over them they would serve our story when we got to a hotel. I looked in my case and found some jeans and a blue polo shirt. I did the same with them, and rubbed the jeans into the mud by the verge so that they were splashed to the knees. I got into the car and changed. It was hardly comfortable. Cars are not great places to dress. I had realised that once some years ago but at least that was in the summer when one could complete the process outside the car.

I wiped my face and hands as best I could with my shirt. Jacqui passed me her blouse and said, "It's less muddy than your shirt. Try it". Even wet I could smell her scent on it. It was comforting and somehow made me feel better. I told her that, and she giggled a bit. "Come on. I'm not taking these clothes off again now," she said.

We switched on the engine and the heating and headed back towards Remantuelle. It was tempting to go to the first hotel but I decided against it.

I remarked to Jacqui, "Keep a close eye on the other cars when we get to the roundabout. They could be keeping a watch for us."

"I don't think so," she responded. "They were worried by your threats. They will wait for us to call. As I was there they will believe we were telling the truth. Anyway, they don't know you are going to stick with me yet."

I hoped she was right. We were exhausted and had pretty well taken all we could. Over the last twenty-four hours Jacqui had seen her Aunt killed. We had found each other again. She had come into our lives and we into hers. We had had the car chase. We had the shoot out. We had the scene with her uncle. And now had dumped the car in the storm.

The storm was still hanging over the peninsula as we moved towards Port Grimaud. It looked as if it were heading away from us towards Hyeres and Marseilles. I was relieved as I drove to the motorway. It is a quick drive out of season.

Soon we were on the motorway and I turned to Jacqui. "I know a hotel in Juan Les Pins. I have never stayed there. Just used their car park. It's modern and a four or five star. I suggest we head there. We should make it about ten fifteen or so and I can't think of one in Frejus. Out of season, the one in Juan will be open and have space. There is a conference centre there but I can't believe the conferences fill it to capacity, and there may be none on now."

I gave Jacqui the name and she took out my mobile. Having called the operator and got the number, she dialled it. She booked the room, apologising for the fact that we would be wet and muddy as we had got caught in a storm in the mountains and had to change a wheel. They were understanding and sympathetic on the phone. Jacqui insisted that we needed nothing other than a warm room and a hot bath. I agreed. I was maybe hungry, but I needed to warm up and sleep for tomorrow was going to be a busy day.

THE ROAD TO MONTE CARLO

We got to the hotel at Juan at around 10.30. A bit later than I thought but the weather was still bad. The storm seemed to have swung round and moved our way again. We were both exhausted as I parked in the hotel car park and grabbed our luggage.

There were some astonished looks as we walked in through the swing doors. At reception, I quickly explained who we were and a Mr and Mrs De Roche were signed in at top speed. We were whisked up to a room on the seventh floor and soon had thankfully locked and bolted the door to the whole world. And I had carefully placed the "do not disturb sign" on the door.

Jacqui just sat on the bed, her head in her hands. I quickly went to the bathroom and turned on the bath water. I checked that it was hot and added some of the bath foam they provided. I then went back into the bedroom and picked up Jacqui. She did not protest. She was just too exhausted, both mentally and physically.

I sat her down in the bathroom and slowly undressed her. Her T-shirt, her bra came off first. Then I gently eased down her trousers, then her tights and panties. I looked at her body. Her skin was smooth and a light olive in colour. Her hair dark, but wet and straggly from the rain. It fell down on her shoulders. There were streaks of mud on her forehead, her eye make up was smudged, her lipstick non-existent. Somehow though, she smiled at me weakly, the steam from the bath revitalising her a bit. I switched off the taps for the bath was now almost full. I picked her up and gently placed her in the warm water and soft suds.

She lay there for a while. Her hands idled over her body. The water lapped up and down over her as she moved and relaxed. The suds parted giving a tantalising snapshot of one bit of her or another. Then she stood up. She took the bar of soap and gently rubbed it all over her body.

I watched as the soap moved round her neck, between her breasts, over her arms and down to her waist. She glided the soap slowly over herself as if in a daze. At times her hand stopped. At others it retraced its moves. Gradually the foam enveloped her before it slipped down her body in one long continuous slow and lethargic flow. It found new routes. It retraced old ones.

Having soaped half her body, she lent forward and tackled the rest of herself. She brushed the soap over her stomach, between her legs and over her thighs. Occasionally she sighed. At times she blinked. Always she seemed to relish in the quiet peace and the soothing touch of the soft, smooth, gliding substance that she controlled.

I moved forward and took the soap, tackling lastly her calves and her feet. Without being asked she lifted one foot after the other to the edge of the bath. She continued to look at me dreamily. She moved, as I needed without me asking. We did not say a thing as I drew in her scent, felt her body and feasted on every part of her.

She was enveloped in the soft foam and sat back down in the water with a sigh of contentment.

The soap washed away in the warm water. It caused the final suds to disperse. Gradually the water became clearer and the outline of her body appeared. The slim waist. The rounded breasts. The long legs. The dark thatch of hair. The water moved gently backwards and forwards with her breathing. It sought out each part to fondle. It slipped over the softness of her skin. She shut her eyes dreamily and smiled secretly to herself. Her hands ran from her thighs up her body and then she placed them behind her neck. She yawned silently.

I picked up the shower and tested the temperature of the water. I ran it over her head and then took the shampoo, carefully caressing it into her hair and feeling its texture slowly change. As the water washed away the shampoo, her hair regained its softness and lost the bedraggled look.

Last of all she rinsed her face, picking up the shower to cleanse it all over. Then she stood up and showered the last of the soap and foam from her body before stepping out of the bath into the large white towel that I held. I dried her gently, slowly patting her all over and feeling her relax into my arms.

She picked up the towel and wrapped it around her. "You get washed darling, while I dry my hair."

I emptied her bath and stripped naked. I am tall, over six foot. I weigh around eighty-five kilos. I guess I am well built. I have blue eyes and fair hair with a trace of red. My hair was slightly long, over my shoulders and half way down my ears. I had grown a moustache for this job, but hated it and planned to shave it off as soon as possible. In fact I had grown it when I left England, and Jacqui had commented on it at the time. She did not think it suited me. I was quite hairy, a blonde wiry down covering my chest and sending shoots down my stomach and beyond.

Some of our ancestors came from the Nordic countries and I appear to be a throwback to those times. I did not look much like my father or mother, except that my father is of similar build although a few kilos heavier. I would change my hairstyle. If I cut it short it went naturally darker.

I stepped into the tub, put on the shower and stood under the stream of hot water. I picked up the bar of soap, the very one that she had been using, and stroked it over me. Like her, I started at my neck and worked down. I closed my eyes and remembered the way she had looked and the way I had felt.

I then washed my hair and happily stood under the steaming shower. I felt the weight of the last few hours fall away from me. I returned to my normal self. I was no longer a gunman; a maniac in a car; a madman disposing of the evidence; a conspirator taking on the Mafia. I felt myself returning to my real self. And I realised that I only had been that once since the plan was launched and that had been last night with Jacqui. I hoped that I would not have to revert to those types again, but in my heart I knew that I would do many things that I would regret before this game was played out.

I got out of the shower and dried myself thoroughly. I then walked into the bedroom. Jacqui was already in bed. Her eyes closed, her hair falling luxuriously over the snow-white pillowcase in the King sized bed. She breathed gently, fast asleep. I switched off the lights and quietly slipped next to her. She was naked and I could feel the warmth of her seeping through to me. I lay down beside her and, in her sleep, she curled up into my arms. Her breasts lay on my chest. Her head lay on my shoulder. Our feet, thighs and stomachs touched. I felt myself reacting to her body, and, then like her, I dropped into that deep sleep that only comes from exhaustion.

The sun was shining in through the gaps in the curtain when I woke. I started and saw it was already eight o' clock. I woke Jacqui. "We must leave. We have to get to Monte Carlo and then on to Geneva" I said. "Let me wash first. I have to make a couple of calls. Then we can have a quick breakfast and we must be off by nine."

"I wanted to make love to you. What on earth happened?"

"We did the next best thing," I said, "We were asleep in each others' arms and tonight we can carry on."

After washing, I put on fresh clothes. This time I put on a light pair of trousers, an open necked shirt and a blazer. I needed to look business-like if I was to go to the banks. I thought of dumping my dirty clothes but stuffed them in a laundry bag instead, did the same with Jacqui's and shut them in the case.

I waited for Jacqui to come from the bathroom and get dressed. She was wearing a short red dress. It was plain and full necked. She added a colourful Gucci scarf to it. Once again she looked her usual self. Her face had its natural lively colour, a mixture of olive and health. Her trim figure was accentuated by the simplicity of her dress. It hid no secrets. It told no lies. She was beautiful.

I picked up the cases and left them with the concierge. I told him not to put them in the car. I wanted to make sure that he did not see the clothes we had thrown in the boot. Mine were stained with blood as well as mud. I knew concierges have a habit of looking for anything of interest. I felt we were remarkable enough in the chaos of our arrival and the contrast of our departure. I did not want to be any more of a mystery.

I went to the public phone. It was in a cabin and I could talk in private. I called Madrid. There was an immediate response. "Hi, this is Charles," I said. "I have thought about our discussion yesterday. I think you should dispose of your car. It will only cause you trouble."

"I agree," said my father. "How are you and how's Jacqui?"

"We're fine," I said. "Had a bad night last night but we sorted everything out. There was bad accident near Tropez. Four men in a sedan crashed while chasing a black Mercedes. We had a couple of visitors at the house but they did not stay long. We then met an uncle of J's and got him to sort everything out about the video. We'll be fine. I'll call you again."

"Good-bye," he said. "Take care." He knew that we had had trouble but had managed to survive. I could hear he was worried. He understood I was afraid the call could be traced. I did not know if the lines would be tapped. It was better to speak briefly. The full story could come out later.

Still he knew better than to do anything. We had to go through with what we started.

One of my oldest friends was a girl. She and I had grown up together. We had confided a lot in each other. Her name was Carrie. I called her. "This is a game Carrie. My name is Charles."

"Oh hi Charles, how are your parents? Are they well? I gather they have gone away."

"They are fine Carrie. Do me a favour though. My bank, you do not need to know where, could call you one day. If they do, go to the police and mention my father's name. Then take them to the bank and do as they say. I hope you never have to do this. Don't tell anyone. I love you."

"I love you too. Take care."

Carrie would not do anything to harm me. Carrie was always getting into trouble and I had always protected her. We were the same age. If she was bullied as a child, I would fight for her. If she was in love as a girl, she told me all about it and I comforted her. When she got pregnant at university, I was the one who organised her abortion. And when she got hooked on drugs, I took her away and weaned her off them. We were not lovers. We were the best of friends. I had never asked for anything, but knew she would not let me down. She needed me less these days for she had got married and she had a baby. A nice boy called Charles. Her husband ran a gallery and specialised in modern art. The Damien Hirst stuffed sheep variety rather than designer chic. Not my taste, but he was a great guy. And I hoped we would one day get together again.

The calls completed, I joined Jacqui for breakfast. She was on her second coffee. I asked for croissants and a fruit juice to accompany my much needed morning caffeine injection.

"Who did you call?" asked Jacqui.

"My parents and told them they should get rid of their car. I then called a friend I can trust and have set them up to call in our insurance if ever we need it."

"I know you won't want to tell me who your friend is, but are you sure of them?"

"Yes. But I have worked on a need to know basis. All they know is that one-day an unnamed bank may give them a call and give them some instructions. I have told them they are to follow them, but to ensure that the police accompany them. The police will listen to my friend. For a very good reason."

"What reason?" said Jacqui.

I did not want to reveal that Carrie's father was a senior MI5 officer and that she had had police protection for many years when he was engaged in undercover work in Northern Ireland. As such Carrie would always have a hot line to the police. "Good reasons. Don't worry. My friend will be OK. In addition they do not know enough to trace us or the tape."

"What will we do with the tape?"

"I will put it into the safe at United Bank in Monte Carlo. As I told you before, it is high security. We already have a safe and some papers in it that are part of my father's plan. We need those for they incriminate a lot of people in high places. I'll tell you about them later. Another copy is in Fucquet in Geneva. I will put the second tape there. I will allow you access to both safes. The only other people with full access are my father, mother and myself.

"I will tell the banks that, in the event that none of the account holders, including you, phone over a one year and one day period, then they must call my friend and give access to the safes. So anyone who does anything to all of us is sitting on a one-year time bomb. And I know these banks. They guard the safes with their lives. One false move and their reputation is in tatters and their business goes down the pan."

Jacqui nodded her approval. "Let's hit the road," she said. "It's gone nine." She stood up, drawing appreciative looks from several of the other male guests. I supposed they were the ones who had given us looks of horror when we arrived the night before. Now the hotel people were treating us royally. Yesterday they couldn't rush us out of the lobby quickly enough.

I paid and picked up our cases. I declined the offer of assistance and headed to the garage. The car was hardly gleaming. "I think I am going to take a further precaution. We will hire another car in my name. Let's leave this one in the nearest car park and send a note to the firm to pick it up."

I thought again, "No Juan is too small a place. Let's make the switch further up the coast. Nice would be a good place. We'll make it more difficult for anyone who wants to follow. We can leave the Peugeot here and catch a train to Nice."

We parked the car and walked over to the small station. A slow train was due in ten minutes. We were in luck. We should be in Nice within the hour. We could hire a car from one of the rental firms near the station. The train arrived. It was one of those typically French ones with open sections between the carriages and doors that shut at your option. We sat at the end of a carriage by the window, our luggage stowed in the rack above. A bit smarter than the average traveller but otherwise nothing unusual. We relaxed. Everything seemed to be working perfectly.

It was only when I looked up, after the train had drawn out of Antibes, that I saw them. Two swarthy, badly dressed youths with shaved heads and earrings in their noses and ears. By now my sense for danger was strong. I could not believe that they were from Jacqui's people. They definitely were not police. I suspected that they were thugs. The problem was that we were both armed. Our luggage held incriminating signs of the night before. And we could not afford to lose our wallets. I hoped that the train did not empty. We had to steer clear of trouble.

I kept an eye on them. I noticed some other people moving away from the thugs and decided to act. I whispered to Jacqui, "I am going to have to bluff them. We can't afford to be robbed and we can't afford to be in a fight. If this doesn't work, we are going to have trouble. Call out if anyone comes down the aisle behind me."

She nodded nervously. I got up and walked over to the thugs. One of them took out a flick knife. He opened it and started to run it up and down his boot. His companion put his hand in his pocket.

I stamped on the companion's foot, sat down and drew my gun. They stopped in mid-movement. I waited a moment and then said, "Don't even think of touching me, the girl or anyone else in this train. You're out of your depth. Both of you. You attack me and I will shoot in self-defence. Do as I say, and you'll get out of this alive. Don't question anything I ask, and I won't even hand you over to the police. If I do they'll be really pissed off and throw the book at you. I doubt you even realise who will be in the cells with you. But I can guarantee they won't like you. After a night with them, any prison sentence would appear light punishment."

It appeared to work. They really seemed frightened. I wondered if I had been hardened by the last few days. I sounded in charge. My voice sounded cold. I was convincing and they were scared.

"You're in the wrong place at the wrong time. We've bigger fish to fry than you and if you as much as start to screw up our operation, you're in shit; and up to your necks in it."

That seemed to do the trick. I wondered if they thought I was undercover police or a criminal. I didn't care as long as they left us alone. I turned to the one nearest the door, "Open the doors." He hesitated. I slowly raised the gun till it pointed at his crotch. "The first bullet will get you in the balls; the second will be more painful." He opened the door.

"Throw your knife on the track." He did. "Empty your pockets." Cigarettes, some money and other bits and pieces." OK pick them up. Now go through his pockets and take out anything that could look like a weapon." Another knife. Nothing else. "Throw it out," I said.

I put my hand and my gun in my pocket. The train slowed down We were getting into Nice. "You're not getting out here. The train moves on to Menton in five minutes. You are staying on board. I won't be watching you from the platform, but one of my men will. You won't see them. And you won't hear them. But get out and you'll wake up in hospital. Perhaps a couple of days later. That is as long as they don't hit you too hard."

By now they were petrified. They were just thugs. Stupid, mindless thugs. But they were not our business. We had more important things to do. We got off the train.

"Are you going to watch them?" asked Jacqui.

"No they'll keep clear of us now. We need to hire the car and get to Monte Carlo. It's getting on to eleven and I want to be there in an hour."

At that time of the year the hire companies had a quiet time. It took us about ten minutes to complete all the paperwork and soon we were heading off down to the Promenade Des Anglais. I had chosen a Mercedes Coupe, like my old one. It was more powerful though. I now appreciated the need to accelerate out of trouble as well as away from it.

The Promenade Des Anglais sweeps along the elegant seafront in Nice. The beach at Nice is fine as long as you drive there and find a place to park. Otherwise you have to negotiate a six to eight lane highway between the town and the sea front. It was sunny, quite warm now. The storms the night before had cleared the air. I kept the hood down though, for the late September had an autumnal chill.

Jacqui laid her head on my shoulder and watched lazily as the landscape unfolded. We passed the bizarre onion shape of the Negresco hotel. We circled the port area and headed out of town. The winding road clings to the cliffs and eases its way from Nice right into Monte Carlo. There was little traffic and we sped along without problem. I felt Jacqui shift and thought she had dozed off.

Then suddenly she announced, "Once we have sorted out the bank in Switzerland, can we have a couple of days together? We should think what we are going to do. We need to plan things. But I also want to know what you did in the six months since we left each other. And I will tell you what I did. We have time. We need to be in Cannes on Friday afternoon to get the first seed money. It's no use starting until the weekend. The casinos are not really busy on Thursdays. The professionals and regulars will be there on Friday, Saturday and Sunday. This area is not like Las Vegas where gambling is a twenty four hours a day seven day a week occupation."

"No problem," I replied. "I really don't need to be in Rio now till December. So we have plenty of time. Once we have laundered some of the cash, my father could start to trade financial markets and do so seriously. He had already started to dabble in the name of the companies under one or another alias to get a bit known as an independent. The last time I looked he had got lucky on betting against the Yen and the Franc against the dollar. I suspect we are now worth around three million dollars or so more than we were when we started out. He has been the right way up much more than he has lost on the downside."

The plan was quite simple. My father had set up a money management company. It would be what was known as a hedge fund type operation. He would tell the bankers that he had won new customers as we laundered the money and transferred the funds. That would allow him to raise his sights. Once we had enough money, we would create what was known as a vulture fund. And that would be when our sights really became big.

I told Jacqui, I would run her through the details later, but the hedge fund would borrow money and deal in some very specialised and very high-risk financial instruments. The vulture fund would take stakes in companies and threaten to put them in play, or actually do it. All very legal. All quite risky. But we could end up with a billion or more if we were successful. And I told her of our theory that success was much more assured if one did not fear failure.

She did not quite agree. She wanted us to make enough to get her freedom from her father. I was confident that could be done. She nuzzled me and said, "I hope so. Love you."

We drew into Monte Carlo and I went straight through to the bank. Monte Carlo is a crazy place. A cramped town of hotels, conference centres and banks. Characterless but rich. Snobbish although money bought status. Ruled by the Grimaldis.

The younger Grimaldis populated the scandal hungry tabloid press. Photogenic girls vied for coverage as they roamed through a selection of companions and husbands. At times the husbands were their own. But that was not always the case. The Prince was a bachelor and circled society beauties and models, but to date had remained single. The father had married Grace Kelly and apparently remained devoted to her memory after she crashed to her death on the road from Nice we had just left.

We even found a place to park by the bank. "We should take both tapes," I said. "This shouldn't take long."

We walked in and looked around the deserted lobby. The cashiers were at their desks, but for a reason I have never understood, like cashiers the world over, seemed to work behind signs indicating that they were otherwise engaged. Perhaps they never have enough customers in banks. Perhaps they have no work but are just employed to make the bank look busy. It did not really matter as we were served quickly at one of the two counters that were open for business. The bored looking youth at the counter listened to our requirements, before quickly calling a companion to take us to the vault.

Bank vaults are fun. One day I must find a way to break into one of them and rifle through those safe deposit boxes. But for now, I had business to do and was grateful for the fact that they looked totally secure. We walked past a huge door with a large wheel and an array of levers. We were inside the vault. A grill separated us from the really important stuff. In the old days this would have been the bearer certificates and the gold bars. I wondered if today it was not there just for show. Perhaps that was where the bank stored all its stationary and paperclips. I smiled wryly at the thought.

"Monsieur De Roche. Please may I see your identity?"

My passport was handed over. He officiously looked through it. There were a couple of visas for the United States and one for Hong Kong. The passport was otherwise empty. But then nobody stamps a passport in Europe any more. That meant that we could have a worn passport with hardly any stamps. It makes the forger's job that much easier.

He handed it back to me and took out a key. I nodded and did likewise. We went to the safe and opened my box. In it was a largish metal container with a lid that hinged back half way along its length. There was a combination lock.

I pulled out the container and went into one of the small curtained recesses that were on one side of the vault. I placed the container on the shelf there and opened it quickly. I checked that the curtain was drawn and nobody could see me. I put the video inside the container. It joined a series of papers that we had placed there on an earlier visit. I returned. The container was replaced. We both locked the box. The ritual completed, we rejoined Jacqui. I thanked the official and we left.

"Can you imagine anything more boring Charles? Standing in that cavernous vault all day without seeing any natural light or life outside the building. How do they do it?"

"I've no idea. Maybe they like the boredom. Perhaps they appreciate the isolation. I can't believe that a job there means that one is on the fast track to the top of the bank. Did you notice how his hair was sleeked back? He must have used a pot of gel. He had a comb in his top pocket.

I saw it. Perhaps he has a phobia. Perhaps he cannot stand the idea of having a hair out of place. He needs to comb it every few minutes. Perhaps he does that all day."

"Did your father ever do anything like that when he worked in a bank?"

"I doubt it. He was an executive. He actually came to the bank as a second job. He never had to go through the boring clerical routines that most bankers go through. That guy was just a clerk, and a pretty lowly one at that. Mind you, dad used to say that you could not often spot the difference between the clerks and the managers. He would call the managers "clerks with a company car." He really was fairly contemptuous about the bank and banking in general.

"He used to do his job in half a day and then spent the rest of the time doing exactly what he wanted. He would tell me of colleagues who would drone on to him for hours. When they called, he used to put the phone on mute, lay it on the desk and read. Occasionally he would pick it up and mumble a few words into the phone. He said that any phone call of consequence was always repeated through a meeting, so it was not worth listening to the calls.

"He also used to only read the first and last paragraph of any note. He claimed all the rest was waffle and was included to fill the day. Banks are full of under employed people. They make so much money that they can afford it.

"He spent a lot of his time learning about the markets. He studied how they moved. He reviewed the new instruments that came out. He was always interested in what happened in the treasury field. That's how we plan to get rich. Its putting to use the training he has had over the last few years."

Jacqui laughed. "Your father's a great guy really. I do like him, and also your mother. She saved me when I was in shock in Gassin. I could have flipped."

I nodded in agreement. She was right in her judgement. It was just that my father was too bored and needed to get out. So he ran the scam. And now we were here.

As we left the bank and got into our car, I looked around. Once again I thought that everything seemed suspicious, when you suspect something. I looked through the rear window at the men in the car behind. I wondered what nationality they were. They did not look French. Swarthy but not tanned. I shrugged my shoulders and did not even mention my uncomfortable thoughts to Jacqui.

We headed out of Monte Carlo and into the mountains. I watched the rear mirror but noticed neither the car that was parked behind us at the bank nor anything else that looked remotely suspicious. By now it was approaching midday and I wanted to make it in time to Fucquet's in Geneva.

The road through the mountains can be slow and often there are heavy lorries that get in the way. That day it was quiet and empty as we sped up towards the Swiss frontier and the Mont Blanc tunnel. It got cooler as we got to the higher altitudes. The air was crisper. The sky was brighter. The clouds were less menacing and soon cleared.

The windy road pulled from one side of the mountain to the other. The odd house or farm populated the fields on either side. The trees climbed at odd angles out of the hillsides. Green and brown were the prevailing colours. Somehow the brown of the trees looked cleaner than in the towns and the cities. The leaves still clung obstinately to the branches before their autumn demise. They were green and brown, turning russet in the sun. Canopies of colour that stretched far in the distance in their last exhibition before they departed. Then the gaunt nudity of the trees would menacingly replace this calming scene. And then the mountains would no longer be harbours of peace. They would be acres of gloom. At least until the snow in the winter covered this challenge and left its own individual imprints on the land.

Jacqui saw me looking at the landscape. "It's beautiful. It's so peaceful," she said. "Sometimes I think we should go into the mountains and find a little village, one with a church. And a few houses. Then we could be there together and go for walks in the hills. We would be alone. There would be no threats. Would we be bored? Or would we survive?"

"In time I suggest we would need to change" I said. "I cannot see us living in total isolation although, after the last few days, I could do with a break."

"After the last few months also," Jacqui responded. "I lived a life of hell. They watched me day and night. They even posted a guard in the grounds in front of my bedroom. They did not trust me for one minute. They thought I would try to escape. Their only mistake was to give me the freedom of the house. That allowed me at least to get hold of the tape. I wonder if they played the one I put in its place?"

"Why? You never told me about that."

"Oh, it was a cartoon video. One about cops and robbers. Goodies and baddies. Pirate. Of course! It appealed to my sense of humour."

I laughed. "That's appropriate."

I looked again in my mirror and told her of my suspicion at the bank. She looked around and stared out of the back window.

"I doubt we are being followed. They would not want to try anything now as they know that we are getting in touch. There is always a danger that some of my father's enemies try to get hold of me. But I doubt it. Usually they leave the women alone. It's a sort of code of conduct. You know how the Mafia believe in the purity of women, although if they thought of it, my sex has provided a fair number of the most evil people in the world."

I slowed down, leant over and kissed her. "And the most gorgeous."

We were now approaching the tunnel. I disliked tunnels. I find them claustrophobic. The Mont Blanc may be a masterpiece of engineering but that does not make me feel less uneasy. We drove into the eerie artificial light. We noticed the noise of the tyres change as we drove into its depth. I heard a screech behind me as a white Ferrari pulled out and started to pull alongside me.

Another car behind him reacted immediately and I stamped my foot down on the accelerator in panic. However hard I tried, I saw it was impossible to pull away from him. He drew alongside me and then pulled ahead. I thought they were going to try to fence me in. A hand reached out of the window in the car behind. A gun? No, a blue light was placed on the car roof and a siren that started to roar through the tunnel. It was a police car. I could see a second police car a bit further behind.

The car ahead pulled away. I must have slowed down instinctively. It was speeding. It was fast. The police car overtook me. The second police car overtook me. They gave chase to the fleeing Ferrari. Lights flashing, sirens roaring, tyres screeching, throwing shadows across the walls and the roof of the tunnel. I breathed a sigh of relief. "I thought they were after us."

Jacqui held her hand to her chest. "This is getting too nerve racking" she said. "That mountain village is looking ever more inviting. Even though I hate the national dishes in Switzerland, I'd even eat roesti and apfelstrudel every day."

I laughed. "You'd lose your figure in a month."

"Better than my mind."

We relaxed now. We were heading out of the tunnel. There was no sign of the cars. We turned to Chamonix and then headed down from the slopes of Mont Blanc towards Lake Geneva.

Glistening in the valley, the lake with its fountain had always fascinated me. On the one hand there was the manicured surroundings, especially in the gardens near the old League of Nations. In other parts it had a natural beauty, not wild but gentle and feminine. It contrasted with the solid buildings on its quays. It was mocked by the ugliness of the buildings, more modern, generally in the financial centre on the far shore. And after ten at night, it revelled in it loneliness as the vast majority of its law abiding citizens fled the streets and made the place feel like a ghost town.

I parked the car near one of the quays and we crossed the bridge to the financial area. Fucquet was close by. It occupied an island site. And, if you did not know the bank, it would have been difficult to identify where the door was located. It was one of those discrete Swiss banks. It had two principles.

The first was to avoid attention from the general populace. There was no plaque above the door. No garish company logo. No sign that the door was a door and not just another smoked glass window. Its second principle was the principle of total confidentiality and anonymity. It could not prevent two customers turning up at the same time at the front door. But once inside, no customer ever saw another, One was escorted to a waiting room. One left after a check had been run on the other visitors and on the approach to the building. One was only allowed to exit if the whole area was clear.

We were in the room alone for a couple of minutes. Monsieur Pierre arrived and greeted me politely. "I believe you wish to transact some business."

"Yes there are two things I need to do. I have a package to place in the vault in my safe deposit box. And I would also like to open a US dollar call account. I would be planning to wire around a hundred million dollars to it next week. I need access to the deposit box and the account to go to the usual account holders and also to this lady. You do not need to mention her surname in public. Her name for your purposes is Mlle Jacqueline."

"That is somewhat irregular, M. De Roche," said Pierre, nervously straightening his tie and then playing with his solid gold cufflinks.

I frowned. "This is my account. Why is it irregular?"

"We are a reputable bank. We have no problem with your instructions in respect of Mlle Jacqueline. We need to have an identity document that we can copy and hold in our records. It need not be in the name you have given but it must always be used to gain access to the bank. I apologise if this upsets you but we need to know the source of the money for there are regulations covering money laundering. We need to be able to answer questions."

"My dear M. Pierre. I can assure our that the money is totally legal. It will come to you through the United Bank in Monte Carlo. It is not coming in bank notes but by wire transfer. As you know, we have substantial fund management operations. The monies are simply a new account. The client, who is a mutual client, has asked us to operate the cash account with you. For him, a hundred million is nothing. If we are successful in managing it, he promises to grow the account. And that would mean hundreds of millions. It goes without saying that we will be using your bank for some of the dealing. If though, you are concerned, I am only too happy to ask him to go to Pictet. I believe he deals with them as well."

Pierre was no fool. He was not sure if he should trust me. But a hundred million was still just credible as seed money for a fund. We would have liked to make it more but felt that would have raised too many suspicions. This was laundering through the banks – later we would use other routes for the bulk of the money. But, as we had agreed with my father, the arrival of Jacqui and the Di Maglio name, meant we could start sooner than we had hoped.

Pierre had an account for one of our phoney companies. He could not tell who my client was. He knew he could not check out with any client even if he knew their name. Quite simply his clients expected secrecy.

They expected their bankers to ignore what money they moved where. They did not want to be asked if it was right to move money from a charitable trust to a company account. And that was even when the bank knew the account belonged to a drug baron. They knew that any such question would cost them dearly. It would be regarded as evidence of indiscretion. Discretion was bought from Fucquet. In this case the price would be a sub market interest rate on the hundred million and fees for the privilege of holding the account.

It was robbery if it was not accompanied by absolute discretion.

"Perhaps you could consider the question while you complete the formalities for Mlle Jacqueline. She will give you her passport as evidence, but remember that you must always refer to her as Mlle Jacqueline."

This had not been planned but I could see that Jacqui understood why. Her passport was in her real name. The banker would recognise it.

He would have an account for the family. For he was that sort of banker. Not Mafia, but private and discreet. Not immoral, but definitely amoral. Indeed little separated him from his colleagues in the First International Bank in Caymans. Other than one key thing. That was Pierre was bright, very bright. And, as a partner in the bank, he was very rich. And he wanted to remain so to ensure that his successors became even richer when they ran the bank.

He took Jacqui's passport. He glanced at it. I could see his eyes open wide as he saw the full name. It read "Jacqueline Madonna Di Maglio, born 1985 in Manhattan, New York."

"I believe I have had the honour of meeting your father. Is he a resident of Geneva?"

Jacqui nodded and said "But I am not here as his representative. I represent others."

I thought "Bravo, Jacqui. That was a brilliant reply."

For again, one could see Pierre's mind working. The coded message had said that he would have trouble if he talked about this meeting with her father. He might or might not be behind the money. If it were another relative, they might want to keep it secret. Again a door had been closed. Pierre could not even mention the visit, for fear of incriminating himself. He might know that the Di Maglios were as crooked as they come but gone were his fears of money laundering. The Di Maglios did not get caught.

Pierre took the details he required. "I look forward to receiving the money, Monsieur De Roche. If there is any other service we can offer you please do not hesitate to ask."

Casually I replied, "As I said I hope we can trade with you. We are not looking to borrow money – our clients do not want that sort of leverage."

We were in fact looking for such a speculative investment strategy that banks would not be keen to lend to us in any event. And, even if they did, they would want all sorts of controls that we preferred to avoid. We were looking to go into a few investments on a really massive scale. We were aiming at risky investments, which were volatile. So if the asset fell, it would not be difficult to wipe out the capital – for that reason we were only planning on betting the first five hundred million rather than the whole amount.

But if the markets went our way, we could make billions. And that was the plan. Not very challenging – other than in one critical area and that was timing. We had to get the timing right. And, as markets had now benefited from a long run of good news and powerful performances, that was becoming more and more probable.

The Di Maglio name had obviously been worth using for a smiling Pierre took the bait.

"I will make arrangements for our credit committee to review the issue. I cannot see any problem as long as you can keep funds with us to cover future margin; a right of set off will suffice." In other words they wanted some cash to cover their risks if we lost on our bets.

I thought that was excellent – no better and no worse than we had expected. Once we had laundered the initial stake for the fund we would have over a hundred million dollars to use. I knew my father was monitoring the situation in Asia. He wanted to bet heavily against the Thai Baht and the Korean Won. He thought both looked shaky. His plans were very speculative but possible given the fact that we were willing to lose a chunk of our seed money. After all it had not really cost us anything! It was a high risk strategy. It was like playing double or bust. He would buy the most volatile instruments possible for his purpose. If he got it right with a hundred million and the currencies fell twenty per cent as he expected, then he could make well over half a billion on the deal. At least that was the theory.

Pierre pressed the monitor and waited for the all clear. He accompanied us to the vault and then the lobby. Smiling broadly, he shook our hands. He had obviously fallen hook, line and sinker for the story. The Di Maglio bit especially. We should use that again.

As we walked out, I murmured half to myself, "Where now? I would rather we stayed in Geneva. It's been a long day."

"Why don't we try the Bergues? I'm sure they will have room. I'm exhausted too. Will your father be here? We're going to have to meet him. But the meeting can wait till tomorrow."

THE HOTEL

We parked in front of the Bergues. The hotel is one of the older and more elegant ones in Geneva. It is on the Quai that bears its name. I thought of the night before when we had stumbled into the hotel at Juan. Bedraggled and exhausted as we had been, I could not see the Bergues allowing us in had we been in that pitiable state.

As it was we were looking smart. The evening was chilly and one could see that the nights were starting to draw in. It was late September and the summer was over. We both shivered as we pulled the bags from the car. I turned to the doorman:

"Park it please. And can someone take our cases. I'll keep the bag."

I was referring to the holdall into which I had stuffed all our clothes from the night before. We would need to get rid of those but not to the hotel laundry.

We stepped into the foyer and headed for reception. A smart looking girl smiled at us. She wore the standard uniform of the hotel. Fashionable suits in blue with ribbing round the collar and lapels.

"Do you have a reservation?"

"No, we were just driving around and decided to spend a couple of days in Geneva. Do you have a suite overlooking the lake?"

"Let me check. Have you stayed here before?"

"No," I replied. "I am afraid my company usually use the President. I don't though want to use the standard corporate hotel when travelling privately."

I knew the Bergues would be choosy about its guests. I was sure my comments gave me credibility. Again I was depending on the renowned discretion of the Swiss. I was with an attractive girl. They would assume she wasn't my wife. I obviously did not want to meet colleagues. Swiss colleagues would never call to check out how one was travelling. And even if they did, it is doubtful that they would have got a clear response from anyone in a top Swiss hotel.

I sometimes wondered whether Swiss discretion is something that they are born with, or is it something they acquire. It had served us well in the bank and was going to serve us again here. I can only assume that it is inbred, like arrogance in the English aristocracy or chauvinism among the French.

"We can provide you with a suite on the fourth floor. It has a King sized bed, two bathrooms and a good-sized sitting room. It will be eight hundred francs without breakfast."

That seemed reasonable. I nodded. "Could you send our luggage up immediately? Would you like an imprint of my credit card? Do you need my passport?"

The girl nodded to both questions and passed me the forms to fill in. Once completed and with the credit card voucher signed, she relaxed. She now had her guarantee of payment and I was no longer a suppliant asking for a room. I was a welcome guest. As indeed was Jacqui.

We were whisked up to our room. The crisp white bedclothes were already turned down. The room was large and the lake was spread out in front of the windows in both the bedroom and lounge. There were sliding doors between the two, and I thought this might be a good spot to meet Jacqui's father. I had no great desire to visit him on his own territory.

The porter dropped the cases in the bedroom. Having gratefully received his tip, he absented himself quickly. Jacqui flopped down on the bed. "I want an early night," she said, "but first of all I want to freshen up, change and get something to eat."

"Let's eat here. I am sure the food is quite good. It's half five now. How about a drink at seven and then dinner at seven thirty?"

"Done," said Jacqui as she slipped her hands behind her back, unzipped her dress and stepped out of it in one movement. I am always amazed at the ease with which women handle the awkwardly placed zips in their dresses. The very act of opening them is erotic. The movement of the hands pulls their dress tight over their breasts, which appear to swell in their eagerness to escape at least one layer of confinement.

Men are much clumsier. Their trouser zips are far less elegant. They are more prone to getting stuck. But then the breast is more attractive than the male organ. It perhaps makes up for it by being more erogenous. But attractive it is not. On the beaches of St Tropez one saw evidence of this. On the naturist beaches men flapped ridiculously as they pranced around the sand playing beach tennis. Others lost themselves in the multiple folds of their extended stomachs. Girls would wonder up the beaches, averting eyes from the more exhibitionist of the other sex. I recall one, whose member had defiantly been extended quite dramatically by the surgeon, facing the world proudly, if pathetically, in all his flaccid glory.

Mind you the women were rarely any more exciting. Their naked bodies offering less tantalising a view of womanhood than their better-clad sisters in their skimpy bathing suits do. Jacqui looked splendid in a white lace panty and bra. The panties were cut high on the thighs and low on the stomach. The bra was delicate, cupping her firm full breasts with courage and delicacy.

She took off her tights, her eyes sparkling.

"I think we could be later for dinner than we think," I said as I took a step towards her. We clung together and then drew apart

I took off my jacket and felt her hands undo the buttons of my shirt. Her hands went over my chest. I stroked her back and ran my hands along the edge of her bra. I found the centre and pulled the two ends together. The clips were released and the bra fell free. I eased the straps off her shoulders.

She came again into my arms as we stood there by the window of the bedroom. The sun was gleaming red in the distance, just keeping above the horizon as if it wished to spy on our final act. I felt her nipples firm as our chests came together. I had a picture of her the day before still flashing in front of my eyes. I recalled the soapsuds and foam running down her warm wet body in the bathroom at Juan. I shivered slightly, not with cold but with anticipation.

I recalled how she had been lying the night before when I found her fast asleep in the bed. One hand thrown over the white sheets and the other caressing herself gently between her legs. It had been almost as if she was preparing herself to take me, had been thinking of the pleasure to come before being captured by sleep.

I wondered what thoughts were going through her mind. She shared them with me. "Yesterday, I was lying in bed and I could feel myself at the edge as I waited for you. I felt your hands on me just like now." She moved even closer, crushing her breasts up against me. Her nipples hardened even more.

I felt her hands undo my belt and work on the fastening of my trousers. I gently hooked my hands into her panties and eased them down, lowering myself to my knees. I pressed my face into her stomach and kissed her all over. I felt moistness. I felt softness. I felt the odour of woman. She groaned and knelt down next to me, working my trousers and pants down in one go. She remained like that as I stood up and rid myself of the rest of my clothes. By now I was aroused to a state of total desire.

She stood up and we held each other, crushed together. Each part of our bodies pressed in desire. Our pulses racing. Our hearts beating ever faster. Our every nerve was sensitive to its partner in the other body.

We moved as one onto the bed and in a single movement I felt her body and mine join fully together. Her warmth blended with mine. Tightness met my firmness. Eagerness met my longing. We floated pleasingly together. There was an explosion of pleasure as the sun dipped over the horizon. It had satisfied its curiosity and no longer played the voyeur.

We moved gently apart but remained in each other's arms as the dusk drew in and the moon rushed forward to gain sight of the final moments of our delight.

We lay there quietly, still relishing the warmth and softness of our bodies. We had pulled the soft white feather filled duvet over us. We were not so much touching each other as stroking our bodies together.

I could feel every part of Jacqui as if it were part of me. Her hair was falling over her forehead, still smelling fresh from the mountain air. Her face was full of colour, that olive skin blending happily with the sheen of moisture from my kisses and her own perspiration. Her lips glistened red as she ran her moist tongue over them and then returned them for me to do the same.

Her neck and chest showed signs of our lovemaking. The flush of excitement still visible. The mark of the more passionate kisses only now fading. I could see the rise and fall of her breasts as she still panted slightly, not through exertion but through excitement and contentment.

She spoke. "You look so much gentler when you have made love. Your eyes are softer. Your mouth relaxes. Your face becomes that of the boy I knew again. Everything about you is so different from when we are with others. This is the part of you that only belongs to me."

I moved back to her and kissed her again. "I love you so much. I don't want us to part. We will find a way to get your father on side. He will never threaten us."

"He never would have done what he said. He loves me too, but in a way I can't take. It was the same with my mother. She was certain he had her brothers killed and could not live with him. He saw that incident as part of his business life, very separate from his love. When she could not forgive him, he exiled her. So she fled from him and from me. Her fear of him in the end was greater than her love of me. It's the same with me. I will not go all the way with his wishes. He sees the world as one with no half way and therefore if I am not for him I have to be against him."

"Don't worry. We will sort it out."

"I know. I trust you. Or rather I trust us," she said and drew me towards her again. Once again I felt the warmth of her body. It was a different warmth from before. A warmth than comes from the heat of two people in bed together, lying under the light caresses of a feather filled duvet.

Our lips slipped against each other. I gently ran my tongue over her teeth. They were small, smooth and ridged, tasting vaguely of the flavour of peppermint. They were both cool and refreshing. My tongue looked further. It ran over hers. It was a soft, moist and undulating partner.

At the same time my hands were stroking the side of her breasts. She moved her body slightly apart so that I could cup my hands around her full breasts. There was not the urgency and forcefulness of our earlier love making. This time all was slow, gentle and timeless. Our stomachs met. Her flat stomach was so smooth. It seemed to enjoy meeting mine. Perhaps it found that hairless region soothing, leaving it to other parts to feel the rougher and hairier areas of firmness on my torso.

We touched. We stroked. We kissed. My head at times was buried in her breasts. Her face at times moved down my body and kissed my chest. I slowly ran my lips over her ears, blowing gently as I did. We then returned to a meeting of the lips. We felt our bodies together. We took our bodies apart. We touched all the places we had touched before. And slowly did it again and again.

After time had passed we drew together and made the final act of love. Not a wild, passionate and vibrant explosion as flesh met flesh. Rather a quiet, deep feeling, a warm and close sensation of pleasure and tenderness.

Once again we drew apart, and lay together. We held hands and watched the final rolls of darkness draw in outside our window. The day had ended. The night had really begun.

We stayed there for some time. Then got out of the bed together and went to the bathroom. The shower was a large glass cabinet in the corner of the bathroom. We walked into it, hand in hand. I turned the dials and switched on the water.

We both started as the first gush of icy water hit us. It soon turned into a pleasant warm stream. I turned the dial again, gently increasing the temperature. I got hold of the delicately scented soap. We rubbed it over our bodies as if to check that our love making had not forgotten any part.

We then moved together again and kissed once more. The water cleaned all away, and then, as we drew apart, ran satisfyingly down our fronts to complete its task.

We dressed dreamily. I looked at my watch. I laughed. "It's a quarter to nine," I said. We must have been in bed for over two hours. I thought it was less"

"I did too. But then there was no need to rush. We will be late though. Our Swiss friends are not midnight eaters."

"Oh there are bound to be some people eating late. You always find business people in these hotels. They wander down to the bar for a quick drink and end up spending hours there before they head for food."

We dressed. I put on a suit and tie. The Swiss are formal and the large hotels are especially so. We called for room service and told them to clean the clothes we wore that day, and press others we had in our cases.

"I think we'll need to do some shopping," said Jacqui. "We have to dress for the part in the casino. We won't have time in Monte Carlo, especially as we have to call on your bank in Cannes. We need evening dress. The best trick is always to pretend that the gaming is the first part of an evening and not the entire purpose."

"There are plenty of shops here for that. Maybe we should do the shopping tomorrow. I am a fairly standard size and can buy off the peg. You'd look gorgeous in most things, but I rather fancy the idea of a plunging neckline and slit skirts."

"You sound like a dirty old man. I am going to have to put you on rations if you don't calm down" said Jacqui. "You must have had more than the average man today and you can't stop talking and thinking of it. I love it though. As long as you talk and think of me. No wandering off. I am a one man girl and only like one girl men."

"What?" I said jokingly. "I'm not allowed to be promiscuous any more?"

"I don't care about the past," said Jacqui. "But I do mind about the future. You mustn't let me down."

I promised I wouldn't. I didn't want to. In any event I had always preferred being faithful, at least as long as the relationship lasted. And this was one that I wanted to last for a long time, indeed for ever.

I thought back over the past. When had I double dated? In reality quite often. But I usually had only slept with one girl at a time. I half remembered a night with two sisters some time ago, but pushed that even further to the back of my mind. That was an exception. In any case we had all had a lot to drink and been smoking pot. Pot was something that I now avoided. I hated drugs. I had seen what they had done to Carrie. And in any case neither the girls nor I were sure what we had or had not done the next day.

In fact, the drugs had nearly killed Carrie. I had found her one night. She was almost unconscious. Lying in a phone box in London's Notting Hill. Just near the subway where she had bought her latest fix. I had taken her to my flat and cleaned her up. And as she screamed abuse at me when I refused to give her another fix, I had tied her up and put her in my car. She had no choice but to go to the rehabilitation clinic. She recovered from then on. Her parents helped, so did I and other friends. To the best of my knowledge she had not touched drugs since.

Those thoughts flashed through my mind. I came back to reality and smiled at Jacqui as she brushed her hair and put the final dab of lipstick onto her perfect mouth.

Hand in hand, we walked down to the dining room of the Bergues. Many people were already on their coffee, but others had only just started their meal.

The *Maitre D.* rushed up and welcomed us with the sincere insincerity that comes from a lifetime in service. He was keen to offer us a table in full view of all. I declined and took a more discrete one near some diners who looked as if they may leave. I was keen to plan out the next day with Jacqui and did not want to have to worry about prying ears.

Hotel dining rooms are bizarre places at the best of time. Luxury ones like that of the Bergues are more bizarre than most. Bedecked with chandeliers, its thick carpeted floor laps up against ornately decorated walls. It has the vulgarity that comes from sparing no expense. The décor matches in a formal way but not with feeling. It looks as if the whole room was put together after selecting the most expensive of fittings. It was not done to suit a mood. The idea was comfort, quietness and lack of discord. In fact it was like a smart whore, masquerading in refinement as she profited from the vulgarity of her metier.

Our fellow diners were a mixed bunch. Many of the tables were filled with businessmen. They would almost all be bankers. I suspected they were mainly private bankers. Perhaps they were with clients.

I said to Jacqui "Let's try to guess who the different people are at the other tables. I'll start."

I nodded to a table near the door. "I am sure that he is an Italian industrialist. The man with him is definitely a private banker. I suspect he comes to Switzerland each month and brings with him a case filled with notes to deposit on his account. He definitely does not want to be recognised here. He has his back to most of the room. He can leave without anyone noticing him. And that pillar hides him from view when anyone enters."

"Not bad," she said and indicated a table close to us. "I think the man is rich. He's about sixty and he's fat and unattractive. As the woman with him is not even thirty, that means she must be a friend or relative. The body language tells me she is not a relative. They are not at ease with each other. The conversation keeps on stopping and they just stare ahead. I find it strange that she is wearing a fur coat. Normally one would leave it at the lobby. That's safe here especially as fox is not that expensive nowadays.

"I think she doesn't want to show what she's wearing underneath. I don't think she has a dress on. I think she just has undies and tights. She's trying to seduce him. I don't think she's professional. She does not play the part well enough. And she is too old to have just started if she were. They normally would start around sixteen or eighteen and so by now she would be an old hand. That means she would put him more at ease.

"I think they'll leave once he's got turned on. I don't think he finds that easy. I think he picked her up somewhere and suggested the meeting. As the coat's new I think he sent it to her flat and asked that she did not wear anything under it. That's the way he gets his kicks."

"Brilliant," I said. "That's a great imagination. Hold on. Here comes the waiter. We better order."

We both ordered a mixed green salad to start. I asked for veal and roesti, much to Jacqui's disgust as she muttered, "That's cholesterol filled Swiss junk food." She took a grilled sole with new potatoes and mange tout. I ordered a Chablis; they had some good years in the wine list and actually had not gone overboard on the price.

While we waited for our meal, I said, "Let's carry on with the game." In reality we did not want to discuss our plans until our neighbours had left. I thought it quite likely that that would be in the not too distant future. They realised we were talking about the other guests and seemed nervous lest we turn to them. It was strange for they could not hear what we were saying. Perhaps our smiles and laughs disturbed them. We seemed the only people enjoying ourselves that night in that cavernous room. At least the only ones who were enjoying themselves other than through the food.

Several of our fellow guests obviously enjoyed that. Beneath the lustrous pearls and flawless diamonds, sat several large ladies in voluminous costumes. And even these were challenged by their bulk as they wobbled excitedly at the approach of the sweet trolley. The men were slimmer as a group, but the double-breasted suits and triple chins were evidence of a lifetime of serious good living and little exercise.

"Don't sneer at them," remarked Jacqui. "Carry on eating roesti and you could be like them. Especially if you start hitting the chocolate cake or some of the sauces that go with those delicious ice creams."

"Today," I said, "Let me sin. Tomorrow I'll be sensible. But what about the two women over in the corner. They are both young. They look like business people. Both are in suits. Modern cut. Discrete grey. Sheer stockings. Strange though, for the blond girl's shoes are clumsy and the other girl is wearing ones with strange buckles. Hold on they can't be business people. Who heard of a business person wearing an ankle bracelet? And they both have them. Now they are an enigma."

"Perhaps," said Jacqui, "they are just two friends going out together."

"No," I said. "There is something odd about the set up. Their handbags are too big for the outfits. I mean why wear delicate suits, non matching shoes and carry large handbags."

"Mules" said Jacqui. "My God. They are mules. I don't know what they are carrying but they have some merchandise in those bags. They would have been given cash to buy clothes and get their hair done. They've both just been to the hairdresser. But they lack taste and haven't got their act together. It's a give-away."

"Why would they be here? If you were smuggling something, surely you would pass it on as you got over the border. Not in a crowded restaurant."

"They are being set up," said Jacqui. "The police need a success story. The girls will have a couple of kilos of coke each in those bags. I bet it's high quality. The police will have a tip off. They'll be caught."

The girls in question were drinking coffee. The waiter appearing with our wine distracted us. An excellent choice. It was dry with a pleasing flavour. I'm not a great wine buff and dislike the snobbery of the so-called experts. I go purely by taste. I drink vins de table often with as much relish as the expensive varieties. I love finding wines, apparently from a good year, but from an unknown chateau. Those are far better than the type that are so commonly dredged up in boardroom lunches.

Suddenly, I noticed that a tall blond women had walked over to the girls and was talking quietly with them. It was all so blatant. She had an identical bag to the blond girl diner. And then, incredibly, a companion joined her. And that one had a similar, though not totally identical, bag to the second girl at the table.

I pointed this out to Jacqui. She told me to keep our heads down. We saw the visitors leave. Jacqui commented, "They will have switched and been filmed switching. They'll be arrested as they leave the hotel. It will be discrete."

The two girls left their table and headed out of the restaurant. I then noticed a reflection of flashing lights. They did too and seemed to stop. They looked for another exit, but, before they could do anything, the police were there. Inconspicuous in their suits, without talking or drawing attention, they took hold of the girls' arms and drew them outside.

"Poor cows," said Jacqui. "They'll know nothing. The ones who picked up the drugs will tell the police where they were to make the drop but nobody will be there. The police know that although they always hope that they will trace the people behind it all."

"It could be my father," she said with a bitter laugh. "For him, this serves its purpose. It sends a signal to the mules to be careful. They get blasé after a time. And the police will look good in the papers. The usual stories about millions of dollars of drugs being seized. But they know this is the stuff they were supposed to get. It is a cost of doing business. But the press will see it as a crippling blow to the drugs trade. I expect that also helps the pushers; they can up the price on the street for a while. Addicts are easy to panic and the thing they fear most is short supply."

I nodded and told her about Carrie. I missed out bits. I did not say her father was MI5. I kept out her role with the bank.

"Was she a girlfriend?" she asked, trying to disguise her interest.

"No," I said. "More like a sister. We never really kissed except on the cheek."

"I'd like to meet her."

"We will one day. Her husband's nice. A bit too arty for me. But he's good fun. And he is great for Carrie. Adores the baby. As does Carrie. That's one of the reasons why I doubt she will ever go back to drugs again."

I started as a dreamy look came over Jacqui's eyes. I had known this before with other girls. And I knew also that we had things to do that needed us to be alert and in top form. I quickly changed the subject.

"We need to discuss what we are going to do tomorrow. We have to do two things. First we need to stock up. I think we should do that in the morning. The second is that we need to meet your father. I suggest that we do that tomorrow afternoon. The question is how to make the arrangements."

"Have you your mobile. Will it work here?"

"Yes. It will work. But why?"

"I'll phone my father. I'll lay down the conditions for a meeting. It needs to be here and we need to arrange it so that he does not bring any of his henchmen. And I have to make sure that he doesn't try to grab me. We also don't want him to know that we are here now. Otherwise we could have trouble."

"I agree. Make the call today. Tell him that we'll meet tomorrow at 1.30 p.m. Say he will get a call during the morning but don't tell him when. That way the meeting could be in Geneva or somewhere over the border. Don't let him fish for facts. And warn him that his party is over if he double-crosses us."

At that moment, our main course came and we stopped talking. As we tackled the meal, we fell silent. It was not the uneasy silence of other couples. There was no distance in our silence. We were contemplating the next day. We had to succeed or we would lose each other. And neither of us could bear the thought.

"We need to find a way of getting your father to let go without making an enemy of him. He's too powerful for that. And in any case you love him despite all you have been through."

Jacqui nodded in agreement. "It's strange. I know he has done terrible things. I know he is ruthless. I hate the idea that he is in drugs. I wish he weren't in prostitution. I can't understand why he still is in protection rackets and embezzlement. I know why we used to be in those things. It was a matter of survival. Then it became a means to an end. The trouble is that now we could ditch all that and still be super rich. It's as if he could not bear to make the break."

"He's not that different from me and my parents then," I commented. "After all, we decided that we needed wealth and power and realised that we were not going to get it through sweating for others. We have embezzled, although from a bank rather than people. We have killed without provocation, at least one person albeit a slime of the first order. I have now killed in self-defence, but nobody is going to quibble about that. At least not from the right side of the law. Now we will embezzle again to get to our objective. The question is whether we stop at that. Or will I end up like your father?"

"No," said Jacqui. "You have morality. Not hide bound, straight-laced morality. But there are boundaries and you won't cross them. That's why we are alike. I can go against the law. That's easy. The law is not made for people like us. As long as we attack the corrupt. As long as we target big business. As long as we don't harm the weak, then it's OK. The fact is that my father profits from people's weaknesses. And he destroys them. Look at those mules. What stupid tarts! They really make me angry. They should have just stayed at home and married some nice boy. They would have been happy with 2.4 children and a detached house with a nice garden. Now they will be never any better than jail bait. When they come out they will be unemployable. They will either end up in a religious cult or walking the streets. There is little in between for them."

I tended to agree. "Let's hope so. But first of all we better forget about any scruples and get the money in the bank. Then we can decide what to do. Once we have made our fortune and got out of the reach of the law."

By then we had finished our meal. It was getting late and the restaurant had emptied quite quickly. The waiters were starting to hover by our table. All the world over, they do that. It's a polite way to say that the time has come for them to get their tip. They have weighed up the possibilities. They don't see it getting any bigger if they allow you to stay longer.

"Let's go," I said. "That is unless you want a coffee? I know you are going to keep clear of those sweets. I would have had one if you had not shamed me earlier. I'll just have to starve then and be weakened by my sugar deficiency."

"Poor boy," laughed Jacqui. "Get the bill. We have work to do."

I paid the bill and gave a generous tip. The smiles were genuine now. We had gone early and paid well. The smiles were of success rather than gratitude. But that's the best you can get in places like that.

We walked out. Jacqui was wearing a tight short black skirt, with a small slit up the back and topped by a patent leather belt that matched her shoes to perfection. Her perfectly shaped legs were covered in sheer honey coloured tights. They tapered into that pair of black shoes, simple, delicate and yet elegant. She had a plain black top, with a round neck, gently cut but tight enough to reveal her superb figure. A gold choker topped this ensemble. The contrast was superb. Her flawless face and neck surrounded by that mane of black hair blended with the outfit. A mixture of textures, varied yet co-ordinated. Fully dressed, yet as she walked through that dining room, it appeared otherwise. I could see every inch of her body through that ensemble. Others tried to undress her and imagine what she was like. Only I was aware that the perfection was a reality. She was beautiful.

We got back to the room. It was approaching eleven. I handed her the phone. She called the number. I could see she was apprehensive. She frowned slightly and licked her lips time and again.

The phone rang. It rang again. It rang a third time before it was answered. I could not hear who was on the other line, but Jacqui said, "I'll wait."

She turned to me and explained "He's having dinner with some business friends. They are going to tell him I'm there."

Someone came to the phone. "Hello Daddy," she said. "How are you?"

Again there was a comment down the phone. "Daddy, we need to talk. In case you don't know. Maria Angelica and Claudio Pasquale have both had an unfortunate accident. Their car fell off a cliff in the South of France in a storm. They were killed. Luckily though they were not drowned. They already had a few holes in them and so did not feel anything."

She laughed, "No, he doesn't want to work for you. We did not appreciate them. We don't appreciate the fact that you sent others to chase us. We did not mean them to get killed. Look you have now lost six people and your brother and his son also failed in their clumsy attempt. By the way I would retire them. They are a liability. They were so stupid and careless. It was unbelievable."

She added. "We need to meet. I have my own life to live. I am going to prove that I am a real Di Maglio. I want us to talk of my plan. I have joined up with some friends. We are going to amass a fortune. Within a year we are targeting several billion dollars. If we do that, we will consider joining forces with you at that point. But there will be conditions. And they will include legitimising our activities. Can we talk?"

Again there was comment down the phone. She replied, "We will call you tomorrow during the morning. Have your plane on stand-by. You may have to take a half hour flight."

I was pleased with that. It was unplanned but would make him think we were far from Geneva.

She continued, "We will try to get closer. We are not going to harm you. You must promise to come alone. There will be two of us. If you double cross us, you can look forward to spending the rest of your life in prison. The tapes have been copied. They are safe. Nobody will see them unless we fail to do some things on a regular basis. And, unless you can produce perfect voice and DNA prints of us, you cannot so anything to stop it. You can have the original back though. You may need it for your purposes."

Again there was a comment from the other end. "He wants to bring one other. A man called Giovanni. He is his financier. He's not a thug. But my father says that we need a legal agreement and Giovanni is good at those."

"Fine," I said. "I did not think that he would come on his own. Two on two would make him comfortable. Tell him OK but I'll carry an extra gun in that case."

She repeated this down the line. "He says you won't need it. He admires you for what you have done. He'd rather have you on his side. But he says you are a seducer and a bastard for despoiling me." That was said with a broad grin.

"He thinks you are a new one. He does not know who you are. He has you down as Charles De Roche. He is going to be surprised."

She turned back to the phone. "Sleep well. We'll speak tomorrow. Good night."

She put down the phone. "It's strange you know. When he saw you last he thought you were just any other businessman. Now he thinks you are like him in some ways. Just as we were talking over lunch."

"Let's not anticipate too much. We'll discover the truth tomorrow. Now I think we need to get some sleep. We should get to the shops first thing. Say at about half nine. Then we can call your father. I want us to call him at five to twelve. You said in the morning. We'll see him in this room. We had better draw the doors shut though. It would be a bit much sitting him on that sofa and allowing him to contemplate the bed. He still resents the fact that we are sleeping together. Don't get fooled by his bonhomie at the moment."

"Don't worry. I know the score. This has been my life for long enough." I switched on the late news. One could get the French channel from here. There was nothing about St Tropez. A bit about the storms in the Alpes Maritimes and Provence regions. Most about the road accidents they had caused. And a bit about damage to property. That did not surprise me. I thought the sea where we had dumped the car was around forty or fifty feet deep. I had been near that area in a speedboat and knew the prevailing currents went out to sea. The car was unlikely to be washed ashore. And the doors had been locked. I did not think that they would open. Even if they did it would be some time before the bodies floated up. And they would be mostly eaten away by the fish. In fact I suspected they would be skeletons sooner rather than later. The likelihood was that they would be uncovered in time, perhaps next summer, by some sub aqua enthusiast. And by then they would be forgotten, even by their friends.

I put these thoughts away and headed to the bathroom. Once again Jacqui was singing to herself. She smiled at me and I kissed the back of her neck in passing. "Come on," I said. "I think we need to get to bed. Or you'll be too tired to shop tomorrow."

"That's where you don't know me. I am never too tired to shop," she replied.

Once again she was dressed in a black nightdress. This time it was one of her own. It fell to the ground in a flow of silk, and sported a low cut bodice trimmed with lace. "And all I've got," I said, "is a pair of boxer shorts. I don't like pyjamas."

"Well at least they're not going to be hard to take off," she said.

She smiled and looked almost feline. I told her so. The smile became a grin and then a laugh. "You're the one behaving like a wolf," she said. "I am just playing the innocent in a long dress covering me down to my ankles."

"Maybe down to the ankles," I replied, "But there are other bits that appear to have greater freedom."

She stepped forward and roughly tousled my hair. "Brush your teeth and then come to me."

"I plan to," I replied. "And in more ways than one."

GENEVA

We woke around eight o'clock. Both of us felt like our old selves. We now had a purpose and that gave us renewed energy. We called room service and sat in our lounge to eat our breakfast. I thought it better to avoid the hotel lobby. There was always a possibility that Jacqui's father would keep watch and I wanted to retain the element of surprise.

I knew there was a risk that we could meet them in town. But I doubted it. We would be in the shopping area. That was not where they would look for us. They would expect us to be in the financial area. They would have reckoned that we were planning a financial coup. There was no other way to make the sort of money we had talked about, at least not in the time frame that we had discussed.

I was confident that, even if asked, Pierre at Fucquet would be silent. He would feel that he had nothing to gain by being truthful. Di Maglio was an important account but not the largest by far. Jacqui had told me that they only used Fucquet for deposit business. They would hold the odd hundred million dollars there, but no more. The really big fee banking business was done elsewhere. That had been another reason for my readiness to go there. If it had been different I would have looked for another bank. And in Geneva I would have been spoilt for choice.

We left the hotel just after nine. Jacqui had put on a scarf and was wearing my jacket with a turned up collar. She had put her hair up and was wearing sunglasses. I doubted she would be noticed as long as the lobby was crowded. It was a bright but fresh day. So her outfit was not out of the ordinary. A bit eccentric perhaps, but not unusual. I was not in disguise. I doubted Di Maglio knew who I was. There was no reason for him to associate me with Charles Ryder. So nobody would be looking for me. I thought nervously of our last meeting. He had scared me. He scared me less now. That was one of the reasons why I wanted to surprise him. I wanted to be in command, just as he had been when he caught me with Jacqui the time before.

It had all happened just three months after I left Europe. My parents wanted me to be out of the way for a good six months before they stole the money. So we concocted a story about a job in America and off I went to New York. Actually, I had rather liked New York. I got a job with one of the investment banks with my new passport. I had a couple of forged references and they swallowed them without question. The bank was Japanese and I knew they would not check me out. The job I applied for was not sufficiently senior for that. Being employed helped me build up my new identity. And I did not plan to work hard.

In any event I did not have to. One day I was invited to a party and it was there that I met Jacqui. We went out together the following day. I took her to a restaurant in Greenwich Village. The food was fun rather than brilliant, as indeed is the rule in many of the area's restaurants. She lived in mid-town Manhattan. She had a small flat in Trump Tower and I lived a dozen blocks north. My area was a bit less fashionable but very convenient for my investment bank. Like many others it had fled the cold wastes of Wall Street and luxuriated in the more select streets of this part of New York. The first day we just said good-bye with a kiss. The second it had lasted a bit longer. There was more than a sense of attraction. There was a hint of passion. On the third, after a visit to one of my favourite watering holes, an Italian restaurant just off 52nd Street, we spent the night together. From that day on, we were together every night. Until, of course, her father burst into her flat that fateful day.

He had threatened that she would be harmed if ever I returned and I needed to ensure that was not the case. He had been far from gentle with me. Once they had me alone, his men had turned on me. I was kicked in the back of the knee. As I fell down, I felt a boot in my stomach. My ribs ached. Only for another foot, this time in an even heavier boot, to pound into them with even greater force. They kicked me in the stomach and in the back. I felt my whole body ache. I wanted to yell with pain. But I was not going to give them the pleasure of knowing my true fear or of realising my true pain.

They tore off my shirt and one of them picked up a whip. I heard the rope seer through the air. The whistling sound hit my ears seconds before my mind registered the pain. Then again and again the rope lashed out at my shoulders, at my back, over my buttocks. They beat me everywhere. I felt blood flow from the cuts that it caused. Everything went black and I sank into a deep faint.

They had not finished with me yet. They threw water over me to bring me round. But it was for no other purpose than to make me suffer more. They held me between two of them and the third punched me in the stomach and the chest. He did it time and again. He enjoyed it for I could see his eyes glisten with pleasure as I coughed and vomited in pain at his blows.

Then Jacqui's father had told them to stop. He had walked over to me. He said that I now knew what it meant to hurt. If I saw Jacqui again, she would feel the same pain. If I told anyone who had beaten me, she would feel even more pain. Even if she was his daughter, he would do this to her. She had bought shame onto his house. She would be forgiven but only if she had not brought harm as well. And it was up to me to decide if she had brought harm.

That had been enough to scare me, but I still contemplated running away with her. I could not find her though. She no longer lived in her flat. She never turned up in the different places she told me she loved. She was nowhere in the museums or art galleries. She never appeared at the theatres. She was not at any concert. In any event it had taken me weeks to get well again after the attack. I told the police three masked men in Central Park had attacked me. I had said it was while jogging one evening. My description was not helpful. Three men in dark jogging suits, masked and with balaclavas. I only recalled they had called me "Spike" and we all supposed it was a case of mistaken identity.

My Japanese employers were most considerate. They gave me a month's notice when they heard I would be off work for at least two months. Their empathy with their non-Japanese employees was not exactly one of their strong points. Still they had served their purpose and I did not need them any more.

Four months after that, I had to go to the Caymans to prepare for the scam. And then I had met Jacqui again. I was less convinced than her that her father would not harm her. But then the short time I had spent in his presence hardly allowed me to give him the benefit of any doubt. It had taken me two months to get better. Nothing had been broken, but I never knew weals and bruises could hurt so much. Every time I washed, I screamed with pain. Each time I bent down I winced. Now, nothing could be seen except for the last of the cuts, and then only in clear sunlight. The hospitals had been good. The treatment had been effective. But the memory lived on.

With these thoughts to the fore, I headed down to the lobby with Jacqui on my arm. She sensed that something was wrong. She turned to me, "Don't worry. My father will not hurt me. He won't hurt you. He will get used to us. And I know he now respects you. That will help. We'll get through. In the end you may even like him."

I smiled. "I wish I could feel as confident. But we will know by tonight. Let's get out of the lobby as quickly as possible. Keep an eye open for any of your father's people."

Jacqui saw none and so we jumped into a cab and headed to the shops. Luckily Jacqui knew Geneva and we headed to the right boutiques. "Me first," she said. "That will be more work than for you."

The first boutique was staffed by the sort of girls that you only find in a boutique. The first reaction is to ask why they are working at all. The second is to question if their outfits cost more than their likely salaries. The next is to realise that they do it all for a hobby. They are in love with designer labels. Being surrounded by them is the only way that they can survive. They are, almost by definition, beautiful. Often they are failed models. Thus they can show off those near perfect figures with impunity. The excesses of haute couture are safe on their bodies as they flit around their temples in a state of near ecstasy.

There were two girls there. The younger served us and she fitted the role well. She was tall for a model. Her figure was that bit too full. The rounded face gave a hint of plumpness to come. But now, at twenty-two or three, it made her appear sensuous rather than solid. She listened carefully to Jacqui's instructions.

"I need a couple of evening dresses. I like them in black or red. They need to be figure hugging. I want them low at the front and back. They should not have capes or anything like that to go with them. I am normally a size 12. At least when the labels measure true sizes. In some I could be a ten."

"We have a wonderful number from Feraud and another from Versace."

"Can I try them on please?"

The dresses were brought out. They were carried as if they were offerings to the Gods. I was given a chair. I had been delegated to a bit part in this ritual. They expected me to pay. I was the bearer of the credit card, hardly a major role. Jacqui disappeared into one of the little rooms at the back of the boutique.

I heard the rustle of material as she undressed and tried on the first of the dresses. She came out for me to view. She had tried on the Louis Feraud. I thought that was rather apt. After all it had been one of the reserve names we had established for the scam. The Feraud she was wearing then was one my mother could never have aspired to. It was a tight fitting black sheath of silk. The neckline plunged between her breasts so that the bodice seemed to push further up and out than usual. The sheath effect continued down to floor level until mid calf when it flared out. That not only gave it balance but helped direct one's attention to the hips that were swaying gently as she undulated towards me.

"My God," I said. "That's not so much a dress as a seduction kit. That will distract me, let alone any one else in the vicinity."

"It feels good too," she said. "I need to get some smaller undies though. You can see the panty line through the material. That looks terribly naff, a bit tarty in fact. I can get the right sort of stuff at the shop round the corner. They apparently have a full range of La Perla."

She lowered her voice and whispered to me, "They are the hottest thing imaginable in what the assistant has just called my personal accessories."

"You mean panties and bras."

"Yes, it's a rather sweet expression isn't it."

"You may call it sweet. Sounds prissy to me. Still I am only too happy to treat you to some. I'll help you with the fitting."

"You have become a dirty old man. And you're so young. I am going to have to train you. By the time you're forty you'll either be exhausted or impossible. I don't know which."

She turned to the assistant. "I'll definitely take this. I won't try on the Versace. It looked too fussy. Have you got one more in this style?"

"We have a Dior which should fit you perfectly. It is much more expensive than the others are. But it is superb. It is really the softest, most beautiful material. A dream cut. Once one puts it on, I think it will be difficult to ever take it off," burbled the assistant.

As Jacqui headed for the changing room, I glanced out of the window. I immediately recognised him. It was her uncle. It was the uncle whom we had seen in the garage. I didn't think he had seen me. But I could take no chances. I ducked down, my hand inside my jacket to check that I was carrying my gun. I knew I was for I could feel it in my waistband. I checked though nevertheless. Luckily the shop was empty as I crawled to the back. I got up behind a beige silk curtain close to the changing room that Jacqui had headed for.

The door opened and the uncle walked in. An assistant came through the far door and greeted him. She obviously recognised him. "You have come for Madame's robe, Monsieur. It is ready. I will fetch it."

I groaned. It was our bad luck that he had appeared. Especially when he was only on an errand. He had come to the shop by chance. We would lose our element of surprise unless I could stop Jacqui re-appearing. I had to do something fast.

At that moment a car screeched to a halt in front of the shop. Two masked men jumped out. They stormed into the boutique. They shouted, "everybody freeze." One had an Uzi sub-machine gun. The other had a pistol.

The assistant and uncle stopped in their tracks. I could see uncle's hand moving. He raised it slowly, keeping his back turned. It moved up his chest. He must have been wearing a shoulder holster. I thought that this was all we needed. There was a risk that Jacqui would re-appear. There was a risk that she would be recognised. There was a risk that we would have a shoot out. And here I was with an illegal gun. And it looked as if I was in the middle of a gangland shootout.

As uncle's hand moved upwards, I realised that they had noticed what he was doing. It was as if they were waiting for an excuse to shoot him in self-defence. A horrible thought crossed my mind. I wondered if they were police working undercover or really another gang. I decided they must be another gang. Police undercover would not be wearing those masks. "What the fuck do I do now?" I said to myself.

At this point one of the two reappeared with the other assistant and Jacqui. She was in another dress, but I hardly gave it a look.

The man covered her with his gun. "Look what we got here. She's the Di Maglio girl. We got ourselves a jackpot. We blast the old man and can use the girl to get whatever we want. Old man Di Maglio dotes on her."

The other man looked at Jacqui. She looked contemptuously at him.

"Tell your scum to keep his hands off me," she said. "Or you'll be dead, and soon."

Uncle had stopped even looking for his gun. He obviously did not know why Jacqui was in Geneva. It was possible her father had not told him of the pending meeting. Even if he had, they had maybe expected it to be somewhere outside the City.

The man with the sub-machine gun raised it casually. "Say your prayers," he said to the uncle. "It's curtains. With love from Rastinov."

That meant nothing to me. I had no love for uncle, but they were going to shoot him in cold blood. I wasn't sure but I thought he had stopped going for his gun because he had seen Jacqui. I sensed he did not want to start a gunfight with her in the room. The machine gun was rising and was now pointed at uncle's chest. He had turned round. He looked at Jacqui. He seemed to move his lips. I did not know what he was saying. Perhaps he was praying.

The gun finger curled around the trigger. The blast of the bullet caught him in the neck and the gun went flying across the ground. The second bullet tore through the air and hit the other man in the stomach. Another gun, this time it was a pistol, clattered to the floor. Uncle dived to his left and collected the Uzi. I kicked aside the second gunman who was crawling towards his fallen gun and picked it up myself.

I turned to the uncle. "Can you get us out of this? No murder though."

He turned to the older assistant. "Call the police. Ask for Inspector Drozet. And say it was me calling." He then turned to me "I'll sort it out."

I went to the gunman I had kicked. I did not know how bad he was. But he looked pretty grim as he lay there, with his breathing rising and fading in short rasping gasps. The other looked even worse. I did not like it. I was adopting the wrong profile for the future.

The uncle eased over to me. "I don't know who you are. But you'll be OK. There will be no record of this. Thanks. You should be on our side. You're good."

I turned to Jacqui, who had remained remarkably calm during all the commotion. "Is that the Dior? It's rather nice. Less erotic than the Louis Feraud but it suits you. It has class. The other has more style but less class. You should take it. We can then head off to get that stuff from La Perla."

"I'll take your advice," said Jacqui. She turned to the younger assistant who was trembling like a leaf. The poor kid kept turning to the injured gunmen. She gaped at the bloodstained floor. She gasped as she saw the pallid faces of the wounded men, and heard the rasping of their breath. Jacqui interrupted her, "Could I have the two dresses, and I would like to try on some classic plain day dresses. In black and red again. I have all the accessories for that with me."

The sale seemed to jerk the assistant back to reality and she walked to the changing room. She came back to the shop and collected some outfits, soon disappearing again. She was back in her role as if two men bleeding to death in her shop was not unusual. It was beyond me. We were in a side street in Geneva. This sort of thing could happen in Manhattan but not in orderly, law abiding Switzerland. I almost felt I could not take any more of this topsy-turvy state of affairs. I noticed at that point that the older assistant was remarkably calm and had been making a series of phone calls.

She turned to uncle. "An ambulance from the Hopital du Croix will be here shortly. The Inspector and his brigade will come in five minutes. The firm you mentioned will come here to clean the shop. We will close. I can't have any of my customers appearing and seeing this mess."

I turned to uncle. "I will be calling Di Maglio as agreed later this morning. The meeting will take place in Geneva. I will give him a location. We must not be followed. I think you owe us a favour."

"Why did you save me?" he said. "You could have kept quiet."

"I saved Jacqui as well," I reminded him. "And you because you were willing to die to protect her from a gun fight."

He did not react. I think he was puzzled. I left it at that. All the same I turned to him and questioned him about the assistant. She was too calm. She was too collected.

He laughed, "Colette is married to one of us. She is part of the family. Like Jacqui. You saw how cool she was. All our women are like that. They are taught to be calm. It is important in situations like this. Otherwise you could be dead. The other girl is an outsider. That was why she screwed up. Jacqui though guessed what was needed. She acted as if all was normal. It will get the girl over the shock. Although I guess she'll be hit by it all later on. But we can manage that."

The ambulance turned up. The injured were removed. It all looked very efficient. The police arrived. They seemed to be real police. They treated the uncle with courtesy. I was told that I would not be needed. I was told a statement would be issued and it would name an undercover agent as having foiled a murder attempt on a Geneva based businessman. "It is normal to keep the name confidential in cases like this," added the inspector.

I found it hard to understand how the Di Maglios appeared to have even the Swiss police in their pocket. I had this nagging feeling that these were not true police. They rang false. I would have to check this out with Jacqui.

It was at that moment that Jacqui appeared. "I think I've spent enough," she said. "All I need now is some underwear and a shoe shop. Oh and we better get another case for these clothes. And you need to go to a man's shop. There is one close by that will have all you need. I've paid. Let's go."

It all seemed quite normal. But this was the crazy world I now lived in. We went shopping and got into gunfights. I acted like a trained gunman and not like an amateur who had taken lessons in the USA just a few weeks ago. I had to admit those were lessons well worth while. And, to be honest, they had been quite intensive and run by experts in warfare. They were mainly ex-CIA.

In the end, my shopping was uneventful. A couple of evening shirts and an evening suit. I also took some new ties along with a plain black bow tie. And then I got a few casual smart outfits. I had never had designer labels like that, but felt that my parents (for it was their money) would not grudge me this extravagance.

We grabbed another cab for it was approaching eleven. As we returned to the hotel, I shared my suspicions about the police with Jacqui. She shrugged her shoulders.

"You could be right. If it is in the Press tomorrow they were genuine. If not, thank my father for his planning. I knew the boutique. I've been there before. But I never knew the family association. It was just our bad luck that uncle walked in. And his good luck that you were there. The good thing is that will help the meeting with my father."

We handed our packages and parcels to the concierge and told him to send them up to our room. Meanwhile we headed to the lounge and ordered a coffee. The place was deserted. The only other guests were a couple of elderly women. From time to time they exchanged the odd whispered comments punctuated by screechy laughs. Typical of many of the elderly rich the world over, they enjoyed ruining the reputations of friends and acquaintances between sips of coffee and delicate bites of petite sculptured cakes. They were disinterested in us, having glanced over inquisitively on our entrance. They had failed to recognise us and therefore assumed that we were not worth talking about.

I picked up the mobile and pushed the redial button. It took me through to Jacqui's father, for he was the last person we had called. A gruff, sharp voice answered the phone. One word "yeah" came over in a menacing and irritable tone.

"Mr Di Maglio," I said quietly. "We met before. I don't know if you remember me."

"Why should I remember you? You haven't told me who you are," snarled back the voice.

"I saw your brother this morning. He was in a bit of a tight spot. Almost as tight as the previous time we had met, and much more unpleasant. I have also come across friends of yours recently. They had a black sedan. And then there was a couple. I don't think they were married. But now they are eternally together." I grinned to Jacqui and waited for the response.

"You're Jacqui's guy," he said. "Well at least you're better than some of the creeps she has brought home in the past. I could do with someone like you on my side. Where do we meet?"

"I think we need to get something straight first. I don't trust you. Last time we met, you were hardly convivial. I want an undertaking that you will leave us to finish the job we have in hand. That's Jacqui and me. And the job will take up to a year. Only then can we talk of working together. And even then it will be conditional. But the conditions will be set by Jacqui and not me."

He was puzzled. "Where have we met. I don't know you."

As I spoke, Jacqui's eyes widened. She looked shocked. She had not known. I had not mentioned this part of the story to her. She looked progressively more miserable and I thought she was going to start to cry. As I spoke, I took her hand and rubbed it against my cheek and the corner of my lips. "You almost killed me. You and your thugs beat me up. It took me two months to recover. The only good thing is that I then took out a couple of months to learn self-defence and self-protection. That's where I learnt to handle guns."

He was still confused. "I've beaten up loads of people. When was it?"

"You found me with Jacqui. In Trump Towers last year."

"You're that shit," he said. "Mind you, you never cried out even when we kicked the living daylights out of you. That made the boys madder. Hold on a minute though. What are you doing with Jacqui?"

"We didn't plan anything. It was chance. Perhaps it was fate. But now we are together again. And we want to remain so. You are going to have to trust me. We need your word. I hesitate to ask for your word of honour."

"Fuck you," growled Di Maglio. "But I accept. I need to see you and Jacqui. I owe you. Jacqui knows we have honour. So don't say we don't. Or everything's off."

"I'll apologise when you earn it. To date I hardly feel grateful to you. But be warned. If anything happens to either of us, someone special whom you don't control will get a fun video. And you'll have plenty of time to regret it."

"OK where do we meet?" he asked.

"At the Bergues. Ask for Mr De Roche. The name is Charles De Roche. We'll meet in a suite. But it should be you and your adviser. And make sure that there's nobody else. If you double cross me, there's no second chance."

"OK we'll be there in a quarter of an hour." With that he put down the phone.

Jacqui turned to me, "You didn't tell me that you had been beaten up. They hurt you." She was now crying. It was anger rather than anything else. I knew I had to calm her. Her anger would be directed against her father and that was not going to help us in our delicate task. Moreover the old ladies were now looking at us with interest. They sensed scandal.

I nodded to the waiter and told him to put the coffee on our bill. Taking Jacqui by the arm, I led her out to the lift and up to the suite. "He was mad. He was furious. He hurt me because he thought that would keep me from you. I told you about his threats. The beating was his way of taking extra insurance. We need him now though. And in the end, you might be able to get him on your side. I would rather have him with us than against us."

Jacqui nodded. "I know you're right. But how could he do that? Why can't he just let me go? I didn't want you to be hurt."

I blew her a kiss. "Forget it. We need to see that we get what we want in the future. Stop worrying about the past."

I thought she would be all right. We needed to be ready for her father. This was going to be a tough meeting. Above all, we needed to be sure that we had him as an accomplice. He would be useful insurance. The last thing I wanted was for us to be looking over our shoulders and wondering if he or his men were waiting for us. I thought we could manage it as long as we kept our cool.

Jacqui came out of the bathroom. She had made up and looked wonderful again. She was beautiful. Her hair, her face, her body, her clothes were all near perfect. And I loved her. I had never known love before. That mixture of thinking as one. That sense of communicating without speaking. It was the pleasure of her touch, even if it was fleeting and accidental. The wonder of our closeness as we made love.

I started at the sound and answered the phone. "Send them up," I said as I pulled myself back to the present. "It's them. Let me start. But treat him as if all was normal. We need to get it right."

I shut the large double wooden doors that separated the bedroom from the lounge area of the suite. Di Maglio was not going to look at the huge bed. He may have realised that our relationship was hardly going to revert to platonic. On the other hand it was not going to do anyone any favours to taunt him.

There was a knock on the door. It was just a single knock. I drew my gun and went to one side, signalling Jacqui to open. I was sure that there was no threat, but it still paid to be cautious. She opened the door. I recognised Di Maglio. He was medium height, slightly built and had actually a quite pleasant face. Seeing Jacqui he smiled. It seemed genuine to me. He took her gently in his arms and kissed her on her head. "I'm sorry," he said, "I shouldn't have. But I thought it was right for you."

Behind him was Giovanni. He was a small man. His dark suit fitted him quite well. His scrawny neck protruded out of a slightly large shirt collar. His features were bird like. Big thick rimmed glasses sat atop a thin hooked nose. A pointed head accentuated his baldness. And two large protruding ears framed that bizarre sight. Giovanni may have been good at his job, but he was never going to win the Mr Universe stakes. And, unless he was very rich, I doubted he had much success with the girls.

I asked Di Maglio if he wanted a drink. He declined. He looked at me, smiled and held out his hand, "Sorry. I goofed. I should have realised that any boyfriend of Jacqui's would be all right. Giovanni was annoyed. He tells me that I behaved like a fool. I agree. Girls sleep with their men friends nowadays before they marry them. Everyone has a few tries before they find the right one. In my day we had tarts and we married virgins. I should have moved with the times."

He put his arm round Jacqui. And then he smiled at me. He seemed quite likeable. But I knew I mustn't drop my guard. "Look, I've apologised to both of you. That's what Giovanni told me to do. And funnily enough, I wanted to. Not so much yesterday when he told me too. Rather today after you helped my brother. You became one of the family when you did that."

I moved as if to protest. He stopped me, saying, "I know you don't want to be part of it. There will be no force. But the offer's there. Now tell me what this is all about."

I looked him fully in the eyes as I talked. He did not blink or even seem ill at ease. "My father has got his hand on seed money that's going to make us billionaires. You need not know what we are going to do. But first of all Jacqui is going to help launder the seed money. We need to do that as soon as possible. Then we'll get down to the high finance part and make our money. We need to be incognito or the police will be on to us. We have taken steps to make sure that we cannot be recognised. We have insurance. We own some papers that we may be able to trade against if we get caught. If we don't we can use them for our own purposes and make more money. We also now have your tapes. There are two copies. Here though is the original back. That way you will always remember what is in it and how incriminating it is. You will get the copies back once we have got through this. If anything happens to us, they go to the police. And then you're history. Perhaps I should trust you. But it's going to take time."

Her father interrupted me. "You should trust me. I am on your side. Look I explained what happened."

I looked at Jacqui. "What do you think? It's your choice."

Jacqui looked at her father. She hesitated. "No, we keep the tapes. There's no harm. I believe you, Daddy. But I want to be sure that you don't change your mind. And I can't be certain. Too much has happened. I no longer know whom to trust. Other than Charles, and that's because I know what he has done for me. After all he did not need to help me. He did not need to save Uncle Aldo. He could have walked out. And I love him."

Di Maglio nodded. "Do it your way. I understand. Perhaps you are right. You should get proof. If you need anything, call me. You can always get my help if you are in trouble."

I went up to him and shook his hand. "I think I am going to trust you. It may take time. But it will be easier when I am more your equal. And then we can see if we can work together. If we do, we would make a superb team. The De Roches and the Di Maglios."

"What are you doing now?" he asked.

"We have to pack and head off to France. I need to be in Cannes tomorrow morning."

He smiled. He seemed so different from the man I knew before. I thought I was seeing the genuine man. But still I wasn't sure. "I'll book you into the Carlton, if you want."

Jacqui smiled and kissed him. "Book us together. No separate rooms. I love you."

He looked pleased. Even Giovanni was smiling although that hardly improved his features.

"It's been too short," he said. "Let's have lunch together. I need to talk to you about one or two things. I need to warn you about Rastinov."

Jacqui looked pleadingly. I nodded. "But we must leave by two for we need to drive down to Cannes. Tomorrow we have to start the scam and, as you said, Friday night is a good night."

Di Maglio said he knew a good restaurant. "We can have pasta. It is the real stuff."

The lunch was strange. Di Maglio was courteous. Giovanni turned out to be a good table companion. It was less of a lunch than a briefing. And the briefing was all about the family and their enemies. Jacqui was quiet. It was as if she knew what I had let myself in for. They needed me to know. They wanted me to be alert to the dangers. Jacqui could be vulnerable. They wanted me to protect her. And I realised, as the lunch progressed, that I was getting deep into dangerous territory. And there was nothing I could do about it. For the danger came with Jacqui.

I think they saw through my silence. They saw me look at Jacqui. They saw Jacqui look at me. She knew I had come on board. They knew they could trust me. I wasn't a member of the family. But I was now one of them.

A NIGHT IN CANNES

Our journey to Cannes was uneventful. We left later than we had planned. But, out of season, the roads in that area are quite fast. There was no disturbance.

We talked happily all the way. At times we played the radio. There was no news about the shooting. That didn't really surprise me.

We were soon on the motorway, heading towards Cannes. It was early evening as we left the motorway at Juan Les Pins. I liked coming into Cannes on the old coast road. It skirted the harbour, took us past the Martinez and onto the Carlton. I swept into the drive in front of the hotel and handed the keys to the doorman.

"We have a room booked for tonight. Our luggage is in the boot."

He took my name and we headed into the hotel. The Carlton is one of my favourites.

In summer it has a wonderful terrace overlooking the sea. Most people go there for dinner and enjoy the looks of jealousy from their poorer relations on the road outside. Even within the terrace, there is a three tier grading system. First of all, in the best seats are the hotel guests. Then one gets the great and the good from the surrounding area. And finally the carpetbaggers who have saved religiously for a holiday treat. Although not universal, they often dressed in reverse order to their grade. The hotel guests were the most casual and the poorest of the carpetbaggers the most laundered. The male variety sported their well pressed slacks, ironed socks, gleaming white shoes and starched summer shirts. The women washed and ironed their summer dresses to perfection, with the bright colours highlighting the fact that many are already past their prime; indeed a classical case of mutton dressed as lamb.

I was not a fan of dinner on the terrace. I preferred to drive up to Mougins, a small hill village above Cannes. Its collective restaurants have more Michelin stars than almost any other town. Or alternatively, I would wonder over to the port and head to one of the small bistros in the old town. The terrace, though, was a splendid place for breakfast. It served a delightful buffet. If one got up early, there was hardly anyone around. And the sea always looked calm in the morning. The occasional yacht would be setting out along the bay towards the Lerins. But the seafront was empty, and even a passing car rarely disturbed the view.

I used very few of the facilities at the hotel. I felt there though. There was a health club and Jacqui and I decided to go there. Quite simply, the pasta had been enormous at lunchtime and we could not face another meal.

I wanted to get ready for my planned bodybuilding. The entrance hall to the Carlton is large, airy and resplendent in marble. The furniture is plush. And the service is prompt. Di Maglio had booked and obviously also requested VIP treatment. I discovered we were to be his guests for the duration of our stay. The only question posed was whether we had an idea of its length. I suggested it could be through to the end of the following weekend, but offered to confirm during the course of the next week. I was assured that was no bother. I wanted to see how much money we could launder in a week. I was no expert and was surprised that Jacqui felt she could handle around the twenty million-dollar level over a weekend. That seemed a lot to me. She assured me though that she could do even more if there were high rollers about. The key was that you have to bet in line with the others at the table. Otherwise it really looked phoney. And, more importantly, she was keen to get in contact with what she called off table clients. I was to appreciate what she meant by that later.

Our room, or rooms, was superb. An enormous bed dominated a large bedroom. A dozen full-budded red roses decorated a table in one corner. A balcony looked over the sea, giving views of the yacht marina to the left and the old port to the right. A lounge led off the bedroom. The sofas and tables were nineteenth century as was a delightful bureau in one corner of the room. A giant television seemed totally out of place. It reminded me of an office I had once seen somewhere in Europe. Then beautiful Louis XV furnishings co-existed with neon lighting and a bank of screens flashing up to the minute data on world markets.

I looked into the bathroom and saw a circular bath with Jacuzzi. I thought that could be quite exciting. I felt enthused and relaxed. I thought back to earlier in the week when we were faced with the two killers in the house. Since then, I was sure that we had sorted out Jacqui's father. As time went by, I was actually quite getting to like him. I had sorted out Fucquet. My father had already brought on board United Bank. We had opened the accounts at Bankhaus Hochzeit some months ago. In fact, all was ready to roll. Tomorrow we would head for the bank vault and take out the first suitcase of cash. Once that was laundered we would proceed to the next one. Until we had done the entire hundred million. Then we still needed to organise the money we had wired all over the world. But once we had a history of receiving large sums for our account that would be easier through the classical banking routes.

The initial laundering had looked a daunting task. Jacqui was an expert at that and so I felt my fears had disappeared. After all we had easily transferred several hundred million through a myriad of banks. And we had agreed, with Fucquet of all people, to get a hundred million into legal accounts. I had to admit that was mainly on the back of her name and a cock and bull story about a fund management company.

The luggage arrived and I tipped the boy well. I always find that a carefully placed tip at the start of a stay is a good investment. Word quickly gets around and staff immediately treats one with care. Breakfast appears when ordered. Laundry is done instantly, and the room service staff jump promptly to attention. The hotel is in fact a microcosm of the corrupt state. Paying one's dues does not get one the service required; it merely entitles one to it. It is the backhander that oils the wheels.

We unpacked. Jacqui's wardrobe was now quite large. I had a modest four or five outfits, although several changes of shirt. As she handed me her clothes and I hung them up, I realised she had eight short dresses, four skirts, two evening dresses and three pairs of slacks as well as a couple of drawers full of miscellaneous other things. We had had a fair bit of luggage. She had always had one quite large case of clothes from the time we picked her things up from her aunt's house. She had since bought another. And, while I was with her father, she had popped into a shop and stocked up on make up. That had all been stored in a small case she had acquired alongside the large one we had got for her and the smaller suit carrier for my own newly acquired outfits. She looked critically at our luggage and commented that we should dump it in favour of matching luggage during the stay. I had a horrible thought that we might also need to buy an extra case or two if we passed too many shops.

I commented on this to Jacqui, "You are not a serial shopper are you?"

"No, but I hate wearing the same outfit too often. Look, I'm not in the league of the Royal Eurotrash. But I like clothes. Most of mine are off the rack. I have the right figure for a load of the labels. In any case I hate hanging around for clothes."

"I know you have the figure, but let's change and head to the gym.

Otherwise you'll pop out of those evening dresses. That could be fun, as long as we are alone. I mean," I joked "it would be rather embarrassing if that happened in public. I don't know if I could restrain myself."

"Well keep your hands to yourself," she responded. Then provocatively, she calmly unzipped her dress and stepped out of it a single movement.

"Hey that's unfair," I said. "That's harassment!"

"Take off your clothes," came the cool reply. "And get ready for the gym. They've got a mat there for press ups."

"That's hardly compensation."

"But it's all that is on offer for the moment." With that she stripped off her bra and pulled on her leotard.

"That was unfair," I protested. "You're teasing. In any event that leotard is too tight for you. And you know it. You got it on on purpose."

Wide innocent eyes looked at me. "In what way do you mean?" She grinned broadly. "Come on there's nothing a five mile run on a treadmill won't cure. You were telling me you did that regularly."

I pulled on my shorts and a T-shirt, and donned a sweatshirt over it. I followed her as we headed to the lift. Long slim legs at ease in a leotard, over which she had casually flung a shirt. I swore as she walked ahead of me, that she swayed her hips that bit more provocatively than usual. I found myself reacting again. And then in the lift, as we headed briefly to the basement gym, she snuggled up and kissed me. That gave quite a shock to one of the other guests, when we did not notice the lift stopping temporarily on the first floor. His surprised face and his embarrassed "bonjour" had Jacqui laughing quietly to herself.

"Impossible woman," I said to her as we discharged one red-faced companion at ground level. "You are going to get us a bad reputation. They'll all know we are not married. I mean, we were enjoying ourselves."

The gym was quite empty. It was getting to early evening. In a hotel like the Carlton at that time, most guests will be thinking of putting on the calories rather than removing them. Jacqui headed to the cycling machine and I headed to the treadmill.

"I'll show you that I can run five miles," I said. "But it will take me about forty minutes. I don't want to push myself. I have hardly been leading the healthiest of existences over the past week."

"Excuses. Excuses" came the reply. "I will be here in forty minutes in any case. She had increased the resistance on her bike and was now starting to puff slightly as she pedalled away.

I started running and soon was working up a sweat. Two or three kilometres later, I was finding the going much easier and increased my speed. I looked over at Jacqui. The back of her leotard was darkening with perspiration as she pedalled ever more furiously. Her neck and shoulders were glistening with moisture. She gave a gasp and stopped. "Not bad," she said "I did ten miles in that time."

"Don't push yourself too far. Or you'll fall asleep before you get back to the room. Or perhaps I will have to carry you back if you are too exhausted."

I was panting slightly as I exerted myself that bit more with the increased speed. Jacqui moved in front of the machine and I looked down at her. I blinked as sweat ran in my eyes. Suddenly I noticed the treadmill seemed to be going faster. I was finding it difficult to keep up. Glancing down, I saw she had quietly advanced the speed to over fourteen kilometres an hour. I slowed it down quickly.

"Bitch," I said with a growl. "Just wait till I have done my session. I'll spank you to complete the exercise."

"You'll have to catch me first and by the look of things, you won't be getting about too well. I think I will be able to keep you at bay. I guess preferably by moving fast or alternatively by unarmed combat."

"You can't do that."

"You better not tempt me. You don't know everything about me. I've got skills you have not even thought of."

"Really. That might be interesting. I must admit I thought I had seen quite a few of your skills."

"Don't be too sure. I could still surprise you. Finish your run. I am going to do some press ups."

With that she went over to a mat in the corner and started to do a variety of exercises. She had obviously had a personal trainer at some time. Nobody automatically works out that sequence.

I realised that the treadmill was slowing down. I had reached my goal. My T-shirt was now clinging to me. I took a drink of water. Then I wiped my forehead and eyes. Jacqui was still hard at her exercises. I decided I had enough and walked over to her. I noticed we were now except for an attendant sitting at the desk.

"There's a steam room. How about a session in it?"

"Good idea. Have you cooled off? Did the alternative therapy work? Are the hormones quietening down? Can the hands keep to themselves?"

"It'll be an effort," I responded. "But I'll try hard."

We went over to the attendant and told him we would be using the steam room. He reminded us to remove any metal. "Take out your ear rings" he said to Jacqui as he handed her a towel. "They'll hurt you if they heat up. Will you want it for half an hour? I think you will find that enough."

"I would think so," said Jacqui. "Do we have it to ourselves?"

"Oh yes" said the attendant. "We only have the one. One has to pre-book in the daytime. We had a bit of trouble when we allowed free entry. You can imagine what happened. Or perhaps you better not. We don't allow it any more."

We headed to the changing rooms and I noted to Jacqui that I was not the only one aroused by a gym and the female body.

"Careful," came the response, "Or I will be locking you out as well."

I joined her again in the steam room. The heat was intense. The air was thick with steam. I felt the welcome warmth penetrate and relax at the same time. I was sitting with the towel tied around my waist. Jacqui had tied her's toga style.

I felt a hand slide up and down my wet leg. It felt rather pleasant. Then it stopped. One finger started drawing a circle just at the top of my leg. It went round and round. Then it moved up further and further. A cupped hand caressed me gently.

At that point I turned and pulled Jacqui towards me. The toga knot undid. The towel fell to her waist. It settled loosely on her lap. I kissed a breast. It was warm and wet. A pearl of moisture glistened at the end of one of the breast and then dropped down onto the towel. Another was forming and I waited for it to follow the same route. Jacqui shifted and the towel around her waist fell apart. She left it there and took my hand. She ran it along her moist stomach and then roughly pushed it down between her thighs. She was shifting backwards and forwards. Her lips parted in a gentle moan. Was it pleasure? Or was it pain?

I turned more towards her and at the same time shook off my own towel. We were sitting in the steam, just able to make out our bodies in the humid heat. The steam surrounded Jacqui and she drew closer to me. One passionate kiss led to another. My arms seemed to glide up and down her back, round the sides to feel her breasts. My hands went round her waist and then back down to her thighs. My fingers stretched out, and I felt her again as she groaned gently.

Her hands seemed to dance over my body as I gently put my hands beneath her elbows and pulled her to her feet as I also got to mine. We kissed and felt the warmth of our bodies together. They seemed to slip against each other. I felt myself drop into a reverie and heard myself gasp, "I must, please, I must."

"Not here," she said. "Not here." Let's get upstairs. I don't know if the attendant might appear."

I don't know what he thought for we both grabbed out towels around us again and half dressed to leave the gym. Jacqui had just pulled on her leotard. She was hugging her shirt around her for she was conscious of her distended nipples protruding prominently through the light material. I had pulled on my shorts and sweatshirt. The laces of my shoes were open. I carried my other clothes and Jacqui obviously had her lacy panties in her hand. Possibly he did not notice. But he seemed to be perplexed by the speed of our exit.

In a moment, we were in the lift. We clung together pushing our bodies against one another. We hardly cared if it stopped on the way to our floor. There was no way we were going to untangle. Luckily the lift did not stop. Luckily the corridor was empty. We ran through it, holding hands and brushing our bodies against each other.

At the door, I fumbled with the electronic key. Jacqui was leaning against me and was starting to pull at the straps of her outfit. I am unsure if she was pulling it off in the corridor or in the room. But that was of no matter. I was already tearing off my shorts and sweatshirt. Jacqui was naked.

Our bodies were still glistening with the damp, hot heat of the steam room. Our senses were still inflamed by the urgency of our touches in the room and outside it. Our minds were excited by the thought that we had ridden through public areas almost naked and visibly excited. We threw ourselves at each other. This was unlike our earlier lovemaking. We were wilder. We were rougher. We were close to the peak sooner than ever before. Our groans and pants rose to a crescendo as I exploded into her and she held onto me with spasm after spasm. Our passion lasted longer than it had done before. One wave of pleasure after another. One searing feeling of ecstasy after another.

And then we felt the quietness. We felt the closeness. We felt the pain of love. We lay there silently in each other's arms. Our thoughts were joined just as some time before had been our bodies. The clock ticked by, breaking the silence. It intruded into our peace. It cruelly woke us from our reverie. It served to return us to reality. Yet we remained there. We held each other. We looked in each other's eyes. We tasted each other's lips. Nothing was going to make this end until we wanted it to do so.

I don't think either of us knew how long it was till we moved off the bed. We only half slipped out of our reverie as we went to the bathroom and sank into the Jacuzzi. The bed behind us was damp with our sweat and the moisture from the steam room. The Jacuzzi was deep and comforting as we kept our hold on to each other. I did not know how I had lasted the months without her. But I also knew that we had reached a greater intensity of love once we had met again. And that was far deeper than the love we had experienced before.

In time, we stepped out of the Jacuzzi and taking a large, soft and white towel I enveloped Jacqui. I patted her body dry. I dropped the towel and it fell to the ground as she did the same for me. We headed back to the room, clad in the towelling robes provided by hotels.

"Oysters and champagne?" I suggested to Jacqui. She nodded and said, "But make it Bollinger vintage. A really good one."

I picked up the phone and gave the order for two dozen oysters and the champagne. It would be with us in ten minutes assured room service. The spell was now broken. The outside world had truly intruded.

We put on the television and saw it was the news. There were concerns about Asia. The recent crisis was well behind us and stock markets and currencies were soaring again. I realised that the events that we had once discussed at home were quite likely happening again fast. We had then seen the stock market and currency crash in Thailand. That had had a ripple effect throughout Asia. In some cases the currencies and markets went into free fall. In Indonesia the currency fell in value by around 80%. In Korea, the economy had to be bailed out by a mixture of international aid and bank support. Malaysia suffered but set about a home grown cure. Even Taiwan and Singapore crumbled around the edges. Hong Kong clung to the status quo by the skin of its teeth and China itself defended its currency robustly. However, the commentators were still nervous. That did not stop the bargain basement hunters. Investment managers are strange animals. They talk of their long-term strategies, but their jobs depend on the next quarter's performance results. They thus run scared when markets are as volatile as those in Asia were proving to be. Irrespective of the risks, if the markets soar and they are not invested, their performance suffers. And performance is the one thing that really draws in the money from investors. So the markets were soaring. This worried me as our strategy was based on hitting the top and seeing the market fall. Moreover it was key for us to get in near the top. But also to get in when others felt the markets would rise. It was only that that would ensure we could maximise our return.

Our strategy was to bet against the flow in the market and market sentiment. I explained my concerns to Jacqui.

"The way markets are going, we may have to act faster than we thought. I'll talk to my father. He'll have already headed down to Mexico on his way to Rio. We have contingency arrangements and can run everything from the US if required. And he can get back to the US within a month if needed. He should be convalescing a bit and could need me. My stuff can be all done in the States or any other country with a good communications system for that reason. It could increase the chance of detection if we do everything too soon, but in extremes we'll have to take that risk. We can't miss the chance. The markets will now carry on up but they look as if they are going bananas on the upside as much as they did on the way down."

I shook my head in exasperation; "God, investors are stupid."

"What effect will it have on the laundering?" asked Jacqui. "I am going to find it hard to do it quicker in Europe. In Vegas it would be simple. There I can operate 24 hours a day and seven days a week. Off season here, I only really have three evenings and one day to operate on any scale."

"We are caught on that one. I daren't bring the cash into the US. We could be hit by one of those random searches. It's too risky. We are both the right ages for smuggling. And Customs there would love the thought of being behind one of those two way mirrors when they strip search someone like you."

"I think you may be exaggerating. But you're right we shouldn't take any unnecessary risks. I would not recommend a mule. It's easy with drugs, as the mules don't know how to handle them on the streets. And the big distributors always ship a cheating mule. It pays nobody to allow them to stray from their agreement. With money, people are less trustworthy. As you know, money buys you anonymity. And few are as ambitious as you or your parents. They think in the odd million rather than in billions."

"Let's think about it. I could do with a drink though."

As if on cue, there was a tap on the door and room service appeared. The table was wheeled in. It was topped by a silver plate, filled with crushed ice. On the ice nestled two dozen of the finest oysters and tranches of freshly cut lemon. An crystal Lalique ice bucket contained a bottle of vintage champagne. It was Bollinger as requested.

The waiter looked at me and asked if he could open the champagne. There was a risk that he was not going to do a good job. He was totally engrossed with Jacqui. She was sitting on the sofa. Her robe was tied around her. It was loose and gave a tantalising but occasional glimpse of her body. Her hair was tousled and damp from the shower. Without make up, she looked almost child-like in that outfit. The waiter just gazed at her. You could almost hear his mind asking whether she was wearing anything under that borrowed thick towelling robe. The answer was that she undoubtedly wasn't. But he would never know.

I looked at him, and said, "Leave it to me. Do I sign here?" And I thanked him as I directed him away from our space.

Once he had left, I picked up the plate of oysters and placed them on the coffee table in front of Jacqui. I put the long stemmed glasses next to it. I carefully pulled away the foil round the Bolly. Then I unwound the wire around the cork. Without using any cloth, I eased the cork away. It came smoothly. I did not spill a drop as I moved the foaming bottle over the glass.

"I think you've done that before," commented Jacqui.

"With anything you want from fizzy wines through to vintage champers," I responded. "Can be dangerous if one is not careful. The cheaper they are, the more vicious they can be. On that basis this was a low risk one. You do realise this is all on your father. I am assuming he won't mind."

"I doubt he'll notice," she said as she picked up the glass. "Cheers. To Love!"

"To love." I looked at the oysters, picking up a lemon slice. I gently squeezed it over the oyster. The edges curled up slightly. That was a good sign. "I think they're fresh. Let's see if they are an aphrodisiac."

"You're insatiable. Mind you, me too at the moment. So we are compatible. Must be the weather."

With that we ate the oysters and happily sipped at the Bolly. We were quite lazy and chatting idly away when the phone rang. I picked it up. Covering the mouthpiece, I whispered over to Jacqui, "It's your father." I listened carefully to what he was saying. I interrupted him. "Do you believe this line is secure? Could the switchboard be listening in? Should we be having this conversation?"

"You're right. I like people who take all necessary precautions. Get back to me when you can." And then without even a goodbye or a reference to Jacqui, he rang off.

"Strange," I said to Jacqui. "He pretty well cut me off. He wanted to know what we were looking to launder. He said he needed some quick cash and thought that would help us out."

"He'll want it for a drug deal" she said. "I have told him I won't get involved. It's all part of his plan to draw me into the business. I honestly thought he had stopped trying."

"Shouldn't we at least find out what it is about? It might not be drugs. I told you earlier that we needed to launder the cash quickly. Perhaps he could help us out."

She suddenly got angry. She stood up. Her eyes were flashing. Her cheeks went red. She placed her hands on her hips. Her nostrils flared slightly. She glared at me. "I thought you hated drugs. You told me the story of your friend. You know the girl. What was her name?"

She didn't wait for a response. Tears were welling up in her eyes. She was now upset as well as angry. "You can't believe my father at times like this. He is not going to tell you the truth. He'll spin you some cock and bull story. It'll be a property deal. It'll be the need for float in a casino. He'll tell you anything but that it is for drugs. Then when he has the cash, he'll tell you. He'll say we knew. We would be implicated. We would have put our hands in his filthy game. And he'd have won."

She calmed down a bit. "Charles, I know him. I know him all too well. He will not let go. He will not let go of me or the drug trade. He actually likes it. He is indifferent to any damage he causes. He works on the principle that if he does not ship drugs, someone else will. And he knows it makes money. He believes he has a set up that is safe. So he'll carry on. Morality is not an issue. He has none."

"Jacqui, hold on" I said. "I don't like drugs. I think there are ways in the financial markets to make much more money than with drugs. Moreover they are legal ways. Well let's say almost legal ways. The richer you get the better the advice you can buy. And the more you can distance yourself from any blame. We'll prove that to your father. Perhaps he won't come out of the drug trade voluntarily. But he will do so if he has to. The only way that will happen is for him to think he can make more money elsewhere. And one of our conditions, if we succeed, could be just that. We can tell him then that he must legitimise your business or no partnership."

She interrupted me. "You don't understand. You think he will do as you want. He'll run rings round you. You've less than a month or two in this business. You've been lucky. You think you are always going to be so. I was born into it. I have lived through it. I cried over it. I had no mother because of it. I learnt to despise my father because of it. And now he is taking you over as well. No. Please No. I can't take it." She lowered her head in her hands and sobbed uncontrollably.

I went over to her. I put my arms around her. She pushed me away. "Get away. I can't take it. You don't understand. You just don't know how much I hate it all. Charles, you're no different from them all. You are going to be corrupted. You'll be drawn into the business. Leave me. You'll be corrupted by it. I won't have it. I can't. We contaminate anyone who comes in touch with us. Go. Get away."

She was now yelling at me. She gave a wild look of despair and broke down in tears. They were harsh, pained, inconsolable tears. I walked forward again and tried to hold her. "Get away. Leave here. I'm going."

"Jacqui, if you don't want me to do a deal with your father, I won't. Don't get so upset. We can handle this without him."

"Get out," she now screamed. "No, leave me. You won't be able to hold off. You have seen his power. And you are going to want it for yourself. Get out of here. Leave me alone. Leave!"

Once again I tried to approach her. Once again she turned on me. Her eyes blazed with fury. She had no love left. Her hand raised. She hit me over the head. Her hand returned and she hit me again. In a voice that did nothing to hide its fury, she repeated, "Get out of here, you bastard. Leave."

Something in me snapped. I said coldly, "Don't tell me that again or I'll leave. And never call me a bastard. My name is Charles."

"Sod you," she yelled. "Get out of here and then I won't have to call you anything. Charles Ryder was the one I loved. Not Charles De Roche. He has become too like my father. I hate that Charles."

A fury took hold of me. "If that's how you feel," I yelled and stalked over to the cupboard. I pulled on the first clothes I saw, grabbed a jacket and, for some unknown reason, my briefcase. Without a further word or look I walked out. She was left there crying in desperation, or was it anger? I thought, as I left the room, she will never know.

I walked to the lift. I got to the lobby. I said nothing to anybody. I walked out into the road. The cool air of evening hit me. I stopped. I only then realised what had happened. It was only then that I though back to the words that had passed between us. It was only then that I thought over the things that I had done. It was only then that I questioned the decisions I had taken. I wondered if she was right. Had this been a plot by her father? Had he perhaps sought to dupe me? How could I tell? Would I see her again?

I could hardly think. My mind was a jumble of facts. I walked blindly across the road. A car braked sharply. I felt the bonnet against my side. The bumpers hit my leg. I seemed to skid across the road. My briefcase stopped my fall. I hit my head against the kerb and for a moment all went dark. I came to as people ran towards me. The car door was opening. A white faced driver approached. I sat up. I got up. I was unsteady on my feet. I walked to the pavement and over to the railings that separated the road from the beach. Voices asked me how I was. Others questioned if I should not just sit down. Someone called for a doctor.

I turned on them. "I'm OK," I said. "You shouldn't have stopped," I said to the driver. He looked perplexed. I shook off a kindly hand. I walked away. Someone followed me. They remonstrated. I started to run. I needed to get away from people. I did not need them. I couldn't cope with them. They appeared to leave me alone. I realised I had run to the start of the yacht marina. I walked into the park they have there and found a bench. I sat down and looked in despair at the dark sea. Night was in full flow. A starless night beckoned me to nowhere. The clouds hid the moon as if to increase the gloom. It was empty. Mankind had deserted me. I wanted nobody, but now I had that I wanted everybody. I thought I should call my parents. I would need to do my part of the job alone. Yet I no longer had the will. At that point I thought I was going to run away.

I stood up from my thoughts. I steadied myself as I swayed from side to side. I walked on away from the hotel. I found myself in the Rue d'Antibes. I knew I must have walked in an arc. I looked at the closed shops. I saw a few people. I stopped by a pharmacy and looked at myself in a mirror. My trousers were covered in dust and dirt from the road. My shirt was open half way down my chest. The sleeve of my jacket was torn. A bruise was fast appearing on my forehead. My wrist hurt where I held onto my battered briefcase. I walked forward and looked closer. I was dishevelled. I looked ill. My face was pale, whether from shock or despair, or perhaps both. My eyes looked haunted. My heart felt heavy. I heaved a sigh and I rested my forehead against the glass. It was cool and felt better, but only for a moment. Then I sank back into despair. I walked further on towards the port. Hardly anybody was around and those that were steered clear of me for fear that I could be drunk and violent. I realised I was by the bank. I was supposed to get there the next day, not today.

Somehow I turned. I walked back towards the Carlton. Something told me to go there. Something ordered me to return. I fell over something in front of the Hilton. I found myself sprawling again. This time I did not want to get up. I just lay there on the ground. My face was on my briefcase. Then I heard a voice ask if I was all right. I pulled my self up. It was just a passer by being charitable. A couple, perhaps middle aged, who felt sympathy or sadness at my state.

I walked on and came in front of the Carlton again. I stood and looked up the drive into the marbled hall. Something told me to go in. I strode to the entrance. The doorman took one look at my appearance and approached with concern. I brushed him aside. I looked into the lobby. I looked beyond. I saw him then in the lounge. He was with two others. They were drinking and laughing.

I stormed into the lobby. He was drinking champagne. It was sitting in a large ice bucket. He sneered at me as I came in. I walked up to him and looked him straight in the eyes.

He looked at me again. "You look terrible," he said. "You need a drink. Then we make a deal."

I glared at him. "Fuck you. There'll be no deal. I've warned you that I have enough to put you inside. Now I am going to do that. You cannot kill me in a public lobby. And I won't give you the chance. So I'll call the police now. I am going to take them to the place where we hold a copy of the tape."

He looked at me. He was shocked. He had not expected such a reaction. He expected me to be cowed. I saw he was now scared. He couldn't gauge me. I was irrational. I should be petrified by his power. And he sensed that was not the case. For the first time in his life, he thought he had been cornered. This was not what he had expected. He had guessed Jacqui and my reaction. He had been playing a game. It was a game he played well and one he thought he could not lose. After all he did see me just as a lucky amateur. To be honest, it was probable that he was not too far out in his assessment.

I glared at him. "There is one way you can get out of this. That is if you actually leave us alone. I am going to notify one person of a change in plan and I am doing it now. And I am going to do it in front of you. I am going to tell them that they should give the tape to the police if they do not hear from me in any twenty four-hour period. And if you do anything to get in the way of Jacqui or me once again, I will not make that call. And you are dead. Do you understand?"

I opened my case and took out my mobile. I dialled Carrie's number. She answered after a few rings. "It's me," I said. "I am in trouble. You know the package I gave you? If I don't call you in any twenty four hour period give it to our friends in the force."

She had of course no idea what I was talking about but she guessed something was wrong. So she played along in case anyone was listening in. I asked her to repeat the instructions. She did.

"I'll call you tomorrow again," I said. "Good-bye."

I then dialled again, this time the hotel number. Once it had answered, I apologised for a wrong number and switched off the mobile. I turned to Di Maglio. "Even if you tried to get my phone you cannot find out who I dialled. It only recalls the last number. You are now going to have to pray that I don't get separated from a phone for too long. Now go. Oh and by the way are we being bugged? You obviously know what has happened. I can't imagine you've had a cosy chat with Jacqui."

"It's under the phone," he snarled.

"Tomorrow I am getting the place swept by an expert. If you have double crossed me, I'll release the tape."

"There is another under the bed. That was a reserve. These things go wrong. They have a radius of 50 yards. That's enough."

I turned on my heels, disappeared down the lobby and through to the lifts.

LAUNDRY TIME

I walked out of the lift on our floor. I went over to our door. I hesitated. Then I knocked. There was no reply. I knocked again. There was still no reply. I called softly through the door "Jacqui. It's me. I've just seen your father. We must talk."

There was movement inside the room. The door opened. Her face was flushed. Her eyes were red. She'd been crying.

She looked at me. She saw the torn clothes. She looked at the dishevelled look. She winced as she saw the bruise on the side of my forehead. She assumed it was her father.

She sobbed "What's happened to you? Darling. Darling. Come to me. I shouldn't have spoken to you like that. He called after you left and laughed at me. He did do it on purpose. He knows people too well. He wanted to destroy you in my eyes. He knows all that happened. He's in the hotel. The room's even bugged. He knows what he did. I should have helped you understand. I was wrong to push you away. Come to me. Please."

I pushed the door closed and took her in my arms. "I know. I have seen him." And I explained to her what had happened downstairs.

We walked over to the sofa. She noticed I was limping. "What's happened to you? Who did that to you?" I explained about the accident. She went quite white. "You could have been killed."

"I doubt it. It was my stupidity. Let's forget about it. But first of all let's get rid of the bugs. Then I think I need a soak in a bath. I feel foul."

We removed the bugs. They were exactly where he had said they were. I unceremoniously stamped on them. I placed the broken pieces in a bin. I then stripped off, throwing my discarded clothes away in a similar fashion and stepped into the large round circular bath we had enjoyed so much earlier in the evening.

The bruises on my legs were going a variety of shades of purple and black. I knew where the car had hit me and was surprised how far the bruises spread. My right hand was grazed and raw. My head sported a large bump where it had hit the kerb. Generally I felt stiff and shaken. I suspected the car was going faster than I assumed when it hit me. I knew he braked sharply but I guessed I took the full force at around twenty to thirty kilometres an hour. I remembered I had sprawled over his bonnet before falling onto the ground. That had helped. I wondered if I had damaged his car. I had gone off in my daze and not talked to the driver.

"I'll call my father tomorrow and discuss matters. We should move from here. It's a pity as it's comfortable and convenient."

"No," said Jacqui. "My father can pay. That was what they told us on arrival. And we'll make him suffer. I plan to run up a bill that even he will notice."

That rather appealed to me too. "OK. Good idea. How about a night-cap?"

"No. First of all I want to see your cuts. You might need a doctor about that bump."

"I'm all right," I said. "I could do with a couple of pain killers. Otherwise it's nothing major."

"I'll get the pain killers from room service. But no booze. You better stick to a hot drink."

Soon she had me propped up in bed, feeling like an invalid. She had slipped into slacks and a shirt. She had cleaned her face. She still looked pale and a bit worried. She started to paint her toenails. She was using a deep pink shade of nail varnish. I was watching her feet. Her toes waggled provocatively as she sought to quicken the drying process. In the morning I knew she had done both feet, but I fell asleep before the first was complete.

Sleep proved to be a better cure than anything else. When I woke up, I could see daylight through the curtains. Jacqui was beside me. She was still fast asleep. Lying on her side, she faced me with one arm thrown protectively across my body. I gently moved it away and eased myself out of the bed. I winced as I stood up. My head ached. My legs were bruised, and my calves and shins appeared as a mass of purple and black. I was less sore than I expected and walking was no problem. I walked into the bathroom. The bruising of the night before had eased. The left side of my face still bore signs of the fall but it looked less frightening and was already starting to heel.

After a long shower and shave, I felt far better. I picked up the phone in the bathroom and ordered a large English breakfast for us both together with coffee. Then dressed in the white robe I had suddenly discarded the night before, I tiptoed over to the sofa and waited for it to arrive. There was no point in waking Jacqui until that happened. She slept on and did not even hear the gentle tap on the door that announced the arrival of breakfast. I took the table at the door and said I would handle it.

Having wheeled it over to the bed, I kissed her on the forehead and told her to wake up. There is something wonderful about a person as they wake up. The inquisitive, sleepy look. The slight yawn followed by a longer one. In this case, a tousled head of hair being shaken as she entered the world of today. A white pyjama top, slightly ruffled, teasing an outline of her figure. She gradually sat upright. Her nose seemed to twitch as she looked over at the table. "An English breakfast. Great. Orange juice and coffee. Get me a plate full and loads of liquid. I'm just off to brush my teeth."

And with that, she tumbled out of bed and into the bathroom. I could hear her humming and wondered how one could hum and brush teeth at the same time. Still I could find out another time.

Breakfast completed, we headed out to the bank. It was a fine day and we walked the short distance. Halfway there, we passed a shop full of designer dresses. Jacqui noticed one and wanted to try it on. There was no rush and I thought a designer bag would make us look more casual. So we went in, only to leave with a bag containing a tightly cut mini skirt in black, topped by a black and white military style jacket over a white silk top. Jacqui looked pleased.

"Shopping suits you," I commented. "Now, how much should I take. I think the banks are open tomorrow. So we could return but that would make it look a bit suspicious. Should it be two million or more?"

"Let's start with five. If I can clear it today, then we go back. We can always pretend we forgot a document or something. I don't like the idea of taking too much at one time. I would be surprised if I do five in a weekend. The big money will come later."

The vault was easily accessible and I disappeared into the privacy of a side room to take out the appropriate bundles. The money was in thousand dollar bills. Each batch of notes was fifty bills thick. That made a fifty thousand dollars a wad. And I needed to load a hundred of them into my briefcase. It took them at a squeeze.

I had brought the money in two thousand wads. I had had to put them in a small trunk when I left with them in the bank. I had explained that they were office papers, which I would sort out as I established my office. The bank had not cared. They just wanted the rental of the vault. As long as the contents did not smell, they were fairly indifferent.

I had had more trouble on the way over. The money had been in false bottoms in a set of cases. That had been a necessary risk. Luckily the departure from Latin America is not a problem. Almost as luckily, the police swoop in Paris on landing was on two unpleasant looking passengers from first class. To keep my cover, I had squeezed myself into an economy class seat for my alibi (supported by visas and date stamps in my passport) had been that I was a post graduate student in Latin American studies returning from a one year exchange visit between universities.

We got a cab back to the hotel. It felt safer than walking with a five million dollar case. From there Jacqui called the casino at Monte Carlo and put the arrangements in place. It would have been impossible to walk in with the cash and expect everything to go smoothly. We needed to have facilities to unpack the money. Jacqui was planning to play a million at a time in Monte Carlo. Afterwards we would see where the private games of the big rollers were taking place. That's where I would come in. There would be some major arrangements to make.

The plan was quite simple. We could launder a million or so in the casino. More than that was impossible. We would meet high rollers there. They would soon realise that we were laundering money. Among the high rollers would be people who needed cash. They would establish our background and we would arrange to exchange cash for a bank credit. The usual instrument would be a US cashiers cheque or a letter of credit. It could even be a bank transfer. Jacqui would do the negotiations. She was aware of how to make the arrangements although I would have to help with the details. My main role was to carry the gun and the money for the eventual drop.

I now realised why she felt she could do the laundering so quickly. I had thought that we would do it only at the casino. She saw the casino as bait. The real big-ticket stuff would be done privately. I established that there were many people who wanted cash, especially US dollars. The dollar is the most recognised currency. Just as a class of people wish to move illegal cash into legal taxable funds, there is a class of people who wish to move legal taxable funds to third parties in exchange for tax-free cash.

I had commented that these could include drug dealers and other illegals. Jacqui had said that they definitely would not include drug dealers. They all, almost universally, have businesses that generate cash. They would rather want to swap the cash and get it into the system.

I almost suspected that she knew that was not true. But she had to persuade herself that she wouldn't touch drug-related money. I did not feel those qualms. I just wanted to get the cash in the bank without having to answer masses of questions. The only thing I did not want to do was to deal with her father. And that was more because I mistrusted him than because of his business.

As the evening approached, we changed. I was still bruised but felt much better. Jacqui put on the Feraud outfit she had bought in Geneva. It was stunning. I felt jealous about leaving her alone. As she explained, I could hardly leave the cash alone and they would not let me carry a briefcase into the casino.

In any case, she also carried her gun. We had agreed that her risk of being robbed was negligible. I would drop her off at the main entrance to the casino. She would have a bag with the cash. I would have the rest in the car. I would park by the casino. There were people around and I should be safe. The greatest danger would be wherever we had a meeting with our prospective partners. And we had to play that by ear.

"The good thing about it," said Jacqui as we sped along the motorway to Monte Carlo, "is that everybody carries guns and there are always women around. So nobody wants a fight. Also this is a relationship game. All the parties want to do it again tomorrow. If you put one foot wrong, then you're finished. That is if you are not dead."

People were pouring into the casino on the Friday night. I waved goodbye to Jacqui, found a spot to park and waited for her call. She had told me that it would take a couple of hours at the least. The trouble was that I was sitting in a car with millions of dollars in cash in the back seat.

It was strange that I had felt indifferent to the dangers from the Caymans to France. I had not even packed a gun. Here I felt distinctly nervous despite the flood of people and the bright lights of the streets of Monte Carlo.

As night drew in, the crowds thinned. The casino must have been busy given the number of people who appeared to be heading that way. The restaurants and bars were also doing a lively trade even if it was hardly in season. I locked the car from the inside and waited.

I then noticed someone stopping behind the car. He looked in through the back window. I could see his outline in the rear mirror. I eased my hand inside my jacket and grasped hold of my gun. I had put it in the waistband. The jacket of my evening suit was made of too fine a material for me to put it there without it being plainly visible to all and sundry. I held my breath. The figure moved forward. I curled my finger round the trigger. There was a knock on the window. I held my breath again. I thought I must act normal. I opened the window slightly. I looked up. It was a policeman. I quickly let go of my gun. There was no way I was going to shoot one of them.

"Could I see your papers Sir?" he enquired politely.

I fished into my inside pocket and removed my false passport. He glanced at it. "Thank you. Could I see your driving licence and insurance?"

He looked at these in turn. "May I ask why you are parked here. I notice you here half an hour ago. It is unusual for someone to wait here in a dinner jacket for so long."

"I'm waiting for my girlfriend. She's in the casino and should be out soon. I arrived earlier than planned and just parked here to wait."

He looked unimpressed by my answer. Luckily at that moment my mobile rang.

"Excuse me," I said. It was Jacqui. "Hello darling. Good, you're on your way. I'll be at the entrance in a minute or two. Have you already got your coat? That's excellent. See you in a moment."

I turned to the policeman. He was looking disappointed. He saw my bruised face. "Have you been in a fight?"

"Yes," I answered. "But only with my own feet. I tripped over a kerb yesterday in Cannes and fell rather heavily."

He again did not look impressed. He was actually a good policeman. He sensed all was not well. It was just that he could not tell what it was. I would have to be careful he did not follow us. He signalled me to move on and I headed to the front of the casino. Minutes later, Jacqui floated down the stairs and got in beside me.

"That's the first million done," she said. "And I have great news. I met a man called Ali. I know him well. He is in the market for high denomination US dollar bills. And he is willing to exchange it for a wire transfer. We just need to make the arrangements. I have dealt with him before. He never deals in less than ten or twenty million. He charges a commission on large amounts. That's usually two and a half per cent. We can maybe get him down."

"What does he use the money for?" I asked.

"He's quite legitimate actually," Jacqui responded. "He buys property all over Europe. In some countries though the seller will ask for a payment under the counter. Say the property is worth ten million, then they will pay eight million through the bank and two million in cash. The seller has two advantages. The first is that he can reduce his tax bill on any gain made on the sale. Secondly he has an untraceable two million dollars on which he will never pay tax."

"I suppose the buyer pays less taxes on the transaction itself. So that makes sense. But why doesn't Ali get the cash from the bank?"

"They would not hold that sort of cash in the right notes. In any case Ali would not want to draw attention to himself. After all this is strictly illegal. Nobody is going to notice high value cheques passing over his account. He trades in everything. He deals in securities or property. And God knows what else. By the way he doesn't know I have had a bust up with my father. It's better that way. It gives us added protection."

I reflected on this as I drove down to the port. Jacqui had told me to head to one of the large modern hotels that serve as holiday venues in the summer and home to interminable conferences in the winter. There we were to meet Ali for dinner. I was amazed how easy it seemed to be.

We walked into the dining room where Ali had already booked a discreet, corner table. He was not yet there and so we crossed over to the bar. Then he came. A small man with a goatee beard that framed a sallow face. He wore an impeccable evening suit and a frilled dress shirt with a big blue floppy bow tie. When he smiled, he flashed a selection of gold teeth interspersed with tobacco stained ones. He held a cigar in his right hand. Its smoke seemed to wind its way up a yellowed finger and then into the starched cuffs of his shirt.

Jacqui introduced me as Mr Charles. There was no need for him to know my surname.

He held out his left hand, indifferent to protocol and not bothered to move his cigar from the right one. We walked silently to the table.

"We order first," he said. "The food is not too good here. This is a place for business. Good restaurants are too crowded. One can't talk in them for fear of being overheard. Then we talk business."

His English was perfect. He had the clipped accent of a public school. It contrasted with his appearance. He added, "No pork dishes. That's my only concession to religion. Not for any other reason than I hate the stuff."

Once we ordered, Jacqui asked what he was looking for. "I require up to fifty million for a series of deals. I will take part but not less than ten million. I need high denomination notes, minimum of one hundred dollars."

"What are the terms?" asked Jacqui.

"Cash on Monday and I want a fee of two and a half percent," he responded.

"What discounts are you giving for large amounts?" Jacqui asked.

"For you, and for you only, two percent for twenty million in one delivery," he replied.

"Go higher," she responded "And don't forget who I am."

"One and a half per cent over twenty five, I won't go lower."

"What if I offer all in thousand dollar bills," she countered.

That obviously attracted him. I wondered if it was just the bulk or whether he had another reason.

"I will go a quarter lower. So one and a quarter per cent for high values," he responded.

"And if I suggest the whole sum. In thousand dollar bills. New thousand dollar bills," she almost whispered.

He lent forward. "You can give me new bills? Are they forged?"

"No. The real thing. In wads of fifty. One thousand wads of fifty. Yours if you do it for a half a million fee. And it can be done on Monday in the region."

He shook his head. "No, seven hundred and twenty five thousand for the fifty."

"Split the difference. Six hundred," she said, arching her eyebrows. As he looked at her, she lent forward. His eyes travelled down the bodice of her dress and feasted on the show of flesh. She flickered her eyelids. She slowly moistened her lips with her tongue.

He shook his head. "You tease me. Because you are beautiful, I agree. We meet Monday but where?"

"How can you pay?" she asked.

"Transfer to be in an escrow account at United by lunchtime?" he suggested. We can set up the formalities on Monday morning. An escrow account allows money to be held to order pending an event that causes it to be transferred to another party.

"Will they be able to identify it by lunchtime?" I questioned.

"They always have to date," he commented.

"What about the drop?" asked Jacqui.

"At the bank. I have a safe box. We will use one of the private rooms. I put the funds in the escrow. You come to the bank. You show me the funds. I release the escrow and Mr Charles can confirm it has been done."

He turned to Jacqui. "You still have an account at United?"

She nodded. "Same branch."

He continued. "Once Mr Charles has confirmed the transfer, I return to the private room in the vault and we exchange the cash. You, Miss Jacqui, will stay in the room with my assistant until we return. If we are not back in half an hour he will take you outside and shoot you. Just the normal procedures. Mr Charles can keep the money on him all the time."

"Who will your assistant be?"

"My son," he replied.

"It's a deal," came the reply. "The money is in Cannes. We'll pick it up from there. When we come to Monte Carlo, we will be armed and followed by guards. Try anything and you'll be blasted out of the world. Your son meets us in Cannes and accompanies us to our bank there and to United."

"Sensible," he responded. "Miss Jacqui. I would never trick you. Why don't you trust me? We have dealt so often together."

"Don't give me that shit Ali. We never trust anyone. That's why we're still around." Her reply shocked me. She rarely swore.

"Where does my son meet you in Cannes?" asked Ali.

"He should call me on my mobile from the centre of the Rue D'Antibes at nine on Monday morning. I'll write down the number," I said. "That way he is not sure where the bank is and where we are going for the pick up. It's safer that way."

He nodded in agreement as I handed him the number. The rest of the meal passed without further mention of the drop. Ali told us about his past. It was definitely colourful.

He had been born in Alexandria. His father was a shopkeeper. He was one of six children. During the Second World War he worked for the British Army. He was only fourteen then but he started to run errands for the soldiers. As the war progressed he became more involved and spied for them as well. He hinted that he had run a good business procuring girls and boys for the officers. I must have looked shocked for he joked, "Some liked the girls. Some liked the boys. And there quite a few who liked both, perhaps at the same time." He laughed uproariously at this. And laughed even more when he saw my discomfort. "You only like the girls Mr Charles. Well it's a free world. But let others enjoy themselves as they prefer."

Ali said that he was well trusted and respected. When the war was over, he was given a small bounty for his services. Apparently that was the practice then. He bought a property in the Gulf and set up in business. He dealt with the oil companies and supplied them with their daily needs. This time he almost cried with laughter when he realised I thought that meant food and household goods. "No, Mr Charles I don't mean food and drink. I mean bedroom goods. Girls mainly. They would come from all over Asia and earn good money with the oilmen. It was my social duty." He laughed even more. "Better that I supplied them and made three people happy. The men who had spent weeks on the rigs. The women who earned more in a week than they could earn in a year back home. And me, who made my little fee."

He said he got to know the oilmen. As the oil price rose, he spent more of his time as a middleman between the rulers of the Gulf States and the oil companies. He had been involved in arms purchases. He had helped get licences. He had moved into the drinks trade, for smuggling illicit alcohol into the Gulf was also a big business. He was now worth several million. He had never got anywhere near the scale of a Kashoggi, but he was a millionaire. In the process he had had six wives, four of whom survived. The current youngest was just two years older than Jacqui. It was unclear if his wives died of natural causes or whether Ali had a touch of the Henry VIII about him. I suspected it could well be a combination.

Dinner completed, Jacqui suggested we head back to the casino. Ali declined. "At my age you go to bed early. Otherwise you are only good for sleep," he roared, lighting another large cigar. We said our goodbyes and reconfirmed the Monday arrangements. I agreed with Jacqui. It was time for the casino. And this time I wanted to go with her.

As we drove back, I asked what she thought of Ali. "He's been involved in some fairly foul businesses in the past. And he must be a health hazard. But he is a straight businessman. We can trust him. But we need to be careful always. These people can be ruthless and we are dealing big money."

She explained that she had laundered the entire million dollars. She had a cheque from the casino in her bag and we could put that into the bank the next day. "I suggest we take another million each and play that. You do exactly the opposite of what I do. That way we break even. I will play random numbers with fifty thousand dollars at a time. That way it is only obvious to the professionals what I am doing. You should do the same. In reality, we may lose half a million but that is one of the risks of the business. If we spread the fifty over the table the risks decrease. So never put anything on one of my numbers. Around one we will take a break and cash in. Then we can regroup and decide if we call it a day or play the last two million."

"What do I do with the rest of the money?" I asked.

"You should lock it in the car. It's a risk but one should never leave a briefcase with cash in the casino. That's a bigger risk. I'll sort it out before we go into the garage. I prefer to do it away from the security cameras."

She opened the case and said, "How many wads?"

"There are fifty thousand in a wad. Two million is therefore forty wads." She counted, and from time to time placed them under her seat. She then put the last ten or so under mine.

We both rather enjoyed the casino. We played till just after twelve in the end. Jacqui was right about the odds. As we cashed in our chips at the end of the session, my cheque came out at just over nine hundred thousand and her's at just over nine hundred and fifty.

"I know it cost us just under a hundred and fifty this time, but I had to lose some money. I just played a straight wash earlier. One can only do that for a limited time. Shall we do the last two million? There are still loads of people around."

I agreed and we were soon back with the money. Having bought our chips, we joined a table filled with Arabs. They all wore traditional clothes and were gambling heavily. They were drinking whisky. They had a group of bleached blond haired girls with them. They gazed at Jacqui and one leant over, leering down her dress to my fury and asked her something. She smiled and mouthed something to him. As she passed me she muttered, "Filthy oaf. He thinks I am for sale. Keep an eye on him."

I nodded as I headed over to the table. We started playing again. All of a sudden I decided to take a big gamble and pushed chips for a hundred thousand onto a single number. Jacqui looked over in horror and shook her head. The ball spun round and clattered from one number to another. Greedy eyes watched its progress. Hope, despair, anguish, pleading registered on one or another of the faces around the table. Then I gasped, "I've won."

I took half of the money and gambled high again. Everyone was looking at me. The same story. It seemed an eternity before the ball stopped whirling round in the opposite direction to the spinning wheel. It landed and I had won again. I continued playing high for about an hour. Sometimes I lost but I won more often than not. The Arabs were following my every move. I tired and put a smaller stake on the thirteen. I said aloud, just as the ball started spinning "This is going to be the big one." Two of the Arabs, including the one who had annoyed Jacqui, quickly pushed all their stakes to my number. And it failed, as I had sensed it would. One of them burst into fury.

"You said it would win. I placed half a million dollars on the thirteen. I lost."

"Tough," I responded, "Perhaps you shouldn't listen to a man talking to himself."

That drove him berserk. He charged at me but I slipped aside. He charged again and I caught his flailing arms. I pulled the arm back and he yelled in anguish as I brought it down on the side of the table with a thundering crack. The security men walked in and stood in front of me. Jacqui went to restrain me too. "Don't worry. That was revenge. That wasn't anger," I whispered to her. "Teach the bastard right for thinking you could be a tart like the floss he brought to the place."

There was much commotion. People were pushing and yelling all over the place. I picked up my chips, pushing a ten thousand dollar one over to the croupier. Jacqui did likewise and we cashed them in. We went over to the bar.

Jacqui looked at me seriously. "That was stupid. I know you had a run of luck but you must never ever do that again. It is too risky. Tomorrow you could lose a million. Gambling is a mug's game. The odds are stacked in favour of the banker, not the punter."

"I know," I said. "I just got the urge to do that. I've been in a casino before. I've played fruit machines, but never at the table. I hate the idea of losing and so always just watched."

"Keep it that way," she said. "And keep away from casinos. You could become a gambler. And that would be stupid."

"I suspect I am already one," I said ruefully. "This whole escapade is a gamble."

"Of course it is," said Jacqui. "But it is one where we can manage the odds. You were playing like an amateur on a whim. That sort of gambling is stupid."

"OK," I said. "I got one point three million. You got a million. With the money we changed earlier, that means we are at five million one fifty. That's one fifty more than we started out with. I guess it's time to head back to Cannes."

"Yes. And we will have to stay clear of the place tomorrow. We were too high profile today. We may even have to find a new casino next week. Still we can take a rest on Sunday and then do the deal with Ali on Monday. Then we have to think of the balance. But we are well ahead of schedule now."

The drive back to Cannes was uneventful. The hotel was quiet as we returned just before two in the morning. I decided to call my father the next day. I did not want to do it from the hotel phone in any case as the call could be traced. Moreover I knew my parents would have left the US now for Mexico, and soon would be in Rio for their operations.

THE HANDOVER

On the Monday morning, we had breakfasted by eight and were preparing ourselves for the handover. We needed to be in Monte Carlo by eleven at the latest. Jacqui would drop me outside the bank and then park the car. I wanted to spend no time in the street with fifty million dollars in a small suitcase. She would also be parked outside the bank once I had picked up the money. There also I did not want to be hanging around in the street.

I had put on a suit for this part of the deal. It was a pale grey suit with a single-breasted jacket. I again placed a gun in my waistband. As a precaution I taped another one to the inside of my right leg. I had only seen this done in films before and was surprised at how easy and comfortable it was. I took some spare ammunition and placed that in my briefcase. It had in it the five million dollars or so of cheques from the casino evening on the Friday night.

Jacqui had put on the outfit she had bought the previous Friday. The skirt was shorter and tighter than I had realised. I questioned if it did not stop her from moving fast if we had to run. "Not at all." She had replied. "If necessary I'll just pull it up around my waist. I am wearing panties and tights you know. The shoes are a bigger worry. I can hardly run in these heels and it can be painful without shoes. But we'll have to see what happens."

We got the car and drove to the bank. There Jacqui got into the driving seat and I sat next to her. It was five to nine. The roads were quite empty. There were few people around. I could see nothing that appeared suspicious. Jacqui did a check as well and agreed with me. There appeared to be nothing dangerous on the horizon.

At nine o' clock precisely the phone rang. It was Yussef, Ali's son. Jacqui gave him directions and told him that he was to get into the passenger seat in the front and to try no tricks. As a precaution, she also had come armed and now she took her gun out of her bag. She held it with the bag covering it from any curious passer by. She would frisk Yussef when he got into the car.

I stepped out of the car and headed briskly into the bank. The staff welcomed me as an old friend. I suppose that I had been to the bank quite a few times now in the past week or so. I headed down to the vault, and removed the container from my box. I counted carefully out one thousand wads of notes. Fifty million dollars in total. They fitted neatly into my case. In fact it was not that large although large enough to attract attention.

I once again went through the ritual of replacing the container in my safe deposit box. I was offered assistance to carry the case but declined. It actually was not as heavy as I had expected. I told the staff that I had come to pick up different papers that I would need this week for business purposes. I was only using the suitcase as I would be storing them at a friend's. He was lending me some space in his office.

I walked out of the bank and blinked in the morning light. It was a sunny day. There was a chill in the air. Autumn was now well established and soon we would be in the middle of a cold wet Mediterranean winter. I was glad we were planning to be away. A seaside resort in the rain, even a large one like Nice or Cannes, has no charm at all.

I again looked around the half empty streets. There was no sign of trouble. Jacqui had pulled up in front of the bank and a younger version of Ali was seated in the front seat. I walked briskly down the steps and into the back of the car. I put the suitcase on the seat beside me.

"Head out to the motorway. The sooner we are there the safer I will feel. In town it is easier to stop the car. Put on the central locking."

Jacqui obeyed and drove off. I looked at the Arab. "I'm Charles," I said. "You must be Yussef. Sit still. Make no sudden moves. Pray that nobody tries to stop us. Hope that we are not being double-crossed. My philosophy is simple. With fifty million dollars in a case next to me, I will shoot to kill if there is the slightest shred of doubt about you in my mind."

That pretty well put a stop to any social chitchat. Yussef looked straight in front. He hardly dared to shift a finger. I looked him over. I suspected he was harmless. He appeared to have the same build as his father. He had no beard but a moustache that filled his upper lip in an untidy fashion. He had longish hair, part way over his ears and collar. I then realised that he stank. Not a dirty smell, but the result of an overzealous use of strong after-shave or toilet water. It filled the car with its pungent odour. It drowned the delicate smell of Jacqui's perfume. She used one called "Mille" by Patou. They say it's the most expensive perfume in the world. It smelt amazing, of jasmine. His reminded me of over-perfumed toilet cleaner rather than a scent. But I realised I had to bear it till we were on the motorway. I was not going to take the risk of an open window.

We drew onto the motorway. It was nine thirty. We had plenty of time. Jacqui drove at a steady one hundred and twenty or forty kilometres. The roads were quiet. There were enough cars to give me comfort. These days drivers have mobiles and anyone attacking us on the motorway would find it difficult to get away. The police alerted by one or another of the passing cars would catch them at the exit tolls.

We swept past Antibes and then through Nice, passing close to the airport where I had landed not that long ago. I kept a watch on the cars behind us. Occasionally one would come close to us, but then they would either overtake or drop back. If they dropped back, I instructed Jacqui to step on it to see if they followed. None did.

We only stopped to pay the tolls but hardly needed to slow down. Jacqui had pre-prepared the change and the traffic caused no queues at the booths. We approached the Monte Carlo turn-off.

"This is the dangerous bit," I said to Jacqui. "Keep your eyes open and try to avoid stopping at traffic lights. Better slow down before you get to them. Attack is always more difficult if we are moving. Even if we are moving at a slow speed."

Jacqui was doing well. We were now approaching the centre of Monte Carlo. Even on the traditionally quiet Monday mornings, we could expect some delays. Here we could not avoid some stops. I took my gun from beneath my jacket and held it behind a newspaper that had been lying on the back seat. I was nervous. I wondered if every head of hair was not a wig. I questioned why people looked towards us as we passed. I kept a watch out for possible lookouts. I scoured the roofs.

"Up there," called Jacqui. "The man has a walkie talkie."

I followed her look to the balcony of a flat. The man was talking into something and it looked like a walkie talkie.

"I know nothing about it," shrieked Yussef in terror.

"Shut up," I snarled. "Pray. But pray in fucking silence. I don't want a load of bloody wailing." If anything, Yussef seemed more scared than ever.

I called to Jacqui. "Take the next turning but don't indicate in advance and make sure the road is not blocked or a one way."

She turned right and then left. She pulled in front of the on coming traffic at the junction, forcing cars to stop suddenly in noisy protest. She drove down the middle of the road before pulling right at another junction.

"I'll turn left and then left again. By then we should have done a semi circle and find ourselves back on the road again. If there is anything, then I hope we have missed it."

"Well done," I muttered as she turned left again. I glanced back up the road. "There's a lorry that's spilt its load back there. It could have been a trap. Someone knows we are here. Let's get to the bank and into the vault."

We stopped in front of the bank. There was restricted parking. I told Jacqui, "I don't want you alone. I can't see police or parking wardens at the moment. At best we get a ticket. At worst they tow us away. I'll see if one of the bank people will park the car. If not, hell it's only rented."

I got out, one hand on the case and the other on the gun. My jacket covered my gun hand. "Out," I snarled to Yussef. "Walk slowly in front of me." Jacqui was by my side and I heard the doors of the Mercedes lock automatically. "Move," I snarled to Yussef. It was ten thirty and we walked unhindered into the bank.

I was surprised to find Ali already there. "I thought you may be early and so I stopped by before our appointment. Let's get into the vault. It's safer than up here."

Ali had arranged a small private room for us. I placed the case on the table. I locked the door from inside for there was a key there. I turned to Yussef, "I hope you did not find the journey too unpleasant. I was nervous too. That made me rude. I apologise if I offended you. I realised I said some rude things about your religion. I shouldn't have."

Yussef seemed to smile, but he was obviously still petrified. I doubted if he could shoot or even overpower Jacqui. But I kept that thought to myself.

Ali turned to Jacqui. "Are you armed?" She nodded and picked up her handbag.

"Put your gun in my pocket," I said to Jacqui. "There's no need to give Ali a gun. That is if he hasn't one already." We already knew Yussef was not armed. I quickly looked round the room. There were no other entrances and no place to hide a person or even a gun. I opened the case.

Ali picked up several random wads of notes. He counted a few. He had an obvious stab at the number of wads and satisfied himself of the number. He took out an eyeglass of the type used by jewellers and scrutinised a random selection. He took out a pen. I saw it was a light and he used it to check the watermarks on the notes. All in all he spent some twenty minutes hard at work. Jacqui was seated on the only other chair. Yussef stood well away from me.

"It's good," said Ali. "I have set up an account here numbered 6081738. It holds already fifty million dollars from a wire transfer. The money arrived at 10 am today. The bank transfer funds within the branch in real time. I will move the funds to your account and you will see them arrive. The bank will confirm to you in writing that the funds have been moved to your account with finality and irrevocability."

I nodded. The words of finality and irrevocability were important. They meant that the money could not be returned for any reason to Ali's account. He continued, "The manager is waiting for us and will sign the letter of confirmation in our presence."

I queried, "Is one signature enough?"

"You must ask him for a copy of his power of attorney. I suggested he had one ready," he responded.

"How do I know he is the manager?" I asked.

"I assume the fact that he is in the manager's office is not enough. But Mlle Jacqui knows him of old. He is Fruget who has been manager here for four years. He will come back down with us for Jacqui to confirm his identity."

Jacqui nodded her agreement. "Let's go. Ali," I said.

He put his hand in his pocket and removed a gun. He held it by the barrel and made sure I could see his every move. He gave it to his son. "If we are not back in half an hour, kill her. It has a silencer. Then walk out and shut the door behind you. Keep away from her at all times. Or, if you do shoot her, you will be covered in blood and are unlikely to get out. Keep your cool. I think the chances of Mr Charles and I not returning are no less than nil."

I turned to him; "There is an outside chance that we could be attacked in the lobby. If you hear shooting there, keep cool and wait. You have no cash here and so you should be safe."

"Yes," said Ali. "But still kill the girl if I do not return. It may be unfortunate but it is necessary for my protection. Otherwise Mr Charles could have me killed and double-cross us."

We went up to the lobby and into the office of the manager. The lobby was empty. I told Ali to check it out first.

I checked the papers. They were in order. I looked at the screen. Ali asked for the transfer. Account number 6082738 saw its balance of fifty million dollars reduce to zero. Our account number 4179267 was credited. I said to the manager, "I want this instruction completed before we leave the office."

He looked surprised but filled in a form and asked me to sign it. I did as requested. He typed in some details and showed them to me. They were an instruction to pay fifty million dollars to our account in Fucquet. I noticed the manager was careful that Ali did not see these details. He was good at his job. He called in a colleague to authorise the instruction and then said, "I have sent off the payment instruction by SWIFT. It will be with your other bank later today and cover will be in New York this afternoon."

"One more thing," I said. "I want to pay these into my account." He took the five million odd of cheques and again filled in a form for me to sign. He called in a clerk who took everything away and soon returned with a stamped receipt.

We had left Jacqui and Yussef at five to eleven. It was now eleven fifteen. We all three left the office and headed for the lobby and the stairs to the vault. Once again I got Ali to check the lobby and see there was nobody suspicious around. He confirmed this to be the case.

Jacqui was looking a bit tense when we walked in. Mind you so was Yussef. She greeted the manager and nodded to me. I placed the case on the table and pushed it over to Ali. "You can have the case if you want," I said. "The contents include your fee as promised."

"Don't wait for me while I put it away," he said. "We will meet again no doubt." With a nod, he dismissed us.

I walked out with Jacqui, passing her her gun. We walked from the bank. Our car was untouched and we got in. I then saw the sudden movement. Four masked men jumped out of a car that drew up in front of the bank. "Down," I shouted to Jacqui as they rushed towards us. I twisted myself round to get the best view, my weapon ready. They ignored our car and stormed into the bank. "They're after Ali," I called. "Do we go in?"

"We've got to," she said "He'll have taken precautions and we need him alive and safe."

"Let me go first in case there is a trap," I called. I ran up to the bank and, just outside the door, drew my gun. I had noticed a desk by the entrance and I dived for it. I got there and waited for the gunfire. There was none. I tried to fathom the reason for the silence.

A voice called out, "We knew you fuckers were in the car and would come back. Get out from behind the desk and pass over your gun or you die after this kid."

I could now see one of the masked men holding a young girl cashier by the throat. He was armed with an Uzi sub-machine gun. That seemed standard for the type. He was alone, keeping watch on the staff and customers. There were about ten huddled together, clearly petrified. The girl was in a half faint. Her face was white. Her eyes stared petrified ahead of her and she was trembling.

"OK. I'll come quietly. Don't hurt the kid. I'll hold the gun by the barrel and then slide it across the floor to you. My friend will then do the same. She is just behind the door."

I stepped out. I then realised there were two of them. The other was in a corner, half hidden by a pillar. He was on his own but with a clear view of the captured staff and customers. I stepped slowly out, my hands apart and the gun in my left hand. I lowered it to the floor and kicked it across with the side of my foot. At that point, Jacqui came from behind the door. She carried her handbag, but no gun was in sight.

"Push your bag across the room" came the call.

Jacqui bent down, facing the two gunmen. She did it unusually awkwardly. Her skirt rode up her legs revealing her crotch. Her open jacket pulled at the fabric of her silk T-shirt showing a bra strap. I saw the two were distracted and swiftly bent down and drew the gun from my home-made leg holster. The gunman behind the pillar turned to me but he knew it was too late as my gun roared while his was still pointing at the ground. Two bullets hit him in the stomach and had him sprawling. His gun skidded from his hand to the corner of the room as I dived to that same corner to avoid the bullets of his partner.

They missed me as I slid away from the desk area, skidding across the floor and grabbing the sub-machine gun as I hit against the wall. I saw Jacqui had pulled out her gun. She had pushed it into the back of her waistband, hidden from the gunmen's view. Her bullet hit the man and made him pause. But it was not going to stop him. A burst of fire from me that sliced into his legs did and he fell to the ground screaming in agony. Jacqui picked up his gun.

"Frisk them," I called. "And keep a watch on them and the door. Get the police someone." With that I pushed my remaining gun back in my trouser band and eased downstairs. Half way down was a one way mirror that gave a view of the vault. I had noticed that on my trips down. It was a clever security device but also allowed me to see the position of the gunmen before they could see me.

The two gunmen held Ali and Yussef. Both had Uzis and both Uzis were pointing at their captives. A large safe box was open and in front of it was my case. Ali had obviously not yet put the money away when the gunmen came in. They had obviously heard the gunfire and were waiting for an all clear from their comrades. Or perhaps they expected a fight with us. I suspect, from their appearance, that they did not think the latter was likely. I also saw I could not attack them for they would automatically kill their hostages. I had to negotiate.

"We've got your friends and you've two minutes to get out. They are calling the police up there. I don't give a fuck if you go to jail or not. If you shoot one of my friends, I'll kill you both. If you try to use them as hostages, I'll do the same. I have a perfect sight of you and killing you will make me a hero. So decide quickly. Drop your guns and run. Take your friends if you want. Although they are in a bad state and I would think they'd slow you down. But you now have a minute left; at the most."

They knew they could not win. They did not want a murder charge if the police came and that was the best they could hope for if they tried to escape. They wanted to run. They knew they had failed.

"Drop your guns and I'll take you to the door of the bank. From there on you find your own way out. Choose."

They knew they would have to trust me. They had no choice. They pushed their guns away and moved towards me. The moment Ali and Yussef were behind them, I came fully into view. I was holding the Uzi and pointing it straight at them. "OK dumbos. You tried to cross the wrong guy. Who sent you?"

They looked at me sullenly. One said nervously, "We've got to get out of here."

"OK," I said "But you're under arrest. I'm making a citizen's arrest and handing you over."

I turned to Ali. "As the police will be here soon, I'd pack your box unless you want them to ask questions. And by the way I suggest you keep quiet about the fact that we know each other. Play the innocent customer caught in a hostage crisis. Otherwise we could be in trouble."

I walked up the stairs with the two gunmen, having picked up their weapons on the way. They entered the lobby just as the police stormed in. I thought for a moment that the police would shoot me. "I've arrested these two," I shouted.

They grabbed them and marched them to a van outside. I saw a medic come in to look at the two wounded on the floor. I handed the hardware to an inspector. The young girl hostage ran up to me crying and threw her arms around my neck, kissing me repeatedly.

"Hold on," I joked, "Or we'll have to get married. I'm glad you feel better."

The inspector turned to me. "I think we need to have a discussion. And I need to see your licence for that gun."

"I haven't got it with me. I have a Swiss licence. I'm pretty sure I have it at my flat here in Monte Carlo. It may though be with my stuff in Cannes. I am based there at the moment but inspector, perhaps we could talk in private in the office?"

I went there with him. "I am a businessman. I am setting up an investment company with some colleagues based here in Monte Carlo. My girlfriend is called Jacqui Di Maglio. You may know her father. He is from New York. He has a villa along the coast."

The way the Inspector reacted when I mentioned Di Maglio told me two things. The first was that he knew him. And the second was that he knew he was Mafia.

I continued, "There have been a series of threats against the Di Maglio family by some Russian criminals who have based themselves in Western Europe. I know that there has been nothing specific but hints of possible kidnappings and ransom. For obvious reasons such issues are hardly for the police."

The inspector nodded grimly. Once again I tried to read his thoughts. I suspected he thought that he would lose no sleep if there were a few Di Maglios less in the world. He seemed that sort of a policeman. Protect the innocent and zero tolerance for the guilty or suspect.

I nevertheless carried on with my monologue. "As a result, Mr Di Maglio advised me to carry a gun. A handgun that could fit into my briefcase. His daughter also carries a small pistol in her purse although I doubt it is very effective. You will see that one gunman has wounds in the stomach from my gun and the other may have a slight wound from Jacqui's. Obviously the Uzis belonged to the gunmen. There should be four as they were each carrying one."

"Look, everyone in this bank swears that you came to their rescue. You stopped a hostage crisis developing. And innocent people could have been killed," responded the inspector. I noted I was right about one thing. He had no care for ill doers. His sympathies lay squarely with the innocent bystanders who obeyed the law.

He continued: "Produce your gun licences in twenty four hours at the station, and there will be no charges. I need your passports to be surrendered until you do. As an exception I will not take your guns away. I half believe your story."

"Thank you Inspector," I said. "There is one other issue. I would rather have no publicity. It will bring Miss Di Maglio and me to prominence. And that is risky. Do we need to be involved any further?"

The Inspector thought, "I need statements. You stormed the building. I know you had been there earlier. I expect we could conceal your identities, at least officially."

"Inspector," I suggested. "Could it be that the press are led to believe that it was the forces of law and order who acted quickly? Perhaps police doing undercover work? They could pretend they were by the bank by chance and acted quickly. They of course could not be identified for fear of destroying the case they are working on. It would be good for the image of the police."

The Inspector liked the thought. He knew though he had to refer such a suggestion upwards. I left it with him. The important thing now was to get a gun licence. I had my passport and I expected Jacqui had hers in her bag. I called her in and she produced it. A US passport went alongside mine and was handed to the Inspector. He put them in his pocket, walked over to the desk and wrote a receipt. He had to take them out of his pocket again when I asked him to note the two passport numbers on his receipt. Our friend, I noted, was not one for paperwork.

He turned to me. "The staff have been warned not to talk to anyone. They have been told that they would be charged if they revealed any names. As it appears the manager and his deputy are the only ones who are sure of your identities, that is really no problem. The two other customers in the bank are giving their statements. They want to thank you. It's the two who were in the vault. They're a couple of rich Arabs. One stinks like a whore. The other is as smarmy as they come."

I noted another feature of the Inspector's make up. He did not like foreigners too much, and above all he most likely loathed Arabs. That is not unusual in the South of France where racism is quite rife. At that point Ali and Yussef came up from the vault. They were shaken but recovering.

Ali turned to the Inspector; "My car will be here soon. You have my address and will bring the statement there for correction and signature. I hope I do not have further involvement."

The Inspector nodded curtly and then turned his back on him. Ali came over to me, "I owe you," he said in a soft voice. "Jacqui knows where I live. Head over there later this afternoon. Perhaps I can help you further." In a louder voice, he said "if you are planning to leave Monte Carlo later today, perhaps you would do me the honour of having tea with me."

I made to protest, and he stopped me. "Here is my card. I would be honoured if you have the time. But if you are busy, I would understand."

With that he and Yussef walked to their car, which had been allowed to park in front of the bank. I turned to the Inspector; "May we leave?"

He nodded and reminded me, "But I need to see those licences and will later today know more about the issue we discussed."

I was glad he was pursuing that line. It would serve no purpose to have our names all over the papers. I already felt that we had been more high profile than I wanted.

Jacqui and I went over to the car. "Let's go for a drive," I said.

I took the car out of Monte Carlo and headed towards Menton and the Italian border. I then turned up into the mountains and eventually found a place to park. We were on a quiet road, well away from anywhere. The cool breeze from the sea blew gently into our faces. The air was salty, even at that height. We could see gulls circling over the rocks far below. Monte Carlo and the other high rise resorts stuck out of the coastline. Man showed his designs were ugly when set against the beauty of the architecture of a thousand years of natural development.

Jacqui lay back in the open topped car. Her eyes were shut. She breathed in the fresh and fragrant air with relish. "I have to say, life's getting exciting. A bit too exciting for me. I don't think I could live this style non-stop for too long."

I put my arm around her and pulled her towards me. She rested her head on my shoulder and we both sat silently.

"Let's take stock," I said. "We have deposited the fifty million dollars from Ali in the bank. That's now with Fucquet.

"I put the casino cheques worth five million one fifty into United. That's a good reserve. I am glad we used them. They have branches world-wide and so we have access to adequate cash.

"We have the tapes in Fucquet Geneva and United Monte Carlo. Those keep your father in check.

"We still have forty five million to launder. I need to call my father tonight. He will now be in Rio as later this week he has his plastic surgery. I need to talk to him about events in Asia.

"We need two gun permits. Someone is also going to realise that I had two guns. So mine will need to cover both. The only person who would be able to get us those on time is your father. You are going to have to call him."

"Oh no," came the reply. "I want nothing to do with him."

"We're not going to," I explained what I had said to the Inspector. "All depends if he wants things to get tough for him. This is a one off. There are no threats from us. If he thinks he can weather the storm, fine. Then we will have to tap Ali for help. I don't know of anyone else and I'd rather keep our Arab friend at arm's length."

Jacqui nodded. I handed her the phone and she dialled her father's number.

"Hello Uncle Aldo," she said. "Are you still operating the switchboard? I need to speak to my father." There was a pause and then I heard something being said on the other side.

Jacqui replied in a very saccharine like tone, "I don't care if he has no wish to speak to me. I don't care if he doesn't give a fuck about what happens to me. This is business. If he wants police crawling over his villa, hang up. Tell him that I have as much desire to talk to him as he is showing about me." Her face seemed to harden. "This is a trade. I'll stop him having problems as long as he does us a favour."

Again a pause. I recognised the gruff tones of Di Maglio as he came to the phone. Jacqui explained what had happened.

"We did a deal with Ali. There was nothing unusual except word got out. There was an attempted ambush on us but we avoided it. After the switch four goons with Uzis stormed the bank. It was the usual one, United Bank of Europe in Monte Carlo. Two of them got hit. The other two gave up. The police have them. Nobody was hurt and we think the police will keep our part quiet. But they want to know that we were carrying guns legally. Charles said it was to protect me from the Russian Mafia. Do you know the Inspector? Charles thought he knew you." And she gave the details to her father, finishing by adding, "You have loads of fake licences waiting to be filled in. Do that and you should avoid any unwanted attention. If you decide not to, we are not trying to threaten you. We'll try someone else."

There was a response and Jacqui said, "That's a wise choice. OK let me give you the gun details. There are three of them. You know my passport details and Charles is using the one he used at the Carlton. I am sure you have the details. Get someone to deliver them to the Carlton. We are in the room you offered us. But make sure you play no tricks."

Again there was a comment. "I'll pass the comment on to him. But you know my views. You can guess my terms. Thanks for the help. It makes life easier."

With that she turned off the phone. "He will do it. They will be at the hotel tonight by ten. He says he respects you. With experience he thinks you could be a master of crime like him."

"I don't think I want that. I want to do it all legally. I have told you. I want to work in the grey area of banking and finance. There are always rules waiting to be broken and legally. Breaking those rules can make one an absolute fortune. With a good legal team, there is no risk. Bugger your father's drugs and guns. I am going to work with technology and law."

She smiled. "And I am going to learn from you. I want to become a full partner. After all, I have my masters and got my bachelors with twenty. I don't want to be a bimbo."

"I doubt anyone will call you that." I laughed. "Now I think we should call on Ali after lunch. He does owe us and perhaps we can fast track the last bit of laundering. That would allow us to head off out of this heat all the sooner."

"I agree. There's no harm, in seeing what he will say. He knows we did not set him up. He may have an idea who it was. It couldn't have come from our side unless my father was trailing us. But even then he would not have known we had that sort of money on board. And he would not have been so stupid as to hit us in the bank. There were better places en route. Even the ambush in town was amazingly high risk. It all smacks of amateurs. And my father is no amateur nor are most of his associates."

We stayed in the car looking along the coastline. We needed the quiet to recover and recharge. I looked at my watch. It was getting on to three. I realised also I was hungry and thirsty. "No good trying to lunch. Let's get fed by Ali and see what he has to say."

I drove off and headed back to the main road and the turnoff for Monte Carlo. I still kept a careful eye open for all the following traffic. I watched for any sign of trouble ahead. But it went smoothly. Jacqui had never been to Ali's house before but knew the area well enough to direct me. The house was actually on the French side of the border.

We pulled up in front of two iron gates. The house was a fairly classical villa. I doubted it was that big. It may have had five or six bedrooms. It stood in about three-quarters of an acre of well-tended gardens. It had white shutters, black painted railings, carefully sculpted bushes, and tall phallic pines. It gave the impression of being well cared for. The sort of house that will set one back a few million in a place like that. It was convenient for Monte Carlo and a quick drive, other than in the chaos of the peak summer season, from Nice Airport.

I hooted and someone appeared. I noticed that there was a video camera behind the gate. The man approaching talked into a mobile and then opened the gates with a remote control. We drove in and the gates immediately started to close again. I headed to the house. Ali stood there in full Arab dress. Behind him was Yussef in a dark suit. Ali smiled a warm welcome at us. Yussef scowled at me. That didn't bother me, as he was not going to do anything that upset his father.

"Come in," said Ali as he kissed Jacqui on the cheeks and gave me, surprisingly, a warm hug. "What can I offer you?"

"We're starving and thirsty," announced Jacqui. "But Ali, can we have European food rather than spicy lamb and stuff?"

He smiled, "I thought you would eat. They have prepared Scottish salmon sandwiches, some fresh dressed lobster, salade nicoise with fresh anchovies and a cheese board. You can eat what you wish. If you prefer hot food…"

"Ali," said Jacqui. "You're great. Just take us to the table."

"And to drink?" said our host questioningly.

"Could I have some chilled white wine? Charles, what do you want?"

I stopped looking around the house. I had been quite taken by the interior. Ali was obviously a keen collector of antiques. He had a range of beautiful ornaments and decorations from all corners of the world.

Persian carpets adorned the walls and the floors. There were paintings that looked as if they were from the sixteenth and seventeenth centuries, perhaps not from the great artists but definitely from members of their schools. The ornaments ranged from antique hookahs, to fine old English china and on to beautiful carvings in wood and stone.

And in a corner nestled an old writing desk with a bank of drawers and cubby-holes. It was obviously used as indeed it had been for a good two hundred years. Yet it was in perfect condition. Ali was an enigma I decided. The story of his life, the reality of his business and the personality stamped on this property were totally incompatible.

I responded to the question, "I'd love a beer, a Kronenbourg rather than anything else. And I'd love some food. I'm starving."

We sat down and ate. I asked Ali if he recognised the thugs at the bank. He shook his head. "They may have been freelance," he said. "Yussef says he told some friends in the casino that he had to be home early on Sunday. He said that I had a big job for him on Monday. As my Jewish friends would say his stupidity sometimes makes me meshugener."

Yussef scowled at this. I thought our relationship with him was going from worse to worse. At first I thought he just stank. Now I knew he was stupid. We had realised he was sulky. I had also established he was a coward. There was little I could think of in his favour.

Ali continued, "Perhaps someone overheard him. Perhaps he was drunk and said more than he can remember. I do not know. Will you be alright?"

"We will see the police tomorrow and should be able to settle things. If the gunmen were just opportunists, that will make it easier. It would have been harder if they knew us and had targeted us for other reasons."

Ali said, "You defend yourselves so well, I doubt I could help you in that area. But I owe you much. Is there anything I can do?"

"There is one thing," I said. "Can you launder another big sum?"

"How much?"

"We have forty five million."

"Where is it?"

"Same place as before."

"When?"

"Tomorrow?"

Ali thought. "OK. But because I trust you now I will make it simpler. I will take delivery of the cash in Cannes at your bank and bring with me a banker's payment drawn on the United. We can both have it validated in United's Cannes office before we exchange. I will also make sure that Yussef is out of circulation till we have finished the trade. This time there will be no problems."

"Excellent," I said. "Ali that was delicious. I need to head back to Cannes with Jacqui. We should go soon. Why not meet at our hotel. It's the Carlton. The main United Bank branch is nearby and then we can go on to exchange the cash and the payment. I will arrange secure transport. If you want to make things even easier I can assign my safe box in the bank to you."

Ali liked the idea. "Is it secure?" he asked.

"The bank think these are office papers. And the vault is an old one. It's as safe as they make them."

I had carefully once again not told him the name of the bank. I preferred him not to know the real location, at least for certain. I suspected though that he had guessed which one it was.

We all shook hands this time. I even shook hands with Yussef. His warm fleshy and sweaty hand matched my impression of his whole nature. Poor Ali would die a rich man and Yussef would squander his fortune in a matter of years.

THE ROAD FROM FRANCE

We left the house overlooking Monte Carlo and headed up to the main road and the motorway. The blue of the sky was darkening as night approached. The sun decided to show its face for almost the first time that day, as we headed towards Cannes.

But soon it disappeared behind a growing bank of cloud, which in turn shut out the light of the moon and stars. The night adopted a gloomy look. The air felt heavier. The shadows from the headlamps of the cars hurtling along the motorway offered the only light. The world looked a tired place. The shut windows of the car, the roof now firmly closed, acted as a barrier to this depressing landscape. Somehow though they did not shut it out entirely and the sadness of the evening got through to us all the same.

I looked over at Jacqui. She sat there quietly, looking ahead out of eyes touched with sadness. She noticed me catch that look and realised that I had recognised it. She said she was thinking of her parents. Her mother had had the choice between staying with her husband and being with her daughter or losing them both. When she made that choice and left, she had never said goodbye. Since she had left, she had never called, never sent a message or even a card on birthdays. The only sight Jacqui had had of her was in fashion magazines. Her memory of her mother was from Paris Match and Vogue.

Her troubles with her father started when she left for university. It had been almost as if he refused to think she had a life of her own. He had people watch her. He tried to rule her. He sought to bring her into the business. Without a son, he had no natural successor. At first he wanted her to be the first woman Don. Then he decided that was not right. So he said that he wanted her to run his legitimate businesses. She loathed the illegal business and refused to have much to do with it. She had done holiday work for him. She was mainly involved in money laundering, but had also attended meetings at his legitimate businesses. She could not understand why he wanted to retain the old links. He had the largest chain of brothels; he ran the biggest protection rackets and owned the major drug distributors on the East Coast and in the South of the USA. He had similar businesses in France, Italy, Spain and Portugal. He had embraced evil and loved it too much to let it go.

Then she explained how she had come to meet me again. She thought I had deserted her. She suspected that her father had bought me off, for that would have been his style. By the time she met my parents, she was desperate. Her aunt had deceived her. She felt terribly alone. She could not understand why she had trusted my parents. She had acted irrationally at that point, perhaps by instinct. Now she had met me, and she was scared. She knew I would not hurt her, but she was scared she would lose me. Everything was going to change. We either would become very powerful, or she thought in time I would be seduced by her father's wealth.

"It's easy for me as he is a multi millionaire, perhaps a billionaire, through his legal holdings. And, even if he hates me, he will leave the bulk to me. But you aim for that sort of money and you want it in your own right. I can see that's important for you. You are like my grandparents. Nothing will stop you in your fight to satisfy your ambition. So I'll always be a bit concerned."

"I do want to win this battle. It's important for me and also my parents. But I told you that I work within boundaries. It's that that differentiates me from your father. I can't prove it though. I can't guarantee what I would do if we failed. Do you remember the other day when we were going through the mountains near Mont Blanc? Perhaps we would go to earth in a mountain village or a hut on a lonely sea-shore somewhere in the sun?"

She smiled, although there were still signs of sadness in her eyes. "Don't let me down. Let's find the right mountain. Let's get to the right beach."

I nodded. "Let's go up one of those mountains tonight. Book into the Moulin at Mougins for dinner. Make it late, say nine thirty. I need to call Fucquet and then my father. We are going to succeed. And then we can plan our lives."

She looked at me and whispered questioningly, "Together?"

I looked back at her, put my fingers to my lips, and blew a kiss. "As together as we can. And for always."

The sadness was still there, but now it was mixed with hope. I smiled at her again as we drove on and came to the exit road for Cannes and the Carlton. I pulled up in front of the elegant hotel and handed the keys to the doorman. "We will need it again tonight."

We walked through the lobby where just a couple of days before I had confronted Di Maglio. As we walked through a voice called "M. De Roche, I have some papers for you."

The speaker was a tall, dark haired man of about thirty. He was impeccably dressed in a double-breasted pale grey suit. His hand stitched shirt and wine red silk tie fitted to perfection. He bowed to Jacqui and she backed away. "So nice to see you again. When you tire of him, I can offer you a job. You'd earn good money."

Her eyes sparked with fury as she pulled herself back and slapped him full in the face. The smack resounded across the lounge, but not so much as the one that followed. The man reeled back as people around looked on in wonder. Some seemed amused while some seemed worried.

I intervened and took the man by the arm. "What have you for me?"

He threw an envelope at me and in fury spat out the words "Whore. Bitch. Whore" at Jacqui.

I looked at him coolly and he did not expect any trouble. He did not notice my hand go for the barrel of my gun, check that the safety catch was on, and then draw it out like a club. As my hand lashed forward the metal hit him full force in the mouth. His nose and mouth spurted blood as I moved in again and clubbed him under the chin.

I discreetly moved back slipping the gun again into my trouser band. Nobody had seen that it had not been my fists. The suit was now speckled with blood. The shirt and the tie were spattered with it. "I don't know who you are and I don't care," I said coldly. "But if you ever use that language in front of any lady in my presence, you will find it even more painful."

Nobody had heard what he had said to Jacqui. I doubted anyone had noticed the envelope. It had fallen to the ground in the altercation and Jacqui had picked it up during the fight. She was holding it now. I called over the manager. "Get rid of this man. I am amazed you allow such people into your hotel. I will not have people asking such questions. Even as a jest, I do not think it amusing for him to act as if he thinks a guest of your hotel is a whore."

My voice carried. The manager called over the porters and the man was ejected promptly. I knew he came from Di Maglio and wondered what the connection was. Of one thing I was certain. Di Maglio would have sent him to stir up trouble between Jacqui and me. He obviously had some connection with Jacqui's past.

In our room, she turned to me and said, "Let me explain. He is one of my father's people. His name is Marco. He runs the brothels. I guess he is the biggest pimp in town. My father saw him as a suitor for me. He has been chasing me for years. We have been together in a few groups but never alone. I despise him, yet he never gives up. This time though he went too far. He offered me a job when we had finished. Oh Charles, they all think we are going to break up. They are pushing for it."

I sat down on the sofa and pulled her gently down beside me. "Jacqui, there is one big difference between you and me. You never had a family from a very early age. They all let you down. Your mother, your father and your aunt let you down. And I guess a few others we haven't discussed. You don't believe that I won't too. It's natural. I promise you I'll stay with you. You've got to believe me or they will win."

She nodded and smiled, this time without that sad look in her eyes. "You're right. I believe you. But the sooner we get away from them, the better I will feel."

"Jacqui, tomorrow we can clear up the laundry. Let's not say anything to the hotel. I'll book us on the last flight to Paris and London. And then we can get to Rio. We'll go a round about route to Rio. We can easily lose them on the way. And then we'll have six months in peace and quiet. Whatever happens we will not return to France for six months now."

I took her in my arms and gently said, "We'll be happy."

She said, "Have you booked the restaurant?"

I shook my head; "We are going to have to work if we are leaving tomorrow. We'll work off the mobile. I don't want the calls traced."

My first call was to Air France and saw us on the late afternoon flight to Paris. My next was to British Airways and saw us on the last flight from Roissy to Heathrow. The third was to the Ritz where I booked a double room for the following night, and arranged for a hotel chauffeur to meet us from our flight.

Those were the simple ones. My next was to M Pierre of Fucquet. It was late, so I called him at home. His wife answered and he came quickly to the phone. "I see a sum of fifty million has been credited to your account. In addition my partners have agreed the trading facility as we discussed. The facility letter can be made available for signature at your convenience."

I thought quickly. "Could you get it to your London office tomorrow?" Of course, that was possible and I told them to get the manager to the Ritz for seven in the morning so that I could sign the documents. I ran through the clauses that would be included. There was nothing that caused us a problem. Basically we would be able to use our hundred million dollars to finance a one to one and a half to two billion position in the markets. That is called buying on margin. In effect you put up a sum of money to cover the bank's worst case estimate of what can happen to your investments. And they revise the sum each day according to what happens in the markets. Given our plans for such speculative investments the offer was not bad.

While I was on the phone, Jacqui had checked and double checked the gun permits. They were in order. She handed them to me and I placed them in the briefcase. I also put the notes I had written during my phone calls in with it.

She then handed me a newspaper cutting. It had been with the permits. It was an extract from a Geneva newspaper. The bodies of two men had been found in a hut in the mountains above Geneva. Both had been shot in the head. They had other gunshot wounds. Police believed they had been injured in a gangland shoot-out and then executed. Their identities were unknown, but documents found on them suggested they might be Russian. Police were pursuing their inquiries, but had found no leads so far.

I now knew at least that the police were not genuine. They had been Di Maglio's people all the time. I felt little sympathy for the gunmen. I realised though the ruthlessness of the family I was now inevitably associated with. Then my heart dropped. A small cutting was attached from a local Geneva paper. A shop assistant had been killed in a hit and run road accident. It had happened the night of the gun attack in Geneva. The shop's owner had said, "She was a beautiful girl. We are all devastated." The shop was the one we had used.

Jacqui had turned to the phone meanwhile and ordered room service for an hour's time. "I know what you think. It's the way they are. That's why we need to steer clear of them. It's horrible, but doesn't shock me any more. Look, I've left an hour till we eat. That will give you time to call your father," she said. "After that we better pack some of our things and be ready for a quick getaway."

"I don't plan to tell the hotel until I am leaving," I said. "That could stop people following us. We can leave everything ready to be packed. That should not take us long and then we walk straight out of here."

I turned back to the phone and dialled my parents' number in Rio. My mother answered and immediately asked how we were.

"Fine," came back the response. "We're at the Carlton in Cannes. How are you? Is dad on the line?"

"He's just picked up the extension. We're fine. He saw the surgeon today and they will operate tomorrow."

"Is the line secure?" I asked.

"Yes," he replied. "I would know if the switchboard were listening in. And I only took the room today. We arrived without a reservation. There was no need to risk one off season."

"Excellent," I said. I had known that already as they had given me three possible numbers for hotels. If all three had failed, they would have phoned me with the number earlier. "Let me run you through what has happened."

With that I updated them on everything since the last call. I heard them gasp as I ran through the incident in the bank. They did not interrupt until I had explained the arrangements with Ali and Fucquet.

"That is excellent," said my father. "I am watching markets daily. We are in luck if we can act sooner rather than later. I am arranging for a nerve centre to be set up in California in our health club retreat. That's quite normal there. Lots of rich overweight entrepreneurs go there. You can work out for six hours, sleep for ten and still have around seven or eight for trading. And we will focus on Asia. The Far East and London markets will be more important for us than those in the North American time zone. That makes it easier to organise. You did a good job on the bank. One point five billion is fine for a start. It will allow us to gain a track record and have credibility when we move in more of our seed money." He meant that, as long as we made a killing first time round, the banks would expect investors to give us more money. And that cover story allowed us to move our stolen funds into our funds under management.

I then ran him through our plans. "I plan to leave here tomorrow night. We will be in London late evening. If I can take a Boston flight, I will put us on it. I haven't yet booked, as I don't want to leave a trail here. Just in case British Airways call and leave a message at the hotel. We'll spend Wednesday and Thursday in Boston and then fly in the afternoon to La Guardia. We'll cross over to Kennedy and pick up a flight to Rio. So we will join you on Friday night. I'll call you at any rate from Boston. We'll drop the guns off in the Monte flat tomorrow. I daren't dump them, as the police will have the numbers. That means we have to be careful with Ali but we won't tell him we are not armed. I don't think we are at too great a risk there."

"What about Jacqui's people?" asked my mother.

"The father wants to annoy us but not kill us. I think he'll leave us alone now. There's no need for us to contact him. We think he's still in Geneva but it's hard to tell. He has one number no matter where he is. Apparently that number is always manned and always available."

"Call us all the same from London. I'd like to know that you're all right. And be careful," urged my father.

"I'd have called anyway to see how you got on at the doctors," I said.

"You may have to wait a day as the operation will take place late afternoon. You're forgetting time zones," he commented. "If that's all, put Jacqui on for a moment."

Jacqui looked pleased that they wanted to talk to her. They chatted for a while and then she passed back the phone. As I discussed some details of the Asian situation again with my father, I noticed that Jacqui was humming happily to herself while sorting through the clothes. She was already getting ready to pack, folding things together on shelves and arranging her dresses and my suits.

After I had put the phone down to my parents, I called Carrie. Her husband answered and immediately put her on. She had been worried about my earlier call, and I apologised. "I had to call you because I knew you would know how to respond. The call had to appear realistic. I couldn't call the talking clock. In any case in reality the arrangements are as they were before. There is no change although I suspect you guessed that."

She asked me how I was doing myself, adding, "I doubt you have time for girlfriends. You seem too busy for anything but work."

I laughed. "I am in love with this fantastic girl. You and she would get on well together. Like a house on fire. She's with me all the time. So we are living through some strange experiences together."

I noticed once again that Jacqui had overheard me and once again she seemed to be humming happily to herself. I was still talking to Carrie when dinner was delivered. I therefore told her I'd call her in a few days and hung up to her last quip of "Room service at this time. Is it love or self-preservation that is keeping you indoors? Enjoy yourself Charles. Hey if she's American, I could call you Chuck."

I was laughing as I put down the phone and turned my attention to the food.

"Is everything ready?" I asked.

"From my side, yes," she answered. "The rest of the packing will take about ten minutes. I have stacked everything as it goes into the cases. So there will be no delays. I have a few things to finalise in the morning but that will take practically no time."

"OK," I said. "From my side, I think we should leave at eight. We need to drop round the police station and the flat. You haven't been there but the complex is quite near the harbour. Then we get back here to meet Ali at one o' clock. If we have time, I would like to stop off at the airport to pick up our tickets. It is hardly a moment from the motorway and gives us a bit of extra time in the afternoon. I don't know how quickly we will complete the deal with the banks."

She nodded. "So let's set the alarm for six thirty and order breakfast for seven. I wish though we could find a gun for tomorrow afternoon. I'll have to think if I know anywhere where we can get one in the Monte Carlo area. I feel safer armed. In the US there will be no problem getting one, especially with our Swiss permits."

We got to bed early that evening. We made love. I caressed Jacqui with all the gentleness I could. She held me tightly, both while we made love and afterwards as we fell asleep together. It was as if we were finding a more peaceful existence. I hoped this was the case. The next months could be interesting and profitable. But they also gave us opportunity to be together and away from the risks of the Di Maglio family.

The next morning, we set off early. We called the inspector from the car and agreed on a nine o' clock meeting. He sounded relaxed about it all. However, I knew better than to take his tone as proof that all would go well.

As we parked near the police station, we both felt nervous about going inside. After all our lifestyle in France over the past week could hardly be described as lawful. I had pointed out to Jacqui that we had committed two possible murders in the house. We had been involved at the minimum in reckless driving between St Tropez and Croix Valmer. We had been tied up in money laundering in Monte Carlo. We had been carrying guns without a licence. I operated under a false passport. And in Switzerland we were perhaps accomplices to two counts of murder.

In short we had clocked up a few years inside between us, should we be caught. And that did not allow for the fact that I was an accomplice in a major international fraud and had murdered a pilot in the Cayman Islands. In theory Jacqui could also be accused of blackmail.

With that sort of background, police stations are places you drive out of your way to avoid. Still we had no choice. We had both decided we should appear conservative. So Jacqui was wearing a plain black dress one of her designer scarves and medium heeled shoes. I was wearing a dark suit and sober tie. I had my briefcase, still slightly scuffed from my accident in Cannes. The good news was that the bruising in my face had almost disappeared. I also had no problems with the other injuries I had picked up that day.

The inspector received us immediately. He gave a cursory glance at the licences and sent them to be copied.

"That seems fine. We also agree with you that it is not in the interests of your safety to be identified. So we will advise that undercover agents of the police apprehended the gunmen. I doubt also that you will have to testify. The four Russians have confessed."

That was the first time I had heard they were Russians. It tied neatly in with my cover story. But I could not understand how they had got to know about the money.

The inspector then said, "I heard that you had a problem in the Carlton last night. There was an argument with one of Mr. Di Maglio's associates. He was not happy but refused to place charges. Is there anything you should tell me about your relationship with Mr. Di Maglio?"

Jacqui chipped in, "I am a bit estranged from my father. There's been a family row. That's why it's important to look after ourselves. My family may not help."

The inspector looked straight at her, "Is this a private family issue or are we talking of another family?"

Jacqui made to look perplexed, "Sorry, I don't follow you."

"Are we likely to have a bout of gang warfare?" he queried.

Jacqui looked even more puzzled, "How would I know. I'm not the sort of person who hangs around in gangs."

He looked at her impatiently, "Well have it your way. But one step out of line and there will be trouble."

I thought it time to intervene, "Inspector, if we could help we would. But I think you have misunderstood our relationship with Mr. Di Maglio. And I cannot understand the apparent connection you are making between him and crime. As far as I am aware, Mr. Di Maglio is a reputable businessman. Are you saying otherwise?"

The inspector shrugged his shoulders and moved to the door of the interview room. "We have your address here and will contact you if needed. Keep off my patch if possible. I don't know what you do or are doing. But I'm a cop. And I know trouble when I see it."

He walked out without another word. The discussion had hardly lasted a half-hour. We were both pleased to leave the station and breathe in the fresh air once again. I fed a few more coins into the meter and we walked to a cab rank a bit further along the street. I instructed the driver to go to the apartment block.

Our flat in Monte Carlo was small. Two bedrooms and a sitting room. Plus there was a small kitchen and a bathroom. It was no more than a *pied à terre*. Inside it was simply furnished. It looked as it was. A flat that nobody really lived in and one furnished from whatever could be found at the nearest out of town shopping centre. But there was one special feature. Behind a print of Picasso on the wall, was a hook. If twisted a certain way a power point in the wall below came forward. The wall behind was hollowed out. It was the ideal spot for our guns. The set up was good for even the power point worked. People may look for clues behind a picture but they were unlikely to manipulate the hook that held it up.

We placed the guns in their hiding spot and closed up the hole and the flat. We walked out with the usual bunch of letters and circulars that one finds after a long absence. Anyone seeing us would have thought we had just come for that purpose. This time we walked the mile or so to the car. We tried to se if we were being followed but could not see anyone.

"Mind you that proves nothing," I said. "They could work in relays in a place like this. I doubt they have much to do off season."

We got to the car and I tossed the letters into the back. We drove off. "I'll take the low road," I said to Jacqui. "You said you could find me a gun. Where's the best place?"

"Near the airport," said Jacqui. "I hope the place is still there. The good thing is that it gives cover. Officially it's a bar. I know it was there for years but haven't heard of it for some time."

Once again I was following her instructions as we drove along the Promenade Des Anglais towards the airport.

"How did you know about it?" I asked.

"I ran errands for my father. Collecting guns was one of them. A girl is unlikely to be suspect. And we normally carry handbags. And younger girls carry bigger ones than couturier dressed women like me," came the response.

"The cafe's still there," she said, pointing to a normal looking place on the corner. "Let's see if it sells the extras."

We parked in front of the place. It looked normal. "Is Georges still the patron here?" Jacqui asked a sullen looking girl at the counter.

"Yes, he's round the back," came a surly reply.

Jacqui walked straight round with me in tow. A squat fat man in a slightly grubby vest sat there. His gauloise drooped from his open bottom lip, curling smoke into the abundant nasal hairs that merged into a straggly moustache. His top trouser button was undone to reveal an enormous paunch. A pair of old braces held up his trousers. He was balding but kept his hair long and naturally greasy rather than slicked back. It was better that this caricature of a cafe owner did not serve up front. I hoped that he did not cook the food or even touch the croissants. For his stubby fingers were topped by bitten down nails that still retained a thin thick layer of grime.

"You get more beautiful with age, you old crook," said Jacqui.

He looked at her sourly. "The Di Maglio girl. You look like your father wanted. A rich upper class bitch. What do you want?"

"Two guns. We want handguns. Mine has to fit into my bag. We're not fussy as long as they work."

He poked a finger in his ear and tried to excavate whatever was in it. "Who do you want them for?"

"That's not your look out," came the sharp reply. "If you want to do business with us, that's fine. If you ask questions, you'll be in trouble."

"OK. I may have what you want but it'll cost you. Come this way."

And with that, he took us through a door at the side of the room and down a flight of stairs to a cellar. There was a concealed door at the end and he opened that to reveal a good-sized arsenal. It did not take long to find the right weapons. I took an identical one to the gun I had been using and Jacqui took another small handbag sized pistol.

"Give me a price," she said.

"For you darling," he sneered, "I'll make it a thousand dollars a piece or five hundred if you make me happy."

A sharp gesture from Jacqui held me back. Her response was cold. "You'll get a thousand dollars from both of us and we want half a dozen rounds each. And if you as much as breathe on me, you'll feel a few bullets in your gut."

We completed the sale and I handed the man the note. He was surprised to get a single thousand.

"Is it genuine?" he asked.

"Yes," I responded.

"If it's not," he said, turning to Jacqui, "I expect those favours from you."

She walked away. I decided to follow her example. On leaving I turned to him, "We haven't been here. If anyone asks. The girl wanted to use the toilet. We ordered a coffee but didn't drink it. You made us feel sick. OK?"

He did not respond and I did not ask him to.

"What a sleaze," I said as I got into the car. "How on earth could you go back there?"

"You can't be choosers in this game and he had the goods, even if he cheated us on the price. Moreover he's so revolting, that makes him a safer bet from our point of view."

We drove the short distance to the airport and I picked up our tickets to Paris. A voice behind me said, "Don't forget that you can't take arms on board."

I turned to face the inspector. "If you are following me, I'll have you for harassment."

The inspector laughed for the first time and showed me a ticket to Paris. "I happen to be going to Paris. I was only being courteous."

I smiled and wished him a good journey. "I have to say," I added, "I hope I don't have to take up any more of your time."

He looked amused by this, "Me too. But if it must be…"

I returned to Jacqui and asked if she thought that was an accident. She was doubtful, but pointed out we were not doing anything illegal that afternoon. I smiled and said "other than having two guns that are not licensed."

She shrugged her shoulders. "They're after bigger fish. Even if they are on our trail, they'd be hoping to catch my father or something."

"All the same," I said, "we may need to have a sudden change of plan. Let's keep that in mind."

We reached Cannes just after midday and went straight to the hotel. We headed to our room. As it had been made up, Jacqui started packing her two cases. I packed mine. We had actually finished by the time Ali was announced.

We greeted him. He was once again with Yussef who looked even less pleased to see us than on the previous occasion. After a few words of greeting we went to United Bank's palatial offices just behind the Martinez. The manager was waiting for us. The transaction was quite simple. The banker's draft was produced. It was a cheque drawn on United Bank for forty five million dollars. It had two signatures and the manager produced, at my request, the signature book to allow me to validate them and to establish their signing powers.

I warned the manager I would need him to do a money transfer for me later that day. He confirmed that he would be at the bank. He had obviously heard from his offices in Monte Carlo about the sums we dealt in and was treating us with kid gloves. Or he believed we were undercover agents and with that sort of money we had to be important.

Or perhaps he cultivated Ali for his wealth. I could think of three good reasons for his attention. That satisfied me.

There was a cab rank outside and, as is common off-season, plenty of cabs available. That did not stop the driver from looking resentful when he heard we wanted to go to our bank, just a short distance away. In any case he took us there.

We went down in the vault. We went through the usual routine. Ali looked through the contents. Then he handed me the banker's payment we had collected from United. I asked the vault supervisor to arrange for the ownership of my vault to be passed over to my associate and to re-arrange the keys. "My associate will also pay the outstanding fees," I said.

I turned to Ali. "You owe us nothing as you have changed the money without a fee and, more importantly, saved us a lot of problems. Now I owe you a favour and one day I will try to repay it."

We actually shook right hands this time. I knew Ali meant me well. He politely kissed Jacqui on the hand. Yussef pretended we did not exist.

We walked back down to United. The manager again waited for us. "I want you to place this money into my account and remit it to these accounts in Switzerland."

The manager looked at the schedule and nodded. He went out of his office and gave instructions to an employee. Minutes later a series of advices had been prepared. The first was to credit my account at United in Monte Carlo. That brought the total to about fifty million. There were three others, all paid out of the United account I had just provisioned. One was a credit to Fucquet for a further forty five million dollars. The second was a two million dollar one for Bankhaus Hochzeit and the third for a million dollars to United in Geneva. That still left a couple of million in the account in Monte Carlo. I checked the dates for the credits. They were for the next day except for the one in Monte Carlo, which was still for that day. I signed them all and passed them back to the manager.

"I need a receipt for the banker's payment and copies of the transfer advices." I was rather pleased. We now had our war chest ready. The hundred million dollars had been banked. The play had started.

We strolled back along the sea front, arm in arm. It was a pleasant day again and there were few people around. One or two brave souls were on the beach. But Cannes was getting the look of a resort about to change its profile. Soon it would be conferences and expense account dinners. The odd tourist would feel isolated among the deserted daytime cafes and the eerily unpopulated tourist restaurants.

We got to the hotel and I asked the doorman to bring round the car. "I want it there in five minutes," I said. "I just need something from the room."

Everything had gone so smoothly. It wasn't even three. I picked up the phone. "We have a flight to Paris if we want at four thirty," I said to Jacqui. "I'll get them to change our tickets. There's no reason to hang around."

We took our luggage down ourselves. Two of the cases were on wheels in any event. Jacqui carried her vanity case and my briefcase. I had the suit carrier over my shoulder and pulled the other cases along. At ground floor level, the porters rushed to help and we handed them all over with instructions to put them into the car. At reception, I said I did not need to see the bill. They agreed that they would send it to Mr. Di Maglio.

I told the porters in passing that we were off to Geneva for business. Out of the corner of my eye I thought I saw someone sticking something onto one of the cases. I decided to ignore that. I mentioned this to Jacqui as we drove away.

"It will be a bomb or a bug," I said. "Mind you I may be wrong. I'll drive to the corner at Palm Beach and check it out."

I was right. It was a bug. A tracker bug. All the other cases seemed OK.

"I'll hold on to this. It must have been a precaution," I then thought. "If they placed this on the luggage as we left, they can't have expected us to go. We were not expected to notice. I only just saw it out of the corner of my eye and that was through a reflection as something caught the sun. That should mean the rest is safe. We need to drive close to the airport area and plant it on a moving vehicle. That will stop them knowing where we turned off."

As we got to the toll, I had a thought. I pulled in. "Wait a moment," I said to Jacqui, and walked to a police car that was parked near by, its engine running. I went over to the policemen and said, "Excuse me, which exit do I need to take for the airport?"

They looked at me as if I was a fool. "Continue straight on. It's marked and takes you straight to the terminal buildings."

I thanked them, and they did not notice how I dropped the bug onto the floor of their squad car, through the open rear window.

I returned to our car and said to Jacqui, "That could be amusing. Was it your father do you think?"

She laughed and said; "I guess so. He's not going to be happy."

Minutes later we were turning off into the airport. I drove into the car rental return area and handed in the keys. I declined to check over the car and commented that it was unscratched but only had half a tank of petrol. They could add that to the credit card.

We loaded a trolley with our luggage and wheeled it into the airport. I asked Jacqui to hand me her gun. I slipped it into my pocket. With our luggage checked we walked to domestic departures. We had half an hour to spare. "Give me a moment before we leave. But walk through. It's safer." I watched Jacqui through the security barrier and turned to the toilets.

I went into a cubicle. I carefully wiped down Jacqui's gun and then, opening my briefcase, did the same with mine and with the bullets. I then took some gloves from the case, the type used by jewellers to avoid fingerprints on their gold and silver ornaments, and also a band of tape. I taped the guns and cartridges together and tied them to the rear of the cistern in the toilet. I then replaced the cistern top. I was sure they were safe, at least for the moment. I then took out a card I had quietly picked up at the inspector's office and wrote on it the location of the toilets and recommended a search of the cubicles. I addressed the envelope to the airport police, marking it urgent in large capitals. I threw the gloves and the tape into a bin, and walked out of the toilet.

We hadn't needed them after all but I now knew that, whatever the chance of danger, it paid to take all possible precautions. In my new world one only made one mistake.

I was soon through security and back with Jacqui. We had fifteen minutes to wait before we were loaded on to the plane. We sat in the cramped positions that appear to be favoured for domestic flights, doing little else other than browse through the airline magazine. We landed on time at Orly. Once we had picked up our luggage we got a taxi to Roissy. But not before I had slipped my envelope and its warning into the open bag of a flight stewardess talking with her friends near the transit desk. I had done all I could to ensure the gun did not get into the wrong hands.

We arrived at Roissy and managed to catch the earlier British Airways flight. And at just after seven local time I landed again at London. It had been almost a year from my departure. But in that time I had lived a lifetime. And most importantly, I had lived it with Jacqui.

THE ROAD TO RIO

We waited for our luggage in the crowd. People around us milled anxiously as they in turn waited for theirs to appear. We ignored them and talked of our plans for the evening. Should we go to a restaurant or a night-club, or both? The only thing we had to do was to meet the London manager of Fucquet in the morning before leaving.

I wanted to be ready to head off for Boston and had already established that the flight left around ten in the morning.

That would mean that we would have to leave the hotel around eight. I was planning to book our seats from the hotel at the last minute. A mid week flight was unlikely to be full. And I saw no reason to warn anyone with access to the information of our plans. I wanted to avoid being followed, especially after the events of the past few days.

I put my arm around Jacqui. She lent against me, her head on my shoulder. I felt the warmth of her body through the light dress and, almost instinctively, my hand moved up her side towards her breast.

Almost as instinctively, she caught it and whispered, "Do behave. There are women and children around. And most likely a lot of impressionable men."

I laughed and looked around saying "Where?"

I noticed him immediately. He was a stocky man in a grey suit. His whole demeanour said that he was police or some other form of officialdom. I thought it was strange how I now recognised them by instinct. But why was he watching us so closely? Could he have recognised me as Charles Ryder?

I turned away and whispered to Jacqui, "Be careful, we are being watched. I don't know why. Whatever happens, play the dumb bimbo. Don't get implicated."

She nodded and we waited for our cases. They came round in quick succession. I loaded them on to a trolley and pushed them through the blue channel. I was hardly surprised by the hand on my shoulder. Then a voice said, "Would you please step this way Mr De Roche, and you Miss Di Maglio."

If they knew us by those names, there could only be one explanation. The French police had tipped them off. I wondered if the inspector had thought we might be in the drugs trade. He could have had had us followed and then warned them of our arrival. I reflected on that possibility for a moment. It was a bit far fetched, as in such a case he surely would have had us searched before we left France.

"We have had a tip off that you may be carrying illegal substances. Is there anything you would like to tell us?"

I looked as surprised as I could, "That's ridiculous. Who on earth would have tipped you off? We are reputable business people, not drug runners."

Jacqui said, "How dare you make such accusations. Is this somebody's joke or something?"

A man entered the room. "I think Miss Di Maglio that someone doesn't like you very much. He tipped us off that you had drugs in your luggage"

"Impossible" said Jacqui. "I packed our cases myself this morning."

Her voice trailed off. She went white. "They were left in our room. They were locked. But that's not a problem. Have we been set up? Has someone tampered with our luggage?"

That threw me. It was possible. And the only person who could have done that would have been Di Maglio or one of his men. How they would have got into the room I did not know. But I supposed that it was not hard to get some piece of technology that operated the doors. After all they were fairly basic electronic keys that were used by the hotels these days.

"I still say this outrageous," I said. "Why don't you search the cases?"

The customs officers opened the suit carrier. They took everything out and searched every inch of it. They then went through the suits item by item. They found nothing.

They next tackled one of Jacqui's cases. They removed eve rything and searched through the lining of the case. There was nothing there. They looked disappointed I thought. They looked through all the clothes. Again they drew a blank. Jacqui had recovered and went to repack her case. She was pushed away and told not to touch anything. Perhaps they were worried that she had something on her person and would transfer it to the case?

I was now really worried. They were too certain that they would find something. Had we been lulled into a sense of false security when we found the bug? Were we meant to see it so that we did not think of looking through the cases? I cursed myself for my laxness.

The final case was opened. It contained both our clothes and once again the routine search was completed. It revealed nothing.

Then the customs officers took Jacqui's vanity case. They tipped everything out and felt the padded lining. I went cold with trepidation. Jacqui gasped as they produced a knife and cut through the lining. The padding was non existent. Instead the case was lined with plastic bags filled with a white powder. It looked like cocaine. We had been set up.

The customs officers looked overjoyed. They told us that we would be stripped and body searched. They had tipped out most of Jacqui's creams and lotions but found nothing else.

I protested, "you need to test that substance. In any event it must have been planted. We knew nothing about it."

The response was formal. Both Jacqui and I were warned in turn that we would be searched and held in custody while the powder was analysed. Apparently an initial test could be undertaken quickly. In the meantime, they repeated, we would be stripped searched and then body searched.

We were told we could have a lawyer if we required one. I was caught between a rock and a hard place. Any lawyer I knew would not know me as Charles De Roche. I turned to Jacqui and asked if she knew a lawyer in London. She shook her head miserably. She knew her way around France or Switzerland or even the main cities in the USA, but London for her was a shopping centre. She too could not help.

I went into a room and stripped. One of the officers told me to sit on a bench, covered by a paper sheet. He pulled on a pair of plastic gloves and commenced his search. I closed my mind to his actions. I shut my eyes. But I could not shut my mind from what was happening. I thought of Jacqui. This would be worse for her. Someone would pay for this. And they would pay for it with their life.

They told me to dress. I was allowed into a washroom and splashed cold water over my face. I thought I would be sick. But I wasn't. I was seething. I couldn't believe it was Jacqui's father. He would not have risked it while we had the tapes. I also didn't think that he would have done it. After all Jacqui could end up in prison. I ran through the options. Who could it have been?

It needed to be someone who knew where we were. It had to be someone who did not know about the tapes. And it would be somebody who hated us.

The only people I could think of were Yussef and Di Maglio's messenger of the previous night. And I thought Yussef was too stupid to manage such a stunt.

I would have liked to discuss the matter with Jacqui but we were kept apart. I told the customs and police that I refused to answer their questions and they decided not to waste their time. So, with a police guard, I sat alone. I was left with my thoughts of what we should do.

It was a quarter past one in the morning when the senior customs official, the one who had been surveying us at the luggage console, returned. He looked worried. My heart missed a beat.

He said, "We have analysed the substance. And it is not an illegal one. It is a normal household product. I have to apologise for any inconvenience or distress we caused. We acted on a tip off which we had good reason to believe was reliable. We acted, as you may be aware, within our rights and according to the guidelines we are given. I am able to make a copy of them available to you if you need them."

I asked for Jacqui and our luggage. He directed me to the next room for Jacqui and said that a trolley was being sought for our luggage.

I walked into the room. Jacqui sat there with a woman officer. She did not see me enter. She sat there hunched up. Her fists were clenched. Her breathing was heavy. I walked over and sat beside her.

I took her gently into my arms. Her eyes were brimming over with tears. She kept on repeating, "Oh no, no."

"I'll look after you," I said. "Let's get going out of this place. I doubt the car is waiting. We'll get a taxi. Let's get some air."

She walked like a robot. Her face ashen and framed by a wild mass of black slightly curly hair. She still swallowed from time to time as she tried to keep her tears back. I pushed the trolley and could not offer her an arm as we walked out of customs again and into the crowd around the terminal exit.

There was no sign of the Ritz driver. He must have assumed we were a no show. We walked out of the airport buildings into a cold, drizzly London night.

There was no queue at that time of night and we soon were in a taxi, heading for London. I held my arm round Jacqui now and felt her tears on my chest as they soaked through my shirt. The horror had been too much for her. This was an indignity for which she was not prepared.

"Darling," I said, "You have to give me a minute for a couple of calls. It's important to make them."

The first was to the Ritz. I told them we had been delayed and asked them to have the room ready and to check us into the hotel in the room. I did not think that Jacqui would want to be hanging around the lobby, even at that late stage of the night.

I then called her father's number. I now knew it off by heart. I thought I recognised the voice at the other end. "Is that Aldo? This is De Roche. I think I saved your life the other night."

It was indeed Aldo and I continued, "I don't want to talk to Di Maglio. But you have an informer in your circle. Someone who is known to the police and who tips them off regularly. I don't know your business well enough, so it's possible he does that with your agreement. But today he went too far.

"Someone planted white powder in our luggage and informed the British customs of the fact. You might be able to narrow down who it was. Sometime today he was in the Carlton. He knew our room and spent a good deal of time planting the stuff in our luggage. It was a professional job. It may have been the person who put a bug on our cases, one that I got rid of before we hit Nice Airport.

"That person must have tracked our flight details. Perhaps he has access to airport computers. He knew we were going to London. But I only ticketed Nice to Orly. I picked up the other tickets at Roissy.

"He also hates us. He got them to strip search me and Jacqui."

I heard a sharp intake of breath from Aldo.

"And he also asked them to do a cavity search," I added.

At that point Aldo swore.

I added, "Kill him for us, and do it quickly." With that I put down the phone.

Jacqui looked at me through tear-filled eyes. She nodded and sobbed, "And they should do it slowly and painfully, whoever the bastard was."

We did not exchange another word. Her breathing became calmer as we approached the hotel. Her mascara was smudged. She had hardly any lipstick on. Her face still looked ashen. She kept on nervously pulling her hands through her hair.

As we reached the hotel, she pulled her jacket around her and waited for me as I paid off the cab.

We walked over to the lobby. A porter carried our luggage. We were whisked up to our room. The expert eye of the receptionist saw something was wrong. Jacqui was evidently distraught. And I suppose I was visibly still in a cold rage.

Alone, I turned to Jacqui. She said, "I need a bath. Get me a nightdress. There's one in the case." With that she disappeared into the bathroom. I soon heard the running water and the sound of brushing teeth.

Opening our cases, I took out her nightdress. I left everything else packed. There is one thing you can say about the customs, they actually repacked the cases well. I was now certain that we wanted to get out of England as soon as possible. I wanted to change our plans. I had to ensure that we were not tailed.

I walked into the bathroom with the nightdress. Jacqui was lying in foam filled, steaming bath. Her eyes were shut. Her face was troubled. I thought back to the day before and the sadness I had noted. I knew we had to go away. Jacqui was no slouch when it came to handling herself. She could cope with most things. But anybody would be stressed out after the trials and tribulations we had been through.

I also knew that I had pushed myself to the extreme. I was lucky she did not depend too much on me at such times, or perhaps I would have been the first to crack. I stripped off; suddenly feeling soiled by the intrusion of the custom search. I walked over to the shower in the corner of the room. Turning it on full blast, first cold and then hot, I tried to wash away even the thought of this evening's events.

I washed and washed myself from top to toe. I pushed the events at the airport out of my mind, although I doubt I could push them out of my memory. I focussed on the hot water splashing me from top to toe. I felt myself slowly gain control of my feelings. I almost returned to the person that I used to be.

The glass door of the shower opened and I turned to see Jacqui.

She had got out of the bath and had dried herself. She was wearing the nightdress. It was a long black slinky number, one she had worn the other night.

"Let's get to bed," she said, "it's almost two in the morning and you need to be up for a meeting at seven."

I looked at her again. The distress was still in her eyes. It was not as pronounced as earlier. It was not the same as before when she talked of her family. But I wanted to banish it forever. Once again the lonely mountain village or the idyllic beach beckoned as the way to escape. Once again, though, it was clear to me that such an option was not the real solution.

I stood there under the hot water, and looked at Jacqui. I smiled and she smiled back. A quiet, sad smile and it flickered across her face. A smile that touched her eyes and then fled in fear of her sadness. I took her arm in my wet hand and drew her close to me. She walked into the shower, and the rush of water soaked her hair.

It attacked the light, flimsy, silky material of her nightdress. The water splashed off her and me onto the floor of the bathroom. I pulled the door shut behind her and took her into my arms. We kissed not a passionate or sensual kiss. It was a comforting, healing kiss. A kiss that recognised the trauma we had both felt. A kiss that cleansed us more than the water ever could.

I moved away from her. By now the nightdress was soaked. The material clung to her body. Her breasts, the nipples leading the way, caressed the wetness of the material. And, as I looked down her body, I saw the contours of her waist and the sliminess of her hips. I looked at the slender legs and envied the freedom of the warm, wet, clinging fabric to touch every part of her body.

We switched off the shower and dried ourselves on the same towel. Rubbing it around our cleansed bodies. We wrapped it around both of us as we moved closer together. Then we allowed it to drop on the floor, before moving to the bed.

The memory of the evening was banished but had not gone. We had exorcised it from our minds, but not from our senses. We clung to each other and fell asleep, but we knew that we needed to be far away from England before we could expurgate the thought of that evening's pain.

I woke a few hours later to realise that it was dawn. I looked at the clock and saw that it was already past six. I remembered that I had a business meeting with the man from Banque Fucquet at seven. I quietly got out of bed and washed and shaved. I looked in the mirror. I looked haggard. I was tired. I knew I needed to get away. Unless Jacqui felt different I swore that we would. And we would do it that day.

Just before seven, I was at reception. Jacqui had been in a deep sleep in our room. As I had expected, at seven an impeccably dressed man, without a hair out of place or a part of his smooth rotund face missed by the attentions of his razor, asked for me at reception. As I approached him, the sweet smell of an eau de cologne wafted over. His trousers were pressed like a knife-edge. His jacket meanwhile had seen no unwanted crease. His club tie was perfectly knotted over his crisp cotton shirt. And an army sergeant would have been proud of his shiny shoes. If you added to those the solid gold ingot cufflinks, the large gold and onyx signet ring and the mother of pearl tie pin, you had to have a Swiss private banker.

This was the manager of Fucquet's representative office in London. Born into nobility and trained in servility, he made the perfect private banker.

As we had breakfast, I read the agreement. As usual it was penal for us and liberal for them. I really didn't care for our aim was to get the maximum cash possible. As I signed the papers with a flourish, I knew that, as long as we won our first and second plays, we would really be in the multi billion dollar plays. That could even be enough to achieve my father's dream objectives of bringing about a crisis in Asia. If the first play went well, we would be able to mobilise without suspicion, under the guise of more funds for investment from our wealthy backers, the eight hundred million we held in different banks throughout the world. And through such a crisis and with that sort of money, we would become billionaires.

The papers signed, I left my Swiss friend, pleased to have done his day's work before eight in then morning. I knew Jacqui would still be asleep and decided to go for a walk.

I turned left out of the Ritz. The streets were still fairly quiet at that time of the morning. I turned left again into St James' Park and walked down towards the Serpentine. I found a bench and, despite the coolness of a damp English morning, sat there and watched the few passers by.

There were a few joggers, some in shorts and headbands, and others in lurid jogging suits. Some ran briskly along the paths, relaxed and calm as they breathed in the semi polluted air just a few feet away from the growing morning traffic. Some seemed to run in a slow walk, puffing at the exertion of their pedestrian pace. Some walked, having perhaps jogged to the corner of their street, and then out of view preferring a more comfortable speed.

There were people walking dogs. The dogs and their owners often looked remarkably similar, either waddling in unison or alternatively mimicking each other's hairstyles. The poodle owner had frizzy hair. A bushy mane accompanied the Old English sheepdog. A plump little old lady led the podgy Pekinese. While the Afghan hound led its kaftan clad ageing hippie owner through their daily exertions.

I saw the office workers joining this group. They were mainly male, completing some interminable commute from the London suburbs. A few smart suited locals appeared in this group, walking from the mews of Belgravia to the chic of St James.

Not all my fellow companions fitted into these stereotypes. I saw the occasional young girl, still clad in the light clothes of summer, and walking, proud of her new found maturity, through the green. Then there was the odd nanny, sometimes still in uniform, pushing a sleepy child banished from the early morning routines of their busy parents. And finally I saw the old tramps; a few bundles thrust into a pram or hijacked supermarket trolley, walking aimlessly towards some warm vent or perhaps a prime location for begging.

As the crowds increased, the people merged into anonymity. They distracted from the beauty of the grass, still green in the early days of autumn. They irritated the trees, turning russet as they prepared to bare their branches for the winter. And they banished the birds flying around to find a fresh fast food snack from nature, only to replace them with arrogant pigeons looking for a casual hamburger.

I no longer felt at ease and walked back to the hotel, mingling with the crowd and yet totally removed from them. I nodded at the doormen as I entered the proud lobby of my famous temporary residence, and headed back to the few square yards that had been lent me for the night.

Jacqui was still sleeping when I quietly walked in. I picked up the newspaper, left discreetly on the doorknob outside and settled into an armchair. There was no news of murder or robbery, at least none that I recognised. Our friends in Asia had apparently decided that they could put their recent tempestuous markets behind them. They, and all the carpetbaggers they attracted, were signalling their desire to act as irrationally after the crisis they created as they had done both before and during it. Markets were moving ever more crazily higher. That was good. I knew though that this behaviour was playing into our hands and every day was bringing closer the moment when we would need to strike.

Jacqui woke up with a start. She smiled when I went over. "I forgot where we were for as moment," she said. "You look as if you had been up for ages."

"Yes I've sorted everything out with Fucquet. I had breakfast with their London man. And I also went for a short stroll in the park. We should head out to the airport some time. Would you like breakfast? Anything you want to do?"

"Let's talk while I get ready," she said. "I'll skip breakfast I'm in favour of elevenses in Fortnum's. I'd like a coffee though."

I ordered it. "I wanted to go to Boston, but I'd rather cut out as much travel as possible after last night. If you agree, let's head straight over to New York. I think we should get over there by the evening flight. It leaves around half six I think. That would mean that we get there in good time for dinner."

"I agree," said Jacqui. "That means we can go shopping here. I want to head up to Bond Street and get some new cases. And I am going to pack them myself this time. I also need some new clothes. You have a habit of getting me into fixes where I ruin what I am wearing."

"Hey" I said, "what do you mean?"

"I ruined one outfit when we got caught in the storm at Remantuelle. You didn't exactly improve my nightie yesterday when you pulled me into the shower. And I've wrecked a pile of tights. Oh, and I lost half my make up last night at customs," she said. A frown passed over her brow.

And then she added, "I bet it was Marco. He was pissed off with what you did to him. And he may have felt that my approach was pretty final, although God knows he's fairly thick skinned."

"Are you going to find it hard to get over?" I asked.

"Well, it was hardly a pleasure being held on suspicion. And I can tell you that I am no great fan of having a hand in plastic gloves pushing its way around my insides. But I'll be OK." She smiled, "Nothing that retribution and a bit of shopping won't cure."

We walked out of the hotel, arm in arm, then crossed the road and wandered through the side streets to Bond Street. I guessed that Jacqui would find all she needed there.

"Why don't you do your shopping and then we can buy cases. We may need an extra one if you excel yourself," I said.

"Hold on, you need some casual clothes as well. Most of yours are formal. They're much too formal for the US and Rio. You'll need to go into some shops. But I still want those late elevenses in Fortnum's. So let's walk up to Oxford Street and then spend our way down Bond Street."

"Is your credit card able to bear this strain?" I asked.

"Sure, the bill gets sent to my bank and they pay it. My father gives me an annual allowance and so the account is pretty flush still. It could get a bit tight towards the end of the year. But, by then, you'll be so rich that you won't mind buying me a hamburger."

We did as she said and soon stopped at several shops. We seemed to go into a variety of dress shops for clothes.

She went into Versace. It had just opened. And she squealed with delight as she found some casual clothes she adored. She stopped in the White House for a couple of nightdresses and got a fit of the giggles when the assistant asked if it was for her honeymoon trousseau.

She pulled me into a man's shop for some slacks and polo shirts, and insisted that I bought a blouson that was more her taste than mine. She stopped for make up, even though I pointed out to her that we would be able to stop in duty free at Heathrow.

"Too crowded, darling, and the selection is lousy when it comes to make up rather than perfume."

At Louis Vuitton, she enthused over luggage. "We must get rid of that assortment of un-matching things. We look shoddy." And she bought us a set of matching luggage. There were three smart leather cases that luckily fitted one inside of the other, together with a matching vanity case and, from sheer extravagance, a briefcase for me. "Darling, the other one looks as if it has been used as a skateboard."

I thought we had finished as we passed the Burlington Arcade, but she insisted in stopping off at the Ralph Lauren shop for a few odds and ends.

I got her eventually to Fortnum's, just before the lunch time crowd.

"I'll order," she said and promptly asked for a variety of sandwiches and some exotic tea. I have to admit that both were delicious although an unusual combination for a workday lunch.

"I bet you can't even recall what we bought," I said.

"I can," she replied. "And moreover I can do it down to the last item. I got two pairs of shoes. They are Ferragamo court shoes, one a high-heeled black job and the other a medium black pair. The two dresses are a red Dior sheath and a Versace off the shoulder cocktail number. I then got a bustier for fun evenings and a couple of casual tops. There is also a pair of white silk trousers. I also got a black jump suit, very tight and slinky with a plunging neckline.

"I got you a couple of pairs of slacks, a couple of casual shirts and also that blouson that you bought because I like it. Although I am not sure if you'll ever agree to wear it."

"Rubbish, I'll wear it if only to appear attractive to you," I responded.

"Well, I'm flattered. Although is it really because you can't stand the idea of not wearing it because it cost you a small fortune?"

"You make it sound as if I had Scottish blood. I actually haven't."

"Darling with a traditional British banker as a father, you have to be the sort of guy who's careful with money. Don't worry though. Your caution and my extravagance should mean that, if ever we have kids, they will turn out just right."

"Hey my former identity is gone. I am now just Charles, remember. What's this by the way of children? You're not getting broody are you? I know you Catholic girls believe it's a sin to take precautions. I don't want a surprise."

"Charles," she replied adopting a mock Italian accent, "oh per favore, you expect me to take all of the precautions. Think of the shame of me in the chemist shop asking for the pill? And they'll know I am not married. Oh the shame of it!"

"Well carry on being ashamed. It's better than the alternative," I said.

"Mmm. I suppose so. But one day I want a few bambinos. Are you offering to father them?"

"Well, let's get married first."

"That's not a proposal is it?" she joked.

The shop was full by now and we were whispering at our corner table. "No," I said. "But only because this isn't the right time and place. Not because of anything else. I love you. Soon, I'll ask you."

She smiled, lent over and kissed me. "And then soon I'll say yes. But for now it's a secret that we'll keep to ourselves."

Suddenly she got up. "Let's pay the bill, darling. I'm no longer hungry. Let's go."

She said this in a loud voice, smiling happily. The people around looked at us as if we had breached the protocol of the place. They were an unusually sombre and sober crowd even for Fortnum's. It's never a buzz of fun, but usually a bit brighter than it was that day. Two women in fussy suits gave us a disapproving look.

Jacqui gave a wicked smile. I waited. I knew she could act the exhibitionist with an evil sense of humour.

"Darling, we've got to find a hotel. I need a bed and you in it. Let's make love, loads of times," cried out Jacqui in a clear voice that carried, her eyes laughing.

The shocked looks on the faces around her spurred her on. She continued, "Your wife needn't know. Come on. You didn't buy me all these things because you wanted us to eat twee sarnies and drink tea here. Come on. Let's satisfy our carnal urges."

At this, I started laughing. The faces around us were horrified. I quickly threw a couple of twenty pound notes on the table. I assumed the bill would come to less.

And, thinking I should at least join in, I responded in kind with, "Let's run down to the Ritz. They rent the rooms by the hour if you've got a tie on."

"Oh do they?" came the response, "I'll pick one up on my way out."

I grabbed the cases and some of the bags. Jacqui picked up hers. I could see the faces looking at the mass of shopping and wondering if to believe this banter or not.

Jacqui though decided to continue, "I don't know what they put in those sandwiches but I can tell you it works better than anything I've bought in a chemist. Darling, how many girls have you seduced here over a smoked salmon sandwich and a chicken vol au vent?"

Our exit was fast, much to the relief, I suspect, of our fellow diners. I had a feeling that we had given them something to talk about.

"I wonder if any of them will try the sandwiches or the vol au vents. It would be fun to see if they do," said Jacqui as we left the august shop.

"I doubt I'll ever dare to go back there again," I said.

"Oh come on. It's all been too serious recently. We need to enjoy ourselves. I love being outrageous."

I laughed, "I think I gathered that the day we went to the Café del Arte in mid town Manhattan. Your outfit even took them by surprise."

"Hold on," she said, "That was a genuine mistake. I thought I had put on a little top under my jacket. At least I was wearing a bra."

We turned into the Ritz and got our key. I told them we would leave in a couple of hours. The great thing about hotels like that is that they do not hassle you over departure times. There was no problem that we would be around till three or four. They have enough late arrivals to allow them to get rooms ready. That is if they are full at the time.

We went upstairs and Jacqui unpacked. I checked the cases to see that there was nothing in the lining before laying them open and allowing them to be filled. Our luggage had expanded to three cases, a briefcase and a vanity bag. And they were all full.

Jacqui had changed into a mini skirt that left little to the imagination and the bustier that she had bought earlier. She topped this with what she described as gorgeously tarty high heels. She insisted I wore a pair of the slacks she had chosen, as well as one of the shirts. And of course the blouson that she had made me buy.

"I look cool and tarty," she announced as she applied a bright pink lipstick and some extravagant eye shadow. "I feel in the mood to look like that." She fluffed her hair allowing it to fall haphazardly over her shoulders. She did not look tarty in reality, more erotic and exotic. She would turn every head in the plane, some would be admiring and others reproachful. But nobody could have described her as tarty.

She looked at me and said critically, "You'll do. The shoes are a bit conservative but the rest is good."

"OK then. We need to see if we can get on the plane. Let me call," I said.

As I suspected there was no difficulty and Jacqui was overjoyed. "Where will we stay in New York?"

I thought through the different hotels I knew. "I want to ensure that we aren't recognised. Otherwise I would stay in the Pierre," I said.

"Let's stay in the Waldorf Towers," said Jacqui. "I feel like a steak and we could get a table at Smith and Wolenski in the evening."

I nodded in agreement. The Waldorf Towers was just right. It was comfortable and normally quite crowded and impersonal albeit rather pretentious. S&W was one of the best steak places in New York and we had been there before when we had been famished.

"I'll get reception to book the Waldorf. I don't think that they will be indiscreet."

Jacqui nodded and I called down, advising we would leave at four and requesting the reservation. I then took out my mobile and dialled a number. I did not recognise the voice that responded. "Is Di Maglio there?" I said. "Tell him it's from De Roche."

He came to the phone. "It was Marco. He confessed. He did it for revenge. He planted two bugs in your cases. The second is in the handle of the suit carrier. Can I speak to Jacqui?"

"What did you do to Marco?" I asked.

"We beat him up rather badly before he confessed. Then he tried to run away from us. We were on the roof of a block of flats near Nice. I am afraid he fell the whole ten floors. I saw an ambulance," he laughed quite evilly, "but the paramedics weren't called."

I passed the phone to Jacqui. She talked for a few moments to her father and then she said, "I believe you. Why don't you take the opportunity to get rid of the shitty things he ran? If you run that type of company, you will always be involved with the Marcos of this world."

I doubt he responded enthusiastically as, after a few more terse comments, she rang off.

We lazed around for the rest of our time. And then took a cab to the airport. I hardly liked the idea of going through the airport again. This time though we whisked through and were soon in the first class lounge waiting for the call to board the plane.

Jacqui had attracted quite a few glances. The first class lounge in Heathrow's terminal four is a male dominated room. When the stewardess asked for coats and other hand items before we boarded, Jacqui winked mischievously at me and took off her jacket. The mini skirt was mini to the extreme. Her midriff was bare, and the bustier plunged and pushed up her full breasts. The conversation on several tables stopped.

"Aren't you going to be cold?" I asked.

"Perhaps we will have to make mile high love to warm me up?"

I smiled at her, happy that we had moved near to the world where we used to live. I put my arm round her.

"If you are going to misbehave, then I am going to have to cancel the flight and book into one of the cheap hotels around here. That will solve my problem and, with a bit of luck, it could help yours."

She kissed me as we walked on board. It is strange in first class across the Atlantic. Either you are a businessman and work or a super rich from whom everybody accepts outrageous behaviour as normal. Perhaps it is because one needs to be slightly mad, even as a businessman, to pay an airline exorbitant prices for a little more space and slightly less bad food for a few hours.

We landed in New York a couple of hours by the clock after we left London. You don't hang around for your cases when you travel first class and soon we had piled into an airport limousine and were heading through the gloom of New York towards the centre. As we drove up outside the hotel, I leant over and murmured to Jacqui, "Welcome back."

In our room, I called my parents. My father was feeling fine and would be out of hospital in the next day or two. He had to relax but would be fully mobile within a week. And by the end of the month he was likely to be as good as new. My mother was going to do her teeth the next day.

"When are you coming over to Rio? You should have yours done as we planned."

"We'll stay in New York for today and take a plane either tomorrow or the next day. I prefer to book at the last minute as we are scared of being followed. So if you book us a room from tomorrow, we will be safe whatever we do."

We did as we had planned that day. We did get to Smith and Wolenski and did have a huge steak and a bottle of Californian red. It was becoming like the old days and we appeared to have put our recent problems behind us. In fact it was almost as if they had never been.

We were in the hotel again before midnight. We put on Music TV and they were just playing a slow smoochy ballad. I took Jacqui in my arms and we slowly started to dance in the splendour of our boudoir like room.

My hands felt the cool warmth of her bare midriff as I moved them up and down her back and then to below her waist to play with the hem of her skirt. She lent against me, the warmth of her body seeping through my clothes. Her hands moved inside my jacket and gently peeled it off my shoulders.

As it fell on the floor, my hands moved back up over her waist and round to her breasts. This time there was no resistance as I gently caressed her. I felt her move her body so that she pressed up against my cupped hands. I moved round to the back of the flimsy garment and clumsily started to undo the hooks. Her hands moved from my neck and gently removed my hands. The g a rment opened up in an instant, only held to her by my body against hers. I moved a half step away to allow it to fall to the ground.

Her hands moved to the buttons of my shirt and she undid them one by one. At each button she stopped and caressed me gently, until the shirt also fell to the ground and joined her bustier on the floor. I pulled her again towards me and felt her naked flesh against me. She moved her body slowly across my chest until I held her tightly. Then as my hands moved back down her body, she started again.

Her skirt offered no resistance and the narrow band of cloth soon fell to the rest. I knelt down and gently rolled down her tights. She stepped out of them as I caressed her gently, burying my head gently into her body. I hooked my hands round her panties, still kneeling in front of her and slid them over her willing hips and legs.

I pulled her naked towards me and we kissed. At first it was tenderly. And finally quite frantically. Moments later I was stripped next to her. We were on the bed, making love with passion. We tried to get closer and closer. I held on to her body, putting my arms around her and pulling her closer to me. She too seized me and pressed me ever closer to herself.

We made love, a deep passionate tempestuous love. We stayed together for a time afterwards. Then, almost reluctantly, we moved apart. But it was only to lie together and hold each other as closely as one can without making love itself.

That night we came together more than once and the next morning we stayed in bed through part of the morning. We did not want to stay in New York for another night. We knew that we would only try to repeat the sensations of the night before. And we knew that we would only spoil the memory.

In the afternoon, we were on the plane to Rio.

PLANNING FOR A FORTUNE

We landed in Rio on time and a hotel limousine was waiting for us at the exit to customs. I was relieved that nobody even gave us a second look as we walked through passport control. Both of us were on edge as we transited customs but without cause.

We had a wonderful room on an upper floor with a spectacular view. The beach in the distance looked inviting, but I sensed that we had had our holiday in New York. It was unlikely that my father would allow us to forget why we were here. Now that we had funds available well ahead of plan and markets looked ripe for action, he would be single minded in his pursuit of his objective of making that billion dollars plus and more.

True to form, we had only just unpacked when the phone rang.

"How are you both? Come up to my room and have a drink. We can then go and see your father. They are keeping him in a couple of days longer as he says he is in a bit of pain. Men are usually unable to cope with that. And he is a bit of a hypochondriac as well."

"Mother, nice to hear you. Sure, we would love to join you. What's your room number?"

I took the number and Jacqui and I walked up one flight of stairs to my mother's room. It was a suite, a bit larger than our bedroom. They had expected to spend some time in it as my father recovered. My mother looked fit and well, dressed in casual slacks and a light silk shirt. She was small next to Jacqui, who seemed to glisten with health after her day or so of total relaxation.

"You both look well," said my mother. "You gave us a fair share of frights with all your escapades. Are you sure that you haven't been followed here?"

"Positive," I replied. "We checked the airlines and found that there were two planes with masses of spare seats. They suggested we went stand by. So I only booked fifteen minutes before the plane left. I put us in business class and that meant we got on the plane immediately, but were not as visible as if we had gone first. We were on board ten minutes or so after getting to the ticketing desk and perhaps within half an hour of reaching the airport. We also kept a close look on the passengers getting on and off the plane."

"Yes," said Jacqui. "And nobody looked at us. There were a couple of women who glanced over at Charles but I soon put a stop to that. I grabbed hold of him and glared over."

"Hey, why so proprietorial?" I responded.

"Because," she said, "that's my prerogative. I don't share."

"Quite right," said my mother. "You two seem to be getting on fine. Don't let anybody else interfere."

I noted the encouragement. She knew I would make my mind up. She was just signalling that she liked Jacqui.

I poured them each a soft drink and grabbed a beer for myself. "When do we go and see dad?" I asked.

"We can go tomorrow morning, if you want. What time will you two love birds get up then?"

"Oh," responded Jacqui, "we're like a staid married couple. We can be up at the crack of dawn if you want. We go to bed early and rise with the dawn."

"I may be older my dear," said my mother, "but I am not blind or stupid. I dislike hanging around and so suggest that we meet at around half nine in the lobby."

With that we headed back to our room. "Well that put us in our place," said Jacqui. "Don't disappoint her. She wants us to have a good time tonight."

The next morning we went downstairs and saw my mother in the lobby. She was talking to a stranger and she looked agitated. My first thought was that something had happened to my father. I then noticed that the man was holding my mother's arm. And there were two other men who were standing beside her.

I turned to Jacqui. "They could be police. They are definitely not friendly. Let's just stand clear and see what happens."

My mother saw us and I noted the quick warning flash of her eyes. I was right. We had trouble. I was close by. My mother pulled her arm from the man's grip and ran to the door, shouting, "Leave me alone. I've done nothing. I don't know what my husband is supposed to have done. We're just here on holiday."

The man caught up with her and pulled her arms roughly behind her back. I understood fully her message. I pulled Jacqui aside. "Let's go. We should pack. These guys may come back and look for me. I think it's time to stop playing at Charles De Roche. Until I am certain, you are sleeping with Charles Feraud. But be careful how you use that name. I haven't any papers to support it any more."

"What about the Swiss banks?" she asked.

"I need to rearrange the money and fast. I don't want anything in the De Roche name. The money in Switzerland is OK as that is all in the company name. The funds in France are in a joint account under De Roche. They will have to be moved."

We went upstairs and packed. I left the television on as I did but the news had nothing on my parents. A quarter of an hour later we were out of the hotel. I had checked out and hoped that I was off the guest list. I did not know if the police would look for me but I knew, from my mother's warning, that neither she nor my father would mention my existence.

I turned to Jacqui. "We have two options. We can either get out ourselves or we try to spring them from the police. That could be a bit difficult, as we haven't any guns. With guns it would be easier. The UK police are unlikely to be armed although we cannot be certain of any local ones."

Jacqui said, "We should spring them. The De Roche name is dead but you don't need to use it anyway. You are going to have to use a passport to get out of Brazil but in the US I can get you an identity switch without difficulty. I suspect the police will have sealed off your mother's bedroom. There may be things inside."

"Could you dress up as a maid and get in without them noticing?" I asked.

"We could try," she said "but it is going to be tough to brazen that one out. Let's get rid of the cases first."

We got into a cab and drove to the airport. Then, instead of heading to the planes, we took two adjoining rooms in one of the airport hotels. We rented a car and headed back into Rio.

"We need different clothes," said Jacqui "and also stuff for your parents."

In the shops we found all we wanted. We bought dark jeans, dark sweaters, sunglasses and caps for Jacqui and me. Similar outfits that we thought would fit my parents together with a wig for my mother. Jacqui also got hair dye from a pharmacy. "We may need that."

We got a map of Brazil and worked out how we could drive from Rio and head to a provincial airport. That would be a safer point from which to leave.

"I could leave you all there and get false papers. Then I could pick you up," said Jacqui.

"Yes, but first of all we need to spring my parents," I said. "Otherwise we may as well just leave."

We returned to the original hotel, carrying our new clothes. There is never any problem in getting into a hotel if you are smartly dressed. We had soon made our way to the twenty-fourth floor where my mother's room was located. A maid was passing.

"I'll grab her," I said. "It's the only way."

I walked along the corridor behind her. I was lucky as she stopped and unlocked a door to a storeroom near the lifts. She smiled at me as I went past. The smile turned to fear. Her mouth opened to scream, but to no avail. My hand was firmly clamped around her mouth and my arms stopped her kicking and struggling from having any effect. I bundled her into the storeroom and Jacqui hurriedly joined me.

"She's a bit smaller than me. Her clothes are going to be a bit tight," she said.

"We can't help it. You won't wear them for long."

I grabbed a hand towel from one of the shelves and fashioned it into a gag. As I put it over her mouth, I told the trembling girl, "Nothing will happen to you as long as you do all we say."

Jacqui moved forward and stripped off the girl's skirt, blouse, and pinafore. She was a slim girl. I looked at her closely and she blushed as she felt my eyes on her. I smiled. I wasn't looking at her for that reason. It was just that her figure was slimmer than Jacqui's. She was also smaller. I was wondering if the clothes would fit. I had to admit though the body was a rather pleasing one. Jacqui took her slacks and blouse off. And I knew that was an even more pleasing body. The waistband of the skirt fitted, but it was ridiculously tight around the hips. It was also a good inch or two shorter than it ought to have been. The same problem arose with the blouse, which was a size to small and strained over Jacqui's full figure. The maid had been quite a small build, and, although Jacqui had a perfect figure, it was of the 34C variety on a five foot eight inch frame.

"You'll have to do," I said, as I tied up the maid with a sheet. She won't be able to move for a bit. Let's go."

Jacqui opened the store door and picked up a pile of towels. "I can at least cover my boobs if this blouse rips," she said. "Let's hope the skirt is made of stronger material."

I watched her walk down the corridor and then lost sight of her as

173

she turned the corner. I followed at a distance. She was in front of my mother's room and talking to the police guard. He was a local policeman and he was gazing at Jacqui's tight outfit with undisguised lust.

She saw me waiting and winked. I realised immediately what she planned. Soon her hand was running down the policeman's chest, and carrying on further to his crotch. There it stopped, and from the look on his face, must have tweaked him or something. She lent forward and whispered something in his ear, leaning against him and pulling his hand round her waist.

She took the master key she had taken from the maid and unlocked the door of my mother's room. The policeman was too engrossed in her to notice me coming up behind him. As he entered the room, I came up behind and pushed him forward. He stumbled against Jacqui as I closed the door. At that moment her knee rose quickly and caught him squarely in the crotch. He collapsed in a heap, and, by the time he had recovered, looked at me in surprise as a large porcelain vase came crashing down on his head. He collapsed unconscious and bleeding from the wound in the head. We tied him up, but not before searching him.

"Bingo," I said. "He was carrying a gun. At least we are armed. That will help. I'll get the girl. I have an idea. They'll find it hard to get anyone to fully believe their stories."

I went to the storeroom. Jacqui was meanwhile carefully searching the room. I checked that the corridor was empty and carried the girl into the room. It was a risk. But we had been taking risks all along.

"Strip him," I said to Jacqui. "But watch out, he's coming round."

She completed her task and I retied him with some sheets. I then put him on the bed. Jacqui did the same to the girl. I then took another sheet and bound them together. The poor things were facing each other. Their bodies touched and, hurt as he was, the poor cop was reacting quite visibly. Both he and the girl were trying to squirm away from each other. There is no doubt that they would not find it comfortable. And, when found, it would be hard to make up a credible story.

"Did you find anything?" I asked Jacqui.

"That was stupid of them," she said as she produced a handgun from a briefcase. They must have had that on the plane. I wonder how they got through security with it."

"Give it to me" I said and I tied it to my leg. I had to use a piece of sheet that I tore off from the one on the bed. But it was as effective as tape.

"False papers," said Jacqui as she looked through the contents of the case. I think we need these. I can't see anything else. I think its time to go."

I went back to the store and grabbed Jacqui's clothes. She pulled them on and we made sure the maid got a good look at us. On the way out we stopped off in the storeroom and changed into our newly acquired outfits. I shoved our old clothes and those I had brought from the bedroom into a bag. This, in turn, I stuffed behind a pile of sheets at the back of the storeroom.

"No, I am hoping the girl will describe the clothes we were wearing and so it's better that they don't find them too soon. They could also trace the labels perhaps. Mine are all designer stuff and not sold in that many places," said Jacqui. "Let's get them back and let's take them with us."

I did and we exited the hotel as calmly as we had entered.

"I wonder if they'll manage to untie themselves or if someone will find them," said Jacqui.

"I have no idea. He's going to have to explain why he was in the room in the first place. And the poor girl's story doesn't look too credible. I suspect that they are going to be under suspicion. I feel sorry for them, but there was no other way."

"No" said Jacqui. "We had to do it. Poor sods! Now we need to find out where your parents are and how to free them."

We went into a café and saw that the news was on. Sure enough an item about my parents was shown.

"They already have an extradition warrant. They will be flown out this evening. They are being held in a prison in the centre. Let's check the flight times. We are going to have to get them as they are moved to the airport."

We checked these out and realised that they were likely to be moved in about an hour or two.

"We need to be there early," said Jacqui.

"I need a phone though," I said. I found a public one that took credit cards and called Fucquet. I established that the De Roche name as a signature on the account would not lead to its disclosure. I told Pierre that I gathered a relative had been involved in embezzlement but the fund was nothing to do with him and I did not want them to be the subject of any publicity.

It was obvious that he believed the money related to the Di Maglio clan. He was going to keep quiet. Of that there was no doubt.

I called Hochzeit. I had little concerns about them. Although they were the Swiss subsidiary of one of the biggest European banks, they had a powerful reputation for shadiness. They made it clear that they did not care if the money came from Attila the Hun or Adolf Hitler. Bank secrecy was more important than any minor law.

I finally called United and asked them to remit the balance of the funds in their Monte Carlo account to their branch in Geneva. The money would be there the next day.

"I think the cash is OK," I said. "I'm a bit nervous about United, because they are honest. But the risk is only on a few million. The seed money is secure."

I then drove the car to a side street near the prison. We looked at the area.

Jacqui pointed out, "This is a fast road and there are a whole series of side streets that lead to the boulevard on the other side of this block. That gives us the best chance of avoiding being followed."

I added, "With a bit of luck they will not be accompanied. They are hardly categorised as violent. But the police will get their clothes and things before they leave. There will be concern at the break into their room at some point. We just have to hope that it is after their departure from the station."

"If the British police act to form," said Jacqui, "they will leave early and that plays into our hands."

"OK, you sit in the car at that side street. You can park at the meter there. I'll watch the station. As far as I can see they must come out of the front. There appears no rear exit. They have got to turn right, as it's one way. I hit them a block up before they gather speed. As you see me move, pull into the main road and be ready to pick me up and hopefully my parents. If anything goes wrong, you don't know me."

Jacqui nodded and we got the car and parked at the meter, which luckily had remained empty. I walked down the street opposite the station. I had been hanging around for just under an hour when the car pulled out of the station. My parents were in the back. In the front was one of the men I had seen in the hotel. Next to him was a man I failed to recognise. They were not followed and the police appeared totally relaxed. I suspect they thought they had a harmless, if high profile, case of white-collar crime.

As they drew up, I pulled the cap over my face, pulled my gun and calmly shot out the tyres of their car. Before they could even get out, I had the gun inside the window.

"I want your passengers, not you," I said in a heavily accented English. I glanced at my parents. They had been put in handcuffs but were not joined together. "The car keys," I said to the driver. He passed them over and I dropped them down the drain by my feet.

Everybody around the car dived for cover or made himself or herself scarce. It did not look as if there were going to be any heroes on the streets of Rio that day. And luckily there was no heavy traffic. There was no car between the corner where Jacqui was now and the immobilised car carrying my parents to their home country and trial.

Jacqui drew up and my parents read the situation immediately. They jumped into the car. I shot out the remaining tyres. A motor bike cop was now roaring to the scene, his radio blaring. I shot at his bike. I missed but he swerved and went flying across the street.

"The handcuff keys," I snarled. They hesitated. I fired a shot into the floor of the rear seat. That jerked them into action. They handed it to me.

"Adios," I said. And I waved cheerfully to them as they sat in shocked silence in their seats in the now immobilised vehicle.

Jumping into the car, I shouted, "Drive" to Jacqui. Her foot jammed down on the accelerator and the car roared away. At the same time I emptied the gun in the air. Behind me in the one way street, I had caused maximum chaos. The shots had startled motorists and there were a series of minor pile-ups. Passers-by had thrown themselves down on the pavement, fearful of more direct gunfire. Even if the police wanted to get out of the station car park, they would be delayed for precious minutes that would help us get away.

"Left," I yelled and Jacqui swerved into a side street. The left wheels hit the curb but she regained control as she rebounded into the centre of the street.

"Left again," I called. We were on an open freeway already and we tore down it. We turned off the freeway into a side street and went through several more.

"Dump the car here," I called. "Everybody get out."

There was nobody around. I passed the clothes to my parents, keeping watch for danger. "Change here and put your old stuff into the bag."

My mother queried, "In the open?"

I responded sharply, "Do it and do it now. Your clothes are known and these are anonymous."

I unlocked their handcuffs and threw them into the car with the key. They changed. It hardly took a moment. "Walk," I said, "I'm going to destroy the car. That will gain us a bit more time. Nobody will be surprised at a bit of vandalism in this area. There are matches in the car. The previous rental must have been a smoker."

They headed up the street. I opened the petrol tank. I grabbed Jacqui's blouse from the bag and stuffed it loosely down the pipe to the tank. I pulled it out. It was damp with petrol. I eased it in again. Then I threw the bag of clothes into the back of the car and, taking a match from the box that I had seen in the car, I lit the end of the blouse. As I ran away, it was blazing merrily with the flames moving up towards the mouth of the tank.

I joined the others and we ran up the street and then turned left into a side street. "Slow down to a stroll, or we'll attract attention," I said as a huge explosion shook the houses with a deafening roar. "There must have been more petrol in the tank than I thought. It's going to take them a time to identify who rented it. Well, that'll be another De Roche who needs to change his identity."

We went through the maze of streets until once again we came to a main road. There we grabbed the first taxi we could find and told him to take us to the airport.

From the airport to our rooms took hardly a moment. We shut the doors and joined each other via the communicating one. My mother threw her arms round Jacqui. My father hugged me. I kissed Jacqui.

"We did it," I called. "Now we have to get out of Rio."

"I am the least known," said Jacqui. "Moreover, my name is not on any hotel register. I'll hire a car. In the meantime you two should arrange your hair. Mr De Roche should take the grey dye and Charles take the blond. Do your eyebrows as well."

"OK but once you have the car, we move. I don't like the ideas of staying in Rio."

My parents nodded. We went about the tasks with the television on. It carried news of the shooting and the dramatic escape. I switched over to CNN. They were not covering the story as yet.

Then there was a sudden shift on CNN. They had picked up the story. The picture of my parents came onto the screen. It was an old photo that must have been provided by the police in England.

"Did they take a new photo?" I asked. My parents shook their heads.

"Excellent, it will make it more difficult to identify you."

"How did they catch you? Have you any idea?"

"They must have been tipped off by someone. I can't work out by whom though," my father said.

"Think carefully, it's important that we know. It reduces the risks to us all," I said.

My father shook his head. "I really don't know. I'm sure we did everything right."

I noticed that CNN had switched stories and a picture of the car, its tyres deflated, appeared. Then there was another one of two embarrassed looking policemen with no answer when questioned about the lax security.

The CNN reporter said that the police believed that a gang who would seek to find the stolen cash had kidnapped the couple. Police were worried that they would be killed once the gang had accessed their money.

The CNN reporter said that two men in dark clothes and caps had led the raid. One was described as tall and well built, while the other was said to be medium height and slim build. They were described as speaking with a strong Colombian accent. The implication was that the drug cartels could have been involved. The description of the car was much clearer. Obviously it had not yet been found. I was amused that they thought Jacqui was a man, but then she had only been seen behind the wheel of her car.

There was no mention of the policeman and maid at the hotel. I assumed they had not yet been found, or the connection had not yet been made.

Then the CNN reporter started to look at the background of the story. He commented:

"The couple travelled from Madrid to Rio over the last week. They were travelling under a false name. They had changed their identity and were called De Roche. The name was used because it is a quite common French name meaning a rock. It is also known that the husband had sought plastic surgery in Rio and had already had one operation.

The wife had been staying in Rio and was recognised by a former colleague of her husband who was in the city for business. Police had been following her for twenty four hours before they arrested her husband in the early hours of the morning; and then arrested her as she attempted to leave the hotel to visit her husband."

I noted that there was no mention of Jacqui or me. I realised that could be a ploy although I doubted it. I also thought that the fact that the police felt my parents might be killed was a good thing. That could relax vigilance at the airports.

"That's why you were tracked. It was pure coincidence. They will try to find how you got to Madrid, but their chances of success are almost zero. The trail is too difficult and random. It's possible also that they believe the Colombian story. If they do that's good for us."

Everyone agreed. We then described what we had done since the arrest.

I explained how we had raided my mother's room. Both my parents found my description hilarious. The thought of the two in the bed, bound together and almost naked, slightly shocked them.

"The poor girl's reputation will be ruined," they said.

"True," I said and shrugged my shoulders. "But I doubt it will be permanent."

"Now look we found the gun. That was stupid bringing it through security."

"We didn't," said my father. "I bought it in Rio in case we needed it."

I was surprised. I had not realised that they were so concerned about their safety and I had not thought they would even know how to go about buying a gun illegally.

"There was a pile of papers. Do we need them? We took them but did not have time to look at them," I asked.

"They are our old passports and other documents. I decided in England at the last minute that we should keep the old documents and I have been carrying them around with me," said my father.

"That was a bit dangerous. Couldn't you have been stopped by the police or customs and been searched?" I queried.

"I don't think so. At worst we would have been stopped. Police and customs never really look through papers."

"Anyway they will save us quite a bit of bother. We thought we were going to have to get a hideaway for the three of us while Jacqui crossed over the border to get some new papers from the USA.

I can't see any risk in using them for you as they think you are kidnapped and, in any event, they think you are travelling under the De Roche name. They won't be bright enough to look for the Ryders as well, even if they were on alert.

I can't believe that the local police didn't go through your papers. There is no reason why they would have left them in that case. The room did not appear to have been searched. My guess is that they were planning to tidy things up some time today. They seem to have been very slapdash. They had only posted a guard and hadn't planned really what to do about the stuff in the room.

Anyway it's important to move about and get to a safe haven. And the best one will be the health club in California. It's isolated and we will blend in well once we have as tan and that can be arranged almost immediately with a tanning machine."

At that point Jacqui returned. She had hired a car and wanted us to leave at once. "We don't need to check out. That way they will think we are still here. And it is not unusual in airport hotels for people to leave without paying. They took a credit card imprint and they will just pass the bill to the card. The only risk is that they associate me with the De Roche name. In time they may, but for the moment we are OK."

I told Jacqui about my parents' new use of their real identities. She laughed, "That will make the journey easier. But we had better all change identities again in the USA as my name could be uncovered here and then the Ryder name would also be associated with me through immigration."

"I have to use the De Roche name myself as I have no alternative. But I am thirty years younger than the fugitives and so that should not be dangerous. But I'd like to get a new identity as soon as possible. Forty eight hours without trace may make the police revisit their theories."

We took our cases. We had enough luggage for four although my parents had nothing but the clothes they were wearing and the papers I had bought. That would not be a problem as we could stock up again when we got to the USA.

"Let's move then," I said. "Everybody take a piece of luggage. Another good thing about these airport hotels is that, as you either prepay or leave the voucher, nobody stops you if you are carrying luggage. Especially as nobody in places like this is really keen to help you."

Minutes later we were down to the garage and piled into the car Jacqui had rented. It was the sort of medium sized car that everyone ignores on the road. The idea was to drive to Sao Paulo and then take a plane that would bring us to Mexico. From there we would drive up to the US, crossing near San Diego into California.

"We will be a good eight hours on the road. I daren't take the fast road as the police could be watching it. The one I have planned is not bad. Apparently there are a lot of visitors who want to see the real Brazil. And they use these types of road. So that's what we are. Our alibi is that we are

181

nature lovers who are in search of beauty. At least that's an excuse to allow us to explain why we are avoiding Brasilia."

"I gather the road's OK for the first hundred miles. That's good as it will mean that we will be clear of the Rio area that bit quicker. And the further away we are the safer we will be. But we need to be careful. The police will be on the look out for us soon. So we have to exit Brazil. And I would prefer to be out of Mexico. We can stay in the US at the health farm for a couple of months at least. And that will be enough time to kill the enthusiasm of the police."

We headed out of the airport and picked up the right road quickly. In the end the journey was quite fun. Jacqui and my parents had never really talked for any period of time. They chatted away merrily and seemed oblivious of the dangers that we faced. I suspected that was a good thing for, in the event of the police stopping us, I could see no option other than a shoot out. And I did not fancy doing that with only one gun. The one I had taken off the policeman had been emptied in the attack on the car.

I carefully made sure that we did not attract attention. I dutifully obeyed all the rules I could think of.

After three hours I pulled in and let Jacqui take over at the wheel. We had actually covered half the planned distance. I suspected the journey would slow down now for we had got off the main roads and could get stuck behind slow moving trucks and buses at this stage. I suspected that Jacqui's temperament was better suited to such driving.

After a further two hours, we changed shifts again. The night had by now drawn in and there was an ominous silence in the now deserted roads.

"Should we make a stop over?" I suggested. "Any hotel is hardly going to be luxurious, but it may be better than braving these roads."

"No," said my father sternly. "We would stick out like a sore thumb in a provincial off the track hotel. We need to get to the airport and on to a plane to Mexico. We look like adventurers at the moment in these outfits. I think we'll be all right. I find my grey hair rather attractive. I am less certain about your blond curls, Charles. They're slightly effeminate although if you keep your arm around Jacqui, the rumours shouldn't be too convincing."

It was in that relaxed mood that we covered the rest of the journey to Sao Paulo. The first option to leave was by a British Airways flight to Santiago. I took four seats on it, mainly because it left in an hour.

I went back to the others. "We have got four seats on the Santiago plane. The good news is that it will be by BA. The bad news is two had to be economy. I hate to say this, but I think that our senior citizens need to be in the back. We can hardly play the impoverished traveller with the luggage that Jacqui bought. I got these two holdalls for you. We should stuff some casual clothes in them. Nobody is going to worry if you travel light. The back cabin will also be less personal and so you should be able to blend into the background much more easily. Jacqui and I need to change into something smarter."

Everybody agreed with the plan. We watched my parents through customs and emigration. And then, without any problems, they boarded the plane. Finally a Miss Di Maglio and a Mr De Roche went into club class. It was not surprising that there was a Mr and Mrs Ryder in the rear section. The name was not an uncommon sounding one.

Plane journeys are rarely exciting and this one wasn't. We landed and avoided immigration by heading straight to transit. We joined up now as we felt the risks of us being trailed were sufficiently low. The plan was to change airline to make it more difficult to trail us. My father and I went to one of the toilets and got rid of the holdalls, transferring back the clothes into our smart luggage.

Next stop was Lima and we repeated our exercise there for Bogota and then on to Mexico City. By this time we were exhausted and distinctly grubby.

An airport hotel beckoned. I turned to my parents and suggested, "We'll book in separately. That's a safe precaution. Let's meet again at ten tomorrow morning. That will give you time to eat from room service, wash and have a really good long sleep. There's a direct flight to Houston tomorrow and we're going to have to try and get it. If it's full we'll revert to the old plan and drive up to San Diego. The problem is that we're all too tired for too long a drive now. So if we can avoid it, even if it is a bit riskier, I think we should."

Everybody wearily agreed. Half an hour later our room echoed with splashing water. Soon after, a plate of the plastic food that marks a hotel dependent on the transit passenger was served and eagerly consumed. The beds were functional. At least they were clean. And within an hour or so of entering the room, we were fast asleep.

The next morning, I went over to the airport. The planes were only half full and so getting a seat on the Houston flight was easy. I headed back to the hotel. It was with some trepidation that I waited for my parents at ten the following morning. The clock moved on and they did not appear. I paced up and down in reception, impatiently glancing around.

"Sorry we're late. We only realised the time change half an hour ago. We'd adjusted our watches but not enough."

I turned round gratefully when I heard my mother's voice and explained our plans. "I suggest we board at the last minute. Jacqui's upstairs giving herself a beauty treatment. If you want one, Mum, I suspect she has all the creams you would need. We have time."

We all agreed and so the women made up while my father and I watched television. There was no news from Rio. I got the impression that this disappointed my father. It definitely did not bother me.

Even customs and immigration at Houston were pleasant. They believed that we were in the USA on business. Transit was helpful and we got onto a flight to San Francisco.

As it touched down and we drove in an air-conditioned limousine to Union Square and our hotel, I breathed a sigh of relief.

"All right. We have two days here. Jacqui can organise the paperwork. And we will also organise security." They knew I meant guns. I now felt safer when armed. I had dumped our previous weapons before we boarded the plane at Sao Paulo.

"You two need clothes. Dad should see a doctor for a check up. But that would be risky."

"I'm fine," he said.

"Me too," said my mother. "My teeth don't worry me at all."

"I'm not going ahead with the dental treatment. And if you are going to get outfits here in San Francisco then we may do without that trip to Italy you had planned. We can do the haircuts here in any case. I would like to avoid borders for a bit. And, in any event, we can run the Asia business from here if we need to."

I turned to my father, "You're the expert but I reckon they're going to go wild."

"They are," he said, "and they'll go wilder. And when they have gone really berserk, we'll strike. I suspect that is going to be sooner rather than later, but not for a few weeks yet."

CALIFORNIA

That night we all slept the sleep of the innocent. Jacqui must have woken up first. The curtains were wide opened and the September sunshine flowed into the room.

I turned to look for her and saw her walking out of the bathroom. She was dressed only in her panties and bra.

Jacqui noticed the look in my eyes. "Oh no," she said, "I've just done a grade one make up and we need to get out. We've a busy day ahead of us."

"But we've been so exhausted for the last couple of nights that we have just crashed out," I protested.

"Think of me and my body all day," she retorted, "And then we can really enjoy ourselves tonight. I'll even take you to a night-club where you can plot your moves."

I sighed and got up. She looked at me and arched her eyebrows. "Mmm. I must wear these things more often. They appear to have a greater effect than the advertisement claimed." She looked down at them, "Definitely x rated stuff this La Perla."

She turned to me "Come on or it'll be a cold shower."

I dressed, planning for the day. Above all, we needed to get some new papers. We had never thought that we would have to change our identities yet again. That did not matter as far as our finances were concerned. The arrangements with the Swiss banks were such that they had no interest in our real identities as long as we had the passwords or other arrangements in hand to access our accounts. But not everyone was that easy. We needed new passports, credit cards and permits for cars or guns. It was lucky that Jacqui had memorised long ago the names of suppliers of a variety of goods in all the main cities of America as well as key countries overseas.

We would need the papers to get the cards. We would need the papers to get the guns, for now we could not exist without them. We had to get some cash till we got our credit cards.

I marvelled though how Jacqui was able to rustle these up at a moments' notice. She had explained to me that one of the reasons why the Mafia owned some small banks was, in fact, to be able to issue credit cards. In America, you can't exist without a piece of plastic, and it was getting more difficult in Europe and Asia. But in America, large sums of cash created suspicion. So we needed to put our finances in order.

We went for one of those rich American breakfasts that please and add to the obesity of a nation. After that, I called my parents. My father had had all the papers brought to his room and was catching up on events in Asia. My mother said that he was going to be there all day and would use room service. She planned to go shopping and would have liked to meet us for lunch. We explained our unusual shopping list of papers, cards and weapons.

"I doubt we will be able to do all we need in that time," said Jacqui. "But how about getting together for a drink at six or seven? Perhaps six would be better. We can then wonder over to Fisherman's Wharf for a meal."

"OK dear," said my mother. "I'll stock up on clothes for myself and your father. I don't need him there. The way he is these days, he just pulls on what first comes to hand."

We made sure she knew the direction and got a scolding, "Don't be silly. I know the area a bit and can speak a version of the language at least. I'll wear the wig and that black outfit. Nobody's going to recognise me. And I know I have to pay in cash. We have plenty of that for the time being thanks to Jacqui. We must pay her back soon."

"You know you'll have to play the dumb foreigner," I said. "Otherwise they'll be wary of your cash."

"I understood that the first time you said it to me. I may be older than you but I am not yet senile you know. I can fend for myself."

I laughed, "Point taken."

Jacqui had raided her account earlier through one of the cash machines at the airport. So, my mother was stocked up with ten thousand dollars. That should suffice.

We grabbed a tram from the hotel and then a cab to a fairly dubious part of the city.

The grim tenements towered together. The place was grimy. The streets were covered in litter and other evidence of human misery. The needles were propped up against the verges, having abandoned their skeletal hosts long before.

People hung around the street corners. They looked at us as we passed. Their looks were both angry and challenging. We avoided eye contact but the antipathy of the bottom rung of the city's underclass made me distinctly nervous. This was not a healthy district for Jacqui and me. We did not belong here. And this part of the city disliked intruders.

Jacqui looked around it, "I doubt I would come here on my own for fear of being mugged or raped. I wish we were armed but I want our papers first. By the way the man we are seeing works freelance for my father. I doubt he will do anything funny."

The man in question looked like an absent minded university professor. He had white hair that fell over his collar and ears. His face was unmarked. He looked slightly owl like with small wire rimmed glasses and a high forehead. He seemed to be wearing a strange assortment of shabby but clean garments. Brown suit trousers, a cream jacket, a green shirt and a speckled tie. It was hardly haute couture, but it actually suited him.

"Darling, sweetie, hello," he cried at Jacqui in an incredibly camp voice. "Who's the hunk? Is he girl only?"

Jacqui kissed him on the cheek. "I'm fine. The hunk is Charles. He's very conservative and just into me this week. And it's the same the next one as well."

"I hope you're not doing anything naughty. You're pure Italian blood you know. They only marry virgins. I hope your studies didn't teach you bad habits."

Jacqui laughed. "Oh the horror of a good education. I'll have to remain a spinster or marry outside the family. Look, seriously I need your help. I want four new identities. We all need a passport, driving licence, social security and the lot. Give us Italian nationality. That allows us to go freely anywhere in Europe."

He dropped the playful tone, "Were you sent by your father or are you working on your own?"

"We're freelance. We need to change documents. The police are pretty sore with us. I don't think they know I'm involved. They most likely don't know about Charles but they are looking for the other two. There's a full Interpol alert for them."

"What have you brought with you?"

"Their old documents. They are called De Roche," she answered.

"Let me see." He looked at the documents. He nodded.

"These are good. They are fake ones of course. This is very like the real thing. Only an expert forger like me would recognise the difference. I suppose you don't want them back. That will reduce the price."

"Keep them if that's the case," I said. The De Roche ones would not be of any use to us any more. I was indifferent if the man had them. He needed to use the photo in any case. He would then recycle them. He had no interest in talking to the police. And by now, I was certain that the Di Maglios would know who the famous De Roches were. Even if they had not made the connection when they met me, by now they would have put two and two together.

Jacqui was, though, giving him instructions. "You can use the two old De Roche passports on mules. They must be ones that will be caught. So only alter the photo and ages on the documents. Then you can have them for nothing. But don't forget I know the price for these things. I want you to play straight. And I want no calls about our location or new identity. The hunk is lethal if crossed and he delivers."

The man looked over at me. I smiled, "That's right. I do as she says. And even if you only told her father, I would have to assume that you bleated to others. And my speciality is slow and painful, but always fatal."

He knew this was only bravado but he sensed danger. He knew I was not capable of gratuitous violence. He also sensed that I was not adverse to killing if that was needed. I hoped he would take heed although I now thought that her father would not seek to harm us again after what had happened.

"I don't care how I have to use them. The important thing is to use them. A mule does not know who they are working for. The police will think the passports have been stolen and therefore the owners could have been murdered. Police don't look for dead people. Good thinking, Miss Jacqui. They will be with the authorities within the week."

He laughed quite evilly and added, "Have you a passport? I need to copy it. I suppose you will want to keep hold of yours."

She handed hers over. "Yes I do. And don't forget you only use the two older De Roche passports for the mules. Charles' must be used in the normal way so that it is recycled but untraceable. That's important."

He nodded his agreement. "What name would you prefer?" he asked us.

"Something common," I suggested. "How about White?"

"Absolutely not," said Jacqui. "Far too boring."

She reflected for a moment. "How about making us all the Pasquales after your first real escapade with me?" I shook my head.

"How about Thackeray. That's my mother's name" I suggested.

Jacqui laughed. "He's one of my favourite authors. I always fancy myself as a bit of a latter day Becky from Vanity Fair."

I shrugged my shoulders. He smiled, "Always the artist comes out in you Miss Jacqui."

"Better have a name without a connection to the famous De Roches who embezzled a few hundred million," said the man.

I was not surprised that he knew. Jacqui simply ignored the comment and nodded, "Well how about using my mother's family name. That was Rossi."

We all agreed and Jacqui added happily, "At least she will have been some help to me. I can't say she has paid too much attention over the last decade or so."

"Poor bitch," said the man. "She couldn't cope. It was just that her fear was greater than her maternal instinct. And why should it not be so? After all you're a tough enough cookie to fend for yourself. Once she knew that she quit."

For the first time, Jacqui looked at him coldly. "That's not your business. When can we have the papers by?"

"Three o' clock," he said. "Back here."

"No" said Jacqui. "You see us on our turf. This place is dangerous and we are unarmed."

"OK," he replied, "The bar of the Sir Francis Drake on Union Square."

I asked if he could arrange credit cards. He nodded. "I have some in stock. I can get your names embossed and have them for you this afternoon. I'll get one from a different bank for each of you two, and from a third bank for the older couple. I'll put in a large limit, as it's you. Miss Jacqui knows the penalty for non-payment. Their banking business is clean and above board." He laughed, "It's just the collection side is unusual if you have been issued one of our instant cards and don't pay back."

"Fine," she said, "that's all we need. And give me a fifty thousand dollar limit. I have to buy clothes. Do keep to schedule. And do call a gun supplier with the licence details, as we need a bit of hardware. I'll use the usual one for this region. See you at three."

And with that we headed out again. "Who on earth is he and why does he live in this hole?" I asked.

"His name is Benny. He lives here because he likes it. He is admired and respected. Have no illusions he can handle himself. He's no more camp than I am. He gets all the girls he wants here. He auditions them for the bars and like."

Seeing I looked shocked, she said, "It's a better life than the streets. And for the majority of the people around here, that's the only other option."

We walked up the road, looking for a taxi. The chances of finding one were poor. We would need to get into a better area than this before they dared to stop.

We passed a group of youths lounging about by a derelict shop. They saw Jacqui and called out "how much?"

I clenched my fists, but she held me firmly by the arm. I knew it would be stupid to pick a fight. We walked on.

"I said how much you fucking whore?" said the voice. "You, the girl. Not the other ponce."

We realised they were following us. "The hope is that they go away," said Jacqui. "Otherwise hit the ones with knives first. They are usually scared if they see their leader's hurt."

"Are you deaf?" called the voice. "What's the menu. Do you blow? Do you do it straight? Or do you have specials? Answer bitch."

This time, when we did not answer they came closer. "Turn around," said Jacqui "Or they'll jump us. Now play tough."

I looked at them. They hesitated.

"Scram. If you think we came here on foot and unarmed, you should think again."

They were not impressed. One or two were a bit less certain but the other five or six were unconvinced by my bravado.

The voice walked in front. He put one hand towards Jacqui. I had forgotten what she had once told me about being trained in martial arts. She was good.

A foot soared upwards and outwards. It caught the mouth in the groin and he bent double in pain. Then she stepped backwards and launched her whole weight at him. Her feet made contact on his chest as he started to straighten up. He crashed to the ground, hitting the curb with his head. She held her balance, stepping back towards me.

Another youth took out a knife from his belt. I allowed him to lunge at me. I side-stepped gently. As he stumbled past me, I slammed the back of his neck with my hand. I grabbed his jacket and pulled him back. As he faced me, I did a karate chop to his throat. He started choking and dropped the knife. I picked it up, grabbed hold of the voice. He was now stumbling to his feet and I said, "He buys it if you make one false move."

I knew they believed me but thought it better to make sure. I slashed the voice twice across the face. He screamed. Blood flowed out of the cuts. He was sobbing in agony. I moved the knife to his throat.

The gang backed off. The little guy with the knife was stirring. I threw away the voice. He collapsed in a heap.

"I think we move," said Jacqui. "It was mad not to think of transport."

There was a car parked by the curb. I grabbed hold of the little guy who had had the knife. "Whose car is that?"

No answers came from the others.

I slashed the little guy across the cheek. He bled. "I said whose car is that?"

One of the gang said "mine." He was an ugly looking character with buckteeth.

"Give me the keys or he buys it."

They hesitated and I slashed the knife across his stomach, cutting his clothes. The knife most likely grazed him for there was a bit of blood. More importantly he screamed. Buckteeth did not move. The others, though, stepped back. I shoved my captive against buckteeth and he stumbled. I grabbed hold of him.

"The keys," I said and helped the knife to his throat. He passed them to me and I tossed them to Jacqui, "Start it up darling, we're going for a ride."

She got in and started the car. She left the passenger side opened and I took buckteeth around to the door. I pushed him into the road and, as he fell over, got into the car. Jacqui drove off.

"Why is it that we always seem to attract trouble?" I asked.

"I have no idea. I managed to keep out of trouble for twenty-two years of my life. Since I met you, you have got me into enough scrapes to last a lifetime," Jacqui replied.

"It must be my magnetic personality," I suggested.

"If it is switch off the current occasionally," she replied.

We drove the car down some side streets. Once we had got it well away from the main road, we wiped it down and left it so that it obstructed an exit. The police would soon pick it up but they would get no joy from the owner. Punks like that lived by the principle that they did not talk to the police.

We, meantime, had a couple of hours to kill before we met Benny in Union Square. I was hardly surprised when Jacqui decided to look at a couple of the boutiques. She upgraded, or so she called it, the casual part of her wardrobe. And I found myself the owner of a few more shirts and designer T-shirts.

Perhaps her shopaholic attitude was infectious. I now found that I quite liked her approach. It made clothes shopping appear like food shopping. That was necessary and quite fun if you came away with tasty things you had not planned.

At three on the dot, Benny appeared with the papers. Jacqui did not check them but took the parcel. I handed over, as we had agreed, the twenty thousand dollars.

"Good hunting," said Benny. "Next time, though, kill punks like the ones who jumped you. I had to get rid of two of them. Otherwise, if they had found out whom they had threatened, they would have gone round boasting that they had taken on a Di Maglio. We need everybody to know that they can't win if they do that. And a few scratches and bumps is not good enough."

He looked at me sternly and added, "That's precious goods you're looking after. Stop acting as if she's just another broad." With that, he left.

Jacqui went to the ladies and checked the paperwork. She handed me my new passport and a gun licence. We turned out of Union Square and down a side road. We came to a gun shop. It was no back street gun shop, masquerading as something else. This was a real legitimate operation.

"Can we see Mr Renaldo?" asked Jacqui. And I knew that there was a dark side to this shop. This was another part of the Mafia supply chain.

Renaldo came out of the back of the shop and asked us through to what he called the staff quarters. "Benny told me you would call," he said gruffly. "What do you need?"

"We don't want traceable guns. We have the licences Benny made. We need weapons to match and ammunition."

Renaldo came back soon with three guns. The first, a small handbag pistol, looked like the one Jacqui carried before in France. She nodded. The second was a standard revolver, compact but powerful. It also came with a silencer. I assumed that could be useful. Again, Jacqui nodded. The third was a type I had never seen before. It was small and stubby.

Renaldo explained, "It's a man's gun. Takes standard bullets. The good thing is that it's light and can be easily concealed about the person. At least it needs a jacket. You can't conceal anything beneath the sort of light silky stuff you normally wear, Miss Di Maglio."

I turned to him, "Have you got some holsters. A leg holster would be best for the little gun. I'm used to wearing that."

He turned back into the shop. He came back with a simple holster that was attached to the leg by two straps. I nodded. He said, "The main gun should go into your trouser band. Police recognise shoulder holsters. But you need a special belt. This one looks normal, but you shove the gun into this part. It's elasticised. Very strong."

I nodded again. "And what can you do about ammunition?"

Once again he turned into the shop. This time he returned with a box of ammunition. "If you need more, you head for the local supplier," he advised Jacqui. "We have word from your father to see that you are armed. And he is supposed to be also."

Jacqui started at the mention of her father. I was surprised but, on reflection, not astonished by this unexpected benevolence. It was a welcome sign from Di Maglio that he would assist if needed. And I was not keen to refuse help. I knew we might need it.

Renaldo took us to a gun range at the rear of the shop and we loosed off a couple of shots each to make sure the guns were as easy to use as they looked. They were. These were good. I immediately felt safer than I had.

We paid Renaldo. I noted that Di Maglio did not extend his support to that any more. And we left, turning back up the street to the Square again.

"Let's take the cable car to Fisherman's Wharf. We can walk around there until we meet your parents," said Jacqui. So we headed off to the Wharf. I wondered if they would be there on time. I knew my mother would be shopping. I knew my father would be working on the Asian markets. And that meant that they could both easily forget about the time.

As it was, I was mistaken. They were sitting in the bar as planned, chatting away happily, oblivious of the outside world. I have to admit that I was surprised for they had only just got out of the tightest spot of the whole trip. They were more resilient than I expected.

We went to a restaurant by the harbour and acted like any other family. It was strange but I had never done this before with my parents and a girlfriend. They and Jacqui got on like a house on fire.

At the end of the sumptuous meal, my father said, "Let's get back to the hotel and agree what we are going to do about the next few weeks."

We wandered up to the cable car and returned the same way that we arrived. We went to my parent's room.

My father said, "OK what we need to do now is get to the health farm. It's about two hours drive from San Francisco. I suggest that we head out there after a lazy breakfast. Charles, you need to get us a car."

I nodded. He continued, "It's a great place. The complex consists of a series of beach houses. We have one with a large open plan lounge downstairs and two bedrooms upstairs. One has a King size bed and the other two doubles. We'll have the King size, as you two are not married."

He grinned at me. "I assume you don't mind sharing a room if you don't have to share a bed."

It was Jacqui who replied, "Not at all, we can always sleep on the floor between them."

He laughed and said, "Don't worry. I was only joking. You two can have the King sized one."

He continued, but this time in a serious vein, "We'll have our exercises in the morning and then we have our days for ourselves. I will be keeping a close eye on the Asian markets. I hope we can hang around for two months. The markets look fairly hairy but I don't think they are going to crash just yet. We have ordered good monitoring equipment and also communication lines. If we need to we can move things forward from here. I know we will not be able to do so from France. Things are going to happen too early for us to return first."

He turned to me, "I may need you to go to Europe, to Zurich or Geneva, and, once we start, I may ask you to be my ears in Hong Kong. You've met a lot of the people over there in the past and that could be helpful."

"Oh, that's great," said Jacqui. "I would love to go to Hong Kong. I don't know the Far East at all."

"It could be quite boring. Charles will need to put his work first and Hong Kong is not the best place for a girl to wander about on her own. Its not that it's dangerous. It's more that it is fairly boring when you are alone," said my father.

"I'll be alright. Anyway, I can look after Charles."

My mother looked carefully at her and they exchanged a conspiratorial look. I swear they had been talking about us when they had been alone.

My father turned to us. "Are you doing anything tonight? We'll have a drink in the bar."

"We might try a club or two," I said. "We feel like a bit of dancing."

"Well, don't stay out too late. You're the one who will be driving," warned my mother. I noticed once again that she and Jacqui exchanged a private smile.

"We'll be all right," I said. Then I remembered the papers; "Here are your documents. I almost forgot. You are now the Rossis. Blame Jacqui

194

and not me. But don't forget that we booked in this hotel as Biggs. Jacqui thinks that's a pretty crummy false identity. But there must be some real Biggs. We are going to have to pay cash, as we have only got credit cards in our new name."

We headed out of the hotel and took a car to club land. We went downstairs into a crowded night-club and got a table. As they served the drinks, the DJ started to play a slow number.

We got up and danced slowly together, holding each other tight. I loved the way that her body curved into mine. I felt the sensation of the fabric of her clothes with my hands. I pressed her body closer to mine as I moved my hands behind her back. The warmth of her slipped through her clothes onto mine and into my body.

She pulled me closer to her and gyrated gently against me. As I reacted to her warmth and invitation, she rushed her lips against mine and pressed even closer as if to enjoy the surge of excitement that she was sending through my body.

She had dressed that evening in a tight skirt that ended about six inches above her knees. The top she was wearing was held up by two narrow straps and fell around the curves of her body in casual pleasure. She was not wearing a bra, but her breasts held firmly under the flimsy garment. Occasionally a hint of a nipple would peep tantalisingly from under it.

I ran my hands down her back and across her buttocks. I kissed her as we clung tightly to each other.

"You feel as if you've got nothing on under the skirt," I said.

"I have" she replied. "I put on a pair of tights. The skirt is too tight to wear anything else. They'd show through."

"Do you mean to say that I am dancing this close to you while you are half naked?"

"Not all. I have three garments on. There's a pair of tights, a skirt and this silk top."

"I despair. What would you say if I said I was only wearing a shirt and a pair of trousers?"

"I'd prefer if you weren't," came the reply. "Look, I'm a full bloodied girl and am dancing with the man I love. I have no plans to dance with anyone else but you. So you and I have a secret. I am playing tarty and you like it. In fact you rather love it."

I licked my lips nervously. "This is not easy. You drive me wild and you are teasing. That's making it worse."

I felt her pull me closer to her again although the next number picked up the tempo. We swayed to it rather than danced to it, and ignored the now writhing bodies that surrounded us. I smelt Jacqui's hair with its gentle, soft fragrance. I sensed her perfume, a delicate bouquet of exotic flowers that seemed almost overpowering close up and yet almost fleeting as one moved away. It was as if the perfume had found its home and had decided not to leave it.

The music stopped and we went back to the table. The club we had visited was a mixed one. There were lonely business executives sitting at tables, keenly eyeing up the aircrews transiting yet another city. A few lone women prowled around the edges of the crowd that wondered if they were at work or at play. The cool scene brigade drank beer straight from the bottle, their chains and safety pins making strange accompaniments to their designer outfits. And then there was us.

Jacqui was in her disco gear. I was wearing clothes she had bought. My trousers were white and somewhat baggy and my shirt a cool cotton designer creation in a delicate shade of blue. The only strange part of my outfit, if anyone had seen it, was the gun I was wearing in the special holster on my leg. And it was this gun that met Jacqui's hand as her fingers caressed me just below my knee.

"Will there be a time when we don't have to be armed?" she asked wistfully.

"I've a horrible feeling that's only when we are in bed . And even then I keep the gun on the table near me."

We carried on dancing until long gone midnight and then went out into the fresh air. We decided to walk the short distance to the hotel, enjoying the cool air after the throbbing heat and noise of the club.

The next day, we hired the car and drove to the health club. There, lost in the quietness of the late September sunshine, we spent an idyllic time. Our mornings were spent getting fit. We each had our personal trainers. During the afternoons we would head to the sea and walk along the cliffs and beaches of the Californian coastline.

In summer, there were crowds, now during the daytime there was loneliness. Where in summer there was a sea populated by yachts, surfboards and swimmers, the sea birds outnumbered the human presence. Where in summer the beach was a patchwork of brown and red bodies clad in minimalist multi-coloured garb, now it was a golden carpet of sand untroubled by the disruptive impact of human bodies.

In the early sunset, we strolled bare foot through the shallows, indifferent to the sharp chill in the water and the sea's cooling breeze. We stopped, far away from the nearest person, and watched the sun in the distance play with low fluffy clouds. We sat on the sand, holding hands, enjoying each other's presence without a word passing between us. And once we made love in a deserted place against the added excitement of inquisitive grains of sand on our backs and the slight, but real, fear that we would be discovered.

The nights were equally idyllic. The open window let cool breezes play with our bodies. We would get up from the heat of lovemaking and stand naked on the porch. Jacqui called that having an air bath. There was none of the arrogant ostentation of the naturist beaches of Europe; this was a private communion with the stars and the wind.

We sat together in the bath and drew delicate patterns on each other with the soap as the foam dissolved into the water. When this became too much to bear one night, we pulled all the towels on the floor and together reached a damp and ruffled climax of pleasure.

We dressed and undressed at will. And with our growing understanding of each other's physical needs, came a deep personal understanding of each other. During those weeks, we grew to know each other. We stripped each other of the veils and filters that protected us from the outside world. We learnt about our strengths. And we dealt tenderly with our weaknesses. As we moved to a total understanding, we filled the gaps in each other's lives. We became more as one rather than as a couple.

We understood each other's reactions to situations without needing explanation. We anticipated each other's wishes. Yet we never ceased to surprise each other. The variety of life meant that we always found ourselves in some situation that we had never experienced. As we grew together we changed, and the reactions we had had to given events changed. We communicated without talking. We exchanged glances without seeing. Our senses worked in unison.

We did not realise it at the time, but we had blended together in a way that would allow us to react instinctively to the other's needs. And that instinct would bring us closer. It would blend us mentally and physically. And it would protect us when we most needed each other.

Neither of us had known this feeling before. My parents noticed it and left us to bond in these idyllic surroundings. The hills of California beckoned. The sea of California caressed our feet on the calm days and roared angrily through the surf on others. The Californian sun smiled gently at times and then withdrew behind clouds as if angry that we had not smiled back. The Californian wind blew at us, playfully attempting to rid us of our clothes, as if it enjoyed our habit of bathing in its caress.

The days were short. The nights were shorter as we balanced love making with sleep. The time flew by, as we knew total peace. We hoped this idyll would never end, but knew it had to.

We had no intention of asking when that would be. Each added day made up for the years we had been apart. Each stolen touch made up for the miles that had separated us. Each passionate moment made up for the anguish of the months alone.

In the background we saw my parents. Further back we saw the staff. As the exercise toned our bodies, we changed in our minds. We used that cocoon of pleasure to exorcise the past. For Jacqui that was the past of many years. The desertion of a mother, the brutal criminality of a father, the despotism of a dynasty and the loneliness of the Di Maglio name all fled in this peaceful harbour. For me, the chill of fear as we planned our task was now forgotten. The anger of separation became a distant memory. I no longer feared I could lose her, for we had neutralised her father's power and soon would dispel it for good. The grotesque conflicts with Di Maglio's people became inconsequential incidents even if for some they had been terminal. The intrusive thuggery of the punks and petty crooks we had met was banished from thought.

We were not what we had been before we came together. We were not even what we thought we were. We had become different. We were together. And we knew we would remain that way.

We also knew that soon, we would need to break out of this reverie and return to a crueller world. But that was a means to an end. And Jacqui had been brought up with the idea that the end could justify the means. I had been persuaded that that was the case. We were different but we had not totally dispelled the trappings of the past. As the poet said, our child remained the father of the man. Our past remained our present. We had removed it from our minds, but not from our memory.

Now though was the time to continue and enjoy the pleasure of our today existence. Tomorrow we would tackle the challenges of a road without a destination.

ASIA BREAKS

Next morning we switched on CNN to see stories of booming world markets and record turnovers. I watched carefully as the reporters switched to the overnight performances in Asia.

"The Hang Seng index reached a new all time high when it topped eighteen thousand in record trading volumes. The market was spurred on by the announcement of the new five year plan for China which forecasts continued double digit growth of their economy," reported their man in Hong Kong.

Then came reports from the rest of Asia. All of the regional markets had hit all time highs. Most of the currencies were now near their levels of early 1997 again. The crash of 1997 had been forgotten. It had been an aberration. The investment gurus were dutifully wheeled out and did their habitual task of forecasting that there was plenty of upside and little downside risk.

I muttered, "What arseholes. They follow the trend. How they keep in business God only knows."

I was not surprised when a call came from my father. "It's work time. Have you seen the markets? Nobody sees downside. It'll crash by the end of the week. We need to get to work. The holiday's over."

Jacqui was getting out of bed. She stood there as I took the call. "I knew every morning that we could get such a call. I'd hoped we wouldn't. But we have to do it. Then we will find another refuge for a bit."

I agreed. I took her in my arms, playing with my fingers down her naked back. She was still warm from the bedclothes but we resisted the temptation we both experienced. Now we had to be disciplined and make that billion. Then we could be masters again of our fate.

I dressed in a pair of slacks and a white business shirt. Jacqui put on a dress. It was as if we were gearing up for work. We no longer wore the casual clothes that had been our normal attire during the last few weeks. We switched clothes with the ease that we switched our minds. There would be no relaxation now. This was going to be work.

Over the weeks of exercise and relaxation, we had changed. I had put on a light brown tan. I was four or five pounds heavier and yet my body had been toned to a better shape than ever before. Jacqui had still her healthy olive glow. Her slim body did not appear any different but she walked with a greater ease. In short we were both as fit as we had ever been.

My parents were around the table in their room, where a selection of screens were blinking at them. The television monitor was on CNN Business. The Reuters screen was on the currency page. They, too, looked fitter than before. Their clothes also were casual business rather than the relaxed holiday wear of the previous weeks.

My father glanced up at Jacqui and me. He nodded approvingly, recognising that we appreciated the seriousness of the situation.

"I guess it'll soon time to act," I said. "The markets look as if they are out of control."

My father nodded. "Let me recap. If there are any questions, just interrupt.

"At the moment we have a war chest in Fucquet that amounts to ninety to a hundred millions of our money. We have a couple of million in Hochzeit. Our expense money is in United. I am not planning to use that for the moment."

"Could we get Hochzeit to lend us some funds. They may be a bit more relaxed than Fucquet who are incredibly conservative," I suggested.

"No," responded my father. "Hochzeit will take on a lot of risk for us when we use them as our broker. They are safe, as their parent would have to stand behind them even if they lost a major amount. And I suspect that they will. They have a reputation of going with the tide and we will use them to build up some of our positions."

He continued, "I plan to do two things. As stage one we will start a run. We'll target the stock market index through over the counter options."

"What does that mean?" asked Jacqui.

"We will get someone, both Fucquet and Hochzeit in this case, to guarantee us protection from a fall in the markets. The idea is that we will pay them a fee and they will pay us any losses we may incur on investments in selected countries. The technical word is that they will grant us an option. But, in reality, it's insurance."

"But we have no investments in those countries," protested Jacqui.

"They don't need to know that. I am going to invent a portfolio and say that I want them to give me protection against a market fall. For a fee they do that. The markets call that sort of insurance hedging," he replied. "It's normal business practice."

"What sort of rates are we talking about?" I enquired.

"Everybody believes this gravy train is going to last forever. The rates for options on the downside are just crazy. They are terribly cheap at the moment. I believe we can get a guarantee that the market will be at current levels in one month for a fee of around two or three percent of the portfolio insured. I've never seen rates like that before. Usually I would expect to pay a fee of five percent and that would be good," he replied.

I explained to Jacqui, "That means that we would pay them three million dollars for every hundred million dollars insured. If markets. during the next month, fell by say ten percent; they would pay us the loss of ten percent on the hundred million. That would be ten million. If markets rise, they pay us nothing and make a three million dollar profit."

"How deep is the market?" I asked my father.

"I have only some indications at the moment and would need to test prices. I believe though that I could get cover for a billion dollar portfolio for around thirty million dollars. I would hope to be able to go higher, but that may increase the fee."

"Where would the alleged investments be?" I inquired.

"I want to focus on two separate portfolios," said my father. The first will be Korea. That's driven by politics. The second is a south East Asia portfolio taking in the Philippines, Indonesia, and Malaysia. They are the most vulnerable."

"Are you sure of the timing?" I demanded.

He smiled sardonically. "We can never be sure of the timing. Markets are not rational. We'll have to work the rumour mill."

"How do we do that?" I asked.

"By a self fulfilling lie," he replied.

"I don't understand," said Jacqui.

"That's where you two will come in. Charles will call Hong Kong and tackle the local brokers. He will pretend to be a journalist from the Wall Street Journal. We'll borrow one of their real reporter's names. He will ask if it is true that Sebo has gone a big bear on the region and gone short of the currencies in anticipation to liquidating his portfolios."

Sebo was a legendary fund manager. He would be dealing large. It had been rumoured that he was the cause of markets and currencies falling and rising all over the world as he moved his millions and billions around in a series of highly technical but generally ruthlessly efficient moves. The great thing about starting a rumour about Sebo was that there were a whole group of other operators who followed his every move. Sebo was good. But he won more often than he lost simply because a lot of similar funds imitated his moves. When he moved a billion, others in total moved tens of billions. And that meant that the first guy on the block, namely Sebo, made a fortune. He took the position and others moved the market for him.

We had perfected that strategy. We would take the position. We would suggest that Sebo had taken it. He would hear the rumours and see the trend in the market. Then he would really take the position. The weight of his money would move the market. The rumour became the reality. The others would follow Sebo. And there we were just one jump ahead of the leader. It was all so simple that it was amazing that nobody had thought of it before.

If there were a rumour that he was selling and that the herd was behind him, that would cause panic. And if that panic caught on, who knew how investors would react?

I nodded. "Do you think the brokers will believe me?"

"Of course they will. They'll believe any rumour that makes markets move. All they want is to trade. They couldn't care less if the market goes up or down. As long as their clients buy and sell, they make money. There is no money to be made in a stable market. And in any case after the rises of recent weeks, they will naturally believe the big funds could decide to sell."

He continued, "At the same time Jacqui will call the US. I have a list of names. She will pretend to be from the Economist magazine in London. She will ask the trading desks of the currency dealers if it is true that Korea is unable to meet the scheduled debt arrangements. And she will also add in a rumour about troops massing on the border with North Korea. There's always fear of unrest in that region. Her approach should be low key, as if she is unsure of the rumours and checking them out.

"The currency dealers are always looking out for good stories and they spread them like wildfire. It should not be too difficult. I will need to train you both. You have to be word perfect and convincing."

Soon we had got everything off pat. Jacqui and I were put through the loops many times. We had to sound green about the way the markets moved. But we had to sound convincing enough to assure the people at the other end that we were real. And more importantly, they had to be convinced that we would print what they said. If they believed the papers would be full of stories that the big funds were selling, they in turn would sell. And when the serious papers came out the general public would sell. And it was only when the popular tabloids ran scare stories about the fall in markets that it became the time to buy.

My father called Fucquet to see what could be arranged. It was near the end of the day in Geneva, but it would take them all night to sort out a deal of this size. They gaped at the size of the deal we proposed. "We thought you had a small fund," said Pierre.

"We have some large ones as well," said my father with a laugh. He acted as if he was astounded that Fucquet had not realised the scale of his operation. "We have several billion on advisory contracts. It's all private money and the funds are only open to a select few. But we make money. Sometimes we have discretion. At others we manage with the investor. This is one of them."

That was a good story as it brought us back into a profile that Pierre could accept. We did not look like a fund management company moving billions. But we could easily be the hybrid. A small fund manager who advised a group of the super rich. That sort of discrete entrepreneur was not uncommon. Pierre consulted his colleagues about our proposed deal. The people at Fucquet would need to work with their people in the Far East. The way the system worked, Fucquet would look for other banks willing to take on a good part of the risks involved. They were never going to take on all that risk themselves. So they would not accept the deal until they had found some willing partners. They would then run their portion of it for a bit and lay off a bit more, gradually taking their profits as the market moved until they had little or nothing left. The whole process was dependent on the markets moving as they expected. And we had plans that would ensure that did not happen. In that case they would be exposed and lose money.

My father had only mentioned that we had a client who wanted to hedge his substantial Far East portfolios. He did not say whether he wanted to protect against a fall or a rise in the market. That was sensible, as Fucquet would be forced to quote two fees. One would protect an investor who felt he had too little invested in the markets from a rise in the market. The other would do the reverse. And my father was betting on the hope that Fucquet would misread him and therefore give him a low fee for taking on the risk of a fall.

He chatted with Fucquet. They questioned him. He extolled the virtues of the market and expressed the opinion that they were now starting to recognise the real worth of companies in the area. But he assured that he felt there was a bit of a way to go yet. He grinned broadly as he put down the phone.

"They think I represent someone who is under-invested in the area and that I need to protect myself against the market rising as I put more money into the region. The indication is that the cost of insurance against a rise could be five to ten percent, while the cost of insurance against a fall is only two to two and a half percent. They will talk to London and I will call them back in an hour."

He then picked up the phone to Hochzeit and spun them a not dissimilar story. But he concentrated on a fund investing in Korea when he talked to them. He implied it was a vulture fund. It would invest in companies. It would build up stakes in them. And the hope was that would flush out possible bidders. That would cause the prices to soar. The fund would then make super profits. It was pure manipulation of the markets. If it worked, it would be super-profitable.

I turned to Jacqui and said, "Everything is based on fear and greed. It's easy to panic people when that's the case. And that's what he is starting to do."

The conversation with Hochzeit went on for some time. It was obvious that they were willing to deal over the phone. I heard my father talk of two hundred million dollars. Ten minutes or so later, after much haggling, he put down the phone with an air of triumph. "That was hardly a challenge. They have agreed to hedge a two hundred million dollar fund for four percent for a month from today's close."

He saw Jacqui was looking puzzled. "I'll pay them four percent. That's eight million dollars. And they will guarantee to pay me compensation for any fall in the market from today's level during the next month. It's just as we said before. If the fall is less than four per cent, they make money. When it is more, we make money."

"You need to remit the balance to them. We have only two million in our account," I said.

"I'll send them the other six when we next talk to Fucquet," he said. "It's like the old times except this is for us and not for clients."

He called Fucquet later. There was quite a lot of haggling and he had a hard time to complete the deal. But he did, and when he had put down the phone this time, he punched his fist in the air with a triumphant "Yes! Yes! Yes!"

This time, he explained that he had hedged a fund of a billion dollars for just two and a quarter per cent. The fee to Fucquet would be twenty-two and a half million dollars.

We had spent just over thirty million dollars but had opened some one point two billion of positions.

"Jacqui start the New York rumours. Charles will have to wait several hours before he starts his. He'll be working into the early hours of the morning," said my father.

Jacqui was very good. She played her part perfectly. She called all the big banks; one after another while my father monitored the screens. We ate sandwiches and drank bottled water. Otherwise the 'do not disturb notice' kept out all visitors.

The bank trading rooms swallowed every word Jacqui fed to them. There were two reasons. The first was that she sounded great on the phone. That was not training. She just sounded great and the traders liked that. The second was that she was convincing. She managed to spin a story that became credible because of her uncertainty about it. It's no use telling the market something is happening. We were asking the market to confirm that something had happened. And in the end they believed it actually had.

The market was not living in a real world. It was make believe and opinion. And we gave them something to believe in. They lapped it up.

"Look the won is falling a bit. It's starting to come under pressure," called my father.

The won was the Korean currency. I looked at the screen. He was right. It was a small movement as yet, but it was there. Jacqui continued her calls.

"Oh hello, I have been given your name by your corporate people. They said you follow Korea closely. We are just putting a story to bed on Korea. We are being told that there is concern that they may default. It appears that there is also trouble on the border. Have you heard anything?"

"Look lady. Oh shit. Sorry, I shouldn't say that. The market's all over the place. It seems they must be doing something. Someone in the Pentagon has made a comment about monitoring the situation. The Koreans have kept quiet. Look all hell's starting to break lose. I'll have to go."

She called another desk. This time, the response was better, "We sure think so. The market says that's the case. It's always a good indicator. Yes Mam, it's bad out there."

That was a standard monosyllabic and meaningless comment from a trader able to worry governments. And he, and hundreds like him, as planned fed the flames that we had started.

My father smiled broadly as the won began to ease. "Excellent," he said. "I think you should call the US banks in Hong Kong as well. That could put the skids under the currency. Then we'll see the markets really move."

He picked up the phone to United in Geneva. Their dealers there would have already gone home but we were switched through to New York. I had not realised, but my father must have arranged lines for foreign exchange with them.

He asked for a price in won for one month forward. He calmly said "I'll buy a hundred million dollars and sell won for one month." He then added, "There's five million cover in my account. I'll remit a further five million tomorrow to give you extra cover."

They had obviously agreed to deal with him as long as he left some cash in his account. If the deal went wrong, as usual they would ensure he had enough in his account to allow them to reverse it. They believed the money in the account would cover any possible loss.

By now the screens were showing the market getting nervous. A story flashed up on Reuters about concerns emerging about the stability of the won. The unsuspecting Koreans were fast asleep and did not know what was happening. But the market gave all the traditional indications of panic and rumour breeding panic and rumour.

My father had been busier than I thought. He seemed to have a whole number of new contacts. He checked out the position with them and grinned each time a new rumour appeared. As most rumours are by word of mouth and dealers are inventive, the original rumours became part of a bigger machine. As time moved on, it was going to be more difficult to stop the fears that were now taking hold of the market.

He turned to me and said, "You're going to have an easier time with your Sebo rumour. In any event it may become a reality. He must be watching these markets for signs of a turn. It would be logical for him to sell other regional markets at a time like this."

We carried on monitoring markets through the evening. We needed to be ready for the Asian openings. This was after all only the first phase of the exercise. In time we would be attacking the Hong Kong dollar, and if that worked, our killing would be complete.

I saw that my father had done his calculations. "We are still in loss," he said. "But the market has moved three per cent in our favour in Korea. That means that we have clawed back six million of the eight million fees we paid. The Fucquet business is less in our favour. On average we have clawed back half a percent. That's around five million of the twenty-two and half we paid them. The sale of won has moved in our favour and we are up just over a million on that trade."

I added those figures up in my head, "That means that we are twelve million up against an outflow of thirty point five. Our timing has been perfect."

My father nodded, "It is really now up to you and Jacqui to get those rumours going. The journalist story can only hold for the next twenty-four hours at the most. We need the market to get into a panic. Otherwise the stories won't hold. That is unless we fall lucky and the papers actually run them."

As the Far East markets opened later that day, Jacqui and I hit the phones. The markets in the US had been sufficiently volatile to unnerve many of the traders in the Far East.

I called one major house and hit the speaker phone button so that all could hear the panic in their trader's voice. "The place is unhinging. The stock markets are down. The red chips are falling like a stone. The cash market has gone crazy. Nobody can afford those rates. They're going through the fucking roof. I tell you there is a load of longs out there and some big names are going to take a bath. It's going to be in billions. There's no liquidity in the market. You can't sell your positions. It's going to fucking collapse."

I did the same with another, "The foreign exchange markets are falling. Of course they're fucking falling. You can't sell for love or fucking money. Shit the won's crashing again. And the ringit's falling out of bed. Shit it's 1997 again. We're fucking shafted."

Then we couldn't even get through to the traders. They couldn't answer the phones. They were overwhelmed. One, in a panic, accidentally left us on hold and we put it on the loudspeaker. The voices rose to a panic crescendo in the dealing room. The language got fouler. The fear was more open.

"I can't cover dollar spot," yelled one voice.

Another responded, "Then don't answer the fucking phone. They only want to sell. I don't want to take a position."

A third shouted, "We've got one. I've over a billion on the book and it's the wrong way."

A new voice came in. "You're fucking fired then. Bugger off out of here. The prick. The goddam fucking prick. He's taken the sodding won and yen on the book and sold the sodding dollar. What an arsehole. That's blown the bloody bonus, I'll tell you."

Another voice yelped in panic, "If he's long, let's find someone we can short against. There must be a government or central bank who'll take us on. We can't lose the fucking bonus. I've spent it. I bought that motor. That bloody Ferrari."

Someone came to the phone, "We'll sell you anything against the dollar but we're not quoting to sell dollars. The only thing that's holding now is the peg. And I don't know how long that'll be for."

By the peg, he was talking about the Hong Kong dollar. It was pegged to the US dollar. I knew my father planned to smash that one too. I looked at him.

He shook his head. "In the second wave," he muttered, "the run there hasn't started and they'll defend it to the end."

The voice on the phone called to me, "Who are you in any case?"

He'd forgotten I was an alleged journalist and thought I was some other trader. I killed the phone. We had enough and needed to watch the screen.

My father was doing another calculation. The Korean index had gone into free fall. It was down twelve per cent. That made a pay out for us of twenty four million dollars less the eight million cost. The big fund index was down seven per cent and that brought in seventy million dollars against our outlay of just over twenty. On the currency side the won had fallen six per cent. That was a massive fall for a day. We had made a further six million on the currency.

"There's more to come," said my father. "They will fall right out of bed, but we need to keep our nerves, It's going to be a roller coaster market."

We stopped working the phones but watched the screens. Rumour followed rumour. The markets tried to rally but failed. There were onerous warnings from the brokerage houses. Economists started talking again of a global slump. Commentators saw the threat of unrest, as soaring unemployment would surely follow the inevitable series of bankruptcies. Politicians muttered half-hearted words about the fall not being justified.

But in situations like that nobody listens to commentators. Nobody ever listens to economists. And most of all nobody believes politicians. And Finance Ministers or central bankers came to the screen. They claimed unconvincingly that the panic was ridiculous. The market ignored them. It fell further. They all lacked credibility. The market was falling and therefore it had to fall.

We called Fucquet and Hochzeit. They sounded scared. And it was inevitable that they would be. For they were in a serious loss making position. Although they would have laid off a large part of the position, the reality was that they would have carried a good part on the book.

We sympathised and commented on our client's lucky timing. That did not make them any happier. But we did not expect it to. When we saw their anxiety, we pushed in a few more rumours. Some were unbelievable but they believed them. There was nothing that the market would not believe. It had reached the stage of total panic and bad news just topped up the reality of the mess.

The markets went on in steep fall for several days. At times they staged a rally and we held our breath. But then they hit the downward track again. For the odd day they stabilised and then fell further.

We all monitored the screens closely day in day out. Our day started with the opening in Asia and ended as the markets closed in New York. That was almost a twenty four-hour cycle.

We staggered our exercises. Nobody thought that strange. The role of those monitoring the positions was to brief my father as he returned. He was the mastermind. Jacqui also got into the swing as we got the feel of markets and realised how simple it was to make them work as we wished. As we had thought, those who do not fear losses were able to stand above it all and make the gains.

This drama continued for nearly three weeks. We knew that we would soon close. We had to do something over the coming week as our positions would come to an end. All the markets had been in a fifteen-day free fall. The only stable areas were the Hong Kong dollar and the Japanese bank stocks.

Then one evening, we had a meeting to review the position. Once again it was my father who led the debate.

"I've assessed our position. The Korean market has actually fallen less than we hoped although their currency has gone through the floor. The market last night closed fifteen per cent below our base level. That gives us thirty million dollars, less the eight we paid up front. That's a net of just twenty two million dollars. We sold a hundred million dollars of their currency on the foreign exchange and that's down thirty two percent. So we should be able to close out at a thirty odd million profit on that position."

"I thought we'd make more there. In total we just made fifty four million net of costs. I suppose the locals supported the market."

My father nodded, "I underestimated the problems they are facing. They couldn't let their markets fall too far or all their corporate lending would have been called. The banks have all taken security in the form of shares; so the companies must have bought their own stock through some cartel arrangement. I guess it's quite easy to do so in a pretty liquid market like Korea. Still the good news is that we have made an absolute killing on the big fund."

My mother said, "Last time we talked we were nearly four hundred million dollars up on that one. What was the status at the close? Given the free fall last night, I would have suspected we are close to five hundred million now."

"You're pretty close," replied my father. "The total fall has been fifty two percent on the basket of markets we insured through that option. When you see what the downside risk was, you have to agree that Fucquet and their friends were crazy to even consider pricing it like they did. I can't believe how short sighted they were."

"That puts us five hundred and twenty million up, less the twenty two and a half million fee," I noted. "We've cleared just over five fifty million on the whole scam."

"It's just crazy," observed Jacqui. "It was the rumours that moved the market. And we fabricated them to move the markets our way. And we haven't any big, big money. After all we only risked twenty to thirty million. But in the end they actually believed the garbage that Charles and I fed them down the phone."

"Yes," said my father, "if things swing too far one way and markets lose touch with reality, they'll believe anything. Even a lousy story told by a journalist they have never heard of."

Jacqui laughed happily and said, "It's a great way to make money. It's so different from my father. You don't hurt anybody."

But that was not strictly true. People would lose their jobs. Countries would become poorer. But we did not see that. It wasn't like drugs or murder. The harm was lost in the normal sea of human misery. Statistics don't make you feel ashamed. At least not until you've made your money. I did not contradict her. And I noticed my father didn't either. We secretly exchanged looks and I felt a bit ashamed that I had let her easy words pass.

By then I had done the calculations in full. "OK, if we close today at the prices at end of day Hong Kong we make a net five hundred and fifty one and a half million. We always had just over a hundred million in the banks. So all in we have a war chest of six hundred and fifty one million. And we should be able to fast track in the bulk of the eight hundred from the scam. Fucquet would expect our clients to be ecstatic rather than just grateful. And that would mean more inflow of funds!"

We waited expectantly for the next morning in Europe. That took us through another day in the Far East. The markets remained nervous but less frenetic. It was as if they were taking their breath. In the end we managed to close out the positions with a profit of a bit over five hundred and eighty million. Our war chest was getting serious. And we quickly gave instructions for an inflow of funds into Fucquet, making sure that it looked like many clients paying in money. For that we used up to twenty banks to remit through to Fucquet, who in turn were relieved to see more money and the chance to make good their losses. We also built up a second war chest at the United Bank. In total we had just under one and a half billion of fund to play with.

With business like efficiency, we spent a long time in conference planning our next moves. We decided that we were certain that the next things to go would be the Hong Kong peg. My father was also convinced that the Japanese banks were worth a punt. They were heavily geared, had lent money all over the Asia Pacific region and he could not see them surviving unharmed.

"It's just manipulation," he said coolly. "There's no way that their current levels are justified."

We restructured our trading facilities and agreed additional ones by fax with the United Bank in Geneva. Fucquet now held five hundred million of our funds. They would be careful about too much risk now but they knew us and would be trying to recover some of their losses. We pushed a hundred million into Hochzeit. But we put the big money into United. They held eight hundred million now. They were more conservative but they would trade larger than the others for they were by far the biggest of the banks.

As we sat and discussed tactics, my father decreed that it was time to launch a new vehicle, a new Asian hedge fund. He wanted to be close to Hong Kong. "You two are excellent at spreading rumours. That we know. You're a bit young but you can be convincing. In fact, I have to say that you bullshit perfectly. I want you to go to Hong Kong. You can base yourself in the Mandarin and act as our eyes and ears. Oh, and spread rumours to your hearts' content."

We agreed and Jacqui was quite excited to think that she was going somewhere new. So we had our fake business cards printed and called the major brokers in Hong Kong for appointments. They were enthusiastic to see a new two billion dollar plus fund. We explained we were launched by a group of very private investors and would be working on a hundred million-dollar trades.

We asked them to think through regional strategies for us. We told them we were willing to short or go long. But we needed performance and we needed it fast. Our sponsors had given us a limited pool of money but if we performed they would add more. And if the fund performed, more investors would join. So we were on a ride. Performance meant extra funds from the existing investors and new funds from new investors.

They understood what we meant. They knew business was tailing off as it always does in a market slump. Then the markets fall on small volumes and the big investors stay away until the market turns. They were keen to attract us as they saw us as immediate term commission. We would get a good welcome when we reached Hong Kong.

Yes, they were keen. Yes, they were good. Yes, they were willing to act for a commission. We gave them convincing references from Fucquet and United. They hardly checked once they were sent a note saying we had several hundred million dollars lodged in each of the Fund accounts.

The Swiss banks were surprised when asked to confirm this and insisted that we gave them our instructions in writing. Secrecy is inbred and that unusual instruction ran counter to their culture.

My parents, having decided that it was time to move from their California base, rented an apartment down the coast near San Diego. It was useful to be close to a border. This time it would be the Mexican one. And any longer stay in the health resort would appear strange. We had already got concerned that our unusual activity could raise suspicion. But in the end, so many super rich people were there that they accepted our behaviour. They thought we were workaholics and didn't bother as long as we paid our bills.

We all went to Los Angeles and had dinner together before Jacqui and I headed to the airport and caught the United flight to Hong Kong. We were in first class. That fitted our cover to perfection.

SOJOURN IN HONG KONG

The plane came into the new airport at Hong Kong. It lacked the excitement of a landing at the old Kai Tek airport. There, you swooped over and between the houses in a breath-taking dive to the runway stretching out into the sea. The smell of the city would flood in through the ventilation vents as one walked along the somewhat decrepit and crowded corridors to the chaos of immigration and the casualness of customs.

Now we walked along new corridors that were pristine clean and had all the excitement of any of the antiseptic pathways of modern airport architecture. The place was more efficient and we soon were in the hotel car area. The Mandarin had sent, at my request, one of their Rolls Royces to pick us up. We sat back in the leather luxury of its seats, watching the high rise buildings of Hong Kong Island approach us from afar. The weather was fine and warm outside, but we did not feel it in our air-conditioned luxury.

We swept round past the imposing façade of the Hong Kong Bank, vying for position and dominance with the adjacent, taller and slightly more splendid, Bank of China. Then we glided into the drive and drew up outside the main entrance of the Mandarin.

Porters jumped forward to take our luggage. We were ushered in to the lobby, and then immediately up to our room. A plumpish girl of indistinguishable nationality, dressed in a Mandarin uniform, accompanied us. We completed the formalities, as is normal practice there, in the comfort of our bedroom.

Gratefully, we accepted the offer of Chinese tea and quickly unpacked our luggage, which followed us by moments. We decided that we would stroll around the Central District and then eat in the coffee shop, before trying to get some sleep. After the rigours of the overnight journey from Los Angeles, it is difficult to make the jump into the different time zone of Asia.

I called my father and told him that we were in place. He was excited and said to me, "Look at CNN, the markets are going crazy again. They are soaring. It's a technical reaction and we might get another bite at the cherry. I want you to do a trawl of opinion in the morning. Focus on the Thai and Hong Kong markets as well as the four we hit last time. Thailand is up over thirty per cent and Hong Kong by nearly as much. And it looks as if some of the others could increase more than that. Brief me at eleven o' clock your time. And call United in Hong Kong to see what indications they are giving for options and in what size."

I agreed and explained the situation to Jacqui. "We could really make a killing now that we have a big slug of cash to play with. We'll see tomorrow. Let's get out for some air, if that's what you can call it here."

We wondered outside into the warmth of a Hong Kong evening. The streets were crowded with people. All races mingled together in this most cosmopolitan of cities. The endless stream of evening traffic belched out their polluted trails as they ferried their captives from office to home. The larger cars headed majestically up to the Peak. The buses and trams rushed to more humble areas.

The shops of Central were still lit up. They gave little sign of a currency in crisis or an economy under threat. We looked in the windows of the designer shops and Jacqui frowned at the clothes. "A lot of the tacky end of the designer range," she announced. "The stuff isn't as much fun as in Europe. They buy the label rather than the dress. And the prices look outrageous."

"Well," I responded ironically, "Perhaps they'll be more realistic when we have hit their currency."

We wandered up through the streets, past monumental office blocks, populated by banks and other financial organisations. We strolled through shopping malls bursting with small businesses selling all kinds of produce. We loitered in streets awash with scurrying people. And we crossed roads crammed with anything from a Rolls Royce to a rusty bicycle.

Looking up, we saw the sky peep out from behind the odd building. We saw the Peak take on its polluted haze. The sun gave up on the people and concentrated on the roofs of the skyscrapers before moving totally away from the Island. And we walked back to the hotel. The Captain's bar downstairs was buzzing with amiable brokers and bankers, talking sex and sport rather than stocks and shares. The lobby was a gentle flow, with eager staff quickly handling the occasional guest enquiry.

We walked into the coffee shop. It still held the remnants of the local café society as well as the first wave of hotel residents. The locals were dressed in formal wear, while the residents contrasted in more casual clothes. We ate and once again played our favoured game of guessing our neighbours' occupations. Indiscreetly, we joked about them and laughed at the excesses we alleged against them. Nobody else could have torn apart his or her characters so viciously. The game over, we headed upstairs and to bed. The next day was going to be a busy one.

Next morning, we dressed our parts. Our business type suits were no longer crumpled. They had been pressed to perfection the night before. Jacqui's was short skirted and body hugging enough to distract any red-blooded male from the fact that she was not a real expert. Nevertheless she was a good actress.

"You would have made a great con man, or even a broker, you know," I remarked. "You'll never have to starve."

"Hell," she replied, "It's not starving that I want to avoid. Its moderate wealth or things like that. I plan to be super rich."

"Don't we all," I responded. "After all, it's only the super rich that are above the law. Then one doesn't have to pay taxes. One can slide around the strict rules the others have to obey. Breaking the law is stupid when you can manipulate it. One needs, especially in finance, to live in the grey band between the Law and Jail. Otherwise one never gets super rich."

"What will you do when we are all super rich?" she teased.

"We're not doing badly at the moment," I retorted. "After all, we have over a billion and a half to our name."

"No," said Jacqui, "that's not super rich. That's just moderately rich. Super rich is when you have influence. Super rich is when in the future people who are trying to work the system start scare stories. And they are about what you are doing. Super rich is when you buy governments."

"I guess so," I said. "I doubt though that one can arrive at that until one has several billion under one's belt. And, as the pot grows, we will have to be more cautious. Otherwise we become too big for the markets and would be betting against ourselves."

"What do you mean?"

"Quite simply, if we are too big, we would find it hard to find people who could deal with us in a size that mattered. So we would have to change our strategy. We would become longer-term investors. We may play around a bit for fun, but it would be nothing like this. This gives you a buzz because you bet all. Doing it for a hobby would be boring."

"What would you do then?"

"We could make love all the time. That's not going to be boring."

"Even when I am fat after five kids?"

"Hey, what's this about procreation at twenty two?"

"I'm Catholic. Don't forget that. Or when we're super rich and see the Pope, he'll tell you off."

"Look, you've already sinned. So let's sin a bit longer. Then you get one great big absolution. And then we please the Pope."

"But if I'm fat will you fancy me?"

"What do you think?"

"I doubt it. You'd find some little piece to have on the side. Perhaps one of those Asian girls. You know like the one you are ogling at now."

Her eyes flashed. "So what have you got to say?" she asked.

"I wasn't ogling at her. I was admiring her dress."

"The material's rubbish. Her mother made it. It's tight round her bum, which is over big for her size. It's tight round the tits and that's quite an achievement. The slit shows the tops of her stockings. And that's naff. In fact that was a lousy answer."

"I came to the same conclusion as you did. But I had to look to come to it," I replied.

"You're bullshitting me."

"No. I'm actually serious. But Jacqui, no thought police. I know the rules and have no desire to break them. But cool off."

She became indignant. "I am not going to cool off if you salivate after every little tart in the shop."

I stood up. She looked anxiously. Perhaps she thought she had gone too far. I walked over to her chair. I bent over her head and kissed her hair. Then I kissed her neck.

People looked over. There was amusement on the faces of some. There was shock on the faces of others. There was bewilderment on others. I kissed round her neck and then down the open collar of her blouse. In a loud voice, I said, "I love you too. Don't worry I'll never embarrass you. After all your husband asked me to be discreet."

The faces now looked at us in excitement and worse. Jacqui went a bit red. Then she pursed her lips. Her eyes were sparkling with laughter. We had done this before but not in a place where we were scheduled to live for a bit.

"Don't worry about my husband," she said. "After last night I decided to dump him."

I interrupted, "Given his origins, are you going to walk around him and tell him three times, I divorce you, I divorce you, and I divorce you."

She smiled. She was giggling. "No, why divorce him. Bigamy is much more fun."

I looked at my watch. "My God is that the time? I have to fly. I've got to get to Wan Chai and pick up my trousers."

She jumped up too. "Let me come with you. I'd love to see the place. It sounded so exciting. Losing your trousers. And in a convent as well."

As Wan Chai is the pink light district of Hong Kong, our fellow diners were perplexed to the extreme. Jacqui slipped her arm around me and guided me out.

"Are you still mad with me?" I asked.

"No. Sorry. But if you want a quick job, I'll give it. I mean, she can't have been good for anything else."

"Point taken. I love you stupid, and just you. So don't worry. This is one person who is not going to let you down."

And for the first time in my life, I really meant it.

Our room had two lines and three phones. So we both took out the list of contacts we had arranged and got started on the calls. I rang some of the local houses and they were universally bullish. They were seeing big buying orders. The Hong Kong billionaires were buying everything. The Central Bank of China was buying. Even the Swiss, usually so conservative, were alleged to be buying.

Jacqui phoned round the international houses. She also got a consistent story. The Americans were buying and they were buying like mad. Two of the most regarded market strategists had called on their clients to double their exposure to the region. There were rumours of take-overs. That was inevitable. Equity was now undervalued. It had been higher before.

We discussed the two variations.

"There's nothing in common with the stories. Other than the fact that they are all saying the market is flooded with buyers. I find that strange so soon after the fall," she said.

"That's because we have heard fifty per cent bull-shit and fifty per cent real life. The market has short memories. Because it bounced back, it saw the fall as just a correction. And, as everyone makes more money on a rise, they want to be bulls. The brokers all talk of the same key clients. The rise appears to be supported but by the big clients. That means that the brokers are putting their big clients into the market."

"But what will happen?" Jacqui enquired.

"They'll work their way through their client list and bring in the smaller clients. They always work like that. Get the big spenders in first and then work down the list. Finally you get the general public who buy

217

when they see the rise. Then the market will fall as the guys who bought at the start of it all sell into the rise."

"But," I continued, "we still should find out the price of options. And then we will need to phone my father."

I called United Bank. Their Hong Kong office covered the entire Asia Pacific region from Jakarta up to Seoul and down China and Japan across to the Indian sub-continent. They had heard of me and were expecting my call.

"We have a series of portfolios in the region and I want to leverage them. Can you quote me options on a basket of markets in any size?"

"Which markets are you looking at?" came the reply.

"We're thinking of a South East Asia portfolio covering the three tigers in Indonesia, Malaysia and the Philippines. Then we have one in Thailand and another in Korea. Finally we have our Hong Kong Fund."

"What sizes are you talking about?" he asked.

"The South East Asia one is at two billion. The Korean and Thai funds are each three hundred million. The Hong Kong one is at a billion," I hazarded.

"You should use us for brokerage. I don't think we've ever seen your trades," he noted.

I sensed greed in his voice. We could use this to good effect. I lied easily as I replied, "Most of our business has been done through the European houses but we are moving over here. In future, we will be trading here as well. I'll be calling on you about our plans in a few weeks. We just don't want to miss the excitement of this rise and so I'm perhaps jumping ahead of plans and could be dealing today. I'll have to talk to my principals first, though."

He rose eagerly to the bait. "We'll make you a good price and tailor an option for you. You'll see we are the biggest and the best in this place. I'll call back in half an hour."

He took my number and I grinned over to Jacqui. "They really are stupid. They'll swallow any story if they see the hope of a commission at the other end – and they must know of the baths we gave their guys in Europe in the last month."

And they came back with a good price. They thought I was going for a further rise in the markets and had fed that into their price. I knew my father would want me to get the maximum. I asked them to refine the two prices, which they were quoting. One was the premium to benefit from a rise in the market. The other was for a fall. And I suspected the fall would cost less in percentage terms than we had seen the first time round, even though it would cover much larger amounts. They complied and I promised to call back.

I called my father and ran him through the discussions we had had. The market had risen even further that day. He thought it could only rise for a day or two. "I like the quotation you have got. I doubt they'll hold it for too long. It's a bit over the top. You got them really hungry for your business. I suspect their traders have gone out on a limb. Their Head Office would never allow them to quote like that."

He asked me to repeat the terms. We were talking of the same type of deal we had done with Fucquet. It was a bit more expensive. And it was much more speculative. The advantage was that it could make us a lot more money. Or it could, if we got our timing right.

United told us their prices. They would guarantee the two billion-dollar fund for six per cent. They would run the Hong Kong one for three per cent. The Korean and Thai ones would be at five per cent. They would base the guarantee on the prices that ruled at the close of business today.

That meant they would take a commission of a hundred and twenty million on the big fund, thirty for the Hong Kong one and fifteen million each for the others. All in all they would charge a cool hundred and eighty million dollars. But the gains for us could be huge. If all those markets fell ten per cent in the next month we would make three sixty million less the fees paid. A twenty per cent fall would give us seven twenty less the fees.

"We'll ask them to hold as long a possible. You'll need to buy the market because they'll try to hedge through sales to get the end of day prices down once they know you are a bear. Unless you think you can get them to strike at the current level rather than at the close of business."

The strike price would be the base level of the market used to calculate the insurance. If we took the insurance against a fall, they would try to push the market lower. If we took it for a rise, they would buy. They could use some of the fee to cover any possible trading losses.

"Look, ask them to hold their prices as long as you can. Then deal. But place limits to buy in key stocks in each market. Make the limits in line with the current price. Make it all or none. That will make it hard for anyone to actually execute the order. Spread them around the market. That will fuel buying interest in other houses. Spend up to a hundred million on buying, but sell first thing tomorrow if you buy anything."

I made up a list of stocks with him and then called United. "Can you hold your prices until this afternoon. I need one more approval and then I'll be able to go ahead."

There was a short discussion before they agreed. I suspected they would buy and push the market further up. After all, they still thought I was a buyer.

I watched the market continue to rise and talked repeatedly with my father. Jacqui called the brokers we had identified for the support operation and checked progress. She intimated that she could be a buyer.

"We are discussing how much we should take and also the price limits," she told them, "I should be back later today."

Around two I got another call from United.

"It's going to be hard to hold the prices," they said. "When can you give us a reply?"

I asked for another half an hour. They agreed. That brought us to within an hour of the close. And once they set the final market prices in Hong Kong we would be OK. Nobody would dare to sell the other markets so late in the day. I called them, having squeezed another five minutes or so over the half-hour. The market in Hong Kong had moved sharply upwards during that time. It was an incredible nine per cent up on the day.

I gave them the order. "But we thought you were a bull. We thought you were targeting a rise in the market. You can't do that to us."

I responded chillingly. "You quoted me a price. You quoted me a two-way price. You've just confirmed that you can hold it in my size. You will have recorded our discussions. I never advised you what I would be doing. I didn't advise you that this morning or this evening. Are you going to fax me immediately a confirmation or are you reneging on the deal?"

"Could you hold a minute?" he said.

"No," I said. "I need to know if you are sticking to your price now. I need a confirmation on my fax now. And if I cannot have that, I will turn my tapes over to the regulators this afternoon."

I pretended to be indignant, "I have never heard of something so outrageous, especially from United. You are one of our major banks. Your head office will hear of this as soon as they open."

By now he was really worried. He had screwed the deal and now he was at risk of being shut. For that would be the penalty if he reneged. He was not to know that I had no recording. But he would have and I did not think that they would be able to destroy them. Their controls would prevent them.

There was a hurried conversation. I heard yelling. I covered the mouthpiece and said to Jacqui, "Put in a buy order for a million dollars of the top five companies on the list at just one percent below the current price."

That would help support the market if they tried to hit it in the last minutes.

The dealer returned. "We confirm," he said. And it sounded like his last words. His voice was cracked. It most likely was his last words, at least at United. He would have hedged the wrong way and moved the market the wrong way. And he would have done it in size. The double whammy would not be forgiven.

"I want the confirm on the fax now and I want written confirmation this evening. The contract notes can follow. I am very unhappy at your attitude just now. I'll wait on the open line for the fax to arrive and then I'll confirm your fee payments."

It was a good idea keeping him on the phone. It disrupted their office a bit and made it hard for them to trade against me.

The fax came through. We had the option. The pan Asian fund, the Hong Kong fund and the small Thai and Korean ones were all hedged.

I confirmed, "We will pay the fees today, European time, crediting your account at your Geneva office. It is an internal transfer and so you will be able to confirm it at around six pm or seven at the latest. It all depends what time they are available."

I continued, "When can we pick up a written confirmation of the deals?"

When told they would be available in half an hour, I said "We'll be round for them then." And I rang off.

I picked up the phone from Jacqui. It was my father and I confirmed the news. "We'll wait until the close and then pick up the letter. That gives us time to have it in our hands before our money moves. Not that I think that's necessary."

We hung on. The market drifted back a bit but we did not pick up any stock. Quite simply at the end of the day, there were enough buyers around to withstand any pressure that may come from United. Or perhaps I had misjudged them and they were betting on trying to lay off their position rather than upset sentiment.

We went over to their offices. They were just up Queens Road Central. That was close to the hotel. I checked the letter. It confirmed everything. I looked at the conditions. There were no problems. I checked the signature. It was fine. I thanked them and left. They hardly looked a happy bunch of bunnies. But then I doubt they were.

I called the States and asked my father what he wanted us to do. "You've done OK for today," he said. "We wait and watch the markets. Get out to Wan Chai or something and have some fun. I can sort out the cover for United."

"What do you want to do?" I asked Jacqui.

"I feel like doing something outrageous," she said. "I want to dress up and do the town."

"We could have dinner in the Chinese here. The Man Wah is rather good. Do you want me to book it for eight? Then we can have a drink in the Captain's bar first. And we can head off to Wan Chai around ten. It is pretty quiet until then."

"Fantastic," she replied. "Now I want you to wear some of those new clothes. An open necked shirt and slacks will be fine. It will be nice to see you in casual gear again. I am going to dress to shock. Oh and to drive you wild. You'll be eating out of my hand by tonight. Then I'll seduce you."

We got washed and changed. I put on one of the designer shirts that she bought me. It was a red and white striped motif in silk. I doubt I would have bought it myself. But it felt smooth next to the skin, and actually a bit erotic. I put on a pair of slightly loose trousers and beige loafers.

"Hey, you look rather good," came the approving call from Jacqui. She was making up in front of the desk mirror, with one of the white fluffy dressing gowns that they give you in the Mandarin draped loosely around her.

She had painted her nails a bright pink and was applying matching lipstick. Her mascara was a deep black and heavier than usual. It had the effect of making her eyes seem bigger and her lashes longer. She had fluffed out her hair, but at the same time had added a spray that made it glisten in the light.

She didn't look like a businesswoman. She looked exotic, even erotic. She had a mischievous gleam in her face. We had been at work for over a month. We thought we would ease ourselves into things here in Hong Kong, but, in the end, we had had to jump in immediately. This was her way of relaxing. And I knew this was going to be a memorable night.

She stepped out of the robe. Her body shone from the bath oils. She was totally naked and kept her back to me. I was happy to be the voyeur for the moment. She wriggled her bottom at me as she sashayed through the room to the cupboard.

As she dressed, it was like watching a strip tease in reverse. She lent against the wall and put one foot into her panties. She did not move from there to slide the other one in, before languorously gliding them up over her calves, then her thighs and finally waggling her bottom into them. She straightened the thin slip of material that stretched from back to front and smoothed the sides so that they fitted like a glove.

Turning half round so I saw her breasts, she pulled out her bra. She placed it around her waist, back to front and did up the hooks. Then she eased it round her body and up to her breasts. One after another, she allowed them to fall gently into the cups of her bra, before pulling the shoulder straps into place.

She then took a halter necked top from the drawer and stepped into it before drawing it gently and tantalisingly up her body and into place. The top was silk and, when taut, revealed the gentle outline of her bra. However, when it was allowed to be at ease, it covered her body only leaving a gentle hint of the temptations beneath.

The skirt, a mini in black, followed the same route, but just to the waist. She did not need tights. Her legs were brown and firm enough to reject any such artificial supports. She just stepped into a pair of high heels and swirled round to me.

"How do I look?" she asked. She already knew.

"How can I reply? The only answer I could give you needs me to get you to take all that off."

Her smile was triumphant. She picked up her bag and declared, "Now for pit stop one. Let's get to the Captain's bar."

We walked over the lobby to the Captain's bar. We got a fair deal of looks as we crossed the crowded lobby. Or, at least, Jacqui did. She had learnt how to walk elegantly even if she was wearing the tightest of short skirts and the highest of heels. It was an art that many women cannot master. She did and that made the clothes she was wearing look as if the fashion had been designed for her.

"Hey," I said, "I won't dare to go for a pee. Otherwise I'll never make the way through the crowd around you."

She walked into the bar and I followed. The predominantly male company let her through without a murmur. We stood in a corner and I ordered a beer for myself and a champagne cocktail for her.

"Could I have the cocktail in a half pint glass?" she called over. "Not one of the diddly ones you serve others. And could the brandy base be the Courvoisier rather than one of the other brands?"

By this time everyone was looking at her. Her high heels allowing her to tower above some of the barflies. They must have made her some five ten high for she was normally around five eight. And that short skirt and flimsy top gave the imagination less work than normal.

Our drinks came and we touched glasses. I drained part of mine eagerly for I was thirsty. Even I was surprised when I saw her do the same, but with the whole half-pint.

She giggled and said "Oh darling, that's just right. Could I have another?"

A woman drinking half a pint of champagne cocktails is unusual. One drinking double that is unknown. I didn't want to question her, though even I thought it was a bit over the top.

Just as I was about to order, she called out, "Oh darling, I've changed my mind. I'll have a Perrier instead or I'll be anybody's by the time I've finished. I want some drinks at dinner, too, and at those strip clubs you've promised to show me."

A woman planning a heavy drink session in Hong Kong is not that unusual. One talking openly about going to a strip club definitely is. Again we drew attention to ourselves. The population were as fascinated with her as I was.

In the event, dinner was blissfully uneventful. We sat overlooking Hong Kong and enjoyed the view. The food was passable rather than memorable. And we both laid off the wine, although I took a bottle of the local Tsingtao beer. Wine is pretty ghastly with Chinese food – it does not blend well. And in any case it was better to be careful because the night was going to be a long one as we tried out the clubs in Wan Chai.

Taking a cab to Lockhart Road, we entered into one of the clubs there. We went down the stairs. There was a bar round a large dance floor. Three girls danced in vague unison, athletically draping their legs round shiny aluminium poles that were strategically placed at different corners. Bikini bottoms covered their tights and from time to time they would pull down their bras.

It was excruciatingly boring. But then it was not meant to be otherwise. Then the star dancer came on. She was a bit more energetic than the first crew and seemed to pull at her minuscule bra a bit more often.

"They look as if they have all gone to the three step school of dancing," said Jacqui. "How can all these people sit and gape at them?"

"Perhaps they are here for a take away," I said "And all this is a simple parade of wares."

"Well if they learn making love in the same school, they are not going to be worth a postcard home. Some of my father's places are much better. Shall I show them how to dance properly?"

"No fear. We can go dancing if you want but I am not going to have you on that stage."

"Oh come on. Don't be a spoilsport. I won't take off my clothes. I just want to teach them how to dance."

"Absolutely no. Or I leave you here."

She pouted. "All right, but let's have another drink and then head off somewhere for dancing."

I was relieved that she had agreed. I had somehow thought she was going to argue about it. So I turned round and ordered another couple of drinks.

It was at that precise minute that she squeezed through the gap that the dancers had taken and talked to one of the girls behind the bar. I was initially a bit annoyed, but then thought that this could be fun. So I waited.

Our drinks arrived and then I noticed that the music had changed. It was a modern song that I could not place. The rhythm was slow but the beat was strong.

And suddenly Jacqui was up on the stage and pulsating to the music. She swayed backwards and forwards to the beat. Her eyes were closed. She arched her body back from the waist and her hair fell back. It almost stroked the ground.

The room was silent. Silenced by her sexuality. Her body moved up and down. Her hips worked their way round. Her feet glided over the floor.

From time to time there was a tantalising glimpse of underwear as her skirt rode up on an energetic movement. There were intakes of breath as her gyrating body pulled her top and she moved her hands across her body. Her figure, from the slender hips through to the full breasts sprung into view. Their contrast to the androgynous figures of the Thai and Philippine dancers, made the desirable almost unbearable.

One sensual movement followed the other. She seemed in a dream. She appeared to float above us. Then she came back to this world. She cruised around the stage before stopping directly in front of me. There she bent back, her hair brushing the stage behind me. Her legs askew, she proffered herself to me, alone in my corner of the room, as her skirt rode up and the gentle silk suggested a dark shadow of pleasure.

As the beat moved from gentle to fast, she pulled herself up. She did it by instinct as people, hidden from the display, moved forward to share our private moment of public exhibition. And then as the beat went to a crescendo, she jumped from the stage and onto the bar in front of me. She stepped off onto the edge of my chair before sliding onto my lap. Her arms round my neck, she kissed me full on the mouth to the applause of the crowd.

There was a faint smell of perspiration that fought to overcome the gentle fragrance of her perfume. There was a secret shifting of her body as she checked to see how excited I was. And when she realised, there was a more passionate kiss. This time she targeted my ear and neck, before returning to my lips in a rough and violent kiss.

The crowd applauded as we both grabbed a drink. I thought I should be embarrassed but I was not. I was not angry. I was definitely aroused. Her act and the reaction of the crowd had excited me more than I knew.

And the girls in the bar seemed to be infected by the sexual fervour that now permeated the air. They danced with vigour but also with lust. Tonight they too would enjoy what was usually a tedious job.

We left the bar soon afterwards. They refused to let us pay. That was unheard of in Hong Kong. But the orders that evening could well become a record. For the bar was infected with desire after the unexpected floor show.

Our next stop was a dance club where they were playing smooth and smoochy music. We danced together, allowing our bodies to sense each other. My silk shirt and her top of similar material pretended not to exist. It seemed we were already undressed and enjoying the touch of each other's skin.

Through the evening we danced. Sometimes fast and sometimes slow. Our bodies were never apart even if they were not together. And as the evening turned to morning, we were still dancing. And as the morning drew on, we walked outside and got into a red cab. In the back we moved our bodies close together. I smelt her hair, her perfume mixing with the smells of the evening. The slight smell of perspiration from our dancing blended with the intrusive smoke and fumes of the dance floors or bars.

But it was our bodies that continued to build up the desire that we had created earlier in the evening. And that desire had been fed and re-fed since that time. The wonder of her dressing flooded back. The excitement of the Captain's bar blended with the eroticism of the Wan Chai bar. And the close contact of the dance floor still throbbed in the proximity of our thighs and the meeting of our chests in the tightness of the cab seat.

We skated through the lobby and up the lift to the twentieth floor. We closed our door behind us as we entered the room with its king sized bed. Our lips and bodies clung and clung together as we kissed.

My hands went up her back and round to her breasts. With a half cry, I kissed her on the neck. As my lips moved round to the back of her neck, I gently unhooked her skirt and it fell to the floor.

I moved away and kissed her on the breasts and then on her bare stomach. I moved my lips down to between her hips, where I licked and kissed the darkening and ever damper patch that came to greet me.

My hands moved to the straps on her shoulders. At the same time I felt her hands unzip my trousers. She must have already undone the belt for they fell down my legs. She pulled gently way from me. Her shoulder straps were falling to her shoulders and the top was gliding to her waist as she bent down. She kissed me down the inside of one leg, gliding my trousers down and easing them over one foot and then the other. Her lips moved up again, over my waist and chest and back to my lips.

I eased her top over her waist and let it drop down to the ground. She stepped out of it, still kissing me. At the same time she undid the buttons of my shirt and eased it off my shoulders. It fell to the ground to meet the rest of our clothes.

I undid the back of her bra and took it off, dropping it to the ground and relishing the feel of her excited breasts against me. My hands slipped into the side of her panties and I pulled them down, kissing the bottom part of her body as I sank to my knees to help her ease out of them. I was kissing my way back up her body and burying my face and mouth between her legs, while one hand ripped off the rest of my clothes.

I stood up, I picked her up, her shoes falling to the ground, and carried her to the bed. Panting, almost crying, my excitement was only equalled by hers. We had thought and planned this all night. In a way we had started when she had got dressed some six or so hours ago.

I did not so much as feel myself entering her as gliding into her. All that I felt was soft, erotic and desirable. Her body moved to my movement. Her spasms spurred on mine. Her cries called out above mine. We ended the evening in pleasure and felt desire meet its ultimate goal.

HONG KONG STRIKES

That morning we had breakfast in bed. We looked out of our window. We watched the boats and tugs move across the narrow strip of water between Hong Kong Island and Kowloon. We saw the red taxis pick up one group after another as the ferries discharged the workers from Central District and beyond at the unexpectedly decrepit buildings of the terminal. It stood in poverty beside the more modern General Post Office and the towering eminence of the adjacent skyscrapers.

We had no need to rush. And it was with definite reluctance that we got out of bed and prepared ourselves for the start of another day.

As planned, we started to call the brokers as the markets opened. They were quiet at the start of business although the market had drifted back from the close. This was not surprising for United's likely buying had driven the late afternoon surges. The market looked nervous but not over vulnerable.

We called the brokers on our list and asked for their views. They were almost all universally optimistic about markets. The only difference between them was the degree of optimism they revealed. Later in the morning we called my parents.

"Watch the market and add to the position every time it strengthens five per cent," said my father. "In addition start putting around some of those 'is Sebo selling?' lines."

"Surely" said Jacqui, "they won't fall for that again?"

"Don't over-rate the intelligence of the Filth," said my father.

"The filth?" enquired Jacqui.

"It stands for 'Failed In London, Trying Hong Kong" I said. "It's quite apt for the bulk of the traders here."

So we went back to our long watch. It was a dull day , but we knew we had to be patient. In the evening we handed over the job to my father in America. We went out again but this time it was for a quieter time than the night before.

Jacqui was dressed in a business suit, had her hair up and was wearing light make-up. She looked the perfect image of a businesswoman. The

228

restaurant we selected was similarly formal. For we ate in the polite correctness of the grill at our hotel rather than the more trendy places in Wan Chai and elsewhere.

The next few days were similar. The market would rise a few hundred points. The next day it would fall a few hundred more. At the end of the week it was a bit below our option prices, but only marginally.

"They can't hold this too much longer," predicted my father. "It will crack soon. It could go one way or another. We can only carry on asking the questions and waiting."

United called from time to time. It was never the trader who had sold us the options. I sensed that they had not been able to lay off the position to any extent. They were too keen for us to close out. I recounted that to my father and he was pleased. "That shows that they are nervous about these levels. And others must be too or they would lay off the position. Even if it meant taking a small hit. Their management would hate that exposure."

It was some few days after this conversation that the strident ring of the phone woke us. Jacqui and I started. We jumped from the bed. It was my father. He was excited, "Switch on CNN," he instructed, "And look at the news."

Jacqui grabbed the remote control and hit the buttons. The story was from the Middle East. The pictures were of troops and weapons being loaded onto transport planes. The place was Tripoli. The story was clear. Libya, Syria and Iran had signed a mutual accord. Troops were going to Iran to help it defend itself against alleged American aggression. The build up of US forces had been accelerated. The President's office was making threatening noises. The British Prime Minister grinned nervously and said the move was a threat to World Peace.

"What are the markets doing over there?" I asked. I saw it was four in the morning in Hong Kong. It would, therefore, be late afternoon in New York.

"Wall Street's just fallen five hundred points. It could be that they'll soon have to put the circuit breakers into place," he said. That meant that they would stop trading for a period to allow the market to take a breather. It was a process they introduced whenever the market went into a major free fall.

"This could make us a fortune," said Jacqui.

"Well," said my father. "Let's hope that it does. As long as it lasts a couple of days and gets worse, we'll be all right. By the way I have managed to buy half a billion US dollars against the Hong Kong dollar. I want us to go up to four or five billion. That will take around five hundred million of margin. But these sorts of crises always help the US dollar. And if that strengthens it makes the Hong Kong dollar link all that more difficult to defend. This could be the big one."

"We'll start some new rumours here, and we'll ask about the peg all over the place once we have our position. Are you going out a month?"

My father said he was. He was buying the dollars for delivery in a month's time and would therefore have to close his position within that period.

The big game had started.

Once Hong Kong opened, the blood bath started. The market fell by eight hundred points at the opening. Other markets followed suit.

I checked the price of the dollar. It was holding steady. I expected that the pressure on the markets would soon unsettle the rate.

I called all the major banks one after another. I sold as many Hong Kong dollars as they would take from me. In the end I dumped over seventeen billion of them. That was incredible. That sort of activity was rarely seen. The market had to be under pressure.

We found it more and more difficult to deal after that. The banks wanted more security. They got nervous. In the end, I called my father and told him what I had done. I advised where I needed margin. When we added it all up, it amounted to almost half a billion US dollars.

"That's better than I thought," he said. "Now we keep twenty four-hour watch and close contact. Get Jacqui to start up rumours, any way she can. Attack the peg."

The peg, I explained to Jacqui again, was the name given to the official rate hundred million between the Hong Kong dollar and the US dollar. We had dealt at 7.70 forward. If the official rate were abandoned, the Hong Kong dollar would fall and we would buy back the ones we had sold for less than we had got. The difference was our profit.

"Shall we take a value check?" I said. "On the share front, if all markets are down in line with Hong Kong, then we are up just over three hundred million dollars against the one eighty million we paid the banks for the options. On the currency side, we have sold twenty three point one billion Hong Kong dollars. That equals around three billion US dollars. The banks are holding around five hundred million or so US dollars as security on those deals. We would get the security back from the banks when the deals were settled. And we would make or lose thirty million dollars for every one per cent variation in the exchange rates."

Jacqui called our contacts. She asked if they had news of meetings. The meetings were allegedly ones involving the leading Hong Kong financiers and government officials. She knew of no news of any meetings, but the fact that she asked made people worried. They, too, started questioning about a meeting.

The stock markets fell. On average I calculated that they were around nine percent down on the night before and eleven per cent down on the price of our options. We were two hundred million dollars up net of the fees. The currency was stable though. The peg stood.

CNN reported that the British were sending another aircraft carrier to the Gulf. The US announced it was considering freezing Iranian, Syrian and Libyan dollar assets. Iran and Libya announced a ban on all oil exports to the West and a blockade of several of the regions' ports. Venezuela stopped oil exports in sympathy. The markets wobbled again.

Hong Kong put up its interest rates and declared again that the peg was a core part of its strategy. Local brokers started worrying about the possibility of defaults. Malaysia attacked the dark forces of speculation.

"I guess that includes us," I said to Jacqui. "Or at least you because I'm blond."

She was watching the screen with fascination. She called another broker and asked if there was truth in a rumour that the Chinese Finance Minister had called a meeting to discuss the crisis. She asked if it was true that China was going to intervene in favour of Iran.

Minutes later another broker fed the rumour back to her. "That's excellent," said my father. "Rumour breeds rumour. And then the rumours become fact. That's the way this merry go round works."

Other governments in the region put up interest rates. Then the rupiah in Indonesia went into total free fall. It hit 17,000 to the dollar, down from 6,000. It was followed by the baht in Thailand. You could buy won but not sell them. They had ceased to be convertible. The markets went crazy.

I recalculated. I estimated markets were now down another five percent, well over five per cent. In many countries the Exchanges were asked to close but trading continued offshore. And the sudden closures dragged them down even more.

As the markets in Asia closed, the markets in London opened. London slumped seven hundred points and then further to a thousand point fall. That had never been seen before. The market was an amazing twenty per cent down. Those double-digit falls were seen elsewhere. Germany, France, Amsterdam were all down sharply.

Currencies came under attack. Briefly the Hong Kong dollar traded beneath the peg. Then again it breached the peg. Interest rates hit four or five hundred per cent as the market crashed.

It was then sheer and unadulterated panic. And that panic fed panic in Wall Street. The market opened. The market slumped. They stopped the market trading for a bit to try to stem the flood of sales. But it was to no avail. It was a blood bath. There were also rumours of major broker defaults. One of the big banks was calling in all their loans to brokers. Another bank had called to see the Federal Reserve. There were rumours that it was in trouble.

In the afternoon, two brokers announced that they would no longer make prices in Asian stocks. The omens for start of day in Hong Kong, just a few hours away, were very bad indeed.

Once the market opened, we watched the screen flood again with red figures indicating market falls. One stock after another fell through the floor. One market after another panicked.

My father called and told me to check the option. "We should take part of our profits. We don't want to be caught in a squeeze."

I called United and they jumped at the chance of getting me to reverse my positions with them. The fall was now twenty three per cent and we could close out half our positions for a four hundred million-dollar profit. Against that we would have to set off half the fees paid, or ninety million dollars. United were over the moon to close out some of the loss. We had cost them over three hundred million of losses on that half. And we still were running the other half of the stock market positions and the whole of the currency one.

I looked to the news and saw that the President was holding a press conference. He warned that the US would strike if the Syrians and Libyans did not announce their withdrawal within twenty-four hours .The Iranians responded by arresting all United Nations personnel on their soil. At that time there were some three hundred inspectors from the UN in Iran, monitoring their alleged peaceful nuclear enrichment programme. The Libyans called the US a scared capitalist hound and promised war in Iran and in Libya and around the world if they attacked. The UN issued a statement saying they regretted Iran's action and called for calm.

The markets fell further. The tone was bad. Currency rates in Hong Kong came under greater pressure. Then it all happened. The rumour started that there was a flow of funds by local residents into the dollar. The peg was in serious trouble.

The Indonesian rupiah fell even further. The ringit in Malaysia and the dollar in Singapore started to crumble. The panic continued. As we had planned, the roller coaster had begun.

I took again the value of our open stock. "The next twenty four hours will be critical," said my father. "If the index falls to give us a thirty per cent profit on the other half of the stocks, let's take it. I don't want to be greedy."

I checked. The fall was twenty seven per cent.

A medium sized local brokerage house announced it could not meet its obligations and went under. The market panicked. Another admitted under pressure that it was in talks with its bankers. The market went into free fall. The contagion spread. Asia under siege fell through the floor.

When I managed to get through to United's terrified traders, they quoted me a price that indicated the fall was now up to thirty five per cent. They jumped to close the balance of our position. We did it at a profit of an incredible six hundred million plus profit before taking into account the associated ninety million dollar fee. Our second excursion into equity markets had been even more profitable than our first.

We had made over eight hundred and fifty million dollars after our expenses. We were worth over two billion three hundred million dollars even if the peg held.

And it did not look as if it could. As the market closed, there were stories after stories about the massive sale of the Hong Kong dollar. The reserves were strong but they would not last forever. And soon something had to give or the flow of funds had to stop.

As the US ultimatum drew closer, the UN asked for talks. The US extended their deadline by twelve hours but started flying over Iraq and Libya on reconnaissance missions. The atmosphere was tense.

Once again in Europe, markets fell sharply. The panic continued. It allowed no respite. The calls for calm were met with incredulity. There was only one way to go and that was down.

Again the currencies came under attack. We monitored the continued rise in interest rates. They soared. The Hong Kong dollar stopped trading. It was impossible to sell.

We monitored the worsening situation overnight in New York. We had had no sleep for thirty-six hours. Things were tense. Then it happened.

A serious faced announcer advised that, against unrelenting pressure, the official exchange rate, or the peg, was suspended as a temporary measure. That moment the rate slumped to 11.50 to the dollar.

"Close out now," barked my father. "It's going to over do it."

I jumped to the phone and asked for a price against the dollar forward. 12.20 offered not bid. I could buy Hong Kong dollars but not sell them. I asked for size.

"Whatever you want," came the reply.

"Tell me what that means in real money?"

"I'll make it in up to a half billion."

"What price would you make me for a larger deal than half a billion US dollars?"

"12.10 for a billion to close you," the trader responded. He had seen my position with him on the screen and so widened his price as much he dared.

"I sell a billion US dollars and buy Hong Kong at 12.10," I said.

I reminded him again of the confirmation details and looked at my pad.

I needed to buy in total 23.1 billion Hong Kong dollars to close out our positions. I had 11 billion left to buy.

I did that in four deals across the market. And as the rate fell further, I got a better price. In the end I spent just under one point eight billion US dollars. And I had bought back our short position. We had made just over one billion two hundred million dollars in all.

My father yelled, "We've done it. That's just a tad over three point five billion dollars in the kitty."

I was staggered that he had managed to work that out so quickly. Jacqui was beaming and waving her hands about in the air shouting "yeah."

I sank my head in my hands and tried to let it all sink in. Jacqui came round and kissed me on the neck.

I heard my father speak, "Check the faxes and be sure they are accurate. Make sure all the deals are the right way round. We should get the option money tomorrow and the foreign exchange at the end of the month. Check and double-check all faxes. Then ensure that you get all contract notes tomorrow."

The faxes came through. I checked them and confirmed that to him. The figures tallied. We were in the clear. We had the confirmations. We had done it. We had made ourselves multi billionaires.

I looked again at CNN. They had the crisis in the Middle East on the news. It read deadline less three hours. I mentioned this to my father. He shrugged his shoulders, or so it seemed, "The Iranians will capitulate at the eleventh hour."

And within two hours we heard that the Libyans would withdraw. Iran would release its prisoners. The threats were over. Peace triumphed from the latest metaphorical sabre rattling.

The markets started to rally. The energy seemed to have been sapped from the markets. Battered and bruised they stagnated. Then relieved that they had overcome the crisis, they rallied slowly.

We were exhausted. We watched out of habit. But we did not concentrate. We did not care. We had played our hand. And we had had our run of luck. We were not going to risk any more. It had been nearly forty-eight hours since we last slept. It was ten days since we had first traded.

"I'm exhausted," I said. "I can't think. I need to crash out."

"Touch base tomorrow and get some food. Then get some sleep. You both deserve it," responded my father.

We killed the phones. Jacqui looked drained. I looked no better.

"We made it," I said. "We made it."

"What do we do now?"

"First of all we need to get some sleep. Then we have to sort out the details."

We crashed out as we spent our first night as multi-billionaires. I fell asleep wondering what on earth several billion dollars actually looked like. Next day we sorted out the paperwork and arranged the details for the remittance of the profit. The money from the options was available immediately. It was sent through United in Geneva and then disbursed on to a series of shell companies that my parents had been busy forming.

The money from the foreign exchange deals would only be available at the beginning of the following month. We agreed that Jacqui and I should stay in the Far East until that had been finalised. We also agreed that I should continue to maintain our cover and trade for a new group of hedge funds.

We put some business United's way as we reckoned they could have lost half a billion dollars on our option deal. They accepted willingly. They were a large enough organisation to cover that, but it would still make a nasty dent in their balance sheet.

We dabbled around in the market as it fluctuated up and down as one rumour after another took command. But we were only playing in the odd million and the fun was not there. We at least got the satisfaction that we made money.

We kept our workdays short and spent our free time getting the maximum out of the city. It is not a place of great variety outside the bars or restaurants. And we avoided the many invitations to dinner. We did not want to make friends. Quite simply we wanted as few people as possible to know who we really were.

Also, we were conscious that the territory was a place where people talked. We had made millions and billions to their knowledge. And although they had no doubt swallowed the story that we worked for a fund, they would expect us to have a stake. I was therefore concerned, lest we could be a target. And we had no contacts and no means of arming ourselves. We therefore avoided taking risks in the less salubrious areas of the place.

We went to restaurants in Central. We took time out in the hotel health club. We danced in the different discotheques. And we still went down to Wan Chai although Jacqui never did repeat her dance routine. She was asked to do it on many occasions.

In the end the day came for the payment of the funds on the foreign exchange. We checked out with my father. They had arrived. We could head off to the USA or Europe.

Jacqui and I decided that we would head to Europe this time. We decided that Paris would be the ideal spot. At long last, we could go to the theatre and cinema and eat well. And we could protect ourselves there. For the next phase of our plans would be doubly dangerous.

We knew we had weakened United and my father suddenly announced that he had decided to attack them. "If their share price falls, they are bound to be taken over. We can make money out of that. And I have a scheme to tip their share price over the edge," he announced triumphantly.

"They made five forty million dollars profit last year," he said. "They will have been hit by the Asia crisis in any case and we would have hit them badly as well. There is no way that they would have managed to lay off any decent part of the position they took when they dealt with us. And now I have worked out a plan where they are going to get hit again. And that will play into our hands."

"What do you mean? Are we going for another big hit?" I asked.

"No," he replied. "At least not yet. This is the skirmish before the next big one. I am going to launch a new fund and it is going to default; and default big time."

He had established that United would be willing to advance us half the value of the assets of a new fund. His aim was to put the fund's money in turn into some worthless companies, mainly in the exploration business. He had a schedule of some companies that fitted that bill in both Asia and the Americas. Our purchases would make their share prices rise. When we stopped buying they would slump and the fund would default. United would call in their loans but the security would all be worthless and impossible to sell.

"But won't we lose money in the process?" I queried.

"No, not a lot," said my father. "First of all, I will carefully buy us stakes through secret offshore accounts for around fifty million dollars in the target companies before the fund even starts to buy. We'll put around a hundred million of seed money into the fund and it will buy like there's no tomorrow. That will really push up the price of the stocks. Once our original stocks have tripled – and they will – we will sell off our stakes and that will recoup our seed capital."

"How many companies are you actually thinking of buying for the fund?" I asked.

"In so far as the fund is concerned, I have so far identified fifteen to twenty stocks to buy. They are all bombed out and most likely all worthless. Normally United would be suspicious. But as they go up there will be rumours of some sort. And as United think that we have the Midas touch, they could well even buy them for their own account. I can't see them questioning me too much."

"But, how will the companies themselves react?" I queried.

"I have identified ones that are mainly in mining or oil and gas. Fairly unscrupulous people who have large stakes in them also run them. I can't see them issuing any statements knocking their share prices. But that's a risk. We may have a black sheep among them. An honest guy may run one of the companies. But that would be a first in that part of those sectors. In a frothy market I could push the fund's value up to five hundred million. I think the owners and directors of the companies will take advantage of the rise to sell out. So there should be supply at the higher prices."

I thought through the scheme. We would put a hundred million into the fund and United would lend us a further fifty million. As we bought, the share prices would rise and they would lend us even more money. And so it would go on. The share prices inflated ever more; and yet the companies were worthless. In the end United would be lending all the money against the overpriced shares in the fund.

It was a classical pyramid. By the time it came crashing down, United would have lent perhaps two or three hundred million against a portfolio that appeared to be worth five or six hundred million. But once the values fell, they would find the shares impossible to sell. In fact they could even be worthless. For as they sought to sell them, they would force the price even further down. And when the market heard of yet another disaster from United, they would hit their share price. So many incompetent decisions in so short a period of time would never be forgiven.

My father continued, "United are worth five billion dollars on the market. I plan in time to buy around thirty per cent of them but need to see the price well down before we do that. And then I can put them in play and we make money again! I don't want to go above thirty per cent or I may have a problem with the regulators. They could bar me, or rather you, or make us bid for the rest. So I'd rather keep this play down to a billion. I'll use straight cash for this."

I interrupted, "Why did you say me?"

"You are less known than me. You are a mystery financier. You made a fortune in the Far East through your stake your hedge funds and other investments. And you can play the private bit. You know how. You refuse interviews. Carry on using the Rossi name but Jacqui should revert to her real name. That will give credibility to your wealth as the market will think the Di Maglios are involved."

I nodded. Like many of my father's schemes, it was high risk, hardly legal but brilliant in its simplicity.

"Will you be needing us for it?" I asked.

"No, why don't you take a breather and enjoy yourselves. We will move over to Switzerland. I want to be closer to the centre of the action rather than having to work nights here in the USA. Keep in touch though for we will need you when we get onto the United Bank heist."

I agreed. We decided to move to Paris immediately and Jacqui and I grabbed the opportunity to head over there that night. We decided to book into the George V in Paris, near the Champs Elysees in a road that carries its name. I booked a suite as we planned to stay there for some time. And, as I kept telling myself, money was no longer an issue.

The day we arrived in Paris, we saw the Di Maglio family contact and got our guns. We followed the earlier precedent and I took one for normal use and another in a leg holster. Jacqui stuck to her usual handbag size.

But, in the end, Paris was uneventful. We were private and undisturbed. My father was busy designing his new fund and slowly buying in the initial stock to launch the fund.

We enjoyed Paris. We walked around the shops, sticking often to the Faubourg Saint Honore. We went to the opera. We went to the theatre. We went to films. We wandered around parks, We visited the Louvre. In short we changed our life style. From frenetic financiers, we became indolent culture vultures. From being a fair imitation of ruthless gangsters, we became careless lovers in the early Parisian winter months.

But we let down our guard and did not notice. The car screeched around the corner of the Rue de La Paix as we walked down it arm in arm. Our reactions were dulled. As I swung around, a club crashed over my head and I fell stunned to the ground. Jacqui screamed somewhere in the distance. There was a yell of pain from a man.

I heard a scuffle as I slowly drifted back to consciousness. I raised myself to my knees. A brutal boot thudded into my stomach and then again into my face. I crashed down onto the ground as the boot again made contact with my head.

I grabbed hold of the foot and wrenched it towards me. The man was unbalanced and fell crashing to the ground. I pulled out my gun and blasted two shots into him. I aimed low but was unaware where he was hit.

I again heard yells and could make out Jacqui's scream. I looked up and saw two men trying to bundle her into a waiting car. She had somehow opened her shoulder bag and taken out the gun. She fired it into the car. There was a sound of breaking glass and then I saw it flying out of her hand. She gave a sob of pain and then appeared to slump as she received a karate chop to the back of her neck.

Now she was thrown into the car. As its doors closed and it started moving down the street, I pulled up every ounce of strength and rolled into the road behind it.

My gun blasted out, catching it low in the tyres. There was a burst as they exploded and shredded beneath the swerving vehicle. The car veered off the road, the two rear wheels grinding their bare metal rims against the hard surface. It came to rest against a bollard, its bonnet dented and petrol spilling out into the street.

I pulled myself behind a parked car as the bark of an automatic filled the evening air. People around, and there were just a few, threw themselves terrified onto the ground. Glass in the nearby shop windows shattered as they were hit and bullets ricocheted uncomfortably close.

Despite the beating I had received, I was on full alert now. The adrenalin was pumping through me and I was conscious of the slightest movement in front of me and around me as well.

The man I had shot earlier crawled towards me, a gun at the ready. But a blast from mine stopped him in his tracks as he fell to the ground and his gun skidded across the pavement. I saw it was a sub-machine gun and twisted myself towards it. I knew I had hardly any bullets left, if any. And I was not wearing my reserve gun. I had left it at the hotel.

A car came to a sudden halt as it saw this scene, its occupants petrified at the violence they saw. A man at the wheel was blinking in astonishment at the scene in front of him. A woman next to him, her mouth frozen open in a strangled scream.

Someone ran to the car and dragged out the driver, hurling him across the road in a fury. Another person materialised and pulled his woman passenger by the hair, as she appeared to go into a dead faint at the unexpected brutality. Jacqui was being pulled from the car.

I saw that there was blood on her face, which was white with shock. Her dress was torn and filthy with grime from the road. She wore only one shoe. The strap of her shoulder bag was dragged round her neck.

I noted the gunmen were not talking English or French. Their speech was guttural. The language appeared Slavonic. Then I realised they could be Russian. My memory flooded back to the shooting in Geneva. The uncle had mentioned something about a feud. But how had they found us? And what did they want of Jacqui?

I rolled out from behind the car but knew I could not get a clean shot at her captor. I risked shooting Jacqui rather than him. Again the automatic went into action, one bullet missing me by inches as I dived back for cover. A machine gun blasted several shots in my direction. A window behind me imploded into the street. Someone screamed. There were shouts. Someone started crying hysterically.

The abducted car drove off; this time under cover from the repeated shots of the automatic. It kept me at bay. This time I did not have an open view of the tyres to try and stop it.

A motor bike pulled up. I thought it was a policeman but saw it was just a passer by. I went over to him. I threw my revolver down next to the injured man. I knew now it was empty. It could not be traced to me and I did not want to be caught with it. People must have seen me grab the machine gun. I could need witnesses. This looked nasty.

I went to the motor bike, the machine gun ready. The rider was young and in a state of shock. This was not what you expect when riding down one of the smartest streets in Paris. I grabbed hold of the bike and snarled "off." I was menacing enough. I knew my head was bleeding. I saw my shirt was covered in blood. My clothes were dishevelled and dusty from the street. But I needed the bike to follow the car.

He protested for a second before backing off and away at the threat of the gun. He did not know who I was but wasn't going to take any risks. I jumped onto the powerful bike and roared away after the car.

I left behind a scene of devastation. One man who may have been dead. Glass all over the place from broken windows. Blood on the pavement. People in shock, some of them were hysterical. Cars riddled with bullet holes. A car crashed into a bollard with its tyres shot away. Petrol spilling over the road from the damaged petrol tank. Somehow there was no fire, but that could still come. Moments later, I spotted the car at the Louvre, going at speed. My bike roared after it. My gun was still in my hand and it made it difficult to control the heavy bike. I was already weakened by my fall and knew I was going to have to act quickly. I had one advantage. The bike moved faster than the car although the traffic at that hour was quite light.

The car turned right and headed down to the banks of the Seine. It turned up towards Concorde. I followed, gradually reducing the distance between me and the speeding hijacked car. I could not see through the windows but I knew there were three men there and also Jacqui. I did not know if any of them were injured, or just battered and bruised.

The car turned off the Place de la Concorde and turned up the Champs Elysees. I caught up with it just near the Arc de Triomphe. I was doing around a hundred and twenty kilometres an hour as we skidded together into the circular road that surrounds Paris' most famous monument.

The driver noticed me. Whether he recognised me is another matter. If he had I doubt he would have left me alive. I was too dangerous. He would have told one of his companions to shoot me. As it was they must have thought I was a citizen being brave or stupid. Or alternatively, even a plain clothes policeman.

Too late, I noticed the car veering towards me and then it swerved sharply into my path. As if in slow motion, I saw the bike soar into the air and crash towards the centre of the road. I soared with it and then lost contact with it. I felt myself flying through the air and seemed to bounce on the hard road before everything went blank.

SEARCHING FOR JACQUI

I came to slowly and painfully. I was lying in a bed. There were two policemen in the room. They sat on chairs near the bed, stiffly upright in their uniforms. They had not noticed me come round. I closed my eyes again. I needed time to think.

I was in a room on my own. The police were not looking worried. That could mean that they thought I was a victim. I wondered what had happened to the gun. It had not been on my shoulder, but loose in my hand. Had it skidded away and been lost? Or perhaps it had not been associated with me.

I decided that was unlikely. Therefore they knew I had been armed. They must have associated me with the upheaval in the Rue de la Paix. The motorbike alone told them that. They would not have known who I was. I had only worn slacks and a sweater and Jacqui had put my wallet in her bag. They therefore did not know my identity. I was carrying no papers.

It was best that they did not know who I was. I suspected I was badly enough bruised to make it difficult to identify me. I should play dumb. I could pretend to be an American. If Jacqui's identity were known, that would associate me with the Di Maglio world. But I had to be careful. I must not involve the police with anything to do with Jacqui. Like it or not, I was going to need help to rescue her. And that help could only come from one person, her father.

I started to feel my body to see if anything was broken. I could move my toes. I tried my legs. I shifted my back, groaning as if moving in my sleep. Perhaps the police looked at me, but there was no sign of movement from them. My arm hurt but I knew it was in one piece. My shoulder ached. I must have fallen on it. My ribs were painful but that was not surprising given the number of kicks I had been dealt. My head ached but I could turn my neck around. I was able to open and shut my mouth. I was now pretty sure that I was surprisingly enough actually in one piece and without breakage.

I needed to get out of the hospital. I needed to get away from the police. But it was not going to be easy. I did not know how good I would be on my feet. My head still felt bad. I was not in a state to move fast. That meant I needed transport and also a disguise.

I opened my eyes again and met those of one of the policemen. He got up and called to someone outside the door. Police outside the room as well. That was a bad sign.

A doctor came in and looked at me. He called a nurse. They took my pulse and looked into my eyes. There was no sign of sympathy. There was no sign of friendship. This did not look good.

I groaned as they touched me. I worked out that it was better to make out I felt bad. That would make them relax. And that could give me my opportunity to escape. Or perhaps get a message to the outside world.

They left me and I heard the doctor say, "He is not up to being questioned. Perhaps he will be better tomorrow. But he is not hurt badly. How he hasn't broken anything I do not know. He is badly bruised and shaken. That's all really. In a few days he will be all right. Then in a few weeks the bruising will go."

The police stayed with me through the night. I realised I needed to act quickly. I would have to try to escape. I had no alternative.

I woke up later and saw that just one policeman was there. He was dozing in the chair. I wondered if the other had gone for good or just for a few minutes. I was never going to know and needed to act quickly. I quietly lifted myself upright. The policeman dozed on.

I swung my feet out of the bed. I was on his side. There was no evident weapon. Then I saw his truncheon lying on the floor beside him. And next to his truncheon was his service revolver. He must have put them there to make himself more comfortable.

I carefully picked up the holster with the revolver and drew it from its pouch. I checked the safety catch was on. I took it by the barrel and lifted it through the air with all the force I could muster. He started just before the heavy weapon crashed into his skull. I caught him as he fell. I had no interest in letting him fall noisily to the ground. I saw my clothes were actually in the room and pulled them on, torn and filthy as they were. They were better than the hospital robe.

The policeman was groaning. He was gradually coming round. I grabbed a sheet and tied one end around his legs, pulling them up behind him. I then tied him up with the rest of the sheet. He looked like a trussed chicken. He would find it hard to move. I lifted my arm high and smashed him over the head again. I had to be sure that he did not raise the alarm until I had made my escape.

I hoped that I had only given him a headache. I knew that I could have done more than that. There is no way to be gentle in situations like that.

I tucked his gun in my trousers and went to the window. I was several floors up but there was a fire escape to my left. There was a narrow ledge that led to a few feet of it. I shut the window behind me. I eased my way along the ledge and then launched myself at the fire escape. I made it without much difficulty. I ran down. I saw a door. It was open. I slipped inside. To my left was a room marked 'store'. I tried the door. It was open. I hurriedly entered the room and prepared for a long wait.

I was exhausted and needed to rest before making good my escape. I had to work out how. I then saw the phone on the wall. I now knew what I had to do.

I looked around the storeroom. At the rear was a laundry basket on wheels. I took some sheets from a shelf and placed them over the basket. If disturbed, that is where I would need to hide. The folded sheets gave the impression that there was basket full of sheets waiting to be placed on the racks. I would be underneath them, with a gun if necessary. I then looked at the door. I placed a chair against the handle. That would give me a warning and time to hide if needed.

I went to the phone. I knew the number by heart. I thought, though, that I would never need to dial it. I did not recognise the voice that answered.

"I need to speak to Mr Di Maglio. Say it's Charles De Roche. Jacqui is in danger."

Di Maglio came to the phone. "We got ambushed. Read the papers. It was in the Rue de la Paix in Paris. I almost got them. I am in a hospital. The police are looking for me. I just clubbed my guard and got out. But I am still hiding inside the hospital. I need to get out. Can you help me? We can then put the pieces together and find Jacqui."

"Where are you inside the hospital?"

I looked at the phone. It read, 'Storeroom. South Wing. Eighth floor,' I told him.

He was brief. "Stay where you are. We'll get the address by tracing the number. My man will knock on the door. He'll knock twice. One long gap between knocks. So don't blast his head off."

The phone went dead. I pulled the chair away from the door and climbed into the laundry basket. I pulled the sheets into place and waited.

I guessed it would not be long before one of Di Maglio's men came. They would be able to find the hospital easily.

I waited a couple of hours. I resisted my urge to go back to sleep. There was a knock on the door. Then there was a pause. Then came another knock. I drew out my gun. The door opened and then shut quickly. There were two of them.

One called hoarsely, "De Roche."

I answered, "Here." I climbed out of the basket. I trailed my arm with the gun until I checked them out. I then put the gun into my trouser band and pulled my sweater over it.

"You look in bad shape," said one of them. "We've got to get you out. He handed me a long white raincoat. "That'll do for a start."

He produced a bandage and worked it round my head and under my chin. They sprayed my cheeks with a white spray. They looked at me critically.

"You'll do. In case we meet anybody. We got a wheelchair outside. You'll sit in it and we wheel you to the car. If we have to split, run with us. If you can't make it we'll dump you."

I nodded. They checked outside and beckoned me to come. They called the lift. They had a key that allowed them to override the controls and we headed straight down into a basement garage. They walked me over to a car parked close to the lift.

"You go in the boot." I was pushed roughly inside and they shut it. I felt claustrophobic but killed the sense of panic. This was better than the alternative. The car pulled off. It stopped. I heard voices and it moved on. It gathered speed.

It stopped in a side street. The boot opened and they helped me out. They steered me into the back seat without a word. And then they drove off again.

"Where are your papers? Where were you staying?"

I told them and they gave instructions over a mobile phone. "One of our people will pick up your stuff and also Miss Di Maglio's. We'll sort out the bill. If you were as discreet as you said, your sudden departure will raise no suspicions. We'll spin some story and the people we'll use will be known to them," I was told.

They then drove off the motorway and headed to a medical centre. There, outside, stood an ambulance. I was helped into the back and they pulled on uniforms. Both were dressed as paramedics.

"The place is owned by one of Mr Di Maglio's companies. We find it useful to have medical facilities where we can depend on their discretion," explained one of my rescuers.

"Has Di Maglio heard anything from the guys who grabbed Jacqui?"

"Not that he's told us," came the laconic response.

And with that they instructed me to strip and don a hospital robe. I lay on a stretcher. They attached a drip.

"It's just a solution with glucose in it. It'll do you good and makes everything look more authentic if we're stopped. You're a car accident victim returning home."

We then headed back to the motorway and made our way to Orly.

We waited outside the airport until a dark limousine drew up alongside. It delivered our cases and also our papers. One of the men turned to me.

"Are you sure that the Rossi name that you are using is not known to the police? Is there any way that they could have matched you with it?"

We have only been using it for a couple of months. It was organised by Di Maglio's man in San Francisco. It's clean. It has been used in the States to get cards and guns. Then we used it in Hong Kong for business. And finally to get into France. We've had no problems with the authorities in that name."

"Have you had problems with them in France at all?" asked one of the men.

"In Cannes, we were involved in a shoot out with some Russians. I think the head of the special branch there suspected something was fishy about our stories. But he let us go. I don't think he took our fingerprints. If he did, it was without our knowledge. We were using another name then."

He nodded. "And you are certain that the police will not have your details as a result of the crash?"

"We were attacked as we were walking down the road. Jacqui had my wallet in her bag. Otherwise everything was in the hotel. I had nothing with my name on it. I don't know if they traced one of the guns to me. It was supplied by one of your people here. Jacqui arranged it."

He shrugged his shoulders. "Our people would send them on a wild goose chase. They never reveal the true identity of their customers without our permission."

I asked if the kidnappers could have sent the police any papers. He shook his head. "We don't know yet what they want. We can guess though that they are going to want to trade Miss Di Maglio for something. We'll see. They are hardly going to want to help the police. Anything they have they'll try to use for whatever their purpose is."

They then got into the front of the ambulance again and we drove straight to Orly to an area where an air ambulance waited. In the end the police and customs were cursory in their examination of the vehicle. They were used to such events. In any case, even if they had a description, they would never have recognised the ashen faced and bandaged body as belonging to me.

When we landed at Geneva, the approach was even more relaxed and I was soon speeding out of the city on country roads. Wherever Di Maglio was going to hold me, it looked as if it would be well away from the centre of the city. Beyond that I could not tell.

We pulled up and then started moving again. This time our speed was much reduced and we went over several humps in the road. We drew to a halt.

One of my captors came into the rear of the vehicle and unfastened the drip. "No need to change. We'll wheel you in and then get you tidied up. Mr Di Maglio will see you in an hour."

Inside, a man who was evidently a doctor examined me. He shook his head over my bruises and expressed amazement that I had not broken any bones. A nurse cleaned up my face and carefully cleaned out my cuts. They put various creams on my face.

They explained, "These will sting. But they will accelerate the healing. You need to get the bruising down or it will affect your breathing. And it will stop any infection."

I was led to a bathroom. A hot bath was already waiting. The nurse helped me out of my robe. She held me as I stepped into the bath and then sank gratefully into the warm water.

"I can help you wash if you want," she said with a mischievous grin. Rough as I felt, I sensed a reaction at her glance and comment as well as the sight of her breasts and the smell of her perfume as she bent over towards me.

I shook my head. "I wouldn't want to put you to too much trouble. I guess I need a period of rest and calm. I'll need to avoid too much excitement. It's better that I do it myself. But thanks for the offer."

Once bathed, I stepped into the clothes that I had been left. There was a tracksuit and also some sneakers. The nurse was waiting as I came through the door.

"We'll get you some proper clothes tomorrow. We were not sure of your size so we had to get the tracksuit. We knew you were tall and needed a large size. Let me dry your hair so that you look less dishevelled. Don't shave for a couple of weeks until your face is healed."

I was soon deemed suitably prepared to meet Di Maglio. I was nervous at the thought of meeting Jacqui's father. It would be the first time since our fracas in Cannes. I was unsure what sort of reaction I could expect. In the end though, I was unconcerned. My objective was to get Jacqui back safe and sound.

Di Maglio came to me as I entered the room. I was walking stiffly. My back ached and so did my ribs. My head at least was no longer throbbing whenever I moved any part of my body. I also felt quite weak. I suspect that I had not eaten for a couple of days.

"We have a problem," he said. "We need to find Jacqui. We forget what happened before. I won't promise you anything I can't deliver. So I am not going to promise that I won't do it again. I know what you have done. You've killed my people. You saved my brother. And you mean something to Jacqui. You also piss me off. But we need you to help us find Jacqui. And, if you were fit, I wouldn't mind you on our side. You're good."

"I just want Jacqui safe. Once that's done we can go our separate ways. I don't care for your methods. But I have no scruples in this case. We get Jacqui back. And we get her back safely."

"All right," he said. "Let's eat some food and discuss what happened. We'll see if that gives us some clues." He was furrowing his brow. His eyes were anxious. He was really worried. And that worried me.

Aldo walked into the room. He came up to me and then surprised me." He put his arms round my shoulders and kissed me on both cheeks. "I'll work with you. We'll get Jacqui back. You are a good boy. I owe you my life. Until I repay you, I am ready to do all you ask. I am a blood brother. There is only one condition. You never ask me to harm the family."

I smiled in agreement. We went to a table. There were four chairs. Giovanni, Di Maglio's adviser whom I had met earlier, was also there.

"Take your broth. It is good for you. We have arranged special food to build you up again. First of all though, describe the kidnapping."

"I think they were Russians. They could have been some other Slavonic race, but I doubt it. It sounded Russian to me. I recognised a couple of words. Simple ones like 'nyet'. But they definitely spoke with a guttural accent. And they knew who Jacqui was and where she would be. We were being followed. Now nobody knew we were in Paris other than my parents.

We only booked the day of our departure. Jacqui did, though, use the

Di Maglio passport. Therefore, she could have been recognised at Hong Kong or Roissy airports.

We booked into the hotel in my name. They did not ask for Jacqui's details. My guess is that they identified us at the airport. The only other alternative is that we were recognised by chance. But that is so unlikely that I would discount it. We were pretty low key in our approach."

"Rastinov," said Aldo. "It has to be him. All the others would use locals. They alone would use Russians. And it was by brute force. It happened in a stupid place. They loosed off their weapons in a crowded street. That's a crazy approach. It has to be them."

Giovanni nodded, "They have people at Roissy. They would have identified you there. They would have checked the computer to see who was ahead and behind Jacqui at passport control and then traced the names through the major hotels. It's so easy when you know how."

"But why has nobody made contact yet?" I asked. "It's almost two days."

"They would wait at least a week to get us really worried. Then we'll get a message. They may even send a picture or something to make us scared for her safety. The question is what is their game plan?" asked Di Maglio.

Giovanni considered the question. "Jacqui is high stakes. It must be something big. It has to be one of your franchises. I would guess the drugs."

Aldo nodded. "They are trying to corner the market. With our distribution power, they can make a fortune."

I asked, "Then why don't you give them the drug empire?"

They looked at me with incredulity. "Because it makes a fucking fortune."

I turned to Di Maglio. "Trade it and you get Jacqui back. As a daughter as well as out of danger."

"Just stop trying to be smart," he warned with a scowl. "We'll do this our way and, if you don't like that, you needn't be part of it."

I allowed them to continue their conversation, but I was thinking through the options carefully. We could find where they were hiding and try to rescue Jacqui. The chances of that were slim. We could trade in whatever they wanted for Jacqui. The risk was that they would double cross us. So we needed to make sure that we covered that angle.

Then a brilliant idea struck me. It would satisfy Di Maglio and get Jacqui back. We could deliver them what they wanted, get Jacqui and then strike back. We would get back what they had taken by destroying them altogether.

I turned to Di Maglio and explained my options. He nodded. "But how do we get her back?"

"We split up into two teams. The first team delivers Jacqui and the assignment of your agreements with your distributors. The second kills them once you are clear and gets the list back."

He smiled grimly, "And then we will get outright gang warfare. That would not worry me. But we cannot do it for it is dishonourable. And if we lose our honour, nobody will trust us. No my friend, there is only one way out of this. We fight or we surrender. And I will never surrender. So we fight."

"But won't that put Jacqui at risk?"

"Yes. But she is in danger anyway. If we give them what they want, then she is at risk if we renege on the deal. If we fight them she is at risk. And, as you say, she is at risk if we do as they want. They are mindless. They are not men of honour. No, it is inevitable. There will be war until they surrender."

"Surely, in that case the lowest risk strategy is to exchange Jacqui and then fight them. There is a risk but the odds must be good."

"In my world," said Di Maglio, "Things do not work that way. If I renege on my word, then nobody will trust me again. I do not do this to satisfy Rastinov. He is scum. I do not trust him. He fights using women and children. He does not fight man to man."

His voice was raised. He went red in the face. "No. I will fight according to our code of honour."

"What is your code of honour?" I spat. "How can you talk about a code of honour? You kill people with your drugs. You murder people who cross you. You seek to destroy people who anger you. You buy power. What honour can you talk about?"

He now exploded with anger. "You, a financial terrorist, dare talk of honour. You also kill to achieve your way. You destroy to make your billions. You are like us. For drugs, you use money. How dare you talk about me in that way? How dare you doubt my honour?"

"Your honour is worth more to you than your flesh and blood. You would sacrifice your daughter for your honour."

"Yes," he shouted interrupting me, "My honour is worth more. She surrendered her honour. She soiled herself when she slept with you. No decent man in my family would touch her then. Yes I love her. Yes I will try to save her. But she is impure. She has no honour. She let the family down."

"She couldn't let this family down. Your honour is nothing. I know what we have done is wrong. It is a means to an end. Once we have achieved that end, we will live within the law."

Again he interrupted me, "Don't be stupid. You say that now. But tomorrow you will see your chance and you will break another law. She, as well, will do that. She likes the thought of working in your world. She sees it as purer than mine. But my world of drugs equates to your world of money. Don't pretend you are better than I am. We are both lawbreakers. We just work in different fields."

Aldo intervened. "Stop it, both of you. Who cares about right or wrong? We need to do two things. The first is to find out where the Russians are holding Jacqui. Then we try to rescue her. Then we need to destroy them or they will destroy us."

I was breathing heavily. My head was buzzing. I was almost crying in frustration. He looked at me. He was very angry. His eyes were full of distrust. His whole body challenged me.

I stood up. Aldo moved to my side. "Sit down. You need not be friends. But you have to be allies. Perhaps, when you have worked together, you will respect each other. You are bound by one thing. In your different ways, you both love Jacqui."

Giovanni nodded. "I have spies out watching for the Russians. I suspect they have Jacqui somewhere in the South of France. They like that area for it is close to Marseilles. And that is the port they use."

Di Maglio said, "Let's eat. It's stupid to quarrel. We need to work together. Aldo's right. And Giovanni's men are good. We'll find out where Jacqui is. Till then we can't plan our strategy. We can only remember our end game."

The room started moving around in front of me. I saw two Di Maglios. Then there were two Aldos. I steadied myself. Aldo was looking at me; "You need to eat. Otherwise you'll be ill."

Someone placed a bowl of broth in front of me. I started to eat greedily.

"Eat more slowly" said Di Maglio. "Or you'll be ill." Those first words of kindness hit me. I looked at him and saw he was being sincere. I smiled wanly and he smiled back. His face appeared to be smiling, but not his eyes. We would never be friends but at least the smile said we did not need to be enemies.

Five long days passed and we still heard nothing from the Russians. Giovanni announced he had some information that the Russians may be in a town called Uzes in Provence.

He told us, "They have a large estate there and it is usually well guarded. But I am getting information that it is even better guarded than usual. We are trying to infiltrate it to get better information."

They surveyed the estate for several more days. Still we heard nothing from the Russians. I was getting worried and one evening asked Aldo what he thought.

"I can't be sure, but it may be nothing to do with Jacqui. It may be that Rastinov is waiting for something to happen before he delive rs us his terms."

The next day we knew what that something was. We were eating lunch when a message came for Di Maglio. It was simple. One of his planes had landed at a private airstrip in California. It was a big shipment. The plane had been attacked and the drugs on board taken. The plane had then been blown up. A message had been given to the pilot. It was simple. It was outright war.

Give over the right to distribute drugs on the West Coast to the Russians. If this were not done in the next week, the Russians would show how serious they were. They would send a finger of Jacqui for each plane that landed after that week. And when they finished with her fingers, they would send some other part of her. And ominously, they said that they would remove the fingers without anaesthetic. She would be in pain as well as mutilated.

"What do you do now?" I asked. "We have a week."

He looked at me. "We pretend to negotiate. But first we need to see if Jacqui is alive. We'll ask for proof."

He turned to Giovanni, "Do it!"

The next day we made contact. We had them on the speakerphone. In the room were just Di Maglio, Aldo, Giovanni and me. The Russians wanted to send us a video of Jacqui but Di Maglio refused.

"I want to see her alive. You can fake videos."

In the end the Russians agreed. They were willing for an emissary to see Jacqui. But only one person would be acceptable. And they had to be on their own.

And they warned that if there were any attempt to double cross them, they would start sending larger parts of Jacqui.

Then they said something that made my heart stop, "And the first thing will be the baby."

"What baby do you mean?" gasped Di Maglio.

The man at the other end laughed cruelly. "You didn't know she was expecting one. Well she is. Your precious little daughter was banged up, as I believe you call it. Our doctor established that pretty quickly when we asked him to patch her up after we grabbed her. She took a nasty knock on the head."

Di Maglio looked at me with pure hatred. He snarled down the phone, "Her boyfriend will be the emissary. He won't want any harm to come to her and his baby."

"Is that the hero who tried to stop us in Paris?" came the sarcastic reply.

"Yes" said Di Maglio. "That's the one."

"All right. We're in Uzes. You know where. He comes alone. And he must be unarmed. Any slight treachery and we won't show any mercy."

Di Maglio turned to me the moment the phone was cut. "You said nothing about a baby" he said. He had slowly become more amenable towards me. We had not been friendly but at least had co-existed. Now he looked at me in hatred and disgust.

"I didn't know. Nor did she. That's if it's true."

"Could it be true?" he asked.

"We were sleeping together. You know that much already. We have been since we got together again. But we did not plan this. I don't know whether to believe it."

"They don't have enough imagination to pretend that one," said Aldo. "It must be true."

Di Maglio snarled at me again, "if you get her out of there, you marry her. I want no bastard in my family."

Aldo laughed, "That's the first time you've said something nice about him. I thought you felt he was a bastard."

Di Maglio glared at him. "Fuck off" he shouted, and stormed out.

I turned to Aldo and Giovanni, "What do I do when I get to the estate and see Jacqui. What's the plan?"

"When we send you in, we'll give you a small bug. You need to plant it on Jacqui. You have to tell her where the switch is. She'll know when to switch it off or on. They have bug detectors in their places and so she has to be careful. The bug will tell us where she is and so we will be able to try to spring her just before we attack. Or at least before they can react."

"Surely they won't let us get together?"

"If they don't you need to plant it in the house and tell her where it is. She will have to try to find it."

"Won't they expect me to negotiate?"

"Perhaps. But you will not be empowered to. We will negotiate once you return and tell us that Jacqui is safe. That's reasonable. They need to release you before we talk. That gives you protection. So you should be pleased. The way the boss thinks of you, you're lucky he does not put you in there and then pull the plug on you."

I turned to Aldo, who had been silent so far. "What is his reaction going to be? The baby is hardly going to improve his feelings towards me."

Aldo shrugged his shoulders. "I wouldn't bother too much. He'll get round it. We all like the idea of a grandson. He's not going to be an exception. Give him time. And do what he says. He'll be pretty touchy for a bit."

I nodded. "She must be only a month or so pregnant. Otherwise she would have told me if she were late."

I thought back. That meant that any baby would have been conceived in Hong Kong. I wondered when. The news made me want to get to Jacqui fast. I suspect Giovanni realised that.

"You will not try any tricks. You do as we say. Any false move will be dangerous. I mean that. It will be dangerous for you and for Jacqui."

Di Maglio returned. He looked at me. I was still bruised round the face. My back and sides were also bruised. I was much less stiff than before. But I was still not fully fit. "Can you make it?"

This was not a question born out of concern. He wanted to know if I was fit enough because he needed to ensure that his plans worked.

I nodded. "I am going to be all right in a few days and this bit of the battle is hardly going to be strenuous."

"No," he said, "but you need to be alert. It's not going to be easy."

He turned to the others, intentionally excluding me from the conversation. "I want you to get our top people in for an attack. They should be gathered in safe houses in Nimes and Avignon. Get some arranged in the next two days. The people must arrive by Wednesday."

Aldo nodded. "How many will there need to be?"

"Ten in each town," Di Maglio replied. "That will mean there will be twenty five for the attack as we will bring in the team leaders on the day. I need Georgio to be the overall commander. He's the best with his army special services background."

Giovanni nodded his agreement. "What about the snatch squad for Jacqui?"

"He can lead it," he said, indicating me. "And Aldo you will be in there to help him. That will repay him the debt you owe him. Get two of your men to support you."

"Can you manage that?" he asked me.

"Yes. But when do we make the snatch?"

"Just before the main attack or perhaps as it is launched, you lead your squad into the building. If the bug works, we will know where Jacqui is and you will have to find your way there. You have to get her out of the place while the fight is going on. No heroics. Just get her out."

"Why do I need to wait for the battle to start? Would it not be better to try to snatch her before you start? Aldo and his men could be close to the house as back up if I fail. But if I went in alone, I might be able to get her out before they know we are going to attack."

Di Maglio nodded. "It's worth a try. If you get caught keep quiet. You're good at that. Or at least you appeared to be when I last caught you. They'll think you are on your own. They'll suspect it's an amateur doing heroics. They'll most likely kill you, but who cares? We then attack when they are even less expecting us to."

He then turned to Giovanni. "Get a couple of your people then to arrange the safe houses and get the men in there . We will attack in the early hours of Friday. You'll need guns, grenades and tear gas. Get communicators that we can link into. We direct the whole show from here. And get a communicator for De Roche but make it look like a mobile phone. If they don't examine it, they won't know the difference."

"Give us sub-machine guns rather than automatics" said Aldo.

Di Maglio nodded. "Let's get started then. We need to get De Roche there to check on Jacqui. We fly him into Avignon and then get the family driver to take him to the estate. We start to negotiate when he returns. We drag the negotiations out till the Thursday. As we concede points they will get more confident. Then we attack as they relax their guard."

He turned to Giovanni. "Well let's get started and see what we can do. I want him out there for Tuesday, if possible. Otherwise we will have trouble meeting all the deadlines."

THE BATTLE STARTS

The plane seemed to land at Nimes Airport minutes after its departure from Geneva. We were whisked away in the sleek Di Maglio car that was waiting for us.

I'd been briefed about the Russians. They were part of a world wide Mafia that had grown out of the collapse of the old Soviet Union. They dealt with anything that made money. Their arms sales ranged from conventional to nuclear. Their goods ranged from pirated software or music through to hard drugs. Their methods of persuasion ranged from bribery and corruption to murder.

I had also been told what might happen to Jacqui. If we complied she might be let out. If we did not, at best, she would die quickly. If we tried to double-cross them, she would be tortured and perhaps let out, hopelessly deformed. They wanted our network and were not going to play softball.

On the other hand if Di Maglio complied on the drugs network, the view was there would be another attempt at blackmail. They could even hold on to Jacqui and use her as an ongoing hostage. They were not people to play around with. They had no scruples. They had no honour.

I was going into their stronghold unarmed and still weakened from the Paris incident. I was going in to check out Jacqui. We were surprised they had allowed us to do that. If they found me passing the bug, they would kill me. And they could even kill Jacqui. This was a high-risk strategy because a low risk one was not available.

We came to a gate and stopped. The car was looked over. "Tell De Roche to come out on his own," a man called. I walked from the car and headed to the gate. They opened it a bit and led me through the gap. They took me behind a wall so that I was sheltered from the road. I was ordered to strip. It was cold at that time of year and they could have taken me into the gatehouse. But they didn't. I had no choice. I stripped down to my pants and stood there shivering. I was ordered to strip naked. I did so.

They slowly went through each item of clothing. I was relaxed, as the bug was not there. We had guessed I would be searched. I was all right as long as they did not search my person to closely. They did not bother. They handed back my clothes. One bug was in my mouth, attached to one of my back teeth. It was a slim metallic object with a small button at one end. That activated it. There was a second behind my watch. But they hadn't examined that.

I dressed quickly and they led me up the road to a house that could be seen through the trees. The place must have been a farm at one point for the building was quite rambling. It was a linked series of converted barns and stables with a farmhouse on one side. It stood about two storeys high. I noted that there were a series of doors and windows at ground level. That would make attack all the easier.

However, the distance between the road and the buildings was at least half a mile. In the grounds I could see trip wires. In the trees were remote control cameras. And I noticed bumps in the road, which may have been for speed control. But they could also have been used for booby trap bombs and simply de-activated for the time being.

It was not going to be easy to get into this building, I thought grimly. Even with the experts that Di Maglio had proposed.

Once inside, I was led into a long room. There were several people there and they all had one thing in common. They looked at me with undisguised hostility. Then one of them came forward. He was of medium height, sturdy build and thickset. His dark hair was brushed forward as if to conceal a receding hairline. He seemed to have more gold teeth than original ones, and they glinted unpleasantly as his face folded into a permanent sneer.

He held out a hand to greet me. Two fingers ended in stumps just below the knuckle. Scars that continued into the cuff of his Jacket marked the back of the hands. I shook the hand as he rasped a single word, "Rastinov."

He looked me up and down. "You killed one of my men in Paris."

I decided I had to play tough. "You attacked us. I didn't attack you. He had us by surprise. I can't help it if he got in the way."

He did not seem to find this amusing. "We bring you the girl and then you go when you have seen her."

"I want to speak to her."

"You look at her." He laughed a cruel laugh. "We strip her if you want and you can check her out for marks."

I looked coldly. "Then I'm doubly certain. I see her. I talk to her. I want to know that you are not harming her. Or the deal is off."

"What deal?" he snarled.

"The one you are organising with Di Maglio. He won't even consider it if I do not return with the right news."

"Perhaps you don't return?" he said.

I shrugged. "That's life. But if I don't you are all dead."

"What do you mean?" he asked.

"I am sending signals. If they cease he strikes. It will all happen within five minutes. Or perhaps you haven't noticed the planes overhead."

This was a total falsehood. But I had the second bug and, as they hadn't discovered it, I thought I might as well use if for best effect.

"You can't be," said one of the men who had met me at the gate. "We searched you." He was white with fear.

I took off my watch and turned it round, revealing the bug. The reaction was instant. Rastinov nodded to someone. The next thing I saw was a red-hot poker meeting the cheek of the man who had protested. The poker came from the fire. There were several placed in it. The smell of burning acrid flesh filled the air. The poker was drawn over the man's face. As he put up his hands to protect himself, it was lashed at his hands as well. He collapsed in a heap, sobbing in pain.

"Idiot," said Rastinov. "Get him out of here. He has failed me."

The man was removed. "Bring the girl," he said. "Let them talk but don't leave them alone. Then get rid of him. Accompany him back to the gate. I am getting tired of this game."

With that he moved out. Minutes later a door at the side of the room opened. There stood Jacqui.

She was drawn and pale. Her clothes were the ones she wore when we were attacked in the Rue de la Paix. They were soiled with dust and crumpled. I realised she was wearing no make up. Her hair was pulled back and unkempt. She blinked in the light.

"What have you done to her?" I cried.

She moved towards me and saw me for the first time. She called me. As I moved towards her, she was grabbed by the arm and pulled away.

"Stop," shouted a voice. "No closer."

I turned to him in anger. "If you want to proceed, I will talk to her. I will accept you should be here, but I want to talk to her in private. Look at the state she is in. I want to know what you are doing to her. If I can't do that, the deal is off. If that is the case, get me your boss. I prefer to talk to the organ grinder rather than the monkeys."

That succeeded in infuriating them. Then one of them signalled to the others to hold back. He looked at me suspiciously.

258

"I don't trust you."

"That's your problem," I said. "I'm calling the shots now." But I realised that Jacqui was not in a state where she would be of much help. She was in shock. She was fearful. I doubted I could get the bug to her. But I had to try.

I walked over to her. Nobody interfered. I held her in my arms. She shuddered as if afraid. I spoke so that they would all hear, "Has anyone done anything to you?"

She shook her head. "Are you pregnant?" I asked more softly.

She started to sob, "I was" came the reply. "I was." Then she started to shake violently. She clung to me.

I looked over my shoulder. "Leave me with her. Otherwise she'll fall apart."

"She already has," a voice replied. "Just because the cow lost the kid after she was roughed up."

I kept my calm. I needed to help her. Losing my temper would not solve anything. I made a mental note of the man. He would not live for much longer, and I wanted his blood.

I took her in my arms again and whispered in her ear. They thought I was trying to comfort her. But I was giving her instructions. I hoped that the need to do something would help her get better.

"Jacqui, I am going to kiss you. I'll pass you a bug from my mouth. Keep it hidden. There's a button on it to switch it on. Leave it on when you can but be careful there are no detectors around. It will tell us where you are. We are coming in to get you in three days. Just wait for us."

She looked at me with a pained look. She then turned towards me and kissed me on the mouth. I realised then that she understood. I had given her hope. I put my tongue into her mouth and with it passed her the bug. When I saw that she appeared comfortable with it, I stopped kissing her.

I spoke in a louder voice now. "Where do they keep you?"

Then the man, who had spoken before intervened. "Don't answer. That's not his concern."

"We'll get you out of here. Don't worry," I said. And I kissed her again. I held her to me. Then I let her go and stood back. She stood there, half falling down. One of the men took her by the shoulder and pushed her away.

Once she was out of the door, I turned. I was in front of the one who had enjoyed talking about her losing the baby. Without warning, I lashed out at him with my foot and caught him square in the crotch. He fell forward retching and I slammed my fist into the back of his neck. He fell further forward and I had time to deliver one kick to the head before others dragged me away.

"Don't touch a hair on her head. Or that's just for starters," I said in a cold voice as I shook off the men holding me away.

"Rastinov," I yelled. He did not appear. I hadn't expected him to. "Tell the bastard I'll be back. And if she's hurt, he dies."

With that I walked from the room and headed out into the fresh air. One of the men who had accompanied me when I arrived was at the door.

"Don't be stupid," he warned. "Don't try anything or you'll regret it."

I ignored him and walked ahead of him to the front gate. I could feel the looks of men behind me but I did not look back. I though that Jacqui may be watching from some window. But I could not bear to look back. I kept seeing her face. I kept thinking of her gaunt body. I kept feeling her pain. I kept thinking of her loss. She needed to get away and quickly. I knew we had to move fast. But could I persuade her father?

I walked through the door and back into the car. "Airport," I said curtly and fast. "Is there a safe communication link from the car?"

The driver shook his head. "Only the car-phone. You are secure in the jet though."

The pilot counselled against talking from the plane. The messages were scrambled but, as we would be back in the compound near Geneva in under an hour, he could see no point in taking the risk. I agreed with him and remained deep in my thoughts.

The plan was to go in on Friday. That gave us till Thursday to negotiate. But I could see no reason why we could not accelerate things. Jacqui needed help. She was in a bad state. I knew her well enough to know that she could quickly recover. But the longer we left her as she was, the harder it would be.

I would need to use all my powers of persuasion to get Di Maglio on board . And there still remained the question of how that snatch squad got into the Russian's building. I was convinced that the place was booby-trapped. It was definitely filled with the latest surveillance equipment. I suspected it had its own generators. But I had not seen any. I would need to check with Di Maglio. He would have had the place surveyed from the air. Somewhere they must have an Achilles heel and we needed to find it soon.

When I returned to the compound Di Maglio was waiting for me. He was with Aldo and Giovanni. They listened grimly at my description of what happened. When I had finished, I looked Di Maglio squarely in the eyes.

"We should go in sooner. There is no benefit in waiting. Can't you sell it to them that you want to trade with them? We need to get in fast."

He nodded. "You're right. Get the plans of the house and bring Jacques to see me as soon as possible."

"Who's he?" I asked.

"He's our plant. He provides the Russians with produce from his firm. He's a wholesale distributor. He's due in tomorrow."

He saw my astonishment. He laughed. "Don't be angry. We only learnt that last night. We have been planning since. We'll use him as a Trojan horse."

Jacques was a giant of a man. His muscles were toned from loading and unloading trucks. He was amiable. I turned to Di Maglio, "How do you know you can trust him?"

"I trust him," he said. "Also I'll pay him a million dollars to get you safely inside. So he'll come back to pick up his money. And also he'll want to collect his wife and children."

In many ways Di Maglio was as brutal as the Russians holding Jacqui were. I had no doubt about the fate that would face Jacques' family should he double cross us.

"At the moment," said Aldo, "Jacqui is located here. She has been here since around the time you left the Russians. It looks like a barn. It must have a communicating door to the rear of the house. It has a door here," he said pointing to a plan on the table. It also has two ground floor windows, here and here."

"If it were open plan we could use stun grenades to storm it," I suggested.

"We doubt it's open plan. The building has been extensively converted and it would be illogical to hold Jacqui in a large open area. They would want to put her into a small room for added safety."

I turned to Jacques, "How close is Jacques' drop off point to the barn?"

"A good hundred yards," said Jacques.

I thought. "Do you pass in front of it as you approach your drop off point?"

"The road goes round by a drive that leads to it. I guess the drive is about twenty yards long."

"From our surveillance, can we see cover between the closest point on the road and the barn?" I asked Aldo.

"There are some privet bushes here," he said, pointing to an area close to the road. "But they would only provide cover for one."

I turned to Di Maglio, "If we could fit a concealed flap in the back of the lorry I could squeeze through it as we pass by the house. There is a danger, though, from the cameras and from people watching the lorry."

Di Maglio shook his head; "Jacques comes too often. They won't watch him particularly. But we need to create a diversion just in case. We'll stage a car crash and explosion in the distance. There is a winding road here in the hills about two hundred yards from the house. The side is a sheer drop onto rocks. If we drop a car over the cliff and explode it, that will give you the time to get out. At the same time, we'll have some equipment in the lorry that will send a radio surge to disrupt for a couple of seconds all the surveillance equipment. Nobody will suspect anything. It will all happen too fast."

He thought quickly. His logic was irreproachable. Aldo said "What about us?"

"The rest of you will be with me in the lorry. You will be concealed behind all the stuff that Jacques will be unloading. We should build a false back in case I'm not seen. Or if I don't return by the time it's ready for you to leave. You stay in the lorry till you hear shooting. Then you come out in support of me. You'll have to play that one by ear."

Aldo nodded. "The moment the shooting starts, Jacques gets back in the car and prepares to leave. If the back is open, it won't matter. We'll reinforce the cab the best we can. You should get there. We will too."

I turned to Jacques; "Can you jettison the trailer while you are driving?"

He nodded. "As long as I release a couple of levers while I unload. And that would not be a problem."

"Could we reinforce the car so that it can crash through the gates?" I asked.

Di Maglio nodded.

"That leaves the humps. I wondered if they were booby trap bombs that could be activated remotely."

"That'll only be a problem if you are not followed," said Di Maglio. "If that is the case, you'll have to go on foot. We'll have a truck on stand by near the property. It can come closer once the shooting starts and try to pick you up at the main entrance."

I thought through the plan. It seemed flimsy but we really had no alternative. I would wait for the explosion that would take out any casual spectators. At that point I would roll out of the truck. It would be going at around fifteen miles per hour. That was no problem. I would be armed with a sub-machine gun and carry a handgun as well. I would roll into the bush for concealment. As I left the lorry Aldo would activate the radio interference.

I would then enter the barn and seek Jacqui. There was a risk that they would kill her before I got to her. That risk we needed to take. I could not see how I could avoid a shoot-out. That would bring Aldo and his team to our assistance. Jacques would be in the cab and turning round.

Time would be of the essence, as we would be counter attacked quickly. Seconds would mean the difference between life and death. I felt the adrenalin surge through my body. I felt more ready than just a moment before. We would go in the next day.

"And the following morning, we wipe them all out," said Di Maglio. I nodded my agreement.

Giovanni had been listening carefully. He now talked for the first time. "I will organise other action for that day in other parts of the world. We will strike at all their centres until they ask for a truce. The price of the truce will be their agreement of our jurisdiction. They'll agree to that if we have wiped out their leadership. But they won't love us for it. And some day they will attack again. This is going to be a long standing vendetta."

His words struck me as a terrible reminder of the cruel world we would operate in. I knew there was no going back.

That evening I called my father. He was building up his stakes in the different target companies and expected to start the funds in the next week. I decided against telling them of our problems and merely said we had left Paris and were enjoying ourselves at friends of Jacqui in the Chamonix region. We were not that far away in the compound outside Geneva. I left a number, and assured them we were all well. There was no point in worrying them or alerting them to our difficulties.

The next day we set out early. Jacques had already gone for his truck. We arrived at a house near the main Nimes to Uzes road. From the outside, it looked deserted. Inside were four men and an arsenal of weapons. There was a hand held rocket launcher; half a dozen sub-machine guns and sundry small arms.

We all dressed in dark trousers and shirts. We had a matching jockey cap. We were told to blacken our faces. We then armed ourselves. We took spare ammunition packs. I took a service revolver and then a knife, which I placed in a sheath that fitted to my thigh. We waited.

"There he is," said one of the men. In the distance we saw the truck come into view. We bundled into the back of a van and drove the short distance to the main road.

"The transfer has to be as quick as possible," said Aldo. "He will be stopped by a police motor cyclist for one minute and then waved on. That's a precaution in case he is being monitored. In that time we get into the truck. We have to climb over the goods and hide in the false compartment. Charles goes first, as there is not enough space to climb over each other. I go next as I have the radio equipment and need to be as close to the outside as possible for it to work to maximum effect."

The lorry lumbered by and we turned out into the main road to follow it. The policeman appeared. He waved down the truck. It stopped. We pulled behind it and jumped out. We were covered from the road by trees. In seconds we were in the truck and the doors were closed behind us. We moved to the rear and got through the false panel at the back. The last man through pulled it into place. The only exit now was through the moveable panel on the side.

The truck jerked forward again. The van must have followed it for a bit. We could not see. Jacques' voice came through. "I am approaching the gates. I have to get down and let them examine the truck."

We stopped. There was a grinding as the gates opened. We heard voices outside. The lorry inched forward. Again we heard a grinding as we assumed the gates shut. There were more voices. Someone was looking under the truck. Then the rear doors were opened and someone jumped in. Any examination must have been fairly cursory for it was soon over. The rear doors were slammed shut. Someone thumped the side of the truck.

"Move on," they shouted.

We once again edged slowly forward. The truck eased its way over the humps in the road. I counted six. They were not going to be fun at a high speed on the way back. Jacques' voice came through again. "Thirty yards to drop off. Twenty yards. Ten yards." And then there was a deafening explosion in the distance.

"Go, Go, Go," shouted Aldo. I pushed the side panel open. I threw myself out, hitting the grass verge and rolling over behind the bush. I saw a camera behind me but it was pointing down the drive. I moved to the side of the bush. I could not be seen from either the house or the road. There was a plume of smoke in the distance. The truck was in front of the house.

Jacques was talking excitedly to two men there. "Someone has crashed at the rocks," he said. "His petrol tank must have exploded. It gave me a shock. I almost crashed myself."

"The poor sod is a goner," someone said in reply. "Driving today and then gone in a puff of smoke."

The other laughed. "He gave us all a shock. We thought it might be some friends of ours."

"You mean those Di Maglios. The boyfriend was so white when he saw the bitch. I could have pissed myself. I'll tell you one thing though. I plan to fuck the bitch before we kill her. We'll have some fun with her. She's got a good body. She's just got a lousy temper."

I held back. I could see no cameras positioned between the door of the barn and me. The men had their backs turned. Jacques was looking in my direction. I ran forward and edged into the small porch by the barn door.

I unfastened the safety latch on the sub-machine gun and held it against my thigh. A strap from my shoulder suspended it. I gently opened the door. There was a large room. It was empty other than a couple of tables against one end. I closed the door behind me and listened.

I sensed movement behind a door at the side. I looked around the room. There were no cameras. I moved to the door and listened.

I could hear a woman's voice. It was a cold voice. "Eat you stupid cow," it said. "Or you'll be too weak for the men to enjoy."

"Go to hell," said another woman's voice. It was Jacqui's.

I listened again. I could hear no other movement. The chances were that there were only two people in the room.

"Eat the bloody food," said the woman.

"Leave me alone," shouted Jacqui in a desperate voice. That meant she was alone bar the woman. With luck the woman would leave. And with luck she would leave by another door. But I would need to shoot down this door. And I would have to give Jacqui a warning so she kept away.

"Suit yourself," said the woman. "But it won't help you. Once your father gives in, then we kill you. It's just some of the guys want a bit of fun first. I must say I'd rather you than me. Most of them are real bastards."

I heard her move to the door next to me. I let go of the machine gun and drew the knife. The door opened and she left. She did not see me.

My hand grasped her mouth to stop her crying out. The sharp knife cut her throat. The blood gushed out in a flood. There was a strange croak. She was dead. I had never thought I could kill a woman in cold blood. But this one was easy. I was not sure if I could have done it if I hadn't overheard her conversation with Jacqui.

Jacqui looked at me in astonishment. She got up and ran towards me. I saw there was a camera in the room. "Come quickly," I said and pulled her out of the room. I slammed the door behind me. We moved to the porch. I had the machine gun at the ready.

Someone came out of another door. A burst of machine gun fire hit him before he had time to fire the gun in his hand. I raked the door from which he had come with another blast. That would buy us enough time to get out of the building.

The noise of gunfire had put everyone on alert and there were shouts from the main house. I took out one of the grenades that Aldo had given me, pulled out the pin and rolled it across the room. With a bit of luck it would catch some of them. At worst it would create a diversion.

We came out of the barn and hung back in the porch. We were spotted immediately. One of the men unloading the truck yelled a warning before I cut him down with a burst of fire. The side of the truck opened. Aldo and his two companions burst out.

The hand held rocket launcher was put into action immediately. As Jacques turned the truck, the rockets screamed into the house. Explosion followed explosion as I pulled Jacqui across the grass to the truck. She fell and I grabbed her with my spare hand. I pulled her upright and swung her into the truck. As I did, the grenade in the house exploded, blowing out windows and doors.

I lifted Jacqui into the cab and climbed in behind her. Aldo and his companions moved towards us.

Three men appeared, guns blazing, from the side of the house. One of our men fell swearing, blood pouring from his thigh. He threw himself at the cab and hauled himself in. I leant over Jacques who was easing the truck round, and fired at the three. That gave enough cover to Aldo and his companion who joined us.

The doors of the crowded cab were now slammed shut and we drove away from the house. Aldo kept a stream of fire from his window. I did the same from my side as I stretched behind Jacques.

"Get rid of the trailer," I shouted. He pressed a lever and we heard it grinding on the path as it fell away. "That will slow then down," I shouted.

I had noticed some men jump into a four-wheel drive and head after us. "Put your foot down," I yelled at Jacques.

We hit one hump after another. We were jolted backwards and forwards. The weight of Jacques' body winded me time and again. Aldo was covering the far window. On the floor of the cab the wounded man was groaning quietly to himself. Jacqui sat next to the driver, her face pale but her eyes alive again. The second man held her steady as she risked hitting the reinforced windscreen at every bump.

As we came up the gates, we saw another four-wheel drive was parked. Behind it were men waiting with guns. We swerved off the road into the shelter of the trees. I called to Aldo. "Hit them with the rocket launcher."

He grabbed the rocket launcher while the other man helped load it. They were obviously unclear what we were doing and happy to wait for their reinforcements. They understood what was happening too late. As the four-wheel drive that I had seen at the house sped down the drive, I opened fire with my machine gun. I blazed it low, hoping to hit the tyres. Another stream of bullets was coming from the open door at the far side of the cab. Aldo's wounded companion had pulled himself across the cab and was firing too.

The rocket seared across the lawn at waist height and ploughed into the parked vehicle. The explosion tore it apart and blew it into the gates. A second rocket was loaded and blasted into the gates, blowing them open. Aldo dropped the launcher. "That's it," he called. "No more rockets."

The car following us swerved off the road as we jumped back into the cab. "Go," I yelled and Jacques put his foot down and headed to the gates. He somehow manoeuvred a path between the mangled car and the gates. We were on the main road, leaving a trail of destruction in our wake..

"To the house," called Aldo. Jacques retraced our steps and turned off at the side road to our safe house. A truck pulled behind us. I started.

"Don't worry, it's our back up," said Aldo.

We waited a few moments before we heard the hum of the helicopters. Two landed in the field in front of us. The wounded man was carried out. I gently pulled Jacqui to me and carried her from the cab to the other helicopter. Aldo joined us.

As we rose above the house, the cab of our truck was being driven away. The other truck was following. "They'll both go to a yard where they are going to be crushed. It's best to eliminate the evidence," said

Aldo. "And in a few minutes the trailer we left will go up in the air. It was full of explosives with a timing device."

I was hardly listening to his talk as I gently stroked Jacqui's hair. Her head was on my shoulder. She did not say a word. I knew her of old. She was purging the last days from her mind. Once she had done that, her recovery would be swift.

We landed at a small airstrip just on the French side of the border. Di Maglio's jet was waiting for us there. The other helicopter landed. The different passengers were unloaded. There was a small house at the end of the strip. "Let's go there," said Aldo. "We need to tidy up for the crossing. We can't go like this through police and customs."

"Take Jacqui to the bathroom and sort her out," he said. "Some of her clothes are there. We need to leave in half an hour."

He headed to another room with the men. I led Jacqui to the bathroom. There was an old metal bath there. I put in the plug and turned on the water. Hot water gushed out. I turned on the cold tap and, when I was happy that the mixture was right, turned to Jacqui.

"Undress and soak in the bath. We haven't much time."

She did as I said. I went over to the basin and washed away the black cream we had used to camouflage our faces. I stripped off my clothes and put on some slacks and a sweater that I had arrived in. The organisation of Di Maglio was incredible to the last detail. The clothes had already been moved ahead of us from the safe house to the airstrip.

Jacqui was lying in the hot water. Her face was less pale. She stood up and said, "Wash me."

I remembered doing that before after we had been through a fair hell. It this was nothing like that. I washed her gently, pulling the soft soap around her body. I soaped each part of her as she turned round to make it easier. But it was like a ritual. It was part of the cleansing that she was going through. I was there in a support role. I couldn't intrude.

She sat down in the water and watched the soap float to the surface of the water as she gradually immersed herself in the water. Suddenly she got up and shook herself dry. "Can you put on the shower?" she said.

I did as asked and she stood underneath it. Her hair was wet. Her body was starting to look refreshed. She stood taller and firmer now. She sat on the edge of the bath and passed a shampoo bottle. "That's the stuff I usually use. They planned this well," she said, echoing my earlier thoughts.

I washed her hair. She sat quietly on the edge of the bath with her back to me as I gently massaged in the shampoo. Once I had finished, she stood up and allowed the water from the shower to clean it away. She then stepped from the bath and asked me to dry her. I took a large fluffy towel from a rail and patted her dry. She took the clothes and carefully stepped into one item after another. When dressed, she ran her hands through her wet hair.

"Can I dry it anywhere?" she said.

We went outside. The one thing they'd forgotten was a hairdryer. I felt at least that it showed they were human. We towel dried it and she put her hair up. She put some lipstick on. Aldo passed her a coffee and put a friendly arm around he shoulder. She smiled at him.

"Thanks Uncle Aldo," she said. "I needed you."

She then turned to me. Her eyes were brimming with tears. "You, too, Charles. I couldn't have survived without you. The day you came in and I knew you were still alive, I knew I would be safe."

I gasped. I had forgotten. She must have seen me come off the bike. She wouldn't have been told what had happened. She had feared I'd been killed.

She lent against me and I held her protectively.

"Look kids," said Aldo. "Stay with the family. Jacqui let your father see you both. He'll forgive you. You can't change his way of life. But you can influence how he deals with it."

We all headed to the plane and Geneva. Customs and police were as cursory as ever. And the car whisked us back to the compound. Di Maglio was obviously still concerned for we had a car trailing us. There was also a motorbike leading the way with a pillion passenger obviously carrying a gun at the ready.

We drove up to the house. Di Maglio waited at the door. As Jacqui got out he kissed her on the forehead and hugged her. He mouthed something. She lent forward and kissed him.

I followed Aldo who got a hug from his brother. He looked at me sternly. "You are now family. That brings no obligation that you would refuse. We look after each other. You can live your own life. But we need to protect each other."

I shook his hand. He smiled and for the first time the smile was genuine. He clapped me on the back. "Take Jacqui to your room. Look after her. And decide when you two will marry."

And with that he wheeled round and disappeared inside the house.

RETURN TO FREEDOM

Jacqui and I went to the room I had occupied before. It was large and airy with a view of the green fields and mountains that surrounded the house. It had a large double bed with a typically fluffy Swiss duvet.

Jacqui sank on the bed and looked at me seriously. "Did you hear what he said about getting married?"

"Is it his choice?" I asked sadly.

"No, it's ours. But it is important that he said that he'd let me make my choice rather than automatically agree to his."

She looked at me and frowned, "You do love me? You do want to marry me?"

"Yes," I said, "And one day I'll find the right time to propose to you. But it's not here and not now. Once you feel better. Once you are my equal again."

She smiled and said, "It was so sad about the baby."

"When did you get pregnant?"

"Darling," she said, "we were making love all the time in Hong Kong. It's hard to say exactly when. But it could have been that night we went to the clubs and I danced in the one in Wan Chai."

"But weren't you taking any precautions?" I asked.

"Of course," she said, "but I must have forgotten or been careless. It wasn't intentional. We'll plan it next time if we can."

I smiled and took her in my arms. I was just going to kiss her when the phone rang. She picked it up and passed it to me, "It's my father."

"Yes," I answered.

"We are to have a council in ten minutes. You are to come. We have only done part of the job. We have to complete and we will do so soon."

"OK Mr Di Maglio. I'll be there. Should Jacqui come as well?"

"No. I have asked a doctor to take a look at her. She'll be with you in a couple of minutes. Leave Jacqui with her."

I had to agree with the decision but I felt a bit annoyed at the way that he took arbitrary decisions without consulting us. I told Jacqui what was happening and she nodded.

"I suppose that's sensible," was her only comment.

Seconds later the doctor was there. I moved downstairs, telling Jacqui I would be back as soon as I could.

Downstairs five men were grouped around the table. Beside Di Maglio were Aldo and Giovanni. The two others were unknown to me.

Aldo introduced them. "This is Ray and this is Ken. They are both ex Marines and they work for us."

Ray and Ken nodded at me. Di Maglio turned round and immediately took command.

He turned to Giovanni. "Brief us on where you are on the other locations," he said.

"The Russians have three main bases. One is in New Jersey and the other is in Leningrad. The main base is, though, in the South of France. They use Marseilles as their main port. They also have close ties with the Middle East for their arms trade.

We've been monitoring their radio signals and believe that several of their key people on our side of their business will be in the South of France. I guess they're planning an all out war against us."

Aldo interrupted, "Are we all prepared for an attack on our compounds, here and in the US?"

Di Maglio brushed the question aside, "Of course we are. Security everywhere is on top alert."

Giovanni continued, "We have provided the police with incriminating evidence on their New Jersey operations. They have a major depot there and we are going to allow them to capture a hundred million dollars of cocaine tonight. The stuff is shit and not saleable through normal channels. It's stuff we either stole or seized. That should be in New Jersey."

"How many people will that put away?" I asked.

"It will neutralise them all. They and their fingerprints will be on every computer around the world. They become persona non grata although they can change their identities easily of course."

He continued, "We have also planted human remains over on their property. We picked up a couple of stiffs in New York and buried them on the outskirts of their property. It won't do much but it will put on the pressure. And we've organised a lot more dirty tricks."

"What about Leningrad?" asked Di Maglio.

"There's little we can do there," he said. "It's too risky. But Leningrad is arms and contraband rather than drugs. So we can live with them."

He continued. "France is key. We need to storm it and the attack must not be traced. France has Rastinov there and the bulk of his key people will also be present. I can guarantee our intelligence."

Di Maglio asked, "What about the police?"

"They will not respond for an hour. The compound is isolated and we will arrange enough diversions to keep them away. They know who the Russians are and are not going to lose sleep about a bit of gang warfare."

Di Maglio asked, "Do we have the identities of the people we must kill?"

"Yes I have their photos here," said Giovanni. "There is Rastinov. He has two lieutenants that we fear. They are called Krakow and Pastinksy. There is also a killer called Andrei, we don't know his other name. We wanted to kill Krakow's wife, but, from the description, it appears Charles did that for us earlier. She's an evil bitch and bright. Alone without Krakow, she would become lethal. Amazingly he was the one who calmed her down. She was in the room with Jacqui when we did the snatch."

Di Maglio beamed at me. "We knew you could handle a gun. We didn't know that you were also good with a knife. That's tough killing a woman with a knife. There are not many men I would trust with such an assignment. Women can kill men. But men find it difficult to kill women."

I felt uneasy. He was building me up as a prospective son-in-law. He felt I was capable of evil; and he relished in the fact. Yet I did not want to be part of his world. I wanted to be independent. I needed to ensure that we did not get too involved.

"All right Giovanni," said Di Maglio. "When is your deadline?"

"We think the meeting in France will be at the compound. Security has been stepped up and the damage we caused earlier has already been repaired. There has also been no report to the police. We think the last attendees will arrive tonight. The New York raid will take place around ten in the morning our time tomorrow."

"The best time then is tomorrow morning," said Di Maglio. "Nobody will expect us to be back so soon. And the New York raid won't have happened. That would put them on added alert."

He turned to Aldo. "What's our strength on the ground?"

"We are in place in the safe house at Avignon. We have a ten man assault team there. And we have seven of the other team in place at Ales in the safe house there. That's three short and they are only flying in tomorrow. So they would arrive too late. All equipment is ready near

Nimes. We have a series of reinforced four wheel drives and plenty of armour."

"What about the Special Forces?" he was asked.

"We have our special command group holed up in Marseilles. They can be on site in four hours. They would need to pick up their assault gear. That's semi-portable rocket launchers and similar gear. They were instructed to be ready for night attack and will have been sleeping through the day. They can be in place in time."

I was the next target for questions. "Are you fit enough to take a special group inside the compound. Have you ever been parachuted into an area?"

"I am fit enough. I've only parachuted once and that was for charity."

"OK we can sort that out then. Let's take a break and get some sleep. Charles, you sleep in one of the spare rooms. There will be a wake up call at two am. You will have a briefing in the plane on the way out. Everyone get five hours sleep now. We need to be ready for tomorrow. It's going to be tough."

I went up to my room. Jacqui was fast asleep in the bed. As I went out again, a trim woman in a fawn suit approached me. She was the doctor.

"Jacqui will be all right," she said. "I've given her a sedative. I think she'll be out for at least twelve hours. Sleep will help her."

"What about the miscarriage?" I asked.

"She was just a month or so pregnant. Physically that's no problem. Mentally it could be otherwise but I suspect not. She is used to knocks. She should overcome this. But she'll need looking after." She smiled at me. "And it's better if she's looked after by you rather than someone else. So play it safe tonight."

I grinned. "I'll take my lucky rabbit's foot."

"A bullet proof vest would serve you better," she said as she walked down the corridor ahead of me.

I crashed out soon after. Aldo, who brought in some clothes for me to wear, woke me. Once again, I was clad in black. This time I also had a flak jacket. The doctor must have known more about the way they operated than I did.

We ate a light breakfast and then headed out to the airport. In the plane Aldo briefed us.

"The plan is simple. We will have three waves of attack. We are going to parachute you, Charles, and five others into the grounds. You are in charge, Charles. Your role is to cause a diversion. You need to confuse the Russians. Kill them if you can, but you are a diversion.

"While you are causing the diversion, our Special Forces from Marseilles will swoop in. They will storm the house. They are expert at that. And we need them to do their bit.

"The final group will come about five minutes later. In total there will be seventeen men in that band. They will attack and mop up as many survivors as they can. Then they will plant bombs and destroy as much property as possible.

"When the third wave come, you and your men retreat and hold the gate. It is important that our retreat is smooth and fast. Our men will withdraw and you will all be picked up by two vans we will send in.

"They will take you to the safe house between Nimes and Avignon. That's the one you used yesterday morning. The helicopters will come in and fly you out. The only difference this time is that some of you will come back to Geneva and others will be distributed via safe houses to their bases. You, Charles, will come back to Geneva.

Is that all understood?"

"It's very clear. I have no questions. Has anyone else? "I turned to the men who would be with me. There were no questions. I went over and said hello to each of them. The men were tough looking. They were not the sort you would argue with. But I would depend on them for the next few hours.

Some minutes later, Aldo returned. "I'll be in radio contact. Pierre there will act as the radioman. Have you all checked your guns?"

I nodded and watched as all the others did too.

I was helped into a parachute and reminded of the routine. "Alberto will jump with you," he said "And will be there to help you if you have problems."

I nodded. The plane was flying high and the side door was open. There was a flood of cold air through the cabin. Two men stood up in front of us. Then Alberto and I. Then Pierre and the remaining man stood behind us.

The first two jumped. They dived down together, using their arms to pilot themselves close together.

I heard a call. It said, "Jump." I launched myself out and saw Alberto tracked me with ease. Below me, out of the corner of my eye, I saw parachutes open.

I had counted to ten as instructed and pulled the cord. The parachute opened and I soon felt the jerk of the chute as I slowed down and then felt myself floating through the air. Above me I could see two more chutes opening. The plane was nowhere to be seen.

Alberto indicated me to steer to the left and I saw below me the complex. It was shrouded in the dark, the stars hardly lighting up the sky. It was perfect. The plane was too high to have disturbed anyone. And, unless someone was suffering from insomnia and staring up into the sky, we would not be seen. Then when we hit the ground and activated the alarms, the chaos would start.

Ahead of us the first two had landed. Until we got to tree height we seemed to float down. I had followed Alberto's instructions and was heading to a square of lawn around a quarter of a mile from the main house. The first two were there already. Their parachutes lay discarded on the ground. The breeze ruffled the light silk of the chutes.

Suddenly the ground started to come up fast. It hit me hard and I panted as all the breath left my body. It was as if I had just run a fast race. I was stunned. It couldn't have been for long as the last two were still above us. I slipped out of the chute, unhooked my gun and took cover.

As the last two landed, there was still no reaction from the Russians. We must be on the monitor by now. Yet we could see no lights. We could hear no voices. Surely we had not chosen an area that was not covered by security? We grouped together.

"We'll spread out and advance to the house. I don't like the quiet. Be alert everyone."

Pierre was about to call on the radio. I called out, "Radio silence until we know they've heard us. They could pick up the radio."

We advanced across the lawn. "Keep close to the trees. Try to avoid the open. We should get as close as possible to the house. That will cause the most chaos."

We had advanced around two hundred yards before the man on my extreme left fell. A light blazed from the trees, illuminating the entire area. It must have been a trip wire. "Take cover," I yelled.

"Call base," I yelled to Pierre. "It's going to get hot here. We have to hold the area until Special Forces get here."

We edged forward. I saw a movement in the distance and fired a quick burst in its direction. I sensed something behind me and wheeled round to see nothing. I was getting edgy.

Ahead of us was a barn, It was totally separate from the house and I motioned the men to get inside. We could do a lot of damage holed up there. There was no sense in trying to move into the open.

We swept through the barn. It was empty. That seemed strange. Why would there be nothing in there?

It was then that I realised the barn looked smaller inside than it had on the outside. I pulled Alberto aside and told him to check the walls.

He did so but found nothing. I still wasn't satisfied and checked for myself. I was getting doubly suspicious because we were not being attacked. I then realised why the barn looked small. It had a low roof. There were two floors. I did not know what was on the upper floor. It could not be reached from inside the barn. I was immediately scared. This could be a trap. This could be why we had not heard from the Russians so far.

I got the men to follow me and led them quickly from the barn. We waited in the trees nearby. There was still no movement. It was then that I realised why. There was nobody there. The place was empty. Miraculously, nobody was responding to our presence. I did not know how. But that was the only explanation for the inaction.

I told Pierre to radio my suspicions through to the base. In the meantime, I indicated to two of the men to come with me and get closer to the house. The Special Forces would be there in a moment. Alberto, Pierre and a third man were left behind.

The house ahead of us was dark. I could have sworn that it was uninhabited. In the distance I looked at the barn. I still sensed someone was there. I was getting more and more nervous. The silence was unreal.

The barn was much bigger outside than in. It was taller rather than wider. The roof was peaked. Inside it had been flat. Barns don't have closed lofts. The barn must be an escape route from the house. But I still couldn't work it out.

"Back," I shouted. We turned round and headed back towards the wood. Then all hell broke loose. From the house and the barn, now both lit up by powerful floodlights, came a non-stop roar of gunfire. One of our men fell over, his hands clutching his stomach. A red gush spread out from his clasped hands as he sank down onto his knees. He fell on his side. He seemed to have passed out.

We had no choice but to leave him there. We advanced towards the wood, three going forwards and two covering our rear.

In front of us the barn roof slid back and we could hear the whirr of a helicopter. I pointed a sub-machine gun and desperately tried to shoot out the rotors. Now I understood. The silence must have been cover to allow the gang leaders to escape. Once they were out of the way, we would have been attacked. But we had got too close and so they had launched their attack sooner than planned. They would not be concerned, though, for the chances of our disabling the escape helicopter with a machine gun were remote.

It was then that we heard the crashing noise of heavily armed men approaching. Pierre called, "It's the Special Forces". We breathed a sigh of relief.

As they advanced we retreated. A rocket launcher appeared and they lined it up, targeting the helicopter that was starting to rise from the roof of the barn. The rocket passed through the rotors, which shattered against it but somehow did not cause it to explode. We heard the helicopter crash back into the barn as the rocket exploded harmlessly in the distance.

There was now an intense battle around the house and the barn. We retreated to the gate as instructed. I was now bringing up the rear with Alberto.

We approached the gatehouse and were greeted by a hail of bullets. Pierre went down. The man next to him threw himself behind some trees to our left for cover. Everyone else dived behind a ridge and watched, lying on our backs, as the bullets flew over our heads.

I eased myself upwards and saw that Pierre was lying crumpled on the ground. I could see that he was dead. Blood stained his jacket and the back of his head revealed a gaping hole.

We had lost two men, although we could not be certain that the one who had fallen by the barn was alive or dead. The Special Forces were at the house. Soon the main body would arrive. The best thing we could do was to wait for their arrival. They would easily flush out the gunmen in the gatehouse.

So far my advance force had failed in its objectives.

I realised as Pierre fell that we were outnumbered. The Russians had been much better prepared than Di Maglio or his people had guessed. I had already lost one man at the barn. Now I had lost Pierre and with him our radio contact.

I called the four of us to retreat into the woods. There we could take better cover. The man on my far left gave us cover. The people who had been assigned to me were good. They reacted by instinct. It had been obvious from the time of the parachute jump that I was a passenger. I was not the right person to lead these men. I was not even in their class in this type of combat.

My training had been to combat street fighting and terrorism. This was actual warfare. As we withdrew into the woods, the main gunfire came from our side. The Russians were happy to see us retreat and took cover. From time to time a warning blast from them reminded us of their presence. They obviously saw protecting the gate as their primary objective. They also must have been aware of the second force at the house and barn. I hoped we did not have a mole and that they were not also aware of the third force that would strike in a few moments.

We regrouped in the woods. At one point Alberto noticed a remote controlled camera and shot it out. Otherwise there appeared to be no movement.

Behind us, near the house, there was fierce fighting. We could hear explosions and gunfire. We had definitely not succeeded in catching the Russians unaware. Although my group had not been spotted landing, we had been spotted somewhere. I suspected the mystery barn with its false walls was the key. It obviously had been two floors. The upper one was a re-inforced hanger with a sliding roof. There must have been a tunnel from the house to the barn, and I assume it came out at one end behind one of the interior walls.

I thought again about the people whom they had tried to get out in the helicopter. It must have been Rastinov and his key lieutenants. There was no logic in keeping them in the house during a pitched battle. That was the job of the foot soldiers. I doubted they had been much hurt from the accident to the rotors. They would have crashed back perhaps ten feet. That was hardly enough to bruise them.

A movement to our right alerted us. A burst of gunfire was met with an equally vigorous return. We advanced into the wood, but the gunmen had disappeared.

"Let's draw out the ones at the gate." I said. "The main force is going to arrive soon."

We spread out. Three of us swept to the front and one covered our rear. I was in the centre. We crawled out of the wood and eased forward towards the gate. We took cover behind the crest of a slope. Beyond us was the gatehouse and we could see men inside.

"Fire on the gatehouse. If we can draw them out, all the better. But there's no point in going out into the open or we'll just get mown down."

We opened fire. There was a desultory return. They were disinterested in us. We were no problem. They expected us to come out when the men in the house and barn drove back our companions. They obviously felt they could wait.

"It's no good," said Alberto. "We need to contact the others and warn them. They'll expect the gatehouse to be in our hands."

I looked over to where Pierre lay. We needed to get him or his radio. The radio lay a bit away from him. Of course it had a strap. If we could hook that we could get the radio.

"That may work in films," said Alberto, "but it won't work here. Once they see us trying to get it, they will fire on the area and the chances are that they will hit the radio. That is if they haven't done that already."

He slipped out of his heavy gear and just held his automatic against his hip. "Give me cover. I need all you've got and I'll run for it."

I signalled to our rear guard. He, too, came up to us and I then gave the order. Three machine guns spattered out at the house, their bullets smashing against the walls, the metal shutters and the door. Alberto threw himself over the ledge and scrambled over to the radio. In one swoop he had it by the strap as he turned to come back towards us.

We carried on our firing. The men in the gatehouse saw us and started to fire at Alberto. Their shots, though, were random ones and he had dived over the ledge and was back with us before they steadied. Two men came into view but retreated as we targeted them.

The third man returned to take up the rear watch. There was still no movement and all was quiet in front of us. We were still not doing well in our diversionary role. The Russians had outwitted our every move.

Alberto was on the radio and contacted the main force. He turned to me, "One minute before they hit the main gate. They'll attack with rockets. We should open fire but in another direction. The ones in the gatehouse may not then notice the third force approaching from the other side. They will automatically assume that we have been engaged from the rear and suppose that the battle up at the house has gone in their favour."

I nodded. That would make them relax their guard. Some could even move over towards us to see what was happening.

I reversed the stance, leaving one man to cover the gatehouse. We waited another twenty seconds or so and then I gave the order. We fired into the woods, hitting trees and bushes at random.

The man covering the gatehouse opened fire as someone looked out of one of the windows. Then we heard a deafening roar as rocket after rocket pounded into the gatehouse. We whirled around as four or five men stumbled out of the crumbling building. We moved up the ridge and caught them in a hail of fire. At least two seemed to go down. The others rushed towards the building as another rocket hit it. The last we saw of them was as the side of the building collapsed over them.

Our final assault wave moved in. There were shots but only sporadic ones. Alberto was on the radio and said, "We should advance and take over the gatehouse."

We moved forward. Pierre was definitely dead although I bent down to check. I saw from the man by my side that he realised that was a fruitless exercise even as I started to kneel next to the still figure.

We took up our positions around the destruction of the gatehouse. More ammunition was dumped next to us. Almost without a word the new group made their way forward towards the battle that raged around the house and barns. We covered the gatehouse and could only listen to the battle raging in the distance. It grew in intensity. We assumed that the main force had joined up with the others. Alberto was on the radio and indicated yes.

"They are in the house. The barn's destroyed. They say they are taking control. We should be on the alert. Some people may try to get out."

"Have they caught the main targets?"

He shook his head. "Not yet, unless they were in the barn. Someone is checking it over."

We carried on watching. Alberto pointed to the drive. A jeep was heading our way at speed. It contained four people and we knew that they were not ours. "Don't let them get away," I said.

We waited behind the crumbling walls until the jeep was just alongside us. At that point the driver was concentrating on the road in his attempt to get away from the fighting.

The passengers stood no chance. They were totally exposed. Four sub-machine guns raked the vehicle and its passengers with a torrent of bullets. It spun out of control and crashed into the wall on the far side of the gate, knocking over one of the few remaining unbroken sections.

There was no movement. Alberto and I cautiously made our way towards it. We edged round. Two bodies lay beside the jeep. One man was pinned against the steering wheel. A third was slumped across the back seat. There was blood everywhere. The jeep was pockmarked with bullet holes. One man groaned on the ground. Alberto spun round and opened fire on him. He was not going to groan again.

I pushed the man at the back of the car onto his back. His eyes stared up into the sky. He was dead. I moved to the one by the steering wheel and pulled him back. His neck was almost broken off, but that had not killed him. The bullets had done that before he crashed.

The final man was a bit further away and I went to him. As I approached a hand grasped at my leg and almost pulled me off balance.

My instinctive burst of fire missed its mark. But Alberto did not. His rapid burst of fire sneaked past me and into the body, which jerked a couple of times and then lay still.

I looked at the face. "Rastinov," I said. Alberto looked at the others. We knew one. It was Andrei. The others we did not recognise.

"We may not have done too well earlier," I said to Alberto. "But you paid for your meal ticket."

He grinned, pleased at the plaudit. We headed back for cover and waited for our next move. I called the others and told them we had caught two of the targets. They had killed Krakow. There was still one to go.

The fighting ahead was quietening down. The fierce continuous bursts of fire had ceased. Now we had sporadic bursts. "They are cleaning up," said Alberto.

The radio called. We would start pulling out. We called Aldo at base and called for the pick up vans. We had fifteen minutes to wait. The last round had begun.

I noticed the man crawling through the trees first. He was approaching the mound we had hid behind during our sally with the gatehouse. "Pastinsky," I said. "I want him." He was the one who had talked about raping Jacqui before she would die. "I want him to suffer."

"No," said Alberto. "Kill him. We forget vendettas. They mean people die unnecessarily. This is war not gang warfare. Nobody will see how he died. It's not worth making him suffer."

He was right, but I resented it. I knew though I had to do as he said. Pastinsky drew closer and, as I had him in my sights, I squeezed the trigger. I had sighted him low down. Stomach wounds are usually fatal if they come from the stream of bullets caused by a sub-machine gun. They are also very painful.

I caught him as I aimed and he went down screaming in pain. His screams continued for several minutes. Then he turned his own gun on himself. He put himself out of his own agony.

Alberto looked at me grimly. "Never do that again. If he had been braver, he could have done us damage. He could have rolled down the slope again and holed us up. I don't know why you did it. You must have had reason. But you must never do things like that again. It's stupid."

I felt dumb at that. But I knew I had wanted him to suffer. And he had.

The gunfire stopped for a moment and then the explosions started.

One after another came and went. A roar of sheer power. A plume of smoke would be followed by the crash of masonry. "The scorched earth policy has begun," said one of the men. "We need to stand by for departure."

"Cover both ways," I called. "For all we know the Russians could have reinforcements coming."

We continued to do just that. The bombs continued in the distance. The flames shot into the air. They must have fired an ammunition dump for all of a sudden there was an enormous explosion.

"That was more than anything we had," said Alberto as if to confirm my thoughts.

I looked over my shoulder as I heard a noise on the road outside. Alberto did too. "They're our vans," he said.

We waited and saw men coming through the trees. "Our people," said Alberto. He was acting as my minder and was afraid I might be nervous enough to shoot our own side.

I counted. There were seven members of the Special Forces and we had seventeen members of the final team. I noticed they were carrying two of their comrades. I finished counting as one man said, "That's all of us."

We had lost six men. In total eighteen were returning of the original twenty-four. Two were wounded and three more appeared to be walking wounded. I had lost two men out of my six.

We retreated out of the grounds and got into our vans. They sped down the road and out through Uzes until they got to the staging post. We split there without a word. These were not people to dwell on sentimentalities.

In the van they estimated that we had killed at last seventy of the Russians. They were uncertain how many there had been there in total. It had definitely been more than they expected.

We returned to Geneva the same way as the previous day. Aldo was strangely quiet in the plane. I thanked Alberto. He had definitely save my life. Yet I was uneasy. I shouldn't have been there. I was an amateur among professional soldiers. And I had a horrible suspicion that I knew why Di Maglio had sent me.

As we drove up to the house, Di Maglio was waiting. Giovanni was by his side. Jacqui was nowhere to be seen.

"Where's Jacqui?" were my first words. I did not trust him and thought she may have been spirited away.

"She's still asleep. She should wake up soon but she was exhausted. The doctor also gave her some tranquillisers."

I breathed a sigh of relief. She was still here. Soon we could leave.

"How did the other operations go?" asked Aldo.

"Well," replied Giovanni. "You may have had problems but we achieved our objective. And I expect that we will be able to make contact with the Russians soon. We should be able to strike up some sort of workable alliance."

I was staggered. "How can you make an alliance with those people?"

"Easily," he said. "The survivors won't want outright war. At least they are not going to want it for the moment. In fact I doubt they'll want it for the foreseeable future. We'll negotiate a peace with them. We'll make it worth their while. We couldn't negotiate with Rastinov. He was too greedy."

"And what is my position?"

"Let us negotiate over the next few days and then you will be free to go."

I went inside. Di Maglio followed me. Giovanni and Aldo talked quietly together behind him. I kept asking myself why he sent me. He was now talking of negotiating with the Russians. My initial thought had been wrong. I had assumed that he sent me so that I would need his protection against the Russians in the future. But that did not seem the case.

I turned to him. "Why was I sent to Uzes the second time? The first I can understand. But the second was nonsensical."

He smiled an oily smile of incredible insincerity. "What do you mean? I thought you wanted to go."

"That's bullshit. Even if I wanted to go, you would not let me unless you had a purpose."

"I really don't know what you are talking about."

"You are saying you'll strike a deal with the Russians. Once you do that, we won't be in danger from them."

Giovanni intervened. "Given the success of the operations in Uzes and New Jersey, they will agree and we will have peace for many years. They will be pleased that we allow them to prosper. And the reaction gave a warning to the world of the danger of threatening the Di Maglio family. They will have taken note. Everyone is safer."

A thought then struck me. "What would happen if the authorities knew who had masterminded the attacks?"

Giovanni again answered, "They will not try to find out. In reality they know. But they prefer scum like Rastinov to be off the streets. We acted on their behalf as well as in our own interests. Nothing will be done to find the attackers. There will be an official investigation. But there will be nothing else."

I then said, "Look I was little better than useless in the attack. Alberto saved me several times. I also endangered the lives of some of the people. I am not surprised. I was unsuited for that attack. And you knew it."

Di Maglio looked angry. His eyes were blazing. His face grew red. "We sent you in because it made you one of the family. You have been part of three of our operations. You went as our emissary to the Russians. You led the rescue for Jacqui. And you took part in the revenge raid. The first two, you could argue, were nothing to do with the family. But the revenge raid was. And you went past the point of no return in that raid. You are one of us."

"I am not. You don't own me. I don't owe you anything."

He exploded in fury. He was yelling now at the top of his voice. "You owe me your life. You owe me for getting you away from the police in Paris. You owe me for letting you stay with Jacqui. You fucking owe me and so don't forget it."

I clenched my teeth. I had to keep my cool. "You've got it wrong. I am independent. I can't shop you to the police without incriminating myself. That's true. In any event I wouldn't do that. In this case, what you did was right."

"You work for me now," he yelled.

"I work for nobody. I saved Aldo's life. I asked you to help me save Jacqui's. I helped you where I could. But I am not one of your family. And I never will be."

"Then you leave. And you leave on your own," he snarled.

"No, he doesn't," came a voice. We all swung round to look at Jacqui. Her hair was pulled back. Her face was pale. Her eyes were full of anger. Her cheeks flushed. Her breathing got heavier.

She repeated, "No he doesn't. You are not going to manipulate us. Or I will deliver the tape to the police. And you all will go with it."

"Oh fuck you both," said Di Maglio. "I'll just do to you what I should have let the Russians do."

Jacqui's eyes went wide in shock, as she heard that threat. I moved forward. Two men jumped from the shadows in case I was going to attack Di Maglio.

"The tape would be revealed then. You forget I have made arrangements to ensure that is done."

"With your little junkie friend?" he said. I stopped dead. How on earth did he know about her?

"If you touch her or any of her family, you're dead," I said.

Giovanni intervened. "Let's cool it. This is stupid. Charles you are bound to us. But you don't have to work for us. You have ties. We fought together. And you have ties through Jacqui."

He turned to Di Maglio. "We must stop threatening each other. Jacqui needs to leave. She must be able to come back. We need to trust each other. This is the wrong way to go about it."

Jacqui leant against the doorframe. I suspected she was still weak from her drugs. I was about to go over to her, but Di Maglio beat me. "Sit down. Perhaps I got too angry. I said things I should not say. I want you and Charles with me."

"No," said Jacqui. And she shook her head. "I am going with Charles. We need our own life. We are able to support ourselves."

"How?" he said. "Because you made some money in Hong Kong? That won't support you."

"I think it may," I said.

"No," he replied shaking his head. "Not in the way that Jacqui needs to live. You need to be more than a millionaire for that."

"But we are. And that's many times over. Even billionaires."

He looked doubtful. Giovanni looked at me questioningly. Aldo looked surprised.

"Look," I said. "You fight in a world of drugs or prostitution and then moved into legitimate businesses. We work in the grey world of finance and will then move into the fully legitimate area. We have a few more moves to make in the grey area but they are low risk. The big risks have been taken and we are talking of having made billions."

Giovanni said, "What did you do?"

I turned to him. "Give us three months and we will explain all to you. But my way of life is safer than yours. And I guess it is even more remunerative."

He nodded. Di Maglio said, "I don't believe you."

I looked at him and smiled, "Give me the three months. If Jacqui and I are not worth a billion dollars at the end of it, then I will work for you. If we are worth a billion, we remain family but independent."

Aldo came in. "That sounds fair." He was a good guy Aldo. He also had a soft spot for Jacqui. That helped.

Giovanni nodded eagerly. Di Maglio considered the options. He nodded. He turned to Jacqui. "Do you agree?"

She nodded. Then she said, "But you must give me your word of honour that you will do nothing to seek to stop us or worse."

He nodded. "I agree. If you can do better outside our business, all the better. We always need to diversify."

Giovanni said, "Both of you should stay for another week or so. By then we will know what is happening on the Russian front. Then you can go your own ways safely."

I nodded and put out my hand to Di Maglio. He hesitated, then took it. "I could get to like you, you bastard," he said. "I can see why Jacqui does."

He kissed her on the head. They then left and we were alone again.

Jacqui moved towards me. "You went on the main attack. You were the advance guard. You shouldn't have gone. It was too dangerous."

"I did not really think. I guess in many ways I had no choice. The good thing is that I got back. And soon we can go."

She had stood up and was swaying a bit. I took her in my arms and held her fiercely for a few minutes.

"Let's go back to the room and get you to bed. Then you can eat there and in a couple of days you'll be fine."

She let me lead her back to the room. She stayed there for two days. We then started to go for walks around the grounds. They were well guarded. We hardly saw the others. They were busy at work.

I called my parents and my father said that he was close to action. I agreed that we would join them in a few days. They did not realise that we were just a few miles away. It was better to keep them and the Di Maglio family apart.

I was surprised that they had based themselves in the President. It was a bit further up the Quai from the Bergues. But they said it offered easier communications than the more old fashioned hotel of my choice.

It was six days from the attack on the Russians. Jacqui and I had been wandering in the grounds. As we walked back to the house, Giovanni joined us. "You can leave when you please," he said. "We have drawn up terms with the Russians."

"What are they?" asked Jacqui.

"We take half their supplies up to five hundred million dollars each year for the next three years. We've arranged the price and the quality."

"Will they keep to the terms?" she said.

"Sure. They screwed up and could have been destroyed. We are too strong for them. All they want to do is generate cash so that they can buy up Russian industry. We allow them to do that and take out the downstream risks. We can sell as much of the shit as we can find. So we'll make the same money as them in the end. Everyone wins."

"Including the kids who die?" I suggested.

"That's their choice," came the callous reply. "They could die in a car crash or from tobacco just as easily."

There was no use debating. I did not want to get involved. Nor did Jacqui. I was relieved we could leave.

The next morning we had a surprisingly friendly goodbye from Di Maglio. We headed to the President and my parents. The final stages of the scam could now begin.

WAITING FOR THE STORM

As the car dropped us outside the Hotel President, my parents were just returning. They had evidently been for a walk. They both looked fit and healthy. My mother had updated her wardrobe again in Geneva and was wearing slacks and a fur coat of the kind you can only buy in the German speaking areas of Europe.

When they saw us they looked horrified. "My darlings," said my mother, "What on earth have you been doing? You are both so pale and drawn. Jacqui, what has happened to you? You look unwell."

"We have had a tough time, perhaps we should explain. Let's check in and then have a coffee together. We'll unpack and then come over to your room."

My father said, "We are on the top floor. We have a suite there. See if they can do one for you."

In the end they could only do us a double room on the top floor. No suites were available except on the lower ones. We took the double as it gave a good view of the lake.

I had ensured that both Jacqui and I were armed. I still was not totally certain that we were as safe as Di Maglio had alleged. I also suspected that we had a secret bodyguard. The two men who had driven us to the hotel were hardly chauffeuring types with their broad shoulders and athletic builds.

We unpacked and headed over to my parents' room. I stopped in front of the mirror as we went out. "You know, they are right," I said to Jacqui. "You are pale and your eyes are tired. You have more make up than usual. Otherwise I think you'd look even more exhausted. I'm also pretty drawn. This is not a life style for us. I think financial racketeering suits us better."

She agreed and we went into my parents' suite for the inevitable interrogation. Sitting in the comfortable sofas, we explained what had happened.

My mother clutched my father's hand as I explained about the kidnapping in Paris and my eventual escape to the Di Maglio compound.

"It's like a bad film," my father said. "It's a world I never thought existed. But, if we could tie in their cash and ours, we could take on the biggest in the land."

"No," I said. "Be careful. That sort of money isn't dirty, it's foul."

Jacqui took up her story. She explained how she had been taken to the house near Uzes. She talked about the treatment she had been subjected to. She told of new horrors. She had been injected with a truth serum to get her to give away secrets that she did not know. She had been subject to electric shock torture when that did not work. Then she explained how she had realised she had miscarried as a result of that torture.

"I suspected I might be pregnant just before the kidnapping. I was fairly certain a week or so later. Then I knew I'd lost it."

I put a protective arm around her as her voice choked. My mother came forward and knelt in front of her. "Don't worry. You're young enough to have as many children as you want. Just wait until all this is sorted out." I knew her gentleness at this point meant much to Jacqui. My mother stroked her cheek and smiled at her. "Just consider it fate. It's not your fault. They did not want you. They wanted your father. And it wasn't his fault. They are people who don't play by the rules. But how did you get away?"

I picked up the story and explained how we entered the grounds with Jacques and how we managed to get away with Jacqui. I then mentioned the attack on the house and its destruction.

"My God, I saw the pictures on the television. They said it was gang warfare between major drug cartels," said my father.

"They were right. It was. In reality Jacqui's incident was just a distraction."

"You should never have been there," remarked Jacqui. "My father deceived me again."

"We have to put that behind us," I said. "Unfortunately we need him. So we cannot reject the past. We cannot ban him from our life. But we have an agreement. He doesn't realise we have already achieved the objective. We already have a billion. But we need to finish the work. And I wanted him at arm's length for that period."

"I think you're right," said my father. "Three months will be plenty. That takes us almost to the spring. By then we will all be free and part of the establishment."

I changed the subject. "Where are you with United?"

"I've expanded the target list of companies for the fund to thirty three. Originally I had selected fifteen to twenty but I've found a few more since then. I knew five of them already. They are Far East based stocks, all are oil exploration, but their prices have slumped as a result of the Asia crisis. So they came into play."

"How much have you put in?" I asked.

"I've invested eighty million so far. That's more than I planned. But I even managed to do it as the markets have drifted down. So our average prices are just a bit higher than the current market prices. I must be close to mopping up all available stock soon. I plan to carry on doing it slowly. I am spreading the orders around the market carefully. That slows one down."

"How long will it go on for?" asked Jacqui.

"I think we'll hit over a hundred million invested," said my father. "I will then start the fund with United's backing. They are ready to support us up to five hundred million dollars as long as they have twice that in assets in the fund. They expect that will protect them, even if the stocks are high risk."

"How long will it be to get everything ready for the launch though?"

"I suspect about three weeks. That means just after Christmas. That's a good time as it avoids any year end balance sheet considerations that United may have. And all their managers will be greedy in the New Year as they face up to their New Year's business targets. That's when their judgements are the most flawed."

"But what should we do over the next few weeks?" inquired Jacqui.

"It sounds as if there will be little for us to do. In fact, I doubt we are needed," I said. "Look we both need a rest. Can we drop out?"

"Where?" said my mother, "After recent events, I am a bit wary about letting you out of my sight."

"It depends on Jacqui. But this is an ideal time for the West Indies. I would quite like to get us a small boat and spend a couple of weeks on it. I don't know if there will be anything good to charter though."

"That's a fantastic idea," said Jacqui. "I'd love it. I need some new summer things. I could get those here."

I was pleased she looked enthusiastic again about our plans. I made some calls and soon found a company with boats to charter. One was available. It had three cabins. It was fast. It had a two-man crew. It was available from the following Saturday for two weeks. I booked it immediately and arranged to confirm all.

I booked the flights too. We would fly into London and then out by

British Airways. This time I had booked us first class. We wanted to have the maximum comfort. We would stay one night in a hotel and then spend the next two weeks sailing around the coast off Barbados. It was just what we needed.

As a precaution, I called Di Maglio and told him of our plans. He would check out the charter company and make sure we had the right crew. He would also arrange for us to have guns in Barbados in case we needed them.

"Alberto will meet you there. He will be in contact with you should you need him. It's better to be safe. You need the holiday. We won't disturb you."

He called me back later. "I have arranged for your crew. They are our people. There will be just two people. They will be discreet. They are good people. And one is a good cook. I have told them to give you all the privacy they can. They need not spend the nights on the boat if you are in harbour. I want them around though. I just want to make sure that there are no slips. You'll like them."

I realised that it was sensible. We needed the protection. He understood his world. And we would be on holiday. I was willing to tolerate his interference in this case. I explained what he had done to Jacqui and then to my parents. They too were relieved and felt it for the best.

The next day we all went shopping. Jacqui was already returning to her old self. She simply raided the shops for summer clothes. She knew exactly where to go. Geneva was one of her cities. We even went back to the boutique where we had first met with the Russians. This time though there were no disturbances. The owner recognised us, but said not one word about the incident or her erstwhile assistant.

I also was kitted out although Jacqui was less enthusiastic about many of the men's clothes. The designer labels for women were, in her mind, better prepared for the affluent winter sun seeker. Men, they assumed, would just wear their summer clothes again.

That night we went out into the old town of Geneva for dinner in a small trattoria my father had discovered in a quiet side street in the old part of town. Anybody watching us would have thought we were just another family. We looked well-to-do with both Jacqui and my mother sporting designer labels. Neither wore much jewellery. So we did not draw unwelcome attention to ourselves.

If they had looked closer, they may have wondered why Jacqui and I were looking quite so tired. Perhaps they would have jumped to the wrong conclusions. We were winding down quite quickly after the stresses of the last weeks. It was only when we had slowed down that we realised quite the strain we had been under.

That night, we talked for the first time for a long time of our future. We both liked the idea of being based in London. "If we are going to work in finance, that's the best city. Frankfurt is inflexible. Paris is full of amateurs. Milan is a children's playground and New York a regulatory nightmare. Only London gives the global reach."

We wondered where we would live. We talked of the places we would go. I named my favourite restaurants. We talked of the small ones we knew around Covent Garden. We both knew the fun places like Langans near the Ritz, the Oxo tower by the river, the RSJ by the National Theatre, Amaya in Belgravia or the Bombay Brasserie in Gloucester Road. Those were the places where even the famous were allowed privacy. Neither of us fancied the affected charm and ostentation of the so-called celebrity haunts where mediocre food was blended with pretentious wines.

We talked of the theatre and opera. We talked of films. We decided we would chose London. One could fly anywhere from there. And one could do anything when based there.

The next day we headed to that city. Our four pieces of luggage were not the same as those that had followed us half way around the world. Jacqui had replaced them. In any case we needed to leave our winter clothes behind. My parents placed them in their closet. They would await our return.

"Christmas we can spend together," my parents had suggested. "Geneva would be fine unless you want to go up into the mountains and do some skiing."

"Let's take a rain check. We could head over to Austria. Lech in the Tirol usually has snow at this time of the year. But they may be fully booked. Or the snow could be lousy. Let's wait and see."

We all said our good-byes at the airport. I noticed Alberto two rows behind us but we pretended not to know each other. It served no purpose and could be dangerous if someone were to follow us. I was learning fast the tricks of my new life.

We landed in London and headed to transit. I had no wish to go through immigration and customs. I felt though that our passage this time would have been easier.

We flew over to Bridgetown sitting together in the comfort of our first class seats. We selected our movies and watched them between the selection of courses that were offered to us. We drank our champagne and dutifully accepted the regular offers of water from the hostesses. "It's strange," I said. "Air hostesses are all supposed to be young. Yet the bulk here are not. Is it because the business has been around for a long time? They were all young with Concorde but have stayed on since."

We had noticed Concorde parked like a souvenir on the tarmac. Jacqui said, "There is a difference. Concorde's paint covers up its age. That one looks as if her make up will crack. Mind you, if you want to letch over them, the pretty ones are in the popular cabins. You can go for a walk if you want."

"No," I said. "I won't even look at the menu. I have you. My appetite is satisfied."

"Actually," she said, "We've been quite moderate these days. I just have been too bushed. You have too. But we can make up for it now. We can have two glorious weeks of sail, sun, sand and sex. That'll make us feel better."

As we landed in Barbados, it looked as if we could be wrong. The sky was overcast with heavy cloud and Bridgetown looked like a provincial English town on a poor summer day.

"It's often like this," said Jacqui. "It could have been sunny this morning. Then it clouds over. It means that you build up a tan in the morning and then make love all afternoon. At night, nobody cares as long as it doesn't rain."

She was right. We headed to our hotel, which was down the coast from the capital. I had been there once before.

It held the same pre-Christmas crowd it had no doubt held for many years. The American widow with three engagement rings of decreasing age. The aged impresario, possibly down on his luck, angling for a bank balance. The octogenarian millionaire who was accompanied by a busty blond wife some fifty years his junior. City slickers and their limpid girlfriends who had jumped for the discount offered before the season really began.

"I am going to dress up tonight," announced Jacqui. "It's time for a grade one evening."

I groaned. "Aren't you tired? Shouldn't you take it easy?"

"Not the least. We're on holiday now. And they have a band. It's hardly going to be about bopping the night away. Half the guests will be shoving their resuscitators and oxygen tents under the table in case of need. But we can smooch. They most likely think we are lovers. I am not wearing a ring. That means they expect us to be naughty."

Jacqui produced the dress she had bought on our first visit to Geneva. It was a tight fitting black sheath of silk that clung to her body like a second skin. The neckline plunged between breasts that seemed to rise triumphantly from its folds. The sheath effect continued until mid-calf when it flared out to floor level. She could wear no bra under the plunging neckline and panties would have left a mark on the thigh hugging material. She wore tights on their own as the only way to overcome this problem.

As she moved, her hips undulated under the seductive material. Her body flowed underneath it as if eager to escape its limited constraints. Her hair was loose and fell over her shoulders. The make up was gentler as the excitement brought colour back into her cheeks.

I was a poor relative by her side. I was dressed in slacks, a blue silk shirt and a blazer. I looked like a banker on holiday. She was anybody's dream woman. She was the epitome of the male fantasy.

We walked out of our room in the grounds. Each room was located in its part of a small bungalow. The main restaurant overlooked the sea, tranquil now below an umbrella of unthreatening cloud. The restaurant was full and most guests were already on their starters. The band was taking up their position, as they had no doubt been doing for some twenty good years.

We were placed at a secluded table in a secluded corner of the restaurant. There we would be allowed to look into each other's eyes until we tired or were disturbed. Behind us we could hear the monotonous hum of polite conversation as strangers and married couples sought to get to know each other. Occasionally an excited laugh would rise above the murmurs, but it was most likely only a reaction to the wine rather than to a witty remark.

We ate and talked. We ignored the crowd. Some sat in embarrassed silence and looked on us as strange beings who actually appeared to have no difficulty in talking to each other. Others appeared to have been together for so long that meaningful conversation had ceased long ago. The music echoed vaguely in the background. It was not meant to dance to. The tempo would become more fitting as the evening wore on.

Jacqui nevertheless took me onto the empty dance floor. The music was slow and languid and I went to take her in my arms for a slow and sentimental dance. But she would have none of that. Her ideas had already progressed beyond such common thoughts. She swayed to the music moving her body with all the eroticism she had portrayed in the Wan Chai night-club. I was a poor imitator. She lent forward and slipped my jacket off my shoulders, throwing it to a waiter who was passing for him to dispose of. She unbuttoned my shirt half way down to my waist and said, "Close your eyes and think of the music. Forget the people around us."

We seemed to move more rhythmically together. Our bodies floated closer and closer. We were holding each other but still apart. Then gradually we moved together still moving our bodies to the gentle beat of the music until we were too close to move except in unison.

Jacqui's arms crept up my back. She tilted her head and kissed me eagerly. I moved my hands to her shoulders and pushed her body closer. I felt her throbbing gently against me. I responded to her in a way that only she could make me.

The band obviously thought this exhibition had gone far enough. They picked up the tempo and sought to attract other guests onto the floor. They were hardly successful as only one other couple did. Jacqui pulled herself away from me and started to show how one should move to music. Even the elderly enjoyed that. The dress she wore was made for dancing. She loved its unrestricted grasp. The voluptuousness of her body was accentuated by its softness.

We danced for an hour or so, returning occasionally to our table for a drink. We then left the restaurant and wandered over to the narrow strip of beach. The clouds were slowly parting. The moon was not visible although one got the occasional glimpse of a star. Jacqui took her shoes off. "Let's paddle," she said.

"But you're wearing tights," I commented. She put her hands under her dress and soon had them rolled up in a ball. She laughed and threw them to me. "A present," she announced.

She hitched her dress up above her knees and stood by the water's edge. I joined her and we kissed, feeling the coolness of the night on the gentle sea that lapped around our legs. "We could go for a swim," suggested Jacqui.

"Not in your dress, and I think there are too many people around for even you to take it off."

"You're right. Let's head back. I can take it off there." She picked her shoes up from the wall on which she had placed them. I followed her and we walked arm in arm back to our room. On the balcony we looked over the sea in the darkness ahead. She breathed in the breeze keenly; slipping her hand inside my shirt as my hand caressed her breast.

She pulled herself gently away. The balcony was not visible from any of the paths that crossed the hotel grounds. She slipped the straps from her shoulders and glided the dress down to the floor. She stepped out of it and tossed it over a chair. She was now naked other than the high-heeled black shoes she had worn. She walked over to me and pressed close. Her body arching onto mine, in a way she knew I would find irresistible.

On the balcony was a settee-like chair that swung from two chains and was topped by a canopy. She moved over to that and sat down. She pulled her legs up and lay back along its full length. Her arms went out to invite me to join her.

My shirt was off in a moment and soon I had pulled off the rest of the clothes. Normally I would have assumed that such a chair, swinging backwards and forwards in the cool evening air, was an impossible place on which to make love. I had forgotten though Jacqui's love of the air on her naked body. I had overlooked how the night air acted on her as an aphrodisiac. And I had forgotten how her tempestuous acts excited me. Together that made any unexpected place an idyllic spot for love making.

We held on to each other, our movement making the chair sway gently backwards and forwards. We forgot about the background murmur from the seaside restaurant, and made love as if for the first time. As we gently eased ourselves apart some time later, the chair was still swinging in memory of the rhythm of our bodies.

The night air was now cool against the warmth of our former closeness. We felt it creep through the heat of each other's passion as if willing to understand its intensity. The clouds parted more and more and let stars peep through. We ignored them all but sensed only the smells of the ocean and the perfume of the grass and trees, as they both mingled with the scents from our bodies.

We went indoors in the end when we were suddenly disturbed by voices. They didn't see us or even dream of our naked existence. But they intruded and scared away the essence of that moment.

Indoors, we were alone and protected from the rest of the world. We tumbled into bed, naked as we were. Our clothes strewn over the room where we had let them fall. Tomorrow we would be on the boat and the ocean would be our only guest.

The next morning we left early and headed down to the harbour. The driver was waiting in the car. As he got out I saw it was Alberto. Neither Jacqui nor I made to recognise him.

Once we had driven away from the hotel, he said, "There's an extra bag with your luggage. It matches the rest perfectly. It contains some odds and ends as well as a couple of handguns for Charles and one for Jacqui. I suggest you hide them in the boat when you are swimming. It is better to distribute them so that you can access a gun on each of the decks."

When we arrived at the boat, I realised it was more comfortable than I had thought. A large sun deck on the rear opened up onto a lounge which in turn led to a bedroom with a large double bed. The top deck had a second wheel house and a similar sun deck. Canopies, that could be drawn back or forward electronically, shaded both.

Then Alberto said, "Here are your crew."

I gasped with surprise as two girls approached. One was small and dark with a trim figure, slightly muscular from regular training. The other was taller with a short bob of light brown hair. She too had a slim trim body. Jacqui looked keenly at them. I thought she would be annoyed at her father. My first thought was that they were here to tempt me away from Jacqui. There was something about them though that I could not place.

"This is Maria," said Alberto indicating the small one. "She is a black belt judo player and one of the best shots I have seen. Her friend is Claire. She is a pentathlon champion. They both have worked for us for about five years and can be trusted. They have lived together for around three years and so get on well. You'll enjoy their company."

"Where will you two sleep?" I asked. "There is only one cabin."

"We plan to sail around Barbados and then over to the other islands. Even at this time of the year, there is plenty of accommodation. So unless you want us on board, we will live on shore. The boat will always be watched and we are fitting it with peripheral radar that will monitor the sea around. That requires you two to do one thing. If you swim off the boat you need to wear one of these watches. They give us a signal that tells us it's you."

"How can you tell someone hasn't got hold of them?" I asked. I knew that we needed to be careful about security now. I want to play doubly cautious.

Alberto looked at me admiringly. "You learn fast," he said. "Next time you won't need me around."

Maria explained, "The watches send a signal that is generated by your body. We will get you to wear them for a bit and the computer will recognise your body rhythm. It's new technology but it's a mixture of your heartbeat, your breathing and your body make up. It's impossible to imitate because there are too many variables."

"What will you do when you are ashore?" I asked the girls.

"Oh, there's plenty of things around for amusement," said Claire. "We won't be bored."

"I wanted to know if we needed you, how we could get hold of you?" I asked coolly.

Alberto nodded his approval again. I was adopting the right no nonsense approach and thinking through the risks of different situations.

"Tell us in advance if you can," said Maria. "Otherwise bleep us. You'll have a bleeper. If for one reason or another, that can't be done, we have the lookout that will always know where we are. He'll contact us."

Our luggage was loaded and unpacked. There were plenty of places to stow things away. Alberto left and said, "See you around." He looked on me as a good pupil now. I was not going to do anything stupid.

We set sail, or rather motor, immediately. The girls knew how to handle the boat. Within the hour, Bridgetown was a distant speck and we were alone on the blue sea. A few other boats on the horizon were our only companions.

I donned a pair of swimming trunks and a T-shirt. I remained bare footed. Jacqui slipped on a bikini. I guess it was four triangles of differing sizes held together by a delicate series of strings. Over that she wore a floor length matching beach dress, with a zip left open to her stomach and a slit up the side to her hips. Once again she managed to find a material that gleamed with eroticism and a cut that accentuated all that was wonderful about her body. Every movement became an erogenous act. I guessed it was going to be hard concentrating on the sun and sea as we had planned.

We headed to the upper deck. On the way I tied a gun beneath the wheel on the lower one, having taped another under the bed in our room. The final one I now taped on the upper deck, beneath the rear seat. I hoped we would not need to use them.

"Wise," said Claire who had been watching us. "I doubt you'll need them. But if you want to survive in this business, you take a few precautions and avoid a few risks. I have checked the boat for bugs. There are none. I have also activated our radar and it is working perfectly. Back in the US we are being monitored at all times."

"Surely people are not going to be watching us on a screen all day and night," said Jacqui.

"No. It's all automated. The radar sends messages by satellite to the base and then a computer reads the signals. It will sound an alert in the event of any strange event. The biggest problem arises if we hit something like a shoal of whales or sharks. The radar finds it hard to distinguish them if they swim too close together."

Maria came up. She was dressed in a halter neck top and a pair of cut off jeans. She had the two watches she had mentioned in her hands. "I need you to wear these for a couple of hours so that we can gather all the data we need to put into the computer. If you can bear to wear them for twenty four hours the risks of us confusing you with others becomes almost nil."

"Let's do that," I said. "They are hardly designer wear but we are not planning to go on shore for a few days. So we might as well eliminate that risk."

"Good," said Maria. "Now where do you want to head. We know a lovely bay at the North of the Island. It has several isolated coves where one can land. The swimming is great off sandy beaches. And then a bit further along, there is a small harbour where we can stop and stay in one of the guest houses overnight."

"Sounds good," I said. Jacqui agreed. "Why can't we stay in one of the coves overnight. I'd prefer to be anchored off the coast rather than parked in a harbour."

"No problem," said Claire. "We'll take one of the motor skis and get to shore. That leaves you two with the other should you need it."

I only realised at that moment that there was a motor ski attached to each side of the boat. They could be automatically loaded into the water. This was a much more sophisticated craft than I had expected.

"Is this a real charter boat or has it been brought over specially?" I asked.

"The latter," said Maria. "We could never get the equipment on a simple hire craft."

I had thought as much and frowned slightly. This was yet another example of the ever-increasing influence of the family on my life. I didn't want to spoil things for Jacqui though and said nothing.

"What about lunch?" said Maria. "The galley is just off the lounge and has limited facilities. If you want anything complicated, tell me in advance."

"Let's have a picnic," said Jacqui. "Just a salad. Have we melons? That would be a nice starter. And some fruit punch. I think non alcoholic as we will be swimming."

"Dead easy," said Maria and headed to the lower deck with Claire. The boat turned back towards the shore and slowly made its way through the water to our lunchtime rendezvous.

We drew back the canopy on the upper deck and Jacqui took off her robe. "Put some lotion on me," she said as she undid the straps of her bikini top. "I want to get brown all over my back as I have this wonderful low cut white dress I plan to wear one of these days."

I gently rubbed the lotion into her back, caressing it into her shoulders. She busied herself with sun block on her face and neck. I knelt down and did the same to her legs, starting with her feet and gradually working up to her thighs. She giggled as I massaged her feet and purred slightly as I moved up her legs. She turned round and let me apply the soft white cream to her front, allowing me to linger over her breasts for just a moment at a time. She then turned her attention to me, rubbing the cream in over my back and chest, before sitting on the deck to do my legs with her head resting against my stomach.

I lifted her off the deck and started to kiss her, raising my hands up her sides.

"Oh no," she said. "This is sun bathe time. Or we go back paler than we came."

The deck had two loungers, each covered by a fluffy white towel. We lay on them, side by side, turning over as the sun heated our bodies. There is something about the gentleness of a Caribbean sun that makes it remove stress and slows down the body and mind. When you add to that the cooling air from a boat moving through the open water, you have a perfect fusion of sun and air.

We read and drank still cold water that Claire or Maria brought up from time to time. As we approached midday, we turned into a secluded cove. It was cut off from the land by a steep cliff and from the next beach by a rocky ledge. The sand was white and sloped gently into the calm waters of the bay.

"It's like a desert island," said Jacqui. "It's just beautiful. It' so peaceful."

We went down to the lower deck and dived into the cool sea. Both Maria and Claire followed us into the water. We swam around the boat. The water was clear and we could see the white sand below. From time to time a shoal of small fish would scurry past us. In the distance was a coral reef.

Maria called over to us, "The cove is free from sharks. They hate to come into the shallows. We crossed the coral reef into the cove at its deepest point. That was about fifteen feet. It gave us enough clearance but should scare off any shark unless something drives it wild."

"What could drive it wild?" asked Jacqui.

"Some kinds of noises could. Blood of course agitates them. But the chances are remote. Mind you I wouldn't swim beyond the reef. That could be dangerous unless one is with an expert. We haven't any snorkelling equipment on board. Do either of you want some?"

"I don't," I said. "I am not too keen on depths."

"I can skip that too. I just want to relax," said Jacqui.

She had not bothered to put on her top and the two girls had done likewise. It struck me as strange. So many things had changed in my life. A couple of days ago I was feeling washed up in Geneva. A few days before that I had been in violent gun battles in the South of France. And now I was in quiet cove in Barbados swimming in the sea with three beautiful women. And it all felt normal.

I noticed Jacqui kept close to me and I was careful to do the same. Maria and Claire got out before us and we could see them on the deck calmly taking off their bikinis and stepping into dry shorts and tops.

"Why do they do that?" I asked Jacqui.

"I doubt they think much of it. I know the type. They work for my father and earn a lot of money. They'll do anything. They know they have a short shelf life. Perhaps they have ten years if they are lucky. In that time they can become millionaires. Afterwards there is no use working on. They slow down then, both sexually and physically."

"You make it sound as if they are totally amoral."

"They are. But don't criticise them. Once they retire, they'll be millionaires. They may be that a couple of times over. They'll only be late twenties. Who else can offer them such an opportunity? It may be corrupt. But it's understandable."

I was amused by this example of Jacqui's casual acceptance of such life. But she was right. The girls knew their attributes and would use them for one end. That end was the achievement of wealth before they settled down to a life that would be comfortable in the extreme. They were all too disciplined to blow it.

We too got out of the water and dried off. We changed on the upper deck. The casual approach of the girls fed through to us. We were as casual with our own nudity as they were with theirs.

We all got on the bikes and headed to the beach. The girls got the food to shore and set up the picnic. Their bike was parked on the beach. Jacqui and I scooted around the bay on ours. Her bikini bottom was matched with a slinky top that was getting wetter and wetter. I had kept my T-shirt on against the now burning midday sun.

The girls called us in. We pulled the bike back onto the shore. Our faces and hair were wet with the spray from the ride. We were soaked from head to toe. Jacqui's shirt was clinging to her. We stripped off and each put on dry shorts and shirts that Claire scooted over to the boat to pick up.

After lunch, we lazed around in the sand. We spent the afternoon swimming and sunbathing. The warm sand was pleasant underfoot. The sun cooled off and we relaxed in its pleasing rays.

As the early evening drew in, we headed back to the boat. We agreed that the girls should take the scooter the mile or so round the bay to the resort. They had radioed in and established that they could get accommodation. We would make ourselves things to eat later.

"There are plenty of eggs and I am a dab hand at omelettes," said Jacqui.

We were alone. It was the first time in several weeks. And more importantly, we were relaxed. The balmy evening air welcomed us to the deck as we watched the sun set in the distance and night draw in.

"Let's go for a dip," said Jacqui stripping off her shirt and shorts. Naked, she headed to the steps and dived into the water. I followed suit and we both swam in the cool water of the evening. We kept close to the boat and to each other. After a few minutes, we came back to the steps. I held onto the side and Jacqui swam up into my arms.

It was strange feeling her under the salty water. I shut my eyes and felt her body brush over mine. I floated onto my back. She floated above me. I held her by the waist as we floated down again. Her body was warm and cool. It glistened as the water lapped backwards and forwards over it. She raised her legs and folded them behind my back. She pushed herself against me. Her wet, salty lips clung hungrily to mine. Her moist body glided against me. She took over control from me as if it were her right.

She tempted me as she floated around me. From time to time, her breasts would stroke against me, the nipples firm as if anticipating my very wish. She raised her legs time and again and clasped them around my waist. Then fighting gently against the buoyancy of the water, she slid herself down me before letting go to run her hands across my naked body.

I stroked her on the back and then wherever she allowed. It was her choice as she angled different parts of her body onto my caress. Sometimes they lingered for more. At others they came for a moment's temptation.

We had time. We were weightless in the water. We were able to come and go to each other without effort. It was tantalising and exciting in the loneliness of the cove. Alone but for perhaps the occasional inquisitive fish, we touched and floated against and on each other time and time again.

Still in command, Jacqui took my hand and pressed it against her. "Come on deck," she said. She led me out of the water. Our bodies gleamed with the salty sea. We moved to the upper deck and she grabbed our towels. They were thick, white and fluffy. She laid them on the deck in a bed like formation and sank back onto them. Her legs apart and her arms up calling to me, she moistened her lips as if concerned that there could be one part of her that could appear less than perfect at that moment.

I groaned and knelt in front of her. Her arms were around my neck. Her body arched to me. I exploded in a frantic desire that matched her own. We sank back into the soft folds of the towels. The sun oil had made her body slippery to the touch. She was still wet from the sea. Her body was warm against the cool evening air. Everything about her was soft, smooth, wet, warm, tender and trusting. I was inside her. Then I felt the cool air as we moved apart. Then I was inside her again, allowing nothing to come between us. She held me tightly. I crushed her in my arms. We tried to get ever closer as our bodies shared their sensations.

We moved together. We breathed together. Our bodies communed together. And we exploded into final passion with a triumphant shared orgasm as a gentle rain came down on us from clouds that had stealthily come to see us while we ignored the sky.

That was the mixture of our life for the next two weeks. Occasionally Claire and Marie would intrude. Usually they did not. We never saw Alberto but I knew he was out there somewhere. It was an idyllic time. It was so different from the time we had spent in California. We went round the islands and found our lonely coves.

We had the discrete company of the girls during the day. And at night we were left to our own devices. We ate every type of omelette under the sun. We stretched even Claire's imagination on salads. We swam. We made love in the open, in the cabin and on the seashore. And then we were brought back to our real world. We were brought back to our real lives.

We had not called Geneva for the whole time, but on the last day we had to. Our holiday was over. It was time to head back to Europe. I could have stayed. She could have stayed. We both could have stayed. But we needed to finish the last part of our scam. We had the wealth and now we would have the power.

THE DEATH OF A BANK

I called Geneva from Bridgetown. The boat was in the harbour. The girls were waiting for their relief crew. I got through to my mother. It was a cold and wet December in Geneva. Then my mother dropped a bombshell.

They had booked a suite at the hotel where we had stayed on our arrival.

"There's nothing to do here until the New Year. And the weather is awful all over Europe," said my mother. "They say they have a couple of rooms at the hotel still but we did not know whether you would want them or would prefer the boat."

"We can see you anyway," I said. "But I think we'd prefer the boat. I don't know if we can keep it. We'll find out."

Jacqui, who I had signalled to get onto an extension, had been listening in.

"Hi, it's me," she said. "If we can keep the boat, that would be great. Otherwise we'll grab a room. I can't say that a cold winter appeals. How can you come here?"

It was my father who now came to the phone. "Hello you two. You both sound like your old selves. I won't ask if you had a good time. We've been working here while you lazed around on your ill-gotten gains. We have put around a hundred and twenty million into the fund. By the way, did you know that we earn almost half of a million a day gross on our cash? And as we are based in Monaco for tax purposes, we don't pay a cent of tax as well."

I had never thought of the money that way, but I had to admit it was quite comforting at a time when most of my friends were dreaming of earning a portion of that each year.

My father continued, "I have told United that we are launching the fund on January 2nd. I have also told them that we have initial subscriptions of over one hundred and fifty million dollars. They think that we are setting up the shares to buy. In fact we have little to do at the moment. We will not pick up much stock over Christmas and we can't launch the fund till after New Year."

I had done some thinking while he was talking. "Why are we earning so little on the cash. The rates seem lousy."

"I'm putting it on short term deposit. We may need access quickly. I believe we will have to take out United quickly. Thirty per cent would cost us around one point five billion at today's prices. We may also have to buy up shares in the bidder to push their price up too. That is what I'm earmarking part of the other billion for."

He then added, "I've shuffled around the money. I have moved it around through such a web that nobody is going to be able to trace it. Or put it this way, if they try they will have to have the law changed in at least four countries including Switzerland, the Cayman Islands, Austria and Jersey. Given that the law changes needed could destroy their banking industries, I can't see that happening."

He continued, "The money is in four banks now. They are all in the top ten in the world and I've got a schedule of them for you. The money is split two ways between joint accounts; one is for us. The other is for you and Jacqui. I put a billion into them each. The other one and a half billion is in company accounts with all four of us as equal shareholders. I want all winnings to be split four ways. That's fair."

"But that's not fair on you," said Jacqui. "I shouldn't have an equal share."

"You can always give it up," said my father with a smile. "I think it fair."

"Me too," I said. "We couldn't have got this far this quickly without you. Let's keep it the way it is."

"And now," said my mother, "Let's stop talking business. Find out what you are going to do and call us back. We leave in four hours. Oh, and arrange for us to be met at the airport tomorrow morning."

"We'll be there. Are you on the evening flight from London?" I asked.

"That's right," said my father. "Can you two get up on time? I doubt you have an alarm clock with you."

"You're right about the alarm clock. But we'll find a way," said Jacqui.

"As long as it's not clubbing till morning," my mother said.

"Are you kidding? The average birthday here in some of the places goes back to the nineteenth century. Tea dances are late nights for half the guests," I responded.

"Oh good, if you are in bed that early, you'll have no trouble getting up in the morning. Go and sort out your boat. And do call us back," said my mother.

We went down to the harbour. Claire and Maria were there.

I said, "Look I know this is organised through Mr. Di Maglio. I want to extend the charter for a fortnight until the 2nd of January. Who do I need to contact?"

"Hey that's fantastic. Can we stay with you?" Maria asked excitedly.

"Of course. If you want," said Jacqui. "You've been great."

They actually had. They were with us all day and left us alone in the evenings. They were friendly without being intrusive. They had forced us to relax. I had been surprised when they stripped off the first day. I had realised since that that was intentional. They wanted to force us into a different world. Indeed most of their actions had been for that purpose. They had succeeded and Jacqui looked now at the days with the Russians as just an interlude. The break had done more good than any doctor could have done.

I had been tense but otherwise less affected by it all. Even Di Maglio appeared to me in a better light. I already liked Aldo and people like Alberto. Giovanni was a strange fish, but not that bad. I realised I was accepting the people around Di Maglio. I questioned how long it would be before I accepted his business methods.

Claire said, "We'll call. They charge premium rates at Christmas. That doesn't bother you does it?"

I shook my head. "But tell me the premium all the same."

Jacqui whispered, "Are you a Scotsman? You heard there are millions coming in each week."

"I know. But old habits die hard." I growled into her ear with mock ferocity, "So don't go and spend your dress allowance in one go."

The girls came back, half an hour later. All was arranged. They were dancing with joy. "They call it work," said Claire, "But really it's a holiday. You should have seen the faces of Alberto and the boys when we told them. They really whooped it up. Alberto's got himself some starlet in tow. She thinks he bankrolls films. She is just a silly tart. He's just taking advantage of her."

"Well if everyone is happy, that's great. Can you arrange everything? We stay in the harbour tonight and tomorrow we sail round to the hotel and moor offshore for a couple of days."

"Done," said Claire.

Once they had left, I went back to the phone and reported back to my parents. "See you tomorrow," they responded cheerfully.

Next morning we were at the airport early. The early morning planes from Europe were all scheduled to arrive on time. We had managed to get into the VIP waiting area with a view of the arriving passengers as they waited for their luggage. I looked casually over the passengers as they arrived.

The tall, dark-haired man stood out from the crowd. His suit was badly cut and crumpled from the flight. His tie was knotted but askew. The stubble on his cheek appeared to be thicker than one would expect from an overnight flight. His shoes were scuffed. He stood by the console waiting for his luggage while I surveyed him from the reception area.

I sensed he was trouble. I always carried with me the bleep for Alberto and I pressed the call button immediately. In moments, Claire was by my side.

"What is it?" she asked.

I was surprised to see her. But I did not question her. "That man over there is out of place here. He looks like one of the Russians. I think I've seen him before but I can't place him."

Jacqui was studying him closely, "He drove the car in Paris. He was part of the kidnap group."

Claire moved away and pulled out her mobile. There was a rushed discussion.

She said, "We could have him stopped at customs, but we need to see if he makes contact. We'll be trailing him. Are you armed?"

I shook my head. "No, but Jacqui has a small gun in her bag. I can't conceal a gun when I am in slacks and a shirt."

"You should have a leg holster," said Claire.

"These trousers would show the gun outline through the material."

"Then you should have them tailored so they don't. You need to be armed in future, even if you have to wear a jacket. We will be a bit stretched till this afternoon when we'll have some support flown in. Alberto will be trailing our friend down there and Maria will go along with him. That leaves me on call and Jamie, our local stringer. But he is pretty inexperienced. Barbados is hardly a hot spot in normal times."

"We need protection for your parents as well," said Jacqui.

"You'll have to do that," said Claire. "They aren't our primary concern. We can only arrange that cover later today or tomorrow."

"All right. Jacqui will stay with them at the hotel and I'll head out to the boat to pick up some clothes and a gun. We can manage it."

"Good" said Claire. "I'll head outside and wait for you. We should go to the boat together."

"No," I said. "You stay with Jacqui and my parents. I'll cover the boat. It's in the harbour and I'm not going to be alone. There'll be people around there. But the road to the beach is lonely. What transport do you have here?"

"I followed in a four wheel drive. It's a Range Rover."

"Look they'll meet you sooner or later. Say you came with transport. Play the Girl Friday act from the boat. But let's keep the Russian and his possible identity to ourselves. There's no use scaring them."

My parents came off the plane. By then the Russian had disappeared through customs and passport control. We waved at them from the viewing area. They waved eagerly back. After we greeted each other and they enthused at how fit we looked. I said, "Look, Jacqui will go with you to the hotel. I have to complete some paperwork for the boat so that it can sail round the island and join us off the coast. I'll be about half an hour behind you."

We packed them into the vehicle. Claire drove them away and Jacqui waved cheerfully at me as they left. When they had gone, I realised that this had been my first moment away from her since we had left Geneva. Suddenly I felt quite lonely.

I pulled myself together and hailed a cab. I told it to go to the port. The boat was moored between two larger ones. The one came from the Cayman Islands while the other was registered in Panama. Like ours, they were most likely charters. I vaulted the short space to the lower deck. We had pulled up the gangplank. I waved at the security guard. He recognised me and let me go unhindered.

Just as I was heading for the cabin, something caught my eye. I flung myself to the deck and felt something streak past my ear. I turned to see a knife humming in the wood of the bulkhead. It was a vicious hunting knife with a long blade. Whoever had thrown it had done it with some force. The blade was at least two inches into the wood. And whoever had thrown it, was coming for me.

I was sprawled on the ground, just a foot or so from the wheel. And beneath the wheel I could see the tape holding one of the guns we had hidden at the start of our trip. I needed more space though to have any chance of getting it before the man got me.

I saw him lunge towards me and somehow scrambled up and out of his way. He was quick for a man of his size. But I realised that he was constrained by the height of the cabin. He must have been approaching seven feet and the ceiling was lower than that. He looked like a weight lifter. He most likely was given the force with which he threw the knife.

He would not want to make any noise and I doubted if he would fire a gun. I didn't even know if he had one. I would find a way to get out of trouble if I got to use ours. The only thing was that I couldn't see how to get to it in time. He came to me again. There was only a rug between us. As he stepped on it I grabbed my end and jerked it with all my strength. He lost his balance and went crashing back. His head smashed against the wall with an almighty crash.

I didn't check to see if he was dazed. The next moment, before he even stood up, I had wrenched the gun from its hiding place and could hear the roar of the bullets as they thudded into his chest. Even then he made an attempt to get at me. But a last bullet felled him. He lay breathless on the floor, blood seeping from his chest and washing over towards me.

I jerked away from the flow of blood and moved to the porthole. The noise had seemed so loud but nobody seemed to notice. I shoved the gun into my pocket and clambered up on the deck. My hand held on to it for I didn't know if others were waiting. I saw someone coming up from the lower deck of the boat next to me.

"What was that noise?" I called over to him. "I thought it was a gun."

We both looked around. There appeared to be nobody on the next boat. In fact the nearest person seemed to be the security guard I had seen earlier. He was a good fifty yards away and appeared unperturbed by any disturbance. "It must have been an engine back-firing," I said.

"I've never heard that noise from an engine," he said. Then he shrugged his shoulders and returned below deck.

I carefully checked the rest of the boat. It was empty. I went to the upper deck and took the gun from below the seat. I used the tape to tie it to my leg. I would risk it being noticed. For the moment I needed to keep alive. And that was more important than raising suspicion.

I emptied the remaining bullets from the first gun and re-loaded it. I grabbed a jacket and put it on despite the heat. I slipped the gun into my waistband. There was no blood on me. I checked carefully. But I needed support. I jumped onto the shore again and headed over to a pay phone by the harbour.

I called the hotel. My parents had arrived. "Could I talk to Claire? She's the girl who drove them."

Claire came to the phone. "I had a reception party here. We have a body to get rid of."

She was quick; "Did he try anything?"

"Yes," I said. "A knife and it wasn't for making sandwiches. I usually forgive people those even if the bread's cut a bit thick."

"Go back to the boat," she said. "Keep watch and stay put. Only let anyone in if Maria or I are with them."

"Keep guard on Jacqui," I said.

"Don't worry, we know our job. Just hold in there as I say."

I slipped back onto the boat. I went to the upper deck, watching the port. I kept myself as covered as possible but there was no sign of any disturbance. An hour went by. I was getting edgy. Waiting was not my strong point. Then Maria appeared with two men I did not recognise.

I went down to the lower deck and let down the gangplank. They went into the lounge cabin. "Shit he's one big bear of a man," said one of her companions.

They checked his pockets. "No papers."

Maria said, "We'd better go out to sea and dump him. Then we'll clean the cabin down. How many times did you shoot him?"

She counted the bullet holes. "Seven times. And nobody heard you. Man you have the devil on your side."

She ruffled my hair. "Go up on deck. I'll get you a coffee. By lunchtime you'll not recognise this place. We'll have to be careful not to leave it unattended. I can't tell who he is but we'll take a shot and see if any of the police records can identify him. I'll also take fingerprints."

I wasn't surprised that they had access to the police computers. In fact nothing surprised me about Di Maglio. I suspect one cannot survive that sort of life for over thirty years without an amazing network. So the criminals used police intelligence to trace their enemies. There was in reality nothing surprising about that.

Maria came up with a coffee. "When Alberto and Claire have traced our friend at the airport, we'll have a chat. In any event we are going to get more help. We'll be another five on the island if necessary by tomorrow night. These guys with me are just stringers. We can trust them but they are not professionals."

We headed out to sea soon after. About two miles off the coast, Maria started to throw small pieces of the body into the water. Within minutes, there were a group of sharks around the boat.

"They often congregate around here," she said.

Once there were sufficient sharks around we scanned the horizon for other boats. There were none around. Maria's two companions humped up the carcass and threw it overboard. The sharks went into a frenzy as they wolfed their way through the body.

We then carefully cleaned the boat for all signs of blood. One of the men also removed a couple of bullets that had got lodged in the cabin. He then surprised me by producing a filler and some colouring paste to remove all signs of the hole. He did the same for the knife, and then threw that overboard as well. Brushes were applied to the outside of the boat to clean off any traces of blood. A few inquisitive sharks swam by expectantly and one even had a bite at a brush. But they had left us, having devoured the dead Russian.

"We'll head back to the hotel," said Maria. "It's easier to monitor the boat when it's offshore. We can use the satellite tracking equipment. That can't work in a crowded harbour. It's too shallow and closely packed."

We sailed round the island and were in place in the early afternoon. I still had the leg holster and gun. I would have to be careful to remember it if I changed for a swim. Even the aged guests would notice something strange.

Maria was on the radio. I realised that she was talking to Alberto. I joined her. "The Russian has holed up in a house just north of here. We need you to come with us. We think there are three of them only but can't be sure. There'll be the four of us. Claire and Alberto plus you and me. Then the others will keep watch here."

Jacqui joined us. Maria explained what had happened. "We think this may be a maverick gang. They could be a splinter group which wants to upset the deal your father made. In any case, we'll find out tonight. Charles will act as look out while we go in. It's not going to be dangerous."

Jacqui agreed to stay with my parents. She would wait till I returned. We would tackle the Russians early in the evening.

Maria and I headed north to rendezvous with Claire and Alberto. "They are three, unless someone hasn't come out at all today," said Alberto. "They suspect nothing."

We remained hidden. Maria had parked her car next to Alberto's in the quiet private road. "The police occasionally patrol out here. But it's not wealthy enough for them to do it often. The cars can be seen from the road if they look to their left as they round the bend in the road. But there's nowhere better to park that allows us a quick getaway and keeps us concealed from the house."

I sat by the car with the others and we waited till it became dark. Alberto and Claire moved to the house to check it out again. They both had guns drawn and moved quietly and carefully. They hugged the sides of the house and ducked under the window, carefully checking out all entry and exit points.

A car was coming up the narrow road, its headlights blazing sporadically between the trees. Claire and Alberto ducked and disappeared at the far side of the house. Maria and I lay on a gentle slope next to the cars.

"Oh shit, it's the police," said Maria. They came closer and appeared to be passing on down the road ahead. Then they stopped suddenly.

Maria turned to me, stripping off her top and panties. She pulled up her skirt and grabbed me. My shirt was off in a second. She pulled down my trousers and pants in one move.

"Pretend to make love," she said. "Pretend this is an illicit rendezvous. That'll explain two cars."

We twined our legs together. She pressed herself against me. Her slim, wiry figure was warm. For the first time I noticed her perfume, a gentle mixture of flowers against the salt breeze from the sea. Her breasts were hard against me. I felt her pull me to herself.

"Look lover boy, if they search us we have problems. You've a real gun in your leg holster. I have one in my bag. And there are a couple hidden in the car. But if you stood up, you'd look as if you just came from a long walk in the cold. Forget about Jacqui and get excited or we'll be sunk. They're coming."

With that she started to grind herself against me. A small, energetic, damp, inquisitive grind that became more excited for me and, I suspect, for her. I forgot about the approaching men as she and I became more and more entwined. If they had been a bit slower or we had started a bit earlier, we would have taken our simulated love making to its conclusion. But a voice called out, "What's going on up there?"

Maria gave a light scream and clutched her top to her naked body. Her small breasts pointed at the two policemen approaching us. Her legs were apart. Her face looked in horror. She grabbed her clothes and pulled on the skirt and top. She patted the ground, making as if she was searching for her panties. She found them and pulled them on as if in panic.

I yanked up my trousers, pretending to struggle with the zip. One of the policemen tossed over my shirt. "Well who are you two then?"

Maria said, "I work on a boat. It's called the "Lively Princess." It's moored over by the Sandy Lane. He rents it with his wife. Please let us go. We are doing no harm. If you report me, I'll lose my job. And he's going to have some explaining to do. It'll hit the press. He's well known."

This was delivered in a wailing voice. The policeman looked at us. They obviously decided that it was not worth pursuing. "Ah, enjoy yourselves," said one of them. "But in future don't trespass. We'll be back here in a couple of hours. Make sure you're gone by then."

With that, they laughed and headed back to their car. We watched them drive away into the distance. A noise came from the house. "Who's there?" shouted a voice. We froze. "Nothing here," came a call as the door closed and all became quiet.

"That was close," said Maria. She lent over and stroked my chest through the unbuttoned shirt. "Shall we finish it. It was getting rather nice."

"I don't think so," said a quiet voice behind us. It was Claire. "Although you actually were quite convincing. At least you were once you both stopped acting. But Maria, someone else will have to enjoy the climax. We have things to do."

Alberto returned as well. "There is one rear door and the front door. The only other exit points are the windows. They appear now to be all in one room watching television. We go in with stun grenades. We need them alive. They cause us a problem dead, if only because Charles and Maria could be recognised now the police have seen them."

I covered the road and heard them as they went in. There was the blast of the stun grenade and then I waited for the shots. There were none. Everything was silent. Maria called me over.

The three Russians were trussed up. They looked dazed and a bit frightened. Maria said, "I'll search upstairs, just in case. They say there's no one else there."

"Don't take too long," called Claire as Maria indicated for me to accompany her.

We went upstairs. There were four doors at the top of a hall. We hit them one by one. The first was a small bedroom. The second was a bathroom. We then hit another small bedroom. On the fourth room, Maria pushed open the door and appeared to dive straight in.

I glanced nervously through the open door. She was lying on the bed, laughing at me. Her skirt had ridden up her legs and her whole body was inviting me over. "Come on. Let's have a quickie. I feel randy from earlier. Another minute and we would have done it."

She was pulling at her panties as she talked. Her eyes sparkled mischievously. I started forward. Then I stopped. I turned away saying, "I want to, but I better not. We'd both regret it if I did."

She came up behind me, her hands moving down from my chest. "You want me, Come on. I'm not going to regret it."

I shook her off. I wasn't rough. She wasn't insistent. The next minute we were on the stairs. "Nobody around," called Maria. "We can have a go at our prisoners."

Alberto tackled the Russian from the airport. He looked even worse than before. He still hadn't shaved. His clothes were still crumpled. His jacket had been discarded and his shirt tails hung out of his trousers. He had sweated in the heat and the stains on his clothes gave warning of the stale smell that surrounded him.

He was co-operative. He claimed that their boss had sent them. Since Rastinov had been killed, a man called Turpin was their leader. Turpin was a second generation American of Russian origin. He had changed his name to anglicise it. "There's a group who want revenge on Di Maglio. There are five of them in the group. They all were on the drug distribution side. So they lost out on the deal. They want to scuttle it. Our job is to eliminate them."

Alberto accepted this easily. That surprised me, Claire whispered over to me that this tied in with other information they had received.

"Who were you looking for here?" asked Maria.

"Just one man. We call him Boris the Bear. His real name is Boris Mikov. There were two over here. We killed the other one but Boris escaped."

"Describe him," Alberto ordered.

The description fitted the man in the boat. We thought it would. Claire lent over to me. I noticed she touched me on the arm. That surprised me for she had always avoided contact before. It was as if Maria had declared open season and they had both come on heat. It wasn't so much that she touched me on the arm. It was more as if she stroked me. The atmosphere was getting highly charged. I needed to get back to Jacqui and to reality.

Claire said, "That's our man. We got a reading on him earlier from the photo and fingerprints. We scanned them and sent them over the satellite link for checking."

"We know him," said Alberto. "He provided a cholesterol rich lunch for some sharks earlier today." He threw them over the photo of Boris on the deck of the boat.

"What will you do now?" I asked.

"We head back," said the man.

"What about the others in the assassination group?"

"They are all dead already. They didn't even leave New York."

Claire asked, "Are there more?"

He held his hands out, "How could we tell? But we don't think so. This is drugs. It's not a bonbon shop."

"When do you leave exactly?" asked Claire

"There's a plane to Miami tomorrow first thing. If we can get on board, we'll take that," he said.

"We should stay with you. You could have some phone calls. We better all stay." said Alberto. "Four guarding three is easy and safe."

The Russian made a call. There were plenty of seats on the way out and they were all booked in. They would need to leave at seven to make the airport. We would accompany them. Claire and I headed outside and moved our cars behind the house. When the police came later, they would think we had gone.

I called Jacqui and explained what had happened. "We want to monitor the place till they leave. It will be best," I said. She agreed she would get a room at the hotel. Even if they have nothing, I can sleep in the lounge area of your parents' suite."

The Russians were untied. They watched television. We had given instructions that they should not answer the phone. They must not move without our consent. They agreed. They didn't want any trouble. I thought Alberto was being over cautious but decided not to query it. He usually had a good reason.

Alberto said, "There are rooms upstairs. We'll split into shifts. I'll do the first one with Claire. Then Charles and Maria can do one. It's nine o clock now. Charles and Maria should each grab a bedroom and get some sleep. We'll wake you at two in the morning."

"No naughties," called Claire as we headed upstairs.

"No naughties indeed," I said as we headed up the stairs.

Maria said "I'll take the room on the right. You can take the big one. The middle one had only a camp bed. I had not noticed, but did not question her. It had been a tiring day and I could do with a few hours sleep. The sheets were clean. Nobody had slept here. I stripped off, placing my gun under the pillow. I must have soon fallen asleep.

The next thing I remember was a cool breeze on my body. Someone cuddled into the bed beside me. A hand was over my mouth and someone was saying, "Shh. It's just me."

"Maria, we shouldn't."

"Just this once. I can't get you out of my mind. I want you."

I gave in. Any resistance flooded away. I had desired her so eagerly before. Now we came together with our desire heightened by the memory of the sudden interruption earlier in the evening. The thought of the others downstairs, not suspecting what we were doing, further added to the feeling of illicit excitement.

We fell asleep together as Maria mumbled, "It wasn't just tonight. I've wanted to sleep with you since I saw you look at me when I stripped off on the boat on the first day. I am glad we did. Even if it may have to be a one-off."

"Hey, what have we got here?" said a voice. I turned over to see a grinning Claire looking down on us.

"I was uncomfortable. You and Alberto should sleep here. You'll sleep better."

I don't think I'll even comment on that one," said Claire. "Alberto wants to stay up. He's talking to the Russians and getting a lot of information from them. I was looking for you to relieve me."

Maria jumped out of bed and seemed to hop into her clothes. She kissed me on the head. "Sleep tight." Then she was gone.

Claire stood there looking at me. "I didn't think that she could hold back. The poor girl has been celibate for three months. Mind you I have too. Are you exhausted or could you do a little girl a good turn?"

And I found myself, for the first time in my life, without being high from drink or drugs, in bed with two girls on one night. Claire was less excitable than Maria was. She was gentle and comforting. Her naked body was cool to the touch.

She said afterwards, "Most people need a lot of sex after a kill." I had not thought of it that way. I wondered if that included me. It was with that thought that I went back to sleep.

The next morning we all acted as if nothing had happened. I walked down to the shore in the early morning and stripped off before walking into the surf and relishing the cool spray. The girls came too. Alberto was relaxed about keeping guard. The Russians were not dangerous.

The girls joined me and we washed away the evidence of our night together. It would never be mentioned. It was a fleeting episode. I felt a bit guilty. But I knew Jacqui would not know. Alberto may have realised. But he would not talk.

The Russians left on schedule and we were back in the hotel mid-morning. Alberto had been able to get all the information he could from the Russians. That had been the reason for spending the night there. The girls would have helped if needed to get the information. But they were unnecessary. It may well have been the thought of these services they could have offered that turned them to me. I would not ask and I would never know.

We took the scooters over to the boat and climbed on board. I drove one and Claire the other. The two girls then returned and brought my parents to the boat. We decided to cruise around and show them the coast. My father had a mobile and occasionally took calls. But generally all was quiet.

I asked what his plans were once we had returned to Switzerland. He wanted Jacqui and me to continue to act as the formal investment managers for our hedge fund. "You should stick to currencies and blue chips."

He would deal for the other fund, keeping a low profile and operating almost incognito, ramping up the price of his selected stocks and borrowing from United at the inflated prices. When they declared their results he hoped they would take a billion dollar hit. "That will put them into loss for the year. And that will hit their reputation and their share price." We would then enter the final part of the scam.

"But, as you get publicity, someone may recognise you. It will be difficult then to keep the Ryder name out of it. What are you going to do about Associated Financial? If they get to hear about you, that will be a problem. And it is always possible, if they see pictures in the papers, that they could recognise you. Surely the performance of the fund is likely to get you some notoriety."

Associated Financial was the holding company that owned Associated Bank for whom he had worked.

"Let me let you into a secret. I know they've been stalking United for some time. So if we have the thirty per cent, we can offer it to them at a profit and with a bonus. The bonus will be my freedom. It'll work. Don't worry. And I think I can avoid the press."

As usual he was supremely confident about his plans for himself. We did not talk business again but lounged on the boat for the rest of the day. The girls were as unobtrusive as they had been before. They were hardly in evidence. I occasionally watched them for a provocative wiggle. But it was to no avail. Jacqui and I hung around the upper deck. We acted quite demurely in front of my parents.

In the evening, I suggested an early night. My parents agreed as they had flown through the night before. The girls took them back to shore and we remained with our boat and the stars.

Jacqui rested her head on my shoulder. She was so trusting. I felt as if I had been disloyal. But it was done. I stroked her back. I felt pretty tired. This would be the third time today. We remained on the upper deck, looking at the lights gleaming on the shore from the hotels in the distance. The sea lapped against the boat, rocking it backwards and forwards.

Jacqui swayed against me as the boat moved. I swayed against her. We kissed and my hands went instinctively to her back. They then moved round her sides and caressed her breasts through the light material of her dress. She ran her hands down my body, slowly lingering whenever she felt me breathing harder than before. We revelled in the silence. We breathed in the coolness of the evening. We felt the salt on our lips as we kissed. We enjoyed the warmth of our bodies.

A plane droned overhead somewhere in the distance. A noise seemed to come from the shore. But otherwise we enjoyed the splendid isolation of the evening. Without thinking I played with the straps of Jacqui's dress. It was a short blue dress with two straps that tied in a bow on each shoulder. I absent-mindedly undid one and the dress fell away, half revealing her breast as it came into the evening light. My hand went for the other bow and the dress fell away to the waist.

Her fingers undid the buttons of my shirt and pushed that off my shoulders so that I too could feel her full body against me. I eased the dress down and she quietly stepped out of it. We kissed again. Her softness contrasted with both the girls of the night before. Maria with her wiry body appeared androgynous in contrast to the full firmness of Jacqui. And the quietness of Claire contrasted to the silent passion that seemed to exude from Jacqui.

We caressed again and again, gradually taking off the remaining few items of clothing. We stood by the handrail and kissed, nakedness touching nakedness at mouth, breast, hip, stomach and legs. We grazed each other with our bodies, working ourselves up into excitement at the rhythm of our bodies blending with the rhythm of the sea. We stood there for some time, before gently sinking down onto the bare wood of the deck. We touched each other lying side by side. Our hands roved over each other's body.

Then Jacqui stood up and I followed as she climbed onto the upper deck and lent against the bulkhead. I came to her as she stood there, her legs slightly apart and her head held back. We came together gently at first. Then the excitement of a new experience roused us to a crescendo. We came together in a way that removed any longing to revisit Maria or Claire. My third time that day was different from the other two as I learnt the difference between love and lust.

That idyllic night was one of many that we spent that Christmas. We often saw my parents but they knew not to intrude. We saw the girls but they had moved further into the background. I saw the world behind Jacqui. And we came as close as we would ever be. But time was passing by. And we knew as the New Year was welcomed in over champagne on the boat out at sea, that the time was coming to truly put the last act into play.

THE FINAL ROUND

Geneva seemed grey and uninviting in the early morning mist that came from the lake. Its burghers had switched off the Christmas lights with the advent of the New Year. They now got down to the serious business of making money. Fucquet and United were hard at work. They were keen to deal with us.

My father had rented offices, very Swiss and very discrete, for you would not have known who worked behind the main doors or what they did for a living.

Jacqui and I started dealing in the markets in earnest and over the month we made enough money to pay the rent. But that was a side-show. The brokers loved us for, in their words, we churned our funds. Whenever there was an opportunity, we were seen to be hot to trot. They made more money on commission than we made on profit. As we both came out on the right side and with a profit, nobody would care. They also believed that others were doing more with us. We carefully acted as if each broker with whom we dealt were a mere side-show. That made everyone think we were bigger than we were. And it made it easier to finalise the main scam.

My father had already accumulated about a hundred and fifty million dollars of stock in his target companies. He decided it was time to strike. He carefully planted rumours across the markets. We called the brokers we had used and asked them to confirm the alleged rumours. Within the hour we would get calls from others stating the rumour as a fact. The hunger for commission was stronger than the hunger for the truth.

We fed these calls with fresh rumours. Our first target, a Far Eastern oil exploration outfit, was soaring. There was no market. It had a capitalisation of thirty million dollars. That was more than it was worth as its entire assets consisted of an old dredging boat and some lifting gear. The rest of the capital had been diverted to more personal assets of the founder and Chairman. Another target, a Middle Eastern mining concern had struck a rich seam of copper. It could be the largest mine in the world. Nobody seemed to think that the alleged copper find was unlikely and perhaps even not exploitable. But they had not looked carefully at the map. Most of the property lay within Iraq and the owner's title to the property was tenuous at the least.

But we happily encouraged the rises in the shares and then it became time for the new fund to be put into play. My father called United and confirmed the arrangements. He told them he was negotiating some direct deals with some big investors to take in shares. He had convinced them that the fund would go for fast track companies on the way up. The moment they saw what he was buying, United tried to buy for their own account. They would also warehouse stocks to place later, at a higher price, into their client portfolios. Such activity was definitely frowned on and illegal. But we could hardly blame them for not complying with the spirit of the law.

The rumours in the market in our selected shares were stronger than we had expected. By the time the fund had completed the official purchase of all my father's holdings, we had made more profit than we had thought possible. In the end the market value of our original hundred and fifty million of investment was just over four hundred million as the shares were ramped higher and higher. I helped in the process by repeatedly putting in sizeable buy instructions at just under the market price. They were never executed but encouraged others.

United lent two hundred million to the fund. We placed two hundred into its books. The whole four hundred came back to us for the shares we had already bought, albeit through a circuitous route and using almost every tax haven in the world. We had made money unexpectedly on our original purchase. We then hit the market in a big way. We splashed out several hundred million dollars on the back of further loans from United as the prices of our shares soared. The movement was so frantic that I was concerned someone would smell a rat. But they didn't. The financial press merely stoked the speculative flames the next day by reporting the stories that were going around. Our Far Eastern oil exploration company was now worth three hundred million dollars. It had risen ten fold and was the star performer. And we were sure that many in the market were short of stock.

In the end the fund was worth just under a billion and United had lent us five hundred million of them.

We now needed to think of bursting the bubble. It ran for another week without showing signs of slowing down. My father told United we did not want the fund to grow any further although they tried to get him to do so. We knew they were putting all their clients into our shares.

There were still enough buyers around to have sold the shares at a profit. But that would not serve our purpose. The portfolio was worth an alleged one point five billion by now and so their loan was apparently covered around three times.

"This is crazy," said Jacqui. "I can't believe the markets are so stupid."

I had been doing the accounts and liquidating our shares in our other funds at the same time. When the news came, all the markets would fall. There was no benefit at the moment in holding quoted shares. "We have actually made a two hundred and eighty million all told on the other funds as well this month," I said. "That was the last of our holdings I just sold at another profit."

"That wasn't difficult," said my father. "After all you held shares in a rising market."

"It's still a profit," I said. "We are closing in on a net worth of around four billion all told."

We now started to try to burst the bubble, but we did not need to. It all started to go badly wrong when the Iraqis confiscated all the assets of the mining company. There was outcry. There was no logic in that reaction as the assets were just strips of sand. But at the time nobody knew that for a fact.

There were rumours that the company in oil exploration was a fraud. The fund tried to sell at market as if in a panic. The shares sunk like a stone. Over the weekend the press was universally bearish. There would be a run on the fund. They were the biggest of the investors in a portfolio of speculative shares. Its holdings were all going through the floor. We made as if to calm United Bank. We said it was just a hiccup. They were looking worried. I suspected they had more clients than we had thought with stock that now was worth much less than they had paid. The cover on the loan had halved. They no doubt studied the loan agreements and regretted the clauses that stopped them from getting repayment other than from the sale of shares in the fund.

We fuelled rumours of forced sales by the fund at the insistence of their bankers. Wall Street fell sharply on fears of market unrest. The markets were uneasy. Our companies fell through the floor. Panic bred panic yet again. The bulls became bears. The buyers became sellers. The fund was now worth only three hundred million.

We started rumours of other hedge funds with big positions bought on margin. We said those funds were rumoured to be close to bankruptcy. In the state of near panic that then existed in the market, they believed the news. Bad news was received without question. The market was falling. Bad news was needed. We invented some more stories. Some were laughable. Others were simply outrageous. No sane person would have believed half of them. But the market was falling and keen to fall further. So they believed the rumours.

And, all the time, we sold stock we did not own into this falling market. Then we bought it back at a lower price after the market had fallen further. We ran the market. We were like a casino owner with a rigged roulette table. There was only one thing we could do. Make money. And then more money as our success bred credibility. The markets listened to us. We were the masters. We had big money. We had to have connections. And nobody knew the link between us and the mystery fund that was the source of all the market unrest. The whole illogical fabric of the markets played into our hands.

Then there was announcement that one of the fund's companies had been suspended from its local stock exchange. It was a distributor in Latin America, and the rumours that it was about to get some major concessions had been denied. Its shares were now worthless. The others carried on in free fall. One or two were below the prices we had seen when we had bought first of all for our own account. Another of the shares was suspended in its local market. Another slumped to nothing when its Chairman was arrested on suspicion of fraud. The fund was worth seventeen million dollars.

My father called for a crisis meeting with United. They were sitting on a loan of five hundred and fifty million secured by assets worth a fraction of that amount. And this was a bank we thought had already lost a billion in the last quarter in Asia. They knew we had taken profits. They wanted to be bailed out. They asked us to do just that. They appealed to our sense of fair play. They insinuated that we had acted wrongly.

We treated that suggestion with the contempt it deserved. We knew we had screwed them. But they were big boys. They were a bank after all. They knew the rules. We declared that some of our clients had made money. Others had lost. They had lost. That was life. They had to grow up. They did not realise how much we had made out of the ramp. They were not to know the value of the warehousing operations that had provided the original money for the fund.

They tried to play tough. We played tougher. They tried to scare us. We scared them. We pretended to be shocked by their approach. They could not handle that. We lectured them on integrity. We reminded them of the confidentiality clauses in our agreements. We reminded them that Swiss law protected that. They squirmed. We asked to see their Chairman. They withdrew all accusations.

We said we would liquidate the fund in the market. Alternatively we would give them the assets. They asked for the latter in the hope that they could recover some of their losses. It was a forlorn hope. But they could only clutch at straws.

We sat down to assess our situation. Our financial position had improved slightly. We each had just over a billion in our two main accounts. The joint account had now grown to just over two billion.

We guessed that United had lost around a billion to a billion and a half. That would mean that they would post a loss for the year of around a billion dollars. They were a broadly based bank, but their capital would be halved by the losses. They would see their reputation in tatters and their share price would slump. Anyone with a large investment management business was being hit. And United's was larger than most.

We again started our rumour mills. We then came out of the shadows and re-adopted our public role in our other funds. We had been so uncannily accurate in the past that everyone believed us immediately. We asked if it was true that United had taken a bath in Asia on currency options. We indicated that we were gaining clients from United who had put them into speculative stocks at the top of the market. We started rumours about United having burnt their fingers in the stock market.

By the end of the week the rumours had gained such momentum that United were forced to act. The announcement was sombre. United would make losses of one point four billion dollars for the year. They had lost eight hundred million in Asia as a result of the market volatility and six hundred million on unauthorised lending against securities. That had to refer to the fund, but not to my father. We had got them to sign that confidentiality agreement at the outset. Revealing his name to the market meant they would pay a penalty equal to their lending to the fund. And they would break Swiss secrecy laws. That meant our name and links had to remain confidential or they were liable for another five hundred million dollars and more.

Their share price slumped. The press queried if they could survive. The Liechtenstein authorities, for that was the head office of the holding company, issued a nervous statement. In the countries where United operated, everyone protested that they were not the regulator. It was Liechtenstein. And they did not know what was hitting them.

The share price was down by a third. My father said laconically, "Now let's put the buggers into play."

The value of United had now slumped to three point five billion. They badly needed an injection of funds. They continued to fall as we quickly accumulated shares through various funds and companies. We bought as the market fell. It was amazingly easy to accumulate a holding.

The next week United carried on falling and we carried on buying. Then on the Wednesday, we put out an announcement. " Italian American Associates advise that they have acquired twenty nine point nine per cent of United Bank of Europe and will be seeking to open discussions with a view to facilitating a re-capitalisation of the bank and changes to its management structure. Italian American believe that United has a sound business and is keen to help it expand in a prudent manner." The announcement explained that Italian American was a group of interests and mentioned my name and also Jacqui's. The presence of Di Maglio's name raised some interest. There was speculation about regulatory concern.

The impact on United's share price was astronomical. It jumped forty per cent before being suspended by the market authorities pending clarification. We talked to the regulators. They queried our record. We advised of our hedge fund activities. They were hardly keen but the prospect of ridding themselves of a problem definitely made them flexible in their approach.

I took a call. It was Associated Financial in London. The big financial conglomerate were keen to talk off the record about United. I suggested we met. A meeting was scheduled for the next lunchtime. It would be in their offices in London. I alone would attend.

The next morning saw me whisk through customs and into the waiting car from Associated. Their offices were in the centre of the city in a prestigious block, recently refurbished at some expense. The plush carpets and the modern art around the walls were testimony to the fact that they had recently moved upmarket into investment banking.

Sir Piers Rupert-Jones was a throwback from the old school. He was a clearing banker who had found himself at the helm of Associated after all the other directors found they hated each other. It wasn't that he was liked or particularly respected, it was that he was not hated. He had one additional advantage. Every other member of the board thought that he was stupid and could be influenced by them. That had propelled him to the chair as all the board bickered at the last succession.

He was blunt to the extreme. "We are interested in United. The regulators will not be happy with your bid. The origins of your money are too vague. You are seen as speculators. You are hedge fund operators. We are willing to buy you out and bid for United. My purpose is to establish your price."

"We are not interested in doing a deal, Sir Piers. This is a change in focus for us. We are now moving out of the hedge fund market into a more stable environment."

"Look people like you will be bored to death by United. We run companies like them. We have the right people. You people are in your twenties and thirties. Our people are in their fifties. You need grey hairs to run United."

I was rude to the extreme. "But you need balls to buy a stake on the way down."

He frowned. "Perhaps. You beat us to it. It was not that we did not consider the prospect."

"What would you offer? I should at least advise my associates."

"Your stake is worth around one point two billion at today's price. We'll pay you a ten per cent premium."

"No way. I would only take back an offer at around one point eight."

"What about one point five?"

"I think you misheard me. I said one point eight. That's the base line."

"If we said somewhere between, what else would you want?" asked Sir Piers.

"Perhaps a couple of favours?"

"Name them."

"Some time ago, last year, you had an employee called John Ryder."

"I remember him. The shit rooked us for a billion. They almost got him in Brazil. I thought he had been killed by the drug cartel in Colombia or something. We had to keep it quiet as it could have hit confidence. It was a hell of a job downplaying it in the papers. We got our money back from the insurers though."

"I don't think you can assume he's dead. I want his freedom. Then, if he's alive, he can come out into the open."

"What's the link?"

"That's irrelevant. I want his freedom."

"OK. But the insurers lost a billion on that deal and they will want to be repaid. We can give indemnity from prosecution by ourselves but no more. I think he is still wanted elsewhere by the police. Sell for eight hundred million and his freedom. That way we pay your price and get back our billion."

I thought the bastard was not as stupid as they make out. But guessed this was an opening bid. "I could propose it. It's a bit low though. I doubt my associates will be too keen. If you can go higher, there may be an interest. What are the conditions?"

He thought. "Can we take an hour out? I need to talk with my colleagues."

I agreed. He headed out. Someone bought me a coffee. I took a newspaper and waited.

About an hour later, he returned. "We want to know your connection with Ryder."

"His father and mine were great friends. We owe him a favour and want his freedom. He's a good man."

"He's a thieving shit. He cost us a billion."

"You are talking of a claw back through this deal. Or at least you'll claw back a decent chunk of it. But the acquisition is also going to make you some; so you should end up in the money."

"Look, the reality is that we can't get him off the hook."

"Can't you advise that you goofed and he was not the person who took you for the money? If we provided you with new evidence, could you say that the culprit was the other guy – the one you fired for incompetence at the time?"

"But," said Sir Piers, "If we do that, he will be at us with hammer and tongs. His name was Jim someone or other. So we need a way to shut him up. How will we be able to persuade him to be the fall guy? He may be broke and susceptible to an offer."

"He'll not be a problem tomorrow."

"OK, then our deal is we'll let Ryder off the hook for the billion if we can blame it on Jim. But how will you do that?"

"I'll persuade him to take the rap. Money really does talk. But I want one point three from you."

"One point two."

"OK. Done," I said.

"How are you going to silence that Jim? That's a precondition."

"We'll meet tomorrow morning and discuss that."

We shook hands and I left. That afternoon I talked to my father. He was overjoyed.

"So they bought. What about Jim?"

328

He knew where he lived. He even had his address. He gave it to me. I called Di Maglio. He was willing to help. Contract work was up his street. "I'll send over a girl," he said. "It'll be Maria. It will be the one who ran the boat with Claire in Barbados. She will meet you at nine tonight. Where do you suggest?"

We met in a pub near the park. Maria kissed me on the lips. "You've got a job for me. Tell me all about it."

That evening, someone broke into Jim's flat. He was not a pretty sight afterwards. He was less so when the night was over. He was not going to complain because he was past complaining. But more importantly, there were some documents left in the flat that showed he had stolen money from Associated Financial and now it looked, from the large open safe, as if he had been robbed himself. He was a victim in the total sense of the word.

That night Maria came to my hotel and we made love again. She seemed to have a greater need than me. "Last time, you were the killer and needed it. This time it was me. It's not warped. It's just that there is a void afterwards. And sex fills it. All the girls feel it. And some of the men do as well."

The news the next day was full of the brutal murder. The police thought it was sexually motivated. The body indicated a violent and brutal death. The important thing was that Jim would not query any actions taken by Associated. And there was evidence to show he had robbed them and not Ryder as had been believed. The papers wondered where Ryder was and assumed he had been killed. He became a victim of human error!

I returned the next day. Sir Piers was white. "I didn't mean that."

"Bullshit. You knew there was only one safe method of assuring his silence. The police have the papers that implicate him. Now what can you do about Ryder?"

"I have no intention of dealing with you any more. You are beyond the pale."

"You have no choice. If you don't complete this deal, you will be associated with the murder. We have the letters you wrote to the poor sod and we can show the killing was a contract job, especially the recording of yesterday's meeting. I think I forgot to say that I was wearing a wire. And I have experts who know how to manage the recording. Oh, and by the way, there is one letter on your letterhead that you won't have in your files. It's the one that threatens Jim if he doesn't shut up. It's personally signed by you and the signature is genuine."

"But that's a forgery and that's blackmail," he said.

"That's your belief. It may not be mine and it may not be the police's," I said.

He glared at me. Then his face sagged. He knew he had no choice. His voice was cracked and trembling when he spoke again.

"We will advise that the accusations against Ryder were all a big mistake. Jim will have done the fraud and set up Ryder. And the papers found on Jim prove that. But Ryder's departure at the same time as the fraud made us suspect him. We will say he was under stress and went away to get a rest. And that we now understand he panicked when he heard he was wanted. And then just fled. He will be cited as an innocent victim. It's hardly credible. But it won't get much attention other than for the first week or so. So it should work. By the way where is he?"

"You do your bit and leave me to worry about his whereabouts. Oh, by the way, would you like some documents we have on some of your stock exchange trades?"

He went pale again. "What the hell do you mean?"

"We thought you'd be amused by your number four account statements between 1994 and 1998. Especially those relating to the period before you did your take-over in America. You know, the time when the market was surprised by the bid."

"You have those?"

"Sure, and a whole load of affidavits with them. But they are safe and will remain so. That is as long as you do not double cross us. If you do, I guess we'll be together behind bars."

He went white with shock. "I play straight."

"Why don't you put together a document saying what you will do. You will pay us one point eight billion after all and you will give Ryder his freedom."

"But we agreed one point two."

"The price went up when you questioned our methods in getting rid of the guy. We also remembered that we had documents that put you into a bad light. And we were shocked by your threatening letter to the dead man."

"You bastard. You double crossed us."

"You deserve it. You may despise us but you will always lose out to people like us. You got a good deal at the price."

He shook his head. "You can't blackmail me."

"I can and I will. And moreover, I don't give a shit about what happens to you. You have no choice. Co-operate or you suffer. And I mean suffer. I'll release the data we have on you. And I'll do it after I've sold your shares short. Then I make a profit as well. You're not dealing with one of your city school friends now. This is hard ball. And we play it our way. So don't tell me what I can do or can't do. Just be glad if our interests are running in common."

He went pale again. Then he went red. I thought for a moment he was going to have a fit. But he pulled himself together and just said, "You, young man, are a financial terrorist. You will never be accepted in decent society."

"That's decent society's loss. I want that document."

And I got it that evening. I was flying back with my father's pardon. And I had an offer of one point eight billion for shares that had cost us just under a billion. The total kitty had swollen to nearly five billion.

In Geneva, we had a conference. It was a fait accompli that we would accept the deal. It was good to delay the decision though, if only to make Sir Piers sweat on it a bit longer.

"What do we do now?" I asked my father

"We need to restructure our companies and sort out all the funds. Most of the companies we own were just there to confuse anyone seeking to trace any of the money or shares. We need to liquidate them. And we need to get agreements between ourselves. We have to sort out what we will do in the future."

"Do we revert back to being Ryders then?" asked my mother.

"I can't see that happening," said my father, "We also need to live a low key life style. I am not wanted but can hardly be seen as the billionaire owner of our companies. We'll go back to France and get a place in Tropez. It's nicer than Croix Valmer by far. And we need to think where we will go in winter. The South of France isn't an ideal place. I'll be in the background. Charles is the key player. He will have the visibility and he should retain the Rossi name. It's now an established alibi and nobody will recognise him."

"Where will you and Jacqui live?" asked my mother.

"We have to base ourselves in London. It's the financial centre. That buffoon, Piers Rupert-Jones, called me a financial terrorist. We can operate as such from there. But we need to find two types of business. There will be a legal one and the illicit one. It's just like the Di Maglio operation. The only exception is that our illicit one will be financial crime rather than drugs and prostitution."

"We go back to my father and tell him we are worth over two

billion," said Jacqui. "His whole empire is worth around eight or nine. It's taken him a lifetime to get there. He may be persuaded to join in with us and get rid of the drugs and stuff."

"Joining our financial power together would allow us to take a crack at almost anything. With a ten billion plus kitty, we would be as powerful as governments. We could manipulate most markets. That would allow us untold advantages," I said.

"Let's sort out our side first all the same. Then we can get in touch with Jacqui's family on any possible co-operation" said my father. "It'll take us a few months to get straight."

I called back Associated and agreed their offer. That evening we signed the deal. That evening United Bank shares rose again as Associated announced they had acquired our stake and would make a full bid. Associated fell. We knew that would happen and had taken positions to profit by it. Our whole principle had to be to never miss an opportunity, especially if it involved insider dealing and a guaranteed profit.

Jacqui and I headed to London. My parents headed to the South of France. We based ourselves again in the Ritz. It all seemed so quiet after the weeks and months of activity. We were indolent. We found somewhere to live. We watched the markets and made contacts. We saw Di Maglio from time to time.

He treated us with respect. He came to the wedding. The bodyguards came to the honeymoon. We were super rich but that had exacted a price. Neither Jacqui nor I were innocent any longer. We had played dirty. We had used murder. We had stolen.

The Sir Piers of this world would never allow us into the inner sanctums. But they had to deal with us. And, although we had wealth beyond any of our expectations, we wanted more. The game was to get the ultimate power. And that was a game we would start to play in the not so distant future.

And it was some months later in a quiet street in the City of London. A tall blonde man walked down the street. His clothes were expensive. His bearing was confident. The girl with him was glamorous. Their briefcases showed they worked in the City. They must have been from an investment bank for they definitely had money to spend on themselves. They were not recognised as they walked into the bank.

The Chairman greeted them. They went to his office. It was an opulent room with views of St Paul's Cathedral from one window and the Royal Exchange and the Bank of England from the other. "Your principals are willing to pay us three times book for the bank," he said. They nodded.

"I think we should start talking detail," said the Chairman.

"I think we should," said the man. The die was cast. The name was prestigious. The new Rossi and Di Maglio holding company was buying a bank. And that bank would in time cut a swathe through a City that worked to rules by which it would not abide.

The man smiled. So did the woman. The adrenalin was starting to flow again. Underneath the table Charles and Jacqui played footsie to pass time while the Chairman droned on about integrity and loyalty. They were good virtues for the opposition. But never for us.

Printed in the United States
104048LV00002B/99/A

9 781906 221355